NOTES

FROM THE

BURNING
AGE

NOTES
FROM THE
BURNING
AGE

CLAIRE NORTH

orbitbooks.net

ORBIT

First published in Great Britain in 2021 by Orbit

1 3 5 7 9 10 8 6 4 2

A CIP catalogue record for this book
is available from the British Library.

HB ISBN 978-0-356-51475-8
C format 978-0-356-51474-1

Typeset in Bembo by M Rules
Printed and bound in Great Britain by
Clays Ltd, Elcograf S.p.A

Papers used by Orbit are from well-managed forests
and other responsible sources.

Orbit
An imprint of
Little, Brown Book Group
Carmelite House
50 Victoria Embankment
London EC4Y 0DZ

An Hachette UK Company
www.hachette.co.uk

www.orbitbooks.net

For Zara

Chapter 1

Yue was twelve when she saw the kakuy of the forest, but later she lied and said she saw only flame.

"Keep an eye on Vae!" hollered her aunty from her workshop door. "Are you listening to me?"

It was the long, hot summer when children paddled barefoot in the river through the centre of Tinics, a time for chasing butterflies and sleeping beneath the stars. School was out, and every class had found the thing that was demonstrably the best, most impressive thing to do. For the tenth grades about to take their aptitudes, it was cycling down the path from the wind farm head first, until they either lost their courage or their bikes flipped and they cartwheeled with bloody knees and grazed elbows. For the seventh, it was preparing their kites for the fighting season; the ninth were learning how to kiss in the hidden grove behind the compression batteries, and to survive the first heartbreak of a sixty-second romance betrayed.

Yue should have been sitting on grassy roofs with her class, making important pronouncements about grown-up things, now that she was twelve and thus basically a philosopher-queen. Instead, on that day, she was tucked beneath the spider tree reading on her inkstone. She had made it at school out of parts pulled from the recycling tubs, painted it orange and doodled relentlessly on the back. It was slower than most and struggled to do much more than plain text, but she refused to use any other. Sometimes she pretended that the stories she read on it were tracts

1

on meaningful matters that younger children could not possibly comprehend, but mostly she read apocalyptic adventures, tales of teenagers who conquered all through grit, inventive use of grappling hooks and the power of love.

In a world on fire, Kendra and Winn must journey across the bitter European desert to find the last fresh water for their tribe . . .

. . . but all is not as it seems . . .

. . . only friendship can save them!

When we recount the stories of ourselves, we gloss over the acne and hormonal angst, the sloppy first steps into sexuality, the wild pouts and pompous self-declarations. Yue was coming into all these things, but that day even puberty could not disperse the universal cheer brought by sun and wind through velvet leaves.

Aunty Ram, however, could.

"Don't let Vae climb the kakuy tree! And be back in time for supper!"

Like a sleepy lion roused by the cackling of hyenas, Yue lifted her eyes from the inkstone in her lap to behold the sight of her displeasure – her sister. Three years younger, and therefore, in childhood terms, a squalling babe to Yue's majestic maturity, Vae was the perfect age for her wild enthusiasm to charm a naive stranger and infuriate anyone who knew her for more than fifteen minutes. Though they shared the same blue-black hair, squished nose and thumb-pinched chin, the same peanut skin and disturbingly triple-jointed thumbs, they had taken upon themselves the respective roles of older and younger sister with varying glee and earnestness. Whether her hearth-kin had intended to spend so much time congratulating Yue on how mature she was, I do not know. Whether they had meant to encourage Vae's giddy disobedience, I'm not sure either, for I was merely a guest. But the outcome was predictable – a reserved older child who felt constantly underappreciated, and a younger who cried petulantly whenever she was not indulged.

Did they love each other?

Of course they did.

But learning what that truly means would take time, and

though that summer felt as broad as the sky, time was running away like leaves in the river.

"And don't let her eat all the apples!"

Vae already stood in the little wooden gate, hopping from one foot to the other, ready to run. She wore beige shorts that hung a little lower than the knees, hand-me-downs from Yue handed down a little too soon, and her favourite t-shirt, faded green with pale blue zig-zags around the sleeves. She had stuffed her pockets with apples and tied her hair so loosely it was already starting to fall around her ears. What was worse, she had brought a friend – a boy, only a few months older than she, in russet shorts and a plain grey shirt, who shuffled and swayed, uneasy in the porch, as confused by Vae's energy as the snail by the swift.

The boy's name was Ven.

He was me, though I struggle now to remember ever being anything other than an observer to childhood, rather than a participant.

From the soft grass beneath the tree, Yue eyed her sister and myself, imparting, I felt, a clear declaration in her gaze that if we so much as sneezed out of place she would snitch to the first adult we saw, and that should Vae make herself sick gorging on fruit or spinning so fast she became herself dizzy, it was no one's problem but her own. I understood this; Vae was studied in the art of selective ignorance.

"Come on, Yue, we'll miss everything!" Vae shrilled, though quite what "everything" was, no one could fathom. Then she was running up the rubber road towards the server office on the corner, swinging past the egg-like kakuy stone that guarded the forest path without so much as a bow to its guardian form, and shrilling up the muddy track towards the ridge above. I followed, checking over my shoulder to see that our escort was coming, and reluctantly, at last, with studied slowness, Yue folded her inkstone down, slipped it into her pocket, shuffled bare feet into brown sandals and followed at a determinedly sluggish pace.

Yue's hearth was near the top of the hill, with a view down

the zig-zag street to the town below. The cables that ran to the server office came straight in across the valley, draped like a giant's clothes line above the river, too high for vines to tangle but the perfect height for flocks of fat wood pigeons and white-headed crows to congregate at dawn and dusk. When the wind blew right, the sound of running water and bicycle bells swept up the slopes into the forest above, along with every argument, shriek of laughter, out-of-tune melody and yap of barking dog. On second and fifth days, the electric truck came with supplies for the general store; on first, fourth and sixth, the postman came with packages and datasticks loaded with the latest books, newspapers, articles, magazines, animations and games, deposited at the server office to the delight of every bored child in winter. In the bathhouse at the upstream end of town, people gossiped about the price of resin, the quality of the newest strains of myce-lium, the latest soap opera downloaded to inkstone and what the neighbours said. Always what the neighbours said. Tinics was too small a town for any drama except our own.

Our temple straddled the river, raised up above a little water-fall of hollowed pools and smoothly etched rocks. Away from the spinning of the wind farms and the tick-tick-tick of the town's compression batteries, the priests offered up incense to the kakuy of wind and water, the living heart of the mountain and the blessed voices of the trees. They also frequently bored the children by talking about truth, love, harmony and awe, and occasionally delighted them by talking about fire, tornado, famine and fury – all the good stuff we actually wanted to hear.

The kakuy had blessed us, the Medj of the temple intoned. In autumn, the west wind powered inkstone, stove and bulb, and in spring the ice melted and the river flowed strong enough to keep the sewage plant pumping and the biowells bubbling. Life was a circle, in which all things served each other. The people of Tinics took this to heart, and the path through the forest to the wind farm was guarded by stone lanterns lit by bowing devotees with muttered thanks to the kakuy of leaf and soil for sheltering us within their bounds.

4

Up this same pebble-pocked track Vae now bounded, followed by myself and, behind, Yue. Vae had no time for ritual ablations before sacred stone or carved sign, for there was a destination she had to reach immediately, urgently, just in case the whole universe were to shift and dissolve in this instant, taking it away from her.

"Come on!" she hollered at her trailing entourage. "Come *on*!"

At the top of the carefully cut steps through the trees, the path forked, right to the batteries gently cranking up to capacity as the wind and sun charged them for the night, and left down a narrower, goat-cut wiggle through ever thicker shadow into the forest.

"Vae, you ..." Yue began to gasp, but all too late, for down the narrower path her sister plunged without pause. Oak and pine, spruce and beech, the smell of wet, fresh bark in spring, hot sap seeping in summer, and mulching scarlet in autumn. In some places you could swing from the soft silver trunk of the alder as if you were dancing between prayer-wheels at the temple; in others the poplar had bent to create the perfect ladder to the sky. But Vae was interested in none of these – not when the best tree in the forest was waiting just down the path.

I followed as the way curled tight round the strict black stone of the hill, caught my grip on flaking branches that protruded from the rock itself, life jutting out to catch the afternoon sunlight drifting through the leaves. Streams trickled and danced below, heading for the river that fed the town, while above twigs brushed and chattered against each other in the breeze. Soon even the hissing of the batteries and the wind farm had faded, and though I knew Tinics was just a few hundred metres away, any stranger walking through the wood would have been astonished to stumble on humanity hidden behind so much green. The path faded to almost nothing, but this didn't stop Vae, who started scrambling up a fern-crowned slope of iron-flecked stone and daffodil lichen, moving like a spider, limb pushing limb.

"Heaven and earth, Vae!" Yue fumed, but Vae pretended she couldn't hear, because if she could hear she would have to admit that she was being naughty. Better by far to have missed her sister's complaints and apologise later, one foot twisting coyly in the dirt, hands behind her back, chin down, eyes up, a puppy in a muddy skirt.

Crows were cawing above, the busy, bickering racket that they usually reserved for evening squabbles, and for a moment I wondered if the hour was later than I thought and sunset was coming, and realised I'd come without a torch; but glancing at the watch on my wrist I saw it was far too early in the day for the crows to be complaining. Perhaps they too were disturbed by Vae's squealing delight and now bickered to make their displeasure known.

At the top of the highest ridge of the tallest hill, Vae finally stopped before the best tree in the wood. The kakuy tree was a hornbeam, older, the priests said, than even the great burning. As the old countries perished when the seas rose and the desert grew, as the peoples of the world mingled and fought for fresh water and fertile land, the hornbeam had grown, spinning towards the sun above and soil below, its roots entangling with its neighbour like children holding hands. Where humans walked, each tree seemed a separate, swaying thing; but below the forest their roots were one, perfect symbiosis. Truly a great spirit lived in the hornbeam, the people said, a mighty kakuy, so at its base they left their offerings and prayers, and every night before lighting the stone lanterns the Medj of the temple would come to give thanks to leaf and branch.

Vae had no interest in such things, though she was at least well trained enough to sprint round the four-metre girth of the trunk and bow once before the mossy base. Then, like the gleeful heretic she was, she was climbing, scurrying up, one foot in the first V-split of the trunk, a hand swinging for a snowy-lichen-crowned branch, off which she briefly dangled like a monkey.

Yue sighed and tutted, but was far too mature to argue with infants. Instead she circled the tree once, fingers brushing the valleys and peaks of moss-softened bark, bowed, pulled her ink-stone from her pocket and settled in against the base of the nearest non-theological tree to read. Above, Vae had already made it into the spluttering crown of the low trunk, where dozens of thick branches shot up like the frightened hair of a porcupine, and was bracing her feet for another push higher.

I performed my prayers without thinking, distracted, then picked around the base of the tree to see what offerings had been left here by priest and wanderer. The Temple liked to keep things neat, even in the heart of coiling nature, and someone had ordered the items around the trunk to create a pleasing palette of old and new, large and small. Here, a few links of ancient bicycle chain were welded into a bracelet, carefully framing a bunch of wilted lilac flowers. Next to that, the classical offering of grain, fading and spiky on the stem. A flask of home-brewed wine pressed in blood-red clay, probably toxic if more than sipped; a collection of the blackest stones pulled from the river bed; some shards of chitin scraped from the bottom of the resin well; and a little woven hat in blue, spun from the same bio-engineered silk that Mama Taaq grew on her spider tree. I circled the hornbeam, wondered if I should leave an offering and what I might ask for in return, when a glimmer of metal caught my eye. It was a tiny thing that I could pinch between thumb and forefinger like the wing of a butterfly. Someone had polished it up, the track marks of their effort still glistening in oily white. Any ink or pigments on the surface had long since flaked away, but characters were still visible, embossed by a great machine a long time ago. I recognised an archaic script, long since fallen out of use, but taught tediously in school by Uncle Mue through songs and games. Much of the lettering was unreadable, flattened by whatever force had carved out this tiny piece of history and offered it up to the forest gods. A few words I could just about read, picking them out from months of study. I mouthed them silently to myself as I shaped the syllables, dancing over some of the stranger shapes until I had the sound: *Product of China*.

Then Vae called out: "Are you coming?" and she was already halfway to the sky, dangling over a branch with one leg swinging back and forth under its own weight for the mere joy of feeling like she might fall. I returned my shard carefully to the bed of moss where I had found it, gave an awkward, quick half-bow to the tree, then started to climb. I was slower than Vae, but confident. The forest was my home, and my hearth did not teach its children how to dread the world that nourished us. Halfway up, I paused, drooping over a branch, stomach pressed to timber and arms flopping free.

"If you scratch your knees, Mama will be so angry," warned Yue from below, not looking up from her reading.

Vae stuck her tongue out; familiar with the habit, Yue returned the expression, still not lifting her gaze, above and below all such things.

"Yue's boring," Vae hissed. She was disappointed to realise that even in her most dramatic voice her elder sister either hadn't heard her or didn't care. With a haughty twist of her chin skywards, she turned away from the argument that she had most clearly won and resumed climbing. I paused a moment below her as a red-bellied beetle head-butted my curled hand, considered this obstruction to its journey, then climbed onto my skin and resumed its ambling, king of the world.

If you listen for the legs of a beetle over a child's skin, you will not hear it. But listen – now listen. And as well as hearing nothing from my crimson friend, I heard a greater nothing too. The crows had fallen silent. So had the songbirds and white-bellied thrushes, the leg-scratching insects and the little cooing creatures of the underbrush. Only the sound of Vae calling, "Ven! Higher!" broke through the hissing of the leaves.

The beetle reached the other end of my hand and wobbled for a moment on the edge, surprised, it seemed, by a steepness which on the way up had caused it no difficulty.

Now listen.

Listen.

Close your eyes and listen.

Leaf on leaf is the brush of something leathery, dry, living and dying. Below, Yue reads, one finger tapping against her elbow as she cradles the inkstone in her arms, eyes tracking across the words on its screen.

Listen.

And here it is. The crackling snap-snap-snap through the forest. Gases, popping apart, breaking something solid into pieces. A groaning of fibres under pressure and then giving way in a single tear, gushing out smoke and steam. The slow grinding creak of the oldest, weakest trunks finally giving way, the smack as they slash into a neighbour while they fall, the sudden updraught of ash and spark into the sky as the impact throws more flames out, caught in the wind.

The beetle, which had been searching for a way down and found none, reared up, opened a pair of bloody wings and buzzed away, bouncing under its own ungainly airborne weight.

And here it is, the tickle at the end of your nose, the taste of it on the tip of your tongue, the taste of black, a stinging in your eyes, and I realised what it was just as Vae shrilled: "Fire!"

The great forest was burning.

Vae was already halfway down the tree before I started moving, not a child any more but a creature entirely of the wood, of speed and limb slithering from foot to hand to foot. I tried to peer through the leaves, to see how close or how far it was, but Yue was on her feet shouting, gesturing furiously at us to get down, and how quickly the world changed! The sunlight, which had been pools of gold and silver pushing through the trees, was now a million broken shafts in the air, given form and dimensionality by the smoke drifting in with the wind. The noise of flame, which began in bits and pieces, was already an all-consuming roar, a sucking in of wind and an exhalation of fire that left no room to pick out the details of trees falling and earth turning to soot.

I reached the ground a few moments after Vae and immediately regretted it, the smoke now tumbling in thick and black, biting my eyes and prickling my throat. Yue pulled her shirt up across her face, and we copied her, scrambling, blinking, tears running down our cheeks, towards the path. Now I could look back, and see the orange glow beginning to drown out the day, and look below, and see it there too, pushing along the banks of the stream beneath the waterfall, moving so fast, like deer before the wolf.

"Stay close to me," Yue commanded, and for almost the first time since Vae was old enough to say "sister", she nodded and obeyed.

The path down, so easy to climb, familiar to us, was now slow, agonising anguish, every step unsteady, every breath a minute's tick on a spinning clock. Vae slipped and got back up without complaint; Yue grunted as her footing gave way and she caught herself on a root, her face curled in a snarl as if to dare the forest to betray her one more time, and she kept on going. I tumbled after them, on my bum as often as my feet, nettles prickling my fingers and stabbing through my shorts, until we reached the path above the river. Here the smoke was a broiling fog, and I blinked and could barely keep my eyes open, put my hands over my face to try and block it out, peered through splayed fingers and could hardly see a foot ahead of me. The noise of the fire was deafening, and I could feel its heat at my back, moving so fast, a warmth that began as the pleasant glow of the stove on an autumn day and now rose and blistered into a relentless, inescapable grapple that squeezed the life from my skin and the breath from my lungs. I called out for Vae, and thought I heard her answer; called out for Yue and couldn't see her, began to panic, then felt a hand catch mine and pull me along.

I don't know when we got turned around, when we lost our footing. I heard the compression batteries explode on the ridge overhead, a thunder as the overheated gas inside finally ruptured the buried tanks to shower what little of the forest wasn't blazing with mud and torn fibre and metal.

We briefly outran the flames into a little gully, a bowl of untouched elder thorns and purple flowers into which the smoke hadn't seeped. Then we crouched low, our faces crimson smeared with ash, and knew that we were lost. Vae started to cry, silently, and I knew I was mere moments behind, when Yue shook her head and hissed, "Down!"

I thought she meant down deeper into this gully, perhaps burying ourselves in soil and hoping the fire would pass by, but she rose to her feet and instead followed the land down, no path, no easy route, just swinging from tree to tree like a drunken squirrel, propelled by her own headlong momentum towards the bottom of the valley. If we had done this dance by daylight, it would have been ridiculously dangerous; by the light of the fire it felt entirely natural, and we flung ourselves after her, tripping on our own feet and tumbling for the darkness below.

I didn't hear the river over the fire, which now domed above us. Looking up for the first time, I could see actual flames withering the edges of the leaves on the trees in orange worms, spitting and spilling up the branches in fluorescent crimson. Then my feet hit water and sank almost immediately into the grit below. I caught myself for a second, lost my balance, fell onto my hands and knees and crawled after Yue, who was already knee-deep and wading deeper. I followed, catching at rocks and feet slipping, banging on stone as I slithered into the stream. The current caught sudden and hard a little before halfway, flowing freely round grey mottled boulders that had obscured its path. It pushed me to the side, and I pushed back, submerged my face briefly to wash away the burning around my eyes, looked up and for a second through the smoke saw Yue, now up to her waist, reaching out for Vae to my left and behind me. I was half-walking, half-swimming, arms flapping against the current as my feet buckled and slipped on stone, coughing black spit with every breath, ducking my head below as long as I dared only to surface and cough some more in the toxic blackness that raged through the valley. All around was ablaze, too bright to look at, my hair starting to curl from the heat of it pressing down against the river. When I was shoulder-deep, I turned my whole body against the current like a kite against the wind, straining as it tried to snatch me away. I reached for Yue, hoping to steady myself on her, and for an instant our fingers caught before the weight of water pushed us apart. Then she looked past me and her eyes went wide.

11

And there, on the edge of the water, was the kakuy of the forest.

I had seen in temple many different depictions of the kakuy who guarded this valley. In some he was a great wolf; in others a woman shrouded in a cloak of leaves. In some she was a great crow, the same size as the tree he perched on. In others they were little more than an oval stone, with one eye open as if to say, "Who disturbs my rest?" The Medj, when questioned about the true form of the kakuy, always shrugged and said: "How do you describe the colour green, or the taste of water?" The Medj have always had a good line in saying very little the nicest way.

The day the forest burned, he was eight feet tall, with a white belly of warm, wet fur and a back of crimson feathers that billowed and moulted from him as he bent towards the river's edge. His eyes were the yellow of the eagle, his snout was a ginger fox, his teeth were sharp, the claws on his hands and feet were black and curled. He rose up on two legs like a bucking horse, then fell down onto all fours and raised his huge head above a flabby neck as if he would howl at the flames; perhaps he did, but I could not hear him.

At his movement, the whole forest seemed to shudder and shake, and for the briefest moment the flames spun backwards as if the wind would change. The kakuy raised his head and howled again, and I felt the river turn icy cold where it held me and a roar of water surge momentarily higher than my head, pushing me under in breathless thunder before I gasped and thrust upwards and surfaced again.

The kakuy looked at us and seemed to see us for the very first time, and though I know very little of gods and the great spirits of the earth that holds us, I thought I saw in his eyes a sadness deeper than any I had ever known.

Then he too caught ablaze. First a feather, then a tuft of fur. He didn't move, didn't lurch into the water, but his mouth opened and closed as if he were screaming. His eyes rolled huge in his skull, and he spat and foamed and rippled from his hind legs to the tip of his nose as if about to vomit up black smoke from the internal fire of his roasting organs. Like the crisp edge of an autumn leaf, he curled in on himself as the fire boiled from his toes to his top, front legs buckling first, then rear, snout hitting the ground last as he flopped down to his belly, then rolled to his side, black tongue out and lolling, lungs heaving and panting with burning breath until, at last, his eyes settled again on us. They stayed wide as the kakuy died.

Temple histories are judiciously vague as to which came first. Were the kakuy earth's punishment for man's disobedience? Did they wake when the sky rained acid and the forests were blasted pits, to punish humanity for its arrogance, to wipe away the men who had sullied this world? Or did the kakuy wake as the world burned by man's own design, to heal and salve what little remained, rolling back the desert and the salty sea? Ambiguity is often an ally to theology, as Old Lah would say.

I saw the kakuy fall, and when his blackened face hit the ground the whole forest groaned. Even through the fire and the burning, I heard it; the deep-timbered roaring of the trees bending against their roots, the cracking of stone and the rattling of the white-scarred branches, an earthquake that made the fire itself twist and recoil as if in shame at what it had done. Or perhaps I didn't. Perhaps in the delirium of heat and smoke and fear, I imagined it all.

I saw the kakuy fall, and when the last breath left his lungs, the wind whipped across the water as if blasted from the hurricane, and the river lurched and buckled as though the spirits of the deep were wailing for the death of their beloved kin, and I screamed and held Yue's hand tight, and she held mine and we slipped and slid together backwards against the turning of the current.

I saw the kakuy fall, and in that moment my flailing left hand caught another's. Vae's fingers brushed the palm of my hand, scrambling like the dancing feet of the spider for purchase. I snatched after her, caught her wrist, don't let go, don't let go, but the river was stronger than a child's grasp. Her fingers slipped a little further down my hand.

Her fingers have always been slipping down my hand.

Caught, in a final hook, joint-to-joint.

Don't let go, I begged, or maybe she did, it was hard to tell.

Then the river snatched her away.

I saw her go under, feet tipping up as her head fell back. I did not see her hands claw at the burning air. I did not hear her scream. I did not see her rise again to breathe, as the great forest burned.

Chapter 2

This is the history of the Burning Age, as taught by Temple scripture.

There came a time when humankind had dominion over all the earth. With their might, they tore down the mountains and built cities there. With their wisdom, they conquered the seas and skies. Great medicine there was in abundance, and even their gods called humanity special, the chosen creature raised up above all things. For their children, they laboured, to make a better world, and that world would be of man's making.

Yet their children did not give thanks for the labours of their elders, and lo: the skies turned yellow, the air too dark to breathe from the workings of their industry. The cracked earth bled poisons. The sea rose and salted the land, and no wall of man could restrain it. In winter, the ice melted; in summer, the world burned.

"What shall we do?" asked the wisest of the burning ones, but: "Mankind is stronger than mother earth and father sky," was the answer, "and we do not flinch before the fire."

And so the forests were felled and the rain burned the flesh of babes and the rivers ran with lead, and still mankind did not turn from its course, not even when the deserts consumed the fertile plains and the children themselves cried out for change.

"We are stronger than the storm," railed the greatest of the burning ones. "Weakness is the child's error."

It was about the time of the great migrations, when all the nations began to splinter like the burning bough and the wars of water and grain came upon the lands, that the kakuy woke. First they rose from the skeletons of the ocean reefs, glistening bone and acid breath. Then they climbed from the shattered mines, and their eyes were embers of coal and their feet broke the towns beneath their feet. Then they came from the sky itself, upon thunder and lightning they blazed, tearing down the monuments of man and bidding the earth swallow whole the sacrileges of the Burning Age.

The arrogant tried to fight back, as if their weapons were not forged of the same earth which now they sought to harm. They perished beneath the kakuy as the mouse in the eagle's claws. Those who survived fled to the last of the forests and the sacred hidden places, their thousand tongues blending into new language, their ancient ways changing as does the scudding sky.

From their prayers, Temple was born. The scattered people raised their hands to the falling rain and said: "No more will we confront sky and earth as enemy; henceforth, we shall give thanks to she that carries us. The sun will rise and the sun will set, and we will walk within this changing life as creatures of this world, born within her womb."

And at last, hearing their prayers, the kakuy turned their wrathful eyes from the remnants of humanity and left the tribes in peace. Where the great spirits walked, the land grew anew; where they laid their heads, fresh springs rose from the barren mountain. And as the forests grew, so in time the peoples of the world grew again, venturing forth as once their ancestors had, to carve a new world from the ashes of the old. We spread across the land and gave thanks for the harvest and the kakuy, who, their work complete, returned to the hidden places of this world to rest once more between sky and earth.

Let not your hands fell the tree but that another is planted.

Let not your ears hear the rain and think it falls for you.

Let not your tongue speak of conquering the mountain, for it will not shiver when winter comes.

And if your eyes should see the kakuy slumbering in their sacred caves, gentle in rest, remember to bow in prayer, for should they wake again, no tears shall douse the flames.

This is the teaching of the Temple on the history of the Burning Age. In deference to the scholars and priests who penned it, most of its lies stem from ignorance and omission, and the rest are at least well-intentioned, all things considered.

Chapter 3

After a great fire, rain.

Water evaporates, the heat pushing it higher and higher until suddenly it is too high, condensing around particles of soot and ash billowed into the heavens by the blaze.

When it falls, a lake tumbles down on you; there are no gentle drops, no merry dancing puddles. You are caught in a nightmare again, blinded by liquid where a moment before you were blinded by smoke. It is enough to turn the crimson world grey in moments, to bring hypothermia after heat exhaustion, until even your burns are shivering. Here too there is a cycle in all things – water from fire.

As the forest turned to white flaking ash that fluttered like butterfly wings, Yue did not believe that Vae was dead. We clung onto each other and slippery stones, hauling ourselves belly-first onto a little island of lichen and ash, choking on smoke and spluttering in the rain, and could see neither the carcass of the kakuy nor Vae.

We lay there all night, she and I, while the river buckled and roared around us. We didn't speak, didn't dare wriggle from our nested nook together. The forest was a glaring, bitter thing, threads of shimmering orange still peeking through the downpour like scars on the back of a writhing snake. I thought it was angry, thought perhaps the kakuy who'd died was some minor spirit of a lesser tree, and any second now we would look up and in the sky would be two eyes of lightning, talons of flame. The creaking of the burnt-out husks of the doused trees falling went on all night, a deafening eulogy sometimes so near we flinched together, buried our heads in each other so we wouldn't have to see the branches crashing down around us. At other times, it was a faraway chorus, the funeral song of the wood.

In the morning, the first rescue team found us, calling our names, scrambling through the river – take our hands, take our hands. The men and women wore orange, coated in grey, waded through slurry and sludge knee-deep, a soup of rain, river and ash.

"Ambulance!" hollered someone. "Fetch the ambulance!"

The ambulance came as close as it could, where the river met the village. Tinics had survived the blaze with little more than a few sooty scars; fire was a part of forest life, and every hearth was set back a little from the trees, shelters built into the hill itself. But the power was out, the windfarm locked down and blackened, the compression batteries popped from the inside out, and the whole valley lay beneath a snowfall of ash, a hollow of soot and carbon.

"You have to find Vae," Yue muttered as we lay on the stretchers, batting away her oxygen mask. "I was looking after her."

As children, we look to adults to be perfect and say the right thing. Mama Taaq, face streaked grey from dust and tears, should have replied to her shivering, shuddering child: "You did everything right, my darling. You did everything you could and none of this is your fault."

Later she would say those words, but later was too late, because that night all she did was cry and turn away from her still-living daughter to try and find her dead one. These things are entirely natural and understandable – just not to a child.

We were still in the hospital in Tseonom when they found Vae's body, washed nearly seven kilometres downstream. They told the children she looked very peaceful, and when alone in the bathhouse I slipped beneath the water and held my breath until my throat spasmed and my face burned and my chest was a cavity swallowing me from the inside out, and then surfaced, and realised I would never believe anything an adult said ever again. I ran to my hearth and hid behind the rainwater butts and was angry, sullen, resentful, whimsical, manic, full of laughter and profoundly sad, until at last my mother grabbed me by the shoulders as I ran down the path shaded with hanging vines and managed to hold me still long enough to say: "My child lived!"

In a strange way, it had not occurred to me that night that, though one family had lost their daughter, another's son had been saved. It had not occurred to me to be grateful that I was still alive. The next day, we climbed the burnt hill to the plot of earth where Vae's body had been laid for the forest to take her, and my mother spoke of the cycle of all things, as the Medj do, of change as truth and death as inevitable, of there being no life where there was not its ending, and then said the one thing that the Medj always seemed to forget to add at the end of their sermons: "And it is all right to be sad about that."

Yue vanished into her room for the rest of the summer, and neither family nor friends could coax her out. They did not try very hard. People are rarely skilled at dealing with other people's pain. Do you carry on as if nothing had happened, or do you find yourself guilty that you were caught smiling, that you played a game a week after the funeral, or laughed at a joke a month after Vae's body was given to the sky and earth, or did your homework and made a meal because life continues? Grief never leaves, but life layers itself on top of the pain, time forming fresh scabs over bleeding wounds, no matter how much we wish we had stayed in the burning forest.

So summer ended, and life went on, and Yue went back to school. And sometimes she cried. And sometimes she laughed. And the teachers said she should talk to a counsellor, and she did, and the counsellor told her parents afterwards that there was nothing remarkable here, nothing extraordinary or strange. There was a child grieving; that was all there was to it. You do not fix grief; there is no pill. You only wait, and be there, and let time pass.

So we waited, and let time pass, and Yue's grief did not become a performance, did not become an all-consuming thing that defined her. There was too much life to be lived for that to be the sole quality of her nature. Instead, her thirteenth birthday came and went with some merriment and a little quiet, and then her fourteenth, and sometimes she caught my eye in the street and looked away, and I was still a child, still ashamed, so I turned my face from her too and went about my business as if neither she nor Vae had ever played with me in the forest.

Two years after the forest burned, the Medj of the town, bundled in patched beige robes, led the village up to the stump of the kakuy tree to plant fresh ferns in the ash-soil. The summer festival of Tinics had always been one of dancing, of games and competitive music-making, in which the most beautiful ballads had competed with those less tuneful souls who understood that an entertained audience was more likely than a moved one to crown you with a garland of flowers. After the fire, the festival had moved into the temple grounds, and we washed our hands in the little pools of water between the pebble rows and gave thanks to the food gifted us by the nearby towns that understood our loss. The priests spoke of the cycle of all things, and of how all things came back to life, and there had not been any dancing.

The next year, the elders of the village took hands with the youngest ones and circled the remnants of the hornbeam four times one way, then four times the other, then we all spread out to plant our offerings to the forest, and the soil was black as night and parted beneath my fingers at the lightest touch, eager to be fed.

That same night, when the adults were in the town making merry by precious citronella candlelight, Yue returned to the forest. With headtorch on her head and a water bottle in her hand, she set off up the blackened path through the scrubby, chin-high trunks and drooping, soot-scared monuments, heading for the highest ridge. The new trees pushing up from the corpses of the old, arm-thin and pale-skinned, were not yet so tall that she couldn't see her destination nor so frail that she couldn't use them to climb, hand-over-hand, towards the rising moon. She was becoming the woman I would one day meet in the winter wood; an oblong of tight mouth and stern eyes beneath a winding braid of hair. Hers were features most suited for a laughing grandmother's smile, and they would not fit easy with her until she reached that age.

Beneath the earth, roots tangled like lovers, one atop another, feeding the new green, and as the ferns uncoiled their fresh leaves and the ants nibbled at the fallen black trunks of yesteryear, the forest grew. Life had returned faster than anyone had expected. Not the old life; not the crows or the great rumbling bears, but the smaller, faster life that thrived in bracken and fern, that fed on the insects which thrived in sooty soil and loved to lick at dribbling nectar from freshly rising sap. For a few years, blooms of flowers had spread like rain, colours I had never seen before, yellows and oranges, pinks and lavenders, gaudy magenta and potassium blues verging on black. As the trees started to open their canopies again, the shadows would drive the flowers into smaller clumps of colour peeking at the light, the birds would return with their cackling and caws, and the wind would move the leaves in an old, familiar song. Perhaps then, the Medj said, the kakuy would bless us once again with their presence, and the fruit would grow ripe on the branches, and the wind would power our farms again, and our offerings would be rewarded with their grace, now that the hard years were over.

"When my tree carries fruit again," Mama Taaq would say, standing beneath the grey branches of her spider tree, "then I will know the kakuy have returned."

Her tree would not bear fruit for another four years, when the old hornbeam on the ridge finally flowered in spring. Within every living thing there is a kakuy; the soul of the stone polished by the sea, the spirit of the leaf turning crimson as it falls. All that lives must die, but death is not the end of living, and so the forest grew, and life found its path, and one day the great kakuy of the forest would walk again.

That night, Yue climbed up to an ebony monument to all that had been, a squatting shadow on the horizon. Even in death, the kakuy tree fed life: beetles and ants, fungus and moss creeping into every nook and corner, burrowing past the char to sup on the sap that had supped on the earth. Though the forest had crumbled, people still climbed to offer their tributes to the kakuy burned in fire. An apple, rotting, busily consumed by bugs. A fresh pink rose, propped up against the ravaged trunk where once Vae had climbed. A poem, folded, written in an archaic style and asking for romantic fortune and future wealth. A broken mask from some children's play, left in gratitude for who knew what blessing. And there, still glinting through the blackened soot and thick grains of dirt that shrouded it, a little metal shard.

Yue turned her headtorch on to see it more clearly, held it up to the light, ran her fingers over the ridged, ancient words.

Product of China.

She considered it quite a while before laying it down on a scarred old stone and turning her attention to me. I had not been invited to this place, but I also knew what anniversary this was, and Vae had been my friend. I had found my path to the burnt kakuy tree before Yue and stood next to it now, briefly defiant, for this was *my* night and *my* remembrance beneath the stars, and if Yue wanted to interrupt she should have come a year ago, when I first climbed through the dark of the ashen forest to mourn.

That defiance flickered out almost as soon as it had arisen, and for a moment there were just the two of us above the growing trees, fed by star and moon.

Now we stood, the pair of us, blinking in the dark, the light of her torch dazzling me as I flinched away from its glare. It took a moment for her to realise what the grimace on my face meant, and she turned off the beam and shuffled on the spot, momentarily dull as her eyes adjusted to the changing light.

Then we stood again a while, listening beneath the moonlight, as the forest grew.

She held out her hand, and I took it, and together we circled the fat, black stump of the kakuy tree once one way, once the other, and bowed together, hinging from the hips, and straightened up, hands finding each other again.

23

She did not look at me, nor I at her.

The forest grew, and the birds did not squabble in the sky, and after a little while Yue let go of my hand and walked away without a word.

That was twenty years ago.

Chapter 4

There is a cellar beneath an old block in the city of Vien that smells of malt and the sweat of men. One night there – or rather, one very early morning – I found myself sprawled along the long, sticky top of a bar as one man held down the back of my head and my bent left arm, pinning it against me with his own body weight, while another attempted to get a decent grip on my jerking, bucking right hand in order to cut my thumb off.

"No please please I can explain please it's a mistake you don't have to please . . . "

The cellar itself was a historical monument, reclaimed from the silt and crumble-down collapse of an ancient city, restored with stones plucked from the ruins of former monuments, buttressed with timber harvested by the Medj, who bowed to each tree in turn and made libations to the kakuy whose gift they were receiving. Dim yellow lanterns hung across the ceiling, powered by the solar batteries high above, and in each padded booth of low couch and table, a hollow was cut for the communal soup bowl, a heavy wooden board laid for the breaking of bread.

"Help, somebody help me!" I shrieked and gibbered, knowing perfectly well that I was the last in the bar, the keys to the front door in my pocket, the back door sealed. "Somebody help!"

During the day, the cellar hosted activities ranging from a meeting hall for monotheists, calling prayers to the old gods, to a twice-weekly knitting group, some of whose efforts were immortalised on the wall nearest the small stage where a dubious range of musical talent was occasionally demonstrated. Who knew you could knit a lobster? Not me.

At night, it had become a haven, first unofficially and then with a semi-official regularity, for members of Vien's Justice and Equality Brotherhood, two of whom were now attempting to remove my digits with a blunt flick knife.

"Whatever you want I can do whatever you need I'm sorry I'm sorry I'm sorry . . ."

Working in the bar had not been my first choice. The hours were long, the pay merely adequate, and any naive notion I had of doing something with my daylight hours was usually lost to restless sleep as sunlight streamed through the shutters of the hearth I called home. My manager had recognised something desperate in me and, faced with the choice between offering me help or exploiting my vulnerability, had chosen the latter. He was now noticeably absent, and I couldn't help but wonder if I would be berated for getting blood on the counter or not tidying up my own severed digits before locking up for the night.

The two gentlemen involved in the business of mutilation were learning on the job. The one who was holding me cheek-first against the countertop focused with a calm, almost bored, non-chalance on keeping my whole body pressed beneath the steady weight of his own, my wrist twisted in his grip. Meanwhile, his colleague tried to turn my right hand up, so that my thumb faced away from the rack of alcohol on the wall, locking my elbow to reduce any writhing to a limp fish's flipper-flap. He was succeeding too, one twisted fibre at a time, so I fell back on screaming, wailing and pleas for mercy, laced with more than a bit of self-pity as I contemplated the poor life choices that had brought me to this place.

Then a voice said, "What's your name?" and the third party to this escapade – a presence I'd barely noted until now – entered the conversation. His authority was enough to make his colleague pause in his work, the knife biting paper-cut thin into my joint.

"What?" I stammered. "I'm Kadri Tarrad, Kadri Tarrad, I live on Katalinastrasse, I'll do anything, please!"

"Your name is not Kadri Tarrad," tutted the voice, and perhaps there was a nod or an indication of displeasure at this conclusion, because the knife bit hard enough that I screamed:

"Ven Marzouki! My name is Ven Marzouki!"

The blade relaxed. I could feel blood running down my skin, spilling onto the bar, seeping through the thick, gloopy varnish into the wood.

"Where are you from, Ven Marzouki?"

"Lyvodia," I whimpered. I was surprised to find that though I had some control of my breath and voice, there was salt in my eyes and a capillary pulsed in the side of my cheek with such power I felt sure anyone looking at me would see a relentless, pounding twitch.

"You're far from home. Why did you lie?"

"I ... " I tried to turn my head away from the sight of my own blood, couldn't, closed my eyes and received a shaking of my skull for my efforts. "Whatever I've done to offend you, I'm sorry. You'll never see me again."

Another movement; another little signal somewhere outside my line of sight. The weight on my back relaxed long enough for hands to flip me round, now bending me concave, spine digging into wood, knife moving from my hand towards my throat. I caught a glimpse of face and eye, of assailants who were not in the mood for wit, then their boss rose from his chair, stepped around a small, round table, adjusted the collar of his coat and mused: "Are you a spy, Ven?"

"What? No. Please." I was still struggling to steady my breathing. "Please just let me go. You'll never see me again, I swear."

"Why are you here?"

"I work here! I just work here, *please*."

"Why *here*?"

"I don't know! Because they gave me a job, they gave me a job! It's not even a good job, please, whatever you think I've done I'll make it right. I'll leave, I swear by river and road."

The man shook his head, disappointed. The lights in the bar were turned down for the evening, a slick yellow pooling like acid, but I knew his face from the endless Brotherhood meetings in the hall. He was a picture of archival masculinity: 190 centimetres of subtle muscle beneath an orange-brown winter coat; shoulders that ran in a well-defined V up through his neck to a square jaw, chin with a nook in it that seemed moments away from becoming another mouth with its own scowls and grins; eyes the colour of autumn; straight, pulled-back oak hair inclining to grey. His order at meetings was always the same – a glass of pricey white wine grown from the vineyards on the coast, followed by endless chasers of water and the occasional cold floral tea. When party members passed out drunk or vomited in the corner, he would apologise, gesture to others in the assembly, and have the offending drunkard removed and the mess mopped up while we staff looked on in silence, grateful to have clients who looked after themselves. That, until this moment, had been the limit of our interaction.

"You swear like a priest."

I licked my lips, swallowed hard, tried to speak, fluffed the first few words, tried again. "I'll leave Vien. I promise. You'll never hear from me again."

"But I want to hear from you. I want to hear all sorts of things from you. I want to hear about your past, your present, your future. I would like you and I to have a conversation."

His enforcers were built to a different physical spec than his. Whereas his muscle was a careful construct of motion and control, theirs was the heavy wallop of gorged meat and slapping pain. His strength was merely one of many attributes he was proud of; theirs was the one thing in the world that gave them confidence.

"Are you going to turn me over to the guardia?" I wheezed, tongue an inelegant tool in a swelling mouth.

"Why would we do that?"

"I don't know. Because you can?"

"Yes. I can." He sounded almost kind; a disappointed uncle hoping that the vagrant child will have the guts to confess before the truth is dragged out with irons. "But perhaps there is another way."

In the temple, as a child, the Medj told me that everything

has a kakuy inside it, from the smallest pebble in the stream to the rolling black clouds that break on the tip of the mountain. I wondered what it would be like to be a kakuy of some small, thorny shrub, or the spirit of the cavern, and decided it would probably be better than this. Instead my very human form was deposited at a table in the corner of the cellar with the man who was to destroy everything, cradling a bloody thumb and a pounding skull, while he poured me a glass.

"Tell me about yourself, Ven. Kadri Tarrad. Whoever you pretend to be."

"Why?"

"I hold your life in my hand. Isn't that enough? "

I took the offered glass, drained it down. It was the good stuff, the stuff my manager would be angry to find missing. "I used to be a priest. I was training to take the vows."

"How did you go from chanting and waving incense around to tending bar here?"

"I wasn't good at the pastoral stuff. I was a linguist. My expertise was archaic scripts. I served on the academic review board, studying Burning Age heretical material. My job was to go through recovered servers and translate items for assessment as useful, heretical or somewhere in between."

The man poured another glass, barely looking at where the liquid fell. "Where was this?"

"Lyvodia."

"What kind of material did you study?"

I gripped the glass tight, and this time did not drink. My thumb was leaving little bloody marks on the glass, odd droplets and smears on the tabletop. "Whatever came in. We're finding archives and hard drives all the time. Most of the data is irrecoverable, but sometimes you get a lucky hit; a complex that was sealed against the worst, or something in the landfill mines that still carries data. Most of it is of purely anthropological interest – messages between people in offices, pictures of cats, pornography, and so on. You get a lot of porn. But sometimes you get something good, engineering data or a fiction archive, user manuals or location-tagged images we can compare to archaeological digs. My job was to translate the more challenging material for discussion and classification."

"How 'challenging'?" he asked, and there seemed almost a genuine curiosity in him, an academic fascination that did not tally with my present experience of blood and pain.

"Usually bigotry – social media hatred, violence against other humans on an ideological basis – ethnicity, religion, wealth, gender, sexual preference, and so on. Socially endorsed violence makes up more than 97% of heretical materials, in one form or another. It's unusual to stumble across a practical heresy."

"Define 'practical' heresy."

"Why?"

"Because I'm asking."

I rolled the glass between my hands, enjoying the brightness of the fresh blood that stayed behind. "Nerve agents. Ballistic missiles. Chemical warheads. Fossil-fuel fracking, tar sands, deep-sea extraction. Nuclear fission, depending on its use. Things like that. Most of the records left behind are of people justifying their use, rather than actual construction guides. Sometimes you'd be lucky and get a server from an old university or something. Medical information, water purification, materials science, geography, geology, aeronautics – you'd find the occasional wonder."

"Did you ever find anything?"

"Once or twice. Stem cells, quantum computing. Ancient tracts on economic models, demographic analysis, and so on."

"What did you think about it? Classifying the world into the sacred or the profane?"

I stared into the still surface of the glass between my fingers, realised I didn't even like the good stuff, drained it down anyway, felt a glimmer of spite and satisfaction. "I ... it wasn't my job to think about it. I was just a translator."

The man in the tan coat smiled briefly, slipped a little deeper into his chair, one leg crossed over the other. He had tiny teeth in his chiselled face – a strange, baby-like anomaly in what was otherwise a textbook portrait of classic Burning Age masculinity.

"So how did you get from sitting in a dusty library to here, Medj of the Temple of the Lake?"

I looked up quickly, then away again lest he see something in my face that he disliked. "Why do you care?"

"Because if you are still a priest, you could be a spy. And if you are a spy, tonight will be full of regrets."

I licked my lips, pushed the empty glass away. "I stole information from the archives. Classified, heretical information. Sold it."

"What kind of information?"

"Anything. Didn't matter. Anything I could find. I downloaded it to datasticks and sold it to anyone who wanted to buy."

"Why did you do that?"

I didn't answer.

"I know you ran, Ven. I know the guardia are looking for you. I'm a good citizen. I should report you."

"If tonight is going to be full of regrets, I'd rather listening to bullshit wasn't one of them."

To my surprise, he smiled. A little smile – the twitching of lips that are enjoying their control, the flicker of delight in the game – that never left his features. But for a moment there was something human behind his eyes, a hint of someone real. "All right. I'm a bad citizen. I am much worse than the guardia. Is that enough?"

I looked round the room. The two thugs were still leaning against the bar, one now with a drink in his hand, bored, professionally paid not to give a damn, not to listen to things which didn't bother him. I looked down at my fingers, bloody and still bleeding in a crimson tangle. "It wasn't fair," I said.

"I beg your pardon?"

"It wasn't fair," I repeated. "I'm ... I worked hard. I could read nearly half a dozen archaic languages fluently and recognise a dozen more. I studied technical languages, coding languages, so I could piece together information from damaged drives or systems we didn't have an operating platform for. I worked while others slept, or ate, or prayed. I was good. I was better than the rest of them."

"If that's the case, why are you here? Shouldn't you be chanting scripture in some wealthy monastery?"

"They said I was worldly. Too concerned with human things. There was this man in the archives, working with me – 'working'. He didn't do anything. He just talked and talked as if he knew things, talking to hide how ignorant he was, and I did everything and then he talked and took the credit. And when I complained, they said no tree envies another the light. They said it like it mattered, like there was some great meaning in it. Platitudes. Little sayings, said in a certain way, to disguise the fact that they don't believe, they don't care, they don't ask questions. This is the way it is because that's how we do it. Honour the stones, they said. Each stone lives, and we lay them down and walk upon them, so give thanks to the stone beneath your feet. What does that even mean? I just wanted . . . I just wanted them to make people do their jobs, not treat their laziness like it was interesting or okay. I just wanted them to acknowledge that I was better."

"Some people are better."

"Temple says that it is pointless to argue if a shark is better than a bat. A shark cannot fly; a bat cannot swim. Why would we call something 'better' when it is incomparable?"

"What do you think?"

"I think it's shit. I think people who can't do their jobs wrote shit like that to make it okay that someone else is doing their work."

"That sounds a lot like heresy."

"I studied heresy. Heresy is forced sterilisation. Heresy is racial profiling, stock buybacks, election tampering. This wasn't heresy. It was the foundation of the Temple itself. I wanted more. And the only way I could . . . the best way I could see . . . I wanted money."

"Why?"

"Because I *earned* it."

"Monasteries have wealth. You could have left the archives and become some fat Medj living off the donations of ignorant people."

"Not in Lyvodia. The accumulation of wealth is a worldly affair. Wealth begets wealth, not justice or equality. We lived at the mercy of the laity, and what we had that was beyond what we needed, we gave away. Not like here – not like in Maze."

"You could have left. Gone to a university. Taught. Studied. The Medj release far more archaic data than they hoard. You could have had a good life, with your stem cells and your … little victories. Why sell the data?"

"It shouldn't be hidden. Our ancestors died discovering this. It belongs to us."

"That's very noble. I don't believe it."

"Greed is impure," I snapped. "It is one of the impurities. We take only what we need; the rest returns to the earth. That is what the Medj say. Endless anecdotes about … happy deer or motherly owls. They said I wasn't ideologically sound. That I did not understand the kakuy."

"Were they right?"

"I honour the kakuy," I barked. "I have always honoured them."

"Why?"

"What do you mean, 'why'? Because it's right. It's what has to be done. They woke when the earth was on fire, they can return us to the flames any time they please, burn the forests, raise the rivers, they can … " I stopped dead, breathing harder than I expected, gripping my bleeding thumb so tight the arteries of my arm pulsed all the way up to my shoulder.

"That isn't honouring," he murmured. "That's fear. You fear the kakuy."

"Don't you?" I retorted. "They are the world's judgement on our ancestors. They are … they are prison guards."

"I'm not sure you're right." He unfolded his legs, stretched out long, like a cat, folded his fingers behind the back of his head, arched his back, relaxed again, smiled. "But please – carry on."

"There's nothing more to say. They didn't listen to me. They said I was suffering from humanist delusions, putting the benefit of a select number of people above the welfare of the whole. They said I'd spent too much time in the archives, read too many journals about ownership, about fantastical social distinctions, about ... conquering the earth. Taming it. Geoengineering. Solar mirrors. Cloud seeding. Lime in the oceans, artificial eruptions, carbon dumping, land reclamation. Our ancestors were so clever, so *powerful*. They were not afraid of fire."

"But they burned," he replied. A gentle nudge, a casual correction. "They all burned."

"The kakuy burned them. If the kakuy hadn't risen, maybe they could have tamed the world. Maybe they could."

He sucked in his teeth, long and slow. "Now that does sound like heresy."

I stared at the dirty wooden floor, resin and wood pounded tight by decades of stamping feet. "What are you going to do with me? I'll leave Vien. I swear, by ... I swear."

The man nodded, but it did not seem that he nodded at me. He considered the ceiling, stretched again, his body locking into a line from head to toe like the bracing of a bridge, before relaxing back into his seat. "No," he said at last. "No, I don't think so. You will stay here. You will continue to work here. My people will check your story. If it is a lie, you'll die, wherever you go. If not, I will occasionally call on you. That is all."

So saying, he rose at once, brushed the front of his coat with the palms of his hands in a single, slow, smooth motion, nodded at his men and headed for the door. I stood, wobbling after him, blathered, "No, wait, but ... what?"

"Good luck to you, Ven Marzouki. Kadri Tarrad." A half-wave, back turned to me now as he pushed the door open, letting in the cold Vien air.

"Wait, I—"

He was already gone with his guards, leaving me alone in the cellar, blood on the floor, keys in my pocket, nowhere else to go.

Chapter 5

Of the seven Provinces that send their Voices to the great Council in Budapesht, Maze is categorically the worst.

Though it is rich in land and blessed with great rivers and mountains, sweeping fertile plains and tall, noble forests, it has nothing of the cosmopolitan charm of Anatalia or the breath-catching richness of Lyvodia. To the north, it borders the endless black forests where live the nomadic Rus, who shunned the city and the hearth as heresies against the kakuy and returned instead to the horse and the steppe, leaving only scattered offerings of milk and blood upon the earth. To the west, it borders the shrouded lands that run all the way to the isles of the Anglaes, who hide behind their sea wall, maintaining a purity of race and culture that they claim survived even the great migrations of the burning, when all the peoples became one. When the ships of the Anglaes enter the southern seas for diplomacy or trade, or their convoys appear at the mouth of the Rhene River, their ambassadors wash their hands three times before greeting any of the peoples of the Provinces, then three times upon conclud-ing their business, lest the impure touch of the mongrel races corrupt them.

"Let there be peace between us," the Medj always say as they greet the shamans and the priests of these distant lands, "lest the kakuy wake."

However barbaric the peoples of the north may be, on that point at least we could agree. Until, perhaps, now.

Walk through Vien, capital of Maze, and smell the rot setting in.

It is a place of half-remembered monuments, of toppled temples to an ancient god, of the armless statues of forgotten heroes plucked from the mud and set in clusters around the garden parks. Wander past the benches where the lovers sit, beneath bowers of green, paths of scented roses and boxes of carrots and cabbages laid between the lawns, and see here – this figure of time-mottled stone might once have been a great general, or here – he might have been some forgotten king. Now they gaze down at the shrines of timber and mycelium brick grown from the fallen walls of their broken palaces, as though their marble eyes might weep the acid that erased them.

On the west side of the Ube River, great efforts are underway to rebuild some of the former grandeur. The cathedral spire had tumbled when the world burned, but the fallen stones have been painstakingly excavated, and now a new spire rises, and music washes from the open doors. Tourists flood in from Praha and Bukarest to hear the reconstructed ballads of Mozert, Beatless and Beyondsee, performed on the traditional instruments of the time to the booming halls, and several times a year the various monotheist denominations gather for prayers to their one God, calling out in archaic tongues for ancient prophecies to show them the newest way.

By the fat, sluggish river, the great temple of the city flies paper streamers from its wooden porch in spring and rings a booming gong for the dawn of winter, its priests clad in muddy brown bowing to the sun and moon between the high branches of the mottled plane trees. Yet at my first winter festival in Vien, while I had knelt in the snow and given thanks for the ice that keeps the mosquito at bay, for the white that glistens on black, for the fire that drives back the dark, for sunset red and cold dawn light, a novice came to me and exclaimed brightly: "Blessing to keep the flu away? For a small donation, we can offer you the protection of the kakuy for the next three months!"

My jaw nearly hit the floor, for here was the unthinkable: a

36

Medj offering magic, peddling false miracles for cash. In Lyvodia, such a thing would have been outrageous, with both the local priests and, perhaps more relevantly, the local clinics up in arms. As each Province was its own state, sharing those laws in common with its neighbour that were passed by Council, so each Temple of every Province had its own ceremonies and rituals – yet surely none could claim that this was one?

Shuffle from door to door in the bloody winter, and know that beneath your feet the foundations of the city are crumbling like the chalky cliff into the raging sea.

At the spring equinox, when the streets lit up with a thousand lanterns hung from every window and carried by children bouncing on their parents' backs, the puritans came, rallied from the Delta and Damasc, from Anatalia and the eastern lands by rumours of Maze's corruption. They paraded between the dancing crowds banging their drums and proclaiming heresy, heresy, heresy! You who shave your beards, who take medicines for your disease, who feast on milk and meat – heretics all! We are of the earth and from the earth comes all our qualities, so why would you try to alter your flesh or fight nature's course? The cycle is all; you cannot escape it. Heresy!

I followed at a distance until they reached the lines of local Medj in robes of brown and blue, who wound through the streets singing their songs and proclaiming that the path to basically all things – wealth, happiness, romantic fulfilment and good dentistry – came from giving generously to Temple. Come, come, they said. Make your offerings and be free. The bigger the offering, the freer you'll be.

These two factions, each heretical to the other, faced off on the corner of Leostrad and Altkirchweg, trying to outdo the other in chanting, banging of drums and displays of piety, egging each other on to more dramatic protestations of devotion, up to and including banging their heads against the walls until they bled, crying, "Our blood feeds the kakuy!" or "The kakuy will guarantee an easy pregnancy!"

Eventually the guardia had to split them up, and the pundits on the radio could not keep the contempt from their voices. The next day, Brotherhood members painted crimson murals of the fat Medj of the city and the fanatic, emaciated hermit of the south screaming at each other, spit flying from their grotesque, curling lips. The motto beneath simply said "Pray For Us", and people tutted and muttered that really, it wasn't right for those who claimed to be holy to behave that way – not right at all.

Walk through the city, blood pooling in your hand, and sense the thunder that comes before the storm.

The struts of an ancient bridge still stick up from the river, a sign beside their stubby fingers explaining the great engineering of the past, the mighty skills of our ancestors. A dome covered in tall grass where the spotted starlings bicker has been built on a base of marble and steel, and people come from all around to touch the white-polished walls and oooh and aahh and say that truly the builders of the past achieved remarkable things. The Provincial Assembly sits in a former palace, one side tumbled down and replaced with columns of pulped hemp and lime to support the solar glass ceilings where they meld into ancient stone, like the hermit crab nestling its way into the shell of the abandoned snail. On its walls are new reconstructions of ancient paintings – men with hands resting upon the globe they wished to conquer, swords at their sides, moustaches primed and chins high. At the feet of some, the sextant and the lead weight, for these are men who have mastered the earth as well as each other, and thought themselves greater than the fury of the skies.

"Our past was glorious – why should we hide?" demand the Assemblymen, and they have a point, for shame was never as comforting as lies.

In the winding streets far from the river, the hearths are pressed in tight and tall, feeding off each other's warmth in winter and bathing in each other's summer shade. Here are slung lines of laundry when the warm wind blows, and beneath them the shady swag of grape, sweet pea and ivy laced from one door to another. Outside every window run tresses of herbs and fragrant flowers, all the way to the roofs of the packed-in houses, where you may pluck some savoury treat to sprinkle on a hot dish from the stove, or whose scent in spring drives back the freshly spawned insects from the river. Shutters are thrown open so neighbours may call to each other in the morning, and behind each cluster of timber-framed housing is a courtyard where the elders tend the biovats that keep the pipes warm and play cards and argue over who is right about a point of forgotten memory.

The smell of fresh bread greets the dawn, though a new fad seems to emerge every few months as the historian-bakers of the city try to outdo each other recreating some ancient recipe – a sweet treat of cherries and rare, precious cocoa or coffee bean, or a folded pastry of extortionate, crumbling butter. Even the food in Vien looks to the past, with countless festivals where people gorge on milk and venison and sing songs from a time when all men were heroes.

And here a sight unforgivable, for in the doorways of the station sit the homeless men and women, abandoned by their own city. They huddle together on beds of card, until the guardia chase them away. Where should they go? Temple should take them in, but their doors are locked – go away, go away, you are no good here! The Assembly should fund refuges, places of safety, there should be hearths with open doors to give them shelter, but no.

Not any more.

"Maze is not here to empower laziness," proclaims the Chief Minister. "It is upon you to seize opportunity."

The Council has laws about this, enacted across all the Provinces – laws that Maze itself helped draft and ratify, in a gentler time. Inequality breeds contempt, Council says. Did we not learn from the great burning how the richest considered their lives more valuable, their moral worth and social deserts superior to those of the poorest? Did we not watch them build walls to keep out their fellow humans, proclaiming, "He who is rich is better to keep alive than the poorest teacher, doctor, nurse, builder, mother, father or child?"

The sea tore down even their walls, when all was said and done. But we should not wait for the ocean to settle our accounts.

39

"The Council is supposed to be advisory, a source of unification!" proclaims Antti Col, the Brotherhood banner flying at his back. "Instead they are tyrants seeking to tell us how to live!"

As timber falls to build ever bigger and more extravagant homes, where are the libations, the freshly planted saplings and the careful copses to nourish the life of the woods? All gone, all neglected. We take more than we give, and the leaves wither and the river rises; we tip our sewage straight into the fresh water that rises from beneath fertile mud, and the clouds boil and the wind blows icy from the north, and people wonder: are we poisoning ourselves, or will the kakuy do it for us?

What will we do if the kakuy wake?

The kakuy never slept, warns the pious Medj of the south. The wind and the ocean never cease, and the earth is patient. Tread lightly, my brethren. Do not shake the world too particularly when you pass.

No one I met in Vien had ever seen the kakuy.

Some said they weren't even real.

Dawn breaks across the city as I shuffle home through the rising light.

On the east bank of the Ube River, the streets are clean, broad and practical. Bicycle paths weave between the courtyard-shrouding hearths, old brick mixed with new mycelium and solar cell, creating a jigsaw of beige, white, crimson and grey. From the bathhouses and communal halls the morning smell of pine, yeast and tea brewed long enough to turn your insides brown mingled with polite chatter and discreet silences between courteous people. No one had the same burning interest in gossiping about their neighbours as we had in Tinics; to be caught griping about someone's plants dribbling onto your laundry was considered thoroughly unsophisticated, and the people of the west so very much wanted to be sophisticated.

I lived in a hearth like any other, thirteen of us to the tall, winding building. I ate alone, slept alone, declined offers of friendship when given, and rebutted even cordial inquiry with monosyllabic grunts or a shaking of my head. If anyone tried to engage me on questions of politics or faith, I avoided it with a shrug and an "It's not really my business, is it?"

Strangely, this answer seemed to be accepted, though I could hardly imagine anything that might be more my business than the running of the world I lived in.

"Where are you from, with your accent?" a neighbour asked, and: "Lyvodia," I replied.

"Oh, Lyvodia! Lovely place. I go on holiday sometimes there. The people are so . . . so gentle, aren't they?"

By "gentle" he meant "lazy", for there was nothing quite as fashionable at this time as mocking the peoples of another Province. We were all meant to be one, and yet on the radio the Brotherhood howled and wailed against injustice, injustice – the gross injustice of being wedded by Council to Provinces who were lesser than our own!

"Ever going to go back?" my neighbour inquired, voice light as the butterfly, not meeting my eye.

"Not if I can help it."

He smiled and nodded and said nothing more, and after that didn't bother to greet me on the stairs.

So all things in Vien were rotten, including me.

Then, two months after the Brotherhood nearly cut my thumb off in a bar, they came back.

Chapter 6

In the heat of the moment, I had not taken much time to note the features of my assailants. When one of them came up to the counter and ordered a cup of hot rice wine, my stomach recognised him while my mind rebelled. His skin was much like mine, the deep olive that had emerged in those peoples who survived the great migrations, when the old tribal boundaries broke down, but he had dyed his dark hair a streaky crimson and pulled it back into a knot that seemed to elongate his high forehead into a cliff. I poured the drink with clammy hands, took his money, left the flask by his side and went about my business with the small of my back suddenly exposed, every hair on my arms standing tall, fingers clumsy and tongue dull in my mouth.

He watched me, that was all. The cellar was hot and crowded, filled mostly with the laughter of men and a few cross-legged women pressed into time-crumbling walls. The talk was of crop failures and discontent, of political change and social revolution, mixed with the usual hearth gossip and romantic misadventures. The man who'd tried to cut my thumb off did not participate in such things, but neither was he unknown. People who approached the bar nodded at him and turned away; respect without friendship.

I did my best to stay away from his end of the counter, but couldn't for ever. He finished his flask of wine, raised one hand, caught my eye. I approached, fumbled a few words, tried again. "Can I get you something else?"

"You read this?"

He pushed a slip of thin yellow paper over the counter. On it, written in archaic German, was a time and a place. The handwriting was stiff, clumsy – as if each unfamiliar character were copied one line at a time from a dictionary, rather than a familiar, flowing thing. I nodded, swallowed. "Anything else?"

He shook his head, tapped his empty cup three times on the wooden bar as if completing some ritual, rose and pushed his way through the crowd.

Four hours later, I stood in the doorway of an old-town mansion as the evening rain sang down the water pipes and made the reclaimed cobbles shimmer like the sea. I closed my eyes against the night and stamped my feet and puffed into my cupped hands and wondered whether I'd leave with my fingers still attached.

A few streets away, I heard a door slam, laughter, the clattering of a bike pushed along a slippery pavement. Someone tried to sing a few verses of a song – a Temple devotional, slurred and out of tune – before someone else louder and differently inebriated cut in with a Brotherhood anthem, a chorus of mankind's strength and dominion.

A cat meowed and a flock of pigeons darted away from their warm perches in the grassy roof above. Steam trickled from a vent by my feet, laced with the smell of pine.

I checked my watch, wound it, checked it again, found barely thirty seconds had passed, pulled my coat tighter, listened. Behind a shutter, a light turned on, then off again, then back on. A figure moved, looking for something in the dark, disturbed by restless dreams or aching bones. They found it; moved back towards a bed. The light turned off again. At the end of the street, the low whine of an electric truck as it passed by, the splash of sheets of water spilling up from a blocked drain in the reclaimed rubber road, the gentle whoosh of a cooling fan from the server office on the corner. Voices raised in the dark, passing by, fading away.

After fifteen minutes, I thought of going. Even the heartiest of revellers were headed to bed, leaving only the long-night novices about their sleepy prayers, if they bothered to pray at all.

I was half snoozing, swaying where I stood, when the car came. I had seen only a few private cars in my life. In Tseonom, the local clinic had one shared between whichever doctors were on call for the area, and in Bukarest the guardia and a few senior Assembly officials had possessed such things, but that was about the limit of it. Most farming hearths had their trucks and tractors, solar panels pressed to cabin roofs for an emergency recharge should they get stuck in the mud, battery packs swung in the middle of their chassis, but in a city like Vien these things were unusual status symbols, as vulgar as they were secretly, quietly envied.

This car pulled up a few feet in front of me, headlights low, engine silent, and as I approached I had to bend almost double to peer at the reflective windows. Before I could get a good look inside, the door opened, pushing me back, and a voice said: "Oh – he's wet."

I leant down to see the interior of the car. Three grey padded seats lined the back, the middle far smaller than the two either side. In the front were two more seats, both occupied, one by the man who had accosted me at the bar. In the back there was a man, a chiselled slab of human in a high-collared black jacket with translucent seashell buttons down the front and at his wrists.

"Are you getting in?" he asked, when I didn't move.

"Are you going to cut my thumb off?"

"Only if you don't get in. Come on, I have an early meeting and would like to shower first."

If sleep was also on his list of things to do, he did not say. I got into the car, pulled the door shut awkwardly, clung to the seat in front of me, heard his little snort of derision. "Put your seatbelt on."

I fumbled with the belt he indicated, struggled with where my arms were meant to go in relation to the strap. He didn't seem interested in my escapades, eyes fixed on the gently glowing inkstone in his lap. On this occasion he wore a ring, bearing the crossed axe and spade of the Brotherhood, oversized on a little finger. At the clip of my seatbelt locking shut, he looked up as if the sound were an alarm and passed me his inkstone.

"Read this."

It nearly slipped from my grasp, but I held tight, tried to focus on the words through the strange movement of the car. It was written in archaic English and was largely a preamble about following health and safety guidelines as laid out in legislation, and the importance of ear defenders. In the top right corner was a string of numbers and letters, a serial number that made my heart sink. I flipped to the next page, and when this audacity didn't elicit violence, kept reading. Soon the generic business gave way to more meaty topics, including guidelines on angles of ascension and declension, and the necessity of having a good wind sock.

"Well?" asked the man at last.

"What do you want to know?"

"What do you make of it?"

"It's a training manual."

"I was looking for a little more insight."

"It's a training manual for an armament. A mortar. This one is small, transported by one or two people. The explosive can fly over obstacles and be launched while in cover."

"What else?"

"It's a very dull read."

"Is it authentic?"

"I don't know, this is just a transcript, not the original. I'd have to see—"

For the first time since I'd got in the car, the man turned his head to look me straight in the eye. "Is it authentic?" He repeated the question as if confused by my stupidity, baffled that I could still be talking when, clearly, there was nothing else to say.

His eyes were blue, framed by the dark. The low white lights of the city pushed and pulled the shadows across his features as we sped down empty roads.

I looked away, swallowed, kept on reading. "The syntax is right, and the grammar's not bad," I mumbled. "But archaic

English was prone to breaking its own rules. Illustrations are wire-frame renderings, which isn't unusual in technical guides of this time. There's no data degradation I can see, although this is a transcript. But you'd expect something to have been lost, a few areas of missing or corrupted text from the original file, unless you were lucky and the hard drive was kept in natural cold storage that minimised contamination until unsealed. It's also noticeable that there isn't an exploded view of parts. Most manuals of this sort are designed to allow the operator to maintain their equipment in the field. That's . . . curious. Do you have any cross-referencing material?"

"Not yet."

"Then I can't definitively say."

"That's disappointing."

I shrugged. "You'd rather I lie? You don't need much to fake data from the burning; there's still a thriving black market in snake oil and material sciences. Anyone who says this is authentic without cross-checking is an idiot."

I tossed the inkstone onto the empty seat between us, not quite having the guts to throw it in his face. We drove in silence a while, rain running in little sideways-stretched dribbles down the windows, the man from the bar watching me in the driver's mirror from the front of the car. I found my reflection in the moving light across the glass fascinating, a hollow plucked-out version of how I imagined myself. My frizzy dark hair had grown out around my ears, making the face it framed seem smaller by comparison, green-grey eyes sinking into the sockets. The lines on my skin were deep enough to make my features appear crudely plugged together – a modular chin that didn't match the modular eyebrows that someone had glued to a second-hand skull. I tried to see the man behind me in the reflection in the glass, but the shadows of the car were too deep, so it was to nothing much and no one in particular that I said: "The serial number at the top." He didn't move, hands laced across one folded leg, so I went on. "That's a Temple librarian's code. I don't know the database it's from, but I recognise the prefix. Highly classified – heretical. The

46

kind of material that gets locked in an archive in some obscure mountain shrine. I don't know if it's real, and I absolutely don't want to know where or how you got it, but if it's fake, someone's tried very hard to replicate Temple codes."

I turned back to examine my companion, who said nothing. Then he leant across, picked up his inkstone, turned it off, slipped it into a pouch on the side of his seat, smiled at nothing much, nodded at no one in particular and said: "Thank you. We'll be in touch."

The car slowed. I didn't move. He half-turned his head, seemed to look straight through me, waiting. I thought about opening my mouth to ask a question and instead fumbled with the handle of the door and let myself out, shaking and shivering, into the sodden night.

Chapter 7

During the spring festival in Tinics, we would walk into the forest to find the first purple flowers, and it was considered good luck to be the first to spot the buzzing bee or hear the call of the common cuckoo. Even after the forest burned, the Medj took us into its ruins and we would find lesser gifts from the growing land; new green shoots arising from the split-open trunks, or fresh moss on the stone within which lived insect upon insect, so that as your eye adjusted to their tiny wiggling bodies of vanilla, white and grey, you saw more again, and more, zooming down into the heart of the thing as a telescope may look up into the darkness and see nothing but stars.

At the spring festival in Vien, people went to the temples to give offerings of money in exchange for good harvest, and many more protested outside saying it wasn't fair that the priests grew fat on their living while citizens suffered, and Antti Col and his Brotherhood cronies made indignant speeches outside the Assembly about the harvest being man's work, man's toil, the land being carved by our will, not fickle, faithless nature.

And in Tinics – in the place that had been my home – the forest grew.

Between winter and spring, I was contacted four more times by the men from the bar. Each time was the same – a late-night pick-up, an archaic document scraped from ancient servers. Two were definitely false. One was almost certainly the genuine article, which I was ordered to translate in full. All of them were heresy.

On my fifth encounter, I was summoned at 4 a.m. to a hearth near the old palace gardens. It was one of the few fully restored buildings of the old world, complete with tiny blue and green tiles woven into a zig-zag pattern across the floor, banisters of twisted iron, high windows of pure, not even solar, glass, and no more than two or three people living in it. I struggled to imagine inhabiting such a place, uncertain if I should walk on veined white stone or thick red carpet – or how many offerings had been made to the kakuy of earth and sky in thanks for the precious goods that built such a place. Not enough, I suspected. The mind that crafted such things did not have much capacity for humility before the sleepy spirit of the mountain.

Dawn was a thin greyness on the horizon, and beneath the bending branches of the springtime trees the Medj were beginning their morning prayers, the sound of half-hearted chanting carried by a cold, damp breeze to the cracked-open windows of the first floor. Soon the lights would be turned off for the silver day, and the streets would clatter with bicycles and cargo carriers, and the server offices would power up their networks as the bathhouses filled with steam. Facing it all, back to the door and eyes to the window, there he was: my sometimes-master and unknown blackmailer, dressed now in an old-fashioned silver waistcoat, a glass held in one hand, the contents hidden from my sight by the broad curve of his fingers. A long desk of black wood stood between us, its top adorned with red leather – real leather, perhaps, the real skin of an actual animal, kept supple and buffed by I knew not what magic. On it was his inkstone, the words already turned towards me as if conversation were an inconvenience best left for daylight hours. I approached beneath hanging bulbs in resin-crystal fittings, noted the private server and computer on the desk, the pictures on the wall of long-faded heroes' valiant deeds, the abstract illustrations and even one crackling, deep-dark work of monotheism that could well have been genuine, depicting a Christian saint with hands upturned towards a trumpeting angel. I had seen no sign that this man believed in anything at all, and the picture seemed to hang as part of a cultural history, a landmark in the journey of how the world came from there to here.

My observations had taken too long, for now he half-turned from the window to glance at me. "Well?"

I picked up the inkstone, read the first page, flipped to the second, stopped, read again, went back a page, forward a page, stopped. Put the inkstone down and, for the first time since I had met this man, held his gaze.

If this surprised him, he did not show it. Not an eyelash quivered in contemplation. "Yes?"

"It is a military paper on the use of radioactive substances in assassination."

"Is it genuine?"

My lips curled against my teeth, and I did not answer.

Now he turned fully, his shoulders following the angle of his neck as if a rod pinned him to the ground, around which he spun in sections.

"Is it genuine?"

"Probably. I am familiar with at least one of the cases it cites."

"Good. You will provide a full translation by sixth day."

"No."

Not an eye twitched, not a capillary flushed, but the corner of his mouth curled, almost as if he would smile. "No?"

"No. You have an inside source feeding you the kind of heresies that would make Temple inquisition bleed from the eyes, but you need me to verify and translate it. Fine. Pay me."

"Why would I do that?"

"Because my service is valuable to you."

"I think you forget the nature of our relationship."

"I don't. Hurting me doesn't do anything for you. It destroys a resource you want to use. When we met, you called me 'Medj of the Temple of the Lake'. I never said which temple I was from. You knew about me long before you brought the knives out, knew I wasn't Kadri Tarrad. You left me alone until I was useful. You have use of me. I'm not greedy; it won't be too expensive. But I want more. Pay me."

Slowly, he sat down, put the glass to one side, splayed his hands out across the desk one finger at a time. "I can see why you found the limited ambitions of your colleagues so frustrating. How much do you want?"

"Two hundred bi for every translation of fifty pages or less. More to be calculated on a per-page rate based on this figure thereafter. Illustrations still count as pages. And a retainer of one hundred bi a month."

"That is, of course, absurd."

"Any other translator would charge you twice as much and report you for heresy. It's a bargain and you know it."

"Do not overestimate your value."

"I think I have estimated it accurately, based on the current market."

The fingers on his left hand rippled, a motion picked up by his right, little finger to little finger across the desk. For a moment, his eyes looked past me, and I wondered if his thugs were waiting for a cue, knives ready, cracked knuckles and dark eyes. It took a physical clenching of my belly, a tightening of my fists, not to turn to check. Then he appeared to relax, nodded once and said: "Very well. But you will increase your output for us, and if we require other services you will comply quickly and without question – fully paid, of course. Agreed?"

"Agreed."

"Excellent. Take the translation. You will deliver it on fifth day."

He gestured loosely at the inkstone. I picked it up, swiped the files to my own, returned it to the desk, made to leave, found no monsters standing behind me, no cudgels raised to bash in my skull, stopped, looked back.

"What's your name?" I asked.

"You may call me Georg," he replied, and turned to contemplate the rising sun.

So began my involvement with the Brotherhood, heresy and the war.

Chapter 8

When I joined the Temple as a layman of the academic review board, my professor, Lah of the Temple of the Lake, sat me down in their little office above the courtyard of pine and pebble and said:

"In the basement of this temple we have a shelf of hard drives recovered and transcribed from the burning. They contain information on medical experiments conducted on prisoners of war and civilian populations across conflicts down the eras. Nerve gas, bacterial warfare, chemical bombs. Weaponised viruses that turned a body's immune system against itself, killing the young before killing the old. Compounds that sent a person blind, blistering the skin, the lungs; people drowning in their own fluids. Many were tortured; many died. People were experimented on based on their race and sexual orientation, or allowed to suffer with treatable conditions so that physicians could learn how death progressed. They have been declared heretical, abhorrent, but the academic review board has a duty to review heresies on an ongoing basis with one question in mind: Who are we now? Before the burning, it was considered heretical for women to behave in a manner considered male. Then these words changed – 'female', 'male'. They have changed again since that time. What is our new morality? What is our new heresy? What would you do with this information, kin of sky and earth? What would you do for those who lived, and those who died?"

"I don't know," I replied.

"Someone must decide. The burden falls on us. Three thousand words on these points by tomorrow afternoon, please."

That was when I was Ven Marzouki, before I became Kadri Tarrad, before Nadira came to me and said, "If you can stick your thumb in your assailant's windpipe, it really is very effective."

That was before I saw Yue again.

The Temple of the Lake in Bukarest was close to the local Assembly. Every winter and summer, the Chief Minister of Lyvodia would come and make offerings and drink hot tea with the priests and walk the grounds around the wide waters and discuss matters both theological and political. When I was a novice, Ull had only just been elected Chief Minister and felt it important to be seen nodding and paying polite attention to the words of the Medj who prayed beneath the spider-silk tree.

Sometimes, protesters came too, a dozen or so men and women with placards waved outside the temple doors. I was sent to offer them tea, and sometimes they took it, and sometimes they threw the cups on the floor, smashing the thin worked clay, which I swept up and used as ballast at the bottom of potted plants.

"Separation of church and state!" one man screamed in my face, when I asked him if he wanted a biscuit. "The Temple keeps us down!"

"Did you know," I asked politely, "that the idea of 'separation of church and state' is from an era known as the Enlightenment? It was an age in which humankind attempted to redefine its internal relationship with itself – with power and tyranny and justice – and its external relationship with the world, i.e. God, and through God, the planet."

The man just kept on chanting, his spittle flying in my face, which seemed a terrible waste of good tea.

After, as we watched Ull cycle away with his entourage back to the Assembly of Bukarest, Lah stood beside me in the half-open sliding door of their little room by the turned vegetable patch, sighed and said: "It is our own fault that the protesters are here. No one else is to blame."

53

I was silent. It was usually best to be silent when Lah was about to speak of things that troubled them.

"Before the Provinces united – when we were simply Lyvodia and Maze and Damasc and the Delta, and so on – Temple sent missionaries out across the lands in an attempt to convince each nation that we were one, humble beneath mother earth and father sky. Yet our most convincing argument was not one of universal fellowship, of compassion and justice and the beauty of this shared, sacred earth. Our most convincing argument was simply this: do not go to war, lest you wake the kakuy. The kakuy are hardly seen any more, but the memory of the creatures that crushed the cities and scoured humanity from the plains takes a long time to fade, even from the fickle memories of humanity. Fear brought the Provinces together in alliance. Fear created the Council to represent all of us as one; fear created the common laws of Assembly, democracy and peace. But fear is exhausting. Effective, but exhausting. And to the eyes of those who see Council as a tool of oppression, as a mouthpiece for the Temple that helped create it, there is nothing in our prayers that is not poison. They say that Temple inquisitors have infiltrated every corner of the Provinces – that our spies manipulate Assembly and government. When we say no, no, inquisitors are meant to stop the spread of nerve agents and automatic weaponry, all they hear is fear. Fear of the past. Fear of change. Fear of what humanity could be. The kakuy teach us that every breath of air is a gift, that the first shoot of spring green is a wonder to behold. But it is easier to be big and loud in your terror than to be tiny in your gratitude. We are to blame."

"What are we going to do about it?" I asked, young and naïve as I was.

Lah laughed, a single bark in the settling gloom. "I have no idea. Like the peoples of the Burning Age, I fear we see our ending come – and cannot imagine that we ourselves can prevent it. More tea, novice?"

In the years between then and now, only one thing has been consistent: as humankind squabbled and bickered, fought for power, prestige and status, back in Tinics the forest grew.

Chapter 9

This is how I became part of the Brotherhood, sworn to justice, humanism and the triumph of the human race.

From translating texts, I was one night summoned to receive some stolen data myself.

"My usual courier is indisposed," Georg sighed. "You'll have to make the drop."

"Fine. You'll pay me double."

He grinned, less at my cheek and more, I felt, because he had predicted that I would be cheeky and was glad at the accuracy of his guess. "You'll be paid by the hour. It should take you less than two."

A Medj, face hidden in hood and shadow, whispered to me through the side gate of the Temple of the River: "It's worth at least five times that!" but I had orders to only pay nine hundred bi for the datastick they slipped me, and they didn't stay to argue the point.

I knew how it felt to be that scuttling priest, slipping back into their dormitory in temple grounds, and felt neither sympathy nor fear that night.

"Well?" Georg asked.

"It's a collection of books on the theme of self-empowerment through wealth accumulation. 'Visualise yourself rich. Then make it happen. No university will teach you this secret. Belief unlocks your human potential and—'"

Georg waved me to silence. "What a shame," he sighed. "Another waste of time."

From receiving stolen data, I graduated to attending occasional meetings with not only Georg but also Kun Mi, Brika and Tanacha, introduced to me as senior policy figures within the Brotherhood's political wing. They rarely wanted my opinion on their ideas – tightening abortion laws to encourage births, changing laws on inheritance, re-writing press codes to force journalists to merely report what they said rather than comment on its factuality – but occasionally Georg would turn to me and say: "Did they do this in the burning?" and I would answer yay or nay, and very little more was needed from me.

One night, after another such meeting, Georg turned to me and said: "What do you think of those three?"

"I think they're so blinded by their own personal desire to get rich and get respect that they wouldn't recognise a good idea if it punched them in the face."

He beamed, nodded, brisk and bright, and proclaimed: "Yes. That's precisely how I feel on the matter."

And every month or so Georg passed me another document to translate or verify, and there it was at the top of every page, that little line of numbers and letters that marked the text below as classified, heretical, profane in Temple eyes. He never said where these documents were coming from, and I knew better than to ask.

Then one day towards the end of summer, he marched up to where I sat huddled over a stolen text and proclaimed: "You are now making the same wage as a medium-salaried assistant within my office. You will start here full-time next first day."

"Will I?"

"Yes."

"Why?"

"Because you will be quickly promoted, you will be safe, you will be part of one of the greatest movements in human history, and you'll no longer have to mop up vomit from the front step of the bar. Yes?"

"May I have a day to think about it?"

"If you really think it's necessary. I do not."

56

I quit the bar that very night and was moved to a side office in the same magnificent restored building which Georg had made his home. My work evolved again, from collecting data, performing mildly illicit acts and translating heresy to secretarial work for the Brotherhood itself, planning rallies and editing addresses by its elected Voices in the Assembly, researching talking points for debates, and cataloguing a never-ending stream of spreadsheets and databases of members, assets, resources and the occasional enemy.

"That is Ayodele," Georg murmured in my ear one day as we listened to a female voice on the radio proclaiming the need for urgent Temple reform and social dialogue. "She is trouble."

Four weeks later, a file with her name crossed my desk, sealed tight. I steamed it open in the local bathhouse, read it by torchlight, closed it up before passing it on to Georg. A week after that, Ayodele stood down from the Assembly, citing personal reasons, and in the by-election that followed her seat fell to the Brotherhood, and Georg invited me to his office for a toast.

"The good stuff," he explained, as I filled the glasses on the table. "Seeing how far we've come."

In the evening, I still translated archaic texts, ranging from the banal to the petrifying.

hey why arnt u ansring my calls? just call me back ok. I ddnt mean the thing i said. your being a child.

So many ancient servers were full of noise, noise, noise. Broken images of pets, babies and food. Messages from lovers and enemies long since dead, their passions recorded in stiff fonts and binary numbers.

babe i luv u wat u want 4 food? u seen what M said?

Even in the best-kept archives, you had to wade through the voices of the burning, peel back their lives to find the good stuff, the proper heresy for an ancient age.

People believe what they want to believe. Tell them what they want to hear. Social media moves faster than fact-checkers, so as long as you . . .

Improve your Spanish! Tres tristes tigres tragaban trigo en un trigal en tres tristes trastos. En tres tristes trastos tragaban trigo tres tristes tigres.

As the number of neutrons increase in the atom, it becomes unstable . . .

Six months after Georg started paying me for my work, I moved into a Brotherhood hearth built around the columns of what had once been a raised road just for cars. Segments had collapsed down the centuries, leaving only odd standing pillars of the past, on the top of which flocks of sparrows had made their homes, startling in black clouds at the shadow of a predator overhead.

Though this new place was more like the hearths I knew, with shared food at a shared table, there were no women in it, and chores were enforced as icy discipline rather than familial co-operation. The hydroponic walls were untended; the fish tanks empty. Conversation was the same litany of complaints every evening – of men who felt disappointed with their lot, held back from advancement, punished for failing to conform, unable to make something more. Men trapped within a system where the respect of your hearth was considered more valuable than your material possessions; where money did not pass to your children and the generation of wealth was not considered an accurate reflection of your contribution to society.

"I want to be a man," muttered a Brotherhood devotee called Sohrab as we bathed together in the hot tubs below the apartments, the light through the skylight above playing sunset orange and gold across his skin. "There was a time when that meant something. There was a time when it wasn't heresy to be strong."

There were other hearths where the women lived, and perhaps the conversation there was much the same. I had never lived with just one sex before.

When the rain broke, washing away the last heat of sticky summer, Georg stood with the windows of the office wide open, smelling the city open beneath the deluge, hands out to catch the fat drops as they pooled in his palm, and said: "How did air conditioning work?"

"A similar principle to artificial refrigeration," I answered. The sky blistered purple and yellow, ocean grey and midnight blue, as though the heavens had held their breath and could gasp no more.

58

"When a liquid converts to a gas, it absorbs heat. Compounds flowing through a closed system would constantly evaporate and condense. When they evaporated, they cooled the pipes they flowed through. When they condensed, they released the heat to the outside world."

"Why don't we do that now?"

"Temple declared it heresy. They said that the chemicals were dangerous, and that making heat in order to move heat away from you just made more heat, and that if you heated up the world in order to keep your parlour cool, you were not living by the ways of the kakuy."

"What do you think?"

"I think that trying to stay cool on a hot planet by heating up the planet more . . . in the long run isn't a winning idea. It would, as the Medj say, displease the kakuy."

"But if only a few had air conditioning? Only the select? Assuming equality seems the mistake here, not the technology itself." I shrugged, and he nodded at nothing much, contemplating the rain. "Must be damned hot in those priest robes."

"Most Medj like to preach from the shade," I replied, watching the water tumble in sheets from the gutter across the street, a miniature waterfall of reflected light. Tiny rivers bounced and wriggled towards the drains, carrying fallen leaves and the settled dust of summer away.

"Memorise these," Georg said, pushing a datastick into my hand.

Loaded into my inkstone, it revealed a series of names and faces, some posed, others caught on an angle. I studied every feature, lay at night trying to imagine them alive, breathing and laughing, returned to work the next day to find a new suit of finest linen and spider silk on the back of my chair.

"It's a loan," Georg said, with a smile in the corner of his mouth, as I stroked the translucent beetle-black of the sleeve. "Try not to spill wine on it."

That evening we attended a party in a restored villa a few blocks from the Assembly. Every detail had been paid to the recreation, from the wood-panelled walls to the paper books – with actual words printed in them – lining the walls. I ran my finger along the shelf, mouthing the ancient names of Hemmingveg, Jelinek, Attwood, Chang and Koates. I doubted the spines had ever been cracked, smelt the fresh glue in the bindings, wondered how much it had cost to have such extraordinary things made and who had translated them from their ancient texts. Double doors with handles of polished brass opened to reveal a long white table laden with duck, chicken, pork, beef, fish eggs and delicate slices of pink salmon on beds of ice, glasses of bubbling wine and fresh red lobster. I stared in amazement as people went to fill their plates, tried to work out the cost of getting such goods, of transporting so much refrigerated flesh from so far away. Then Georg was by my side and murmured, "Mind yourself," and I closed my mouth and wondered what else he had seen in my eyes.

"Her." A tilt of his chin towards a woman, crystal glass spinning in a gloved hand.

"Minister for Energy, Lerna Binks," I replied.

A half-nod; perhaps thanks for information he did not know, perhaps acknowledgement of a test completed.

"Him."

"Head of northern section railways, Chiwocha Ckahad."

"What do you think of him?"

"That he's never eaten lobster before."

"Have you?"

"No. I've never seen one."

"Then how can you judge?"

I bit my lip, bowed my head. He raised his glass to salute someone of minimal importance who'd saluted him, breathed: "Stay close, always behind, and do not speak until spoken to."

I nodded and followed him deeper into the crowd.

" ... I mean the Assembly in Damasc is hardly functioning at all these days, it's all just talk talk talk ... "

"Council laws, always just more Council laws, don't do this, do do that, do you know I spend more time these days learning Council laws than I actually do running my business?"

"Who do they even think they . . . "

"What do you mean, 'crack the shell'? Oh gosh that's terribly . . . I mean, isn't it . . . ?"

"Do we even need Council? Do we even need the other Provinces? Georg, help us out here, help me explain this to him, he's so . . . "

"Georg Mestri. I see you still know how to throw a party."

"Pav. I didn't expect you to attend."

A moment of panic – I didn't recognise this man with a shock of snow-white hair above a tiny almond face. His eyes were huge compared to his tiny hook nose and tight little smile, and though he was nearly a foot shorter than Georg, he managed to hold the little space he inhabited as though every other person in the room were some distant grandchild and he the progenitor of it all. He smiled at Georg and tipped his glass, which he held between his fingertips with his little finger out, as if trying to counter-balance all that weight of crystal, then glanced at me, eyebrow raised. "And this is . . . "

"Kadri Tarrad, my assistant."

"That's a very nice suit, Kadri."

"Thank you. It's not mine."

Another flash of a smile, and then his attention was back where it belonged, burning straight into Georg's eyes, and though the smile remained it was the grin of the shark that knows no other way to show its teeth. Georg adjusted his weight a little more evenly, a tiny tic in his body that prefaced battle, and I briefly felt relieved – he was as surprised to see this man called Pav as I was. "And how long are you gracing Vien with your presence?"

"Not long. Back to see the old hearth, a few friends – you know how it is."

"Of course. I imagine Council keeps you busy."

"Even on Council we have the occasional holiday."

"Do you? I thought all the pronouncements, the new laws, the 'don't-do-this, don't-do-thats' that you people seem to endlessly impose on the Provinces would keep you up every day and every night."

"Our output is only proportional to your imagination. I had no idea how creative the Assembly of Maze could be in coming up with new ways to undermine their own democracy."

"A democracy controlled by Temple is hardly democracy, wouldn't you agree?"

"When I last checked, it seemed to me that the Vien Assembly had more influence over Temple than any Medj over a Minister. Didn't I read that Antti Col managed to get a priest to bless his car?" Pav's laugh was sharp as the glass he held, a tinkle of playing light, a flash of pointed teeth. It was gone so abruptly, listeners might have wondered if it was there at all. "How is Antti doing, Georg?"

"Looking forward to the elections."

"Of course he is. I'm sure he'll do very well."

"Tell me – do you still pray every morning for forgiveness, Pav? I heard you dress in a special gown and brush your teeth with charcoal – a malicious rumour, I'm sure."

"I pray every morning and every night, just to be safe, but alas, my favourite penitent robes don't always fit in the travel bag. You know I respect you, don't you?"

"You have always been very clear about your sentiment."

"Council cannot stop the people of Maze electing Antti to the Assembly, if that's what they want. But the Provinces were united with one purpose at their heart – that the kakuy must sleep. You can march up and down and throw these delightful parties and make all the noise you want. But if you wake the kakuy ..."

"Have you ever seen a kakuy?" Georg cut in, a little louder, eyes fixed on some different place. "No. Of course you haven't. Neither has Jia, or any of her Council. Neither has anyone in Vien, except in paintings at Temple. So while it is absolutely lovely to see you here, of course – always welcome, please do try the lobster – let's not base our discussions on a hypothetical, shall we?"

Pav's smile curled in tight for just a moment – just a moment – before he relaxed again, tipped the lip of his glass towards Georg in salute, drained the liquid down and turned away.

*

"Who was that?" I asked in the soft, low-lit aftermath of the party. The cleaners were moving across the room, shoving half-chewed meat and bits of bone into compost bags for the biowells, the heat of bodies still sticky in the room.

"Hum?" Georg stood by the window, sipping water, watching the night.

"The man called Pav."

"Ah, yes. He was not invited."

"Who is he?"

"Pav Krillovko. He used to be an Assembly member here, many years ago. A servant of Maze. Now he works in Budapesht as chief of staff for the Voice of Council herself, passing down pronouncements to all the Provinces as if he wasn't once one of us. A waste. He was a good man, before Temple got to him."

"He appeared to threaten you without having the power to act on it."

A snort of laughter. "Quite. That is the Council's way, isn't it? Their power rests on habit. We are habituated to obeying what they say without question, but if a Province chooses not to, to resist, then it turns out the Council is quite incapable of enforcing its pronouncements. Pav knows that. Interesting that he came here in person."

I opened my mouth to ask something more, to blurt out words, questions, and stopped myself. Georg rolled the glass between the palms of his hands as plates of wasted food were thrown into stinking bags for the biopits, and in the world outside even the prowling cats slumbered.

"Good night, Georg," I said.

"Good night, Kadri," he replied, without looking back.

Chapter 10

At the autumn festival, I went out of habit to the temple to give thanks for the gifts of the earth, for the heat of the sun and the cold of the rain. I bowed my head to the wind and was grateful for its touch, but other members of the Brotherhood tutted and shook their heads and said it was rank superstition. Human is the superior species, they intoned. Whether by accident or design, we had only ourselves to thank for our thriving.

Later, I was invited to dine with some of the women of the party. I had almost never seen these mysterious figures, dressed primly in knee-length skirts and tight buttoned shirts. But even the Brotherhood felt it necessary for its members to rest on occasion, so I found myself kneeling at a long, low table decked with beans and lentils, fresh forest mushrooms and apple stew, next to a woman called Rilka. Her short black hair was cut to a line across her shoulders, and she sliced all her food into perfect, tiny morsels, before eating one at a time as if waiting for bitterness.

"We are mothers," she proclaimed. "We have forgotten what it was to be proud of that. You cannot be a real woman unless you give birth. Only then, real."

I did not think she had any children, and she did not look at her food as she nibbled it down.

One night, returning to my room, I encountered on the stairs the self-same gentleman who had been so enthusiastic about removing my thumb from my hand. He saw me, recognised me, smiled. I moved my hands together automatically to bow as he passed by, but instead he held out his right hand, an archaic gesture from another era. I shook his hand awkwardly. He gripped far longer than the archives said he should, squeezed tight until my bones scraped and squelched against each other above my palm, grinned, patted me on the shoulder and let me go.

The next day, I realised he had moved into the room next to mine. In the bathhouse, the others called him Klem, and he was an excellent gardener, tending to each leaf like a tailor to a regal gown. We sometimes smiled at each other in passing and never had a conversation.

Chapter 11

In my ninth month working for the Brotherhood, I met Antti Col. The leader of the Brotherhood should have been a charismatic demagogue, a handsome, striking man able to express the frustration of everyone who felt they wanted more, more, more. Instead, as he strode into Georg's office in a flutter of evening blue and golden lapel pin, he was a diminutive weed next to Georg's spring tree, with teeth like yellow fungi and a foul, ranting mouth.

"Fuck the Assembly," he proclaimed, flinging himself sideways across Georg's winter-green couch. "Fuck the Provinces."

Georg poured him a drink as he ranted, decrying Jia, Voice of the Council, as a stupid little whore. The temples were run by ancient toads, outdated dens for paedophiles, and anyway the streets loved him, and had Georg read the latest reports from Budapesht?

"I have," murmured Georg. "Encouraging."

"Is that what you call it? Fucking cowards."

He drained the proffered drink, didn't seem to enjoy it, waved his glass for a refill, which Georg provided. That too was guzzled, and as he laid the glass down, the angle of his arm drifted towards where I stood, silent in my corner, and for the first time his eyes met mine. "Who's that?" he barked, sober and cold.

"That is Kadri, my assistant."

"Why's he just standing there?"

"He's waiting for instructions."

66

"Fuck off – there you go."

My eyes flickered to Georg, who half-nodded in confirmation. I gave a tiny bow from the waist and closed the double doors behind me on my way out.

On the last day of autumn, I cycle up to the forest's edge where the lumber merchants have sliced away the trees. All has been torn down and spat into machines – even the youngest saplings, the freshest growth. It was a pointless destruction, out of balance with the bargain we once struck with the kakuy. There is low thunder in the distance; tonight there will be lightning bright enough to punch through shutter, window, eyelid and sleep, a gasping awake as the heavens grumble in the fading heat.

The Assembly voted to harvest more timber, more from the forests in the hills above, to fish the rivers harder, deeper, to let the factories drain poisons into the downstream gullies and inlets. At my little desk outside Georg's office, I read the letters of protest from the other Provinces, the Assemblies of Bukarest and Budapesht, and from the Council itself.

"Are they going to do anything about it?" Georg would ask.

"Not that I can tell," I replied.

"Then it's just a waste of words. They will want to buy the things we sell, sooner or later. They'll come round. Temple won't be able to stop them – it doesn't know how."

"I was Temple. They will fight you."

He shrugged. "I don't fear the inquisitors."

At the edge of the devastation is a black line where the still-living forest waits for its fate, leaves brushing together like lovers' skin, roots tangled like claws into black, crawling soil. I watch the darkness and it watches back, and though I do not see the kakuy, I think that tonight he prowls beneath the moon in the form of the great black wolf, and I hear his voice howling and know that in this place nothing new will grow, as if the land were sown with salt.

Three months later, I see Yue.

Chapter 12

And where has Yue been, these twenty-odd years?

Why, she has been in Bukarest, studying, learning, working to become the best.

And then?

She has gone to Budapesht, to work for the Council, bringing the Provinces together in one Grand Assembly, doing so well, our Yue, doing so well.

Sometimes she returns to Tinics, at the spring and harvest festivals.

Then she only came back for spring.

Then she did not come back at all.

Mama Taaq spun spider silk from her tree and stirred the fish tanks at the top of the stream and said well, well. She's doing . . . so well. In time, even the nosiest of neighbours stopped asking about it.

And now?

Why, she is walking in Jia's delegation as it arrives at Vien's central station, a few people behind the Voice of Council herself. She is deputy to Krima vaMiyani, who everyone knows is a spy who pretends she's got an interest in culture and telecommunications. She is smiling politely to Antoni Witt, who is already eyeing up the heresies of Maze and muttering about extraordinary actions and desperate times − comments Antti Col has been quick to pick up on as provocative, dangerous. Council serves the Provinces, he snaps; it does not command them.

She is grown up, and having grown up there is nothing of the fire in her any more. She burned from the inside out, and now there are only cool palms pressed together in polite bow; ice smile and stone gaze. She does not see me – or if she does, she does not make the connection between my face, pressed into the shadows, and the boy who once stood with her by the kakuy tree.

She arrives two weeks after Assembly elections in which the Brotherhood wins the majority of seats in the Vien Assembly. She is here, officially, as part of the Council's overall responsibility to visit the Provinces and engage with the cities, Assemblies and temples.

They are here, unofficially, because the election put Antti Col in the Chief Minister's seat, and Antti Col is a humanist and a heretic.

"Fair reward for fair work!" he chants from the podium in the square. "Recognition of human difference, of the power of our diversity – that there are those born with talent, intelligence, strength, that men and women not the same, that we have our own unique parts to play in the balance of the world! A human balance! A human world!"

Georg does not stand on the podium. It is not his place.

When the speech is done, everyone applauds, except Jia, her followers and Yue.

Antti met Jia at the Assembly building, a vast converted pre-burning-era palace that had at one time held princes and kings, then dinosaurs and skeletons of great beasts. It now held restored statues of ancient gods and nude boys holding spears, and cases boasting a range of anthropological specimens from the history of Maze, from the first clay figures carved in mud to the gold cigarette bowls and restored combustion engines of the Burning Age, each adorned with little plaques explaining the traditions and beliefs of the time.

Antti brought Jia there as a power play, the Council forced to come and pay homage at the upstart's place of work, forced to climb the steps up to the great doors beneath the domed roof and flying flags, forced to wait her turn to see the newly appointed master of the Province, forced to smile when finally let in by a pasty demagogue.

I had never seen Jia in person before. I had voted for her in Council elections several times, and the general view of the Lyvodian Assembly was that she was a decent administrator, keeping the Provinces vaguely united through a mixture of tact and legalism. She was older than I expected, her straight black hair turning grey and swept up into a high, stiff topknot. She walked slow and stiff-backed through the halls, but when she sat, her spine would curve down in a little arch, as if the effort of erection were too much to be sustained. Her eyes were tiny in the almond folds of her long, pinched face, but whenever a camera was near she'd tilt her chin up to force her gaze down, creating the impression of a wider, more trustworthy stare. She bowed a little to any stranger who bowed to her, hands pressed together; bowed more to Assembly members, and noted but did not respond when delegates from the Brotherhood barely bowed at her in reply, their disrespect and disdain visible in every curl of their lips or sideways remark.

I kept out of her line of sight, positioning myself in corners and behind inkstone and briefcase, little more than portable furniture in human form. From here, I watched Yue. She walked some three metres behind Jia, buried in the older woman's entourage. Where Jia's stick-like straightness bespoke a harsh dignity, Yue was a metal string pulled between two rods, humming with a tension ready to snap. Her hair was braided either side, close to her skull; her tunic was crow-black, her hands encased in thin grey gloves. She carried her inkstone like a weapon, ready to draw and smash against her opponents, and her eyes scanned left and right, up and down, taking in everything like a cat who is unsure if it sees prey or a trap.

Everything except me.

For a moment, I thought of calling out to her, stepping out and catching her hand.

I did not.

Somewhere, hundreds of miles away, the forest was coming back to life. Vae never would.

"The mining – strip mining! When the kakuy wake . . ."

"When the kakuy wake, when the kakuy wake, when the hell did the kakuy last wake?"

Voices half-heard through the door, arguments about politics, war, a glimpse of Yue at the back, in the room but not of it, stiff and straight as the winter pine.

"The kakuy don't care about borders; what happens in Maze will affect us all!"

Georg sticks his head out of the room to murmur: "More alcohol. This will be a delight."

I nod and go to fetch another bottle. The door closes tight behind Georg, blocking out the little trickle of sound I had been so attentively noting from the gloom.

I find Krima vaMiyani sat on a long balcony round the side of the room where Jia and her cohorts argued and raged, booted feet up on the railing, a drink of something fruity and full of seeds by her side, hat pulled across her eyes to block out the hard winter sun. Seeing her, I immediately move to retreat, but before I can she says: "Kadri Tarrad, isn't it?"

I freeze, turn, wait.

"Georg's assistant. I've seen you scurrying around in his wake. Do you love him?"

"What?" I blurt.

She tilts the hat a little back from her eyes, revealing eyebrows like razorblades, cobalt-black skin and lips painted shocking crimson, so bright on her face it is almost impossible to see anything but her thin, polite smile. "Do you love him?"

"No. I don't love him."

"Do you believe him?"

"Depends what you mean."

"That's a no, then. Are you greedy? I know you used to steal secrets from Temple."

71

From behind the door to her left, I hear voices raised in a sudden gale, then subsiding again. Her eyes don't leave my face as mine flicker to door, to sky, to my shoes and finally back to her. "It occurs to me," I say at last, "if you could convince me to spy for you between now and the time it takes for someone to miss you, that would probably be one of the fastest recruitments in the history of espionage."

She tuts and shakes her head. "On the contrary. The only way I could recruit you in the few charming seconds we have would be if I had spent months researching you to establish precisely how to leverage my approach. You may experience this moment as an instant, but I know how much work has gone into it. I know that there are gaps in your story, Kadri. Things even Georg doesn't know."

"Perhaps – but I'm not convinced you know them either. All you can see are the empty places, not what should fill them."

"I am chief of security for Council itself. I can find out."

"You can threaten me, of course. But you have to consider how scared I am of Georg. And I am. I am scared of him."

She sighs, shakes her head. The moment is gone. She has lost interest, returned to lounging in the last dredges of sun. Did this encounter even happen? Who's to say.

"Too bad," she muses, soft as autumn rain. "Too bad."

Two days later, Jia was gone, and Yue with her, riding the train back to Bukarest.

"That's enough for now," Georg mused, as I closed the shutters across the study windows. "That's enough."

I nodded, picked up my things, turned to leave, my standard dismissal.

"Will you drink?"

I stopped in the door, turned slowly, looked at him, found myself wanting to look away – a habit I thought I had broken in our months of association. He had turned from his customary position by the window to gaze directly at me, and when I didn't immediately answer he nodded towards the decanter on the cabinet by the wall. I put my bag down, walked numbly to the vessel, poured – one for him, one for me – returned to where he stood, handed his drink over, stood dumb as he held it up.

"You are supposed to chink your glass," he explained. "It is a tradition of the Burning Age."

I knocked my glass against his, surprised at the heaviness of it, the depth of its ring. He drained his drink down in a single gulp, so I followed suit. The alcohol burned all the way to my stomach, a sickly-sweet taste of plum and syrup lingering on my tongue. Georg gestured at his couch. I sat, knees together, hands wrapped round my empty glass, and waited. He slipped into his desk chair, rolling back a little into its tanned depths, watched me, said at last: "What do you believe, Kadri Tarrad?"

I thought about the question a long, long time. I had learned that it was always better to stop and think, where Georg was concerned.

"Nothing," I said at last. "But there are things I know to be true, which you might call beliefs. I know that humanity was once master of this world. I know that there was a time when everyone had a car, and big houses, and ... well, maybe not everyone. But it was the aspiration. We aspired. We made our choices."

"You're just quoting Antti's speeches – my speeches," he chided. "I asked what you believe."

"I told you. Nothing. None of this makes a difference to me. None of this changes a damn about who I am, or what I do."

"That seems ... disappointing. For you, I mean. On a personal level."

I blinked, swallowed every other flutter of feeling that threatened to run across my face. In my time knowing him, I had never heard Georg express anything to do with sorrow, or joy, or any shred of human experience beyond the turning of the sun and the march of an idea. I thought I should say something, claw back the moment to some time before he had found a place in his heart to judge me, couldn't find anything worth saying.

He spared me the effort. "You come from Lyvodia, yes?"

73

I nodded.

"Where in Lyvodia?"

"Tseonom."

"So you would have been a child when the forest burned?"

In the place where the red leaves fall above a roaring river, the kakuy dies. Close my eyes and the forest is in me, burning still. I understand now that it will burn until the day I die.

"Yes."

"Did you see it?"

"Yes."

"What did it look like?"

"It . . . there was a lot of smoke. I saw blackness, but heard the fire. They took the children away. They kept us safe."

In the ashes of the night, Mama Taaq does not comfort her daughter who sits in the back of the ambulance. Tomorrow she will. Tonight Vae has died, and even the adults are human when the rain falls.

"Did they tell you why the fire started?"

I shook my head.

"Do you know?"

"I found out later. The old Chief Minister, he wanted a new . . . something . . . a road . . . but the Medj told him it would damage too much. They said the forest protected the land, and cutting down so much would bring harm and the anger of the kakuy. So he burned it all, because he could, and the kakuy did not stop him."

"No. They didn't."

"Neither did he build his road," I added, a little sharper than I meant, and he replied with a knife-edge look, a cutting into my soul, an inquiry that ripped through my bones and out the other side. "These things have always been . . . obscure," I stumbled. "When the forest burned, the land suffered. Mudslides and floods, crop failures, wild beasts attacking, stinking summers and freezing nights. Was this because the kakuy were wrathful? Or was it because trees have roots that bind the soil together in heavy rain? Temple says that these things are one and the same."

"What do you think?"

I half-closed my eyes. "I don't, any more."

Georg's lips drew in thin, a tiny motion I had learned to recognise over many years. Not exactly displeasure, but a sign of something to come, a change in the air. Then he barked: "Come with me."

I followed, scuttling to keep up as he marched down through the building, to a small triangular door set in the wall beneath a staircase, then down again. The cellar was cold and dry, the walls lined with inactive hard drives, boxed-up files and spare batteries, some large enough to boost a car, some tiny enough to slip into an inkstone. At the back was a low white door, with bolts at top and bottom. I had never been through it, never seen it unlocked, but now it opened with a juddering, time-warped scrape along the earth. Beyond was a smaller room, adapted for storage and then abandoned again, the remnants of fans and coolers still visible hanging from the walls, a shocking waste of valuable resources. In the middle, beneath a long white strip of lights, was a stool, and sitting on the stool was a man.

His nose was broken, the blood across his face so smeared by beating it was hard to tell the source of each splattered bleed. Spit, snot, tears and the broken liquids of shattered bones all mixed together to create rivers through the crimson, and he held one hand close to his chest – a hand from which two fingers and a thumb had already been removed. Klem, my next-door neighbour from the cold, stern hearth, sat against the back wall, reading. Sohrab doodled on his inkstone.

Georg pulled the door behind us closed, shutting in the cold and stink of iron. The bloody man looked up slowly, struggled to find focus, looked away. I huddled against the wall, trying to vanish into it as I had when Yue walked by. Georg said: "He's a spy. Sent by the Council. One of Krima's, meant to undermine us. Council says it doesn't interfere in Provincial democracy, and here he is."

The man shook his head but didn't speak, as if this were an ancient argument between old friends – no point continuing it now. Georg patted him on the shoulder, a gesture he'd performed on me a hundred thoughtless times, a habit that had seemed paternal and now would never be the same again. "Jia thinks Maze is going to split from the Provinces. They think we have fallen to humanism."

I looked from Georg to the man in the chair and back again. The childishness of it struck me suddenly, so hard I nearly laughed, and I had to squeeze my arms around my chest to hold in the bizarre hysteria.

"Would you?" Georg asked, and he had a knife in his hand. I had not seen him pick it up from a shelf or be handed it by my digit-clipping neighbour. It had a wooden handle, a folding steel blade. I took it, resting the tip on my left hand, like a royal sceptre. Georg gestured towards the man in the chair, who coughed on what might have been a whimper, a cry for mercy. I stepped towards him. He started to cry, not loudly, but with hiccupping gasps of breath. Somewhere through the stink of blood there was the high acid of urine and the severed fibres of the butcher's yard.

I shook my head, stepped away.

"No." I turned the blade, offered the handle back to Georg. He didn't take it, one eyebrow raised – another familiar gesture, the mountain buckling before the volcano bursts. "Get him to organise your spreadsheets," I snapped, tilting my chin towards Sohrab, who barely lifted his eyes from his inkstone. "Get him to run your errands or translate archaic text. When these two" – I indicated Sohrab and Klem – "can tell the difference between data corruption from degraded hard drives and random letters thrown in by a greedy forger, then come back to me and I'll do your dirty work."

"You're sacked," Georg replied.

I shrugged, and as no one seemed willing to take the knife, I folded the blade, walked to the door, laid it down. Perhaps the bloody man might make a run for it, have a chance; I doubted it, but he eyed that weapon with a sudden alertness that could be his doom.

"Pack your belongings and leave the hearth," added Georg as I jostled with the warped door, my exit somewhat undermined by its slow drag across the floor.

I nodded, hesitated, put my hands together in front of my heart, and bowed.

Then I turned and walked away from the killing room, leaving behind my boss, two murderers and a living corpse.

Chapter 13

Here I am.

Packing up my life.

The room in the hearth is small and grey. I have not filled it with possessions. Temple teaches us that the valuing of material things is how the Burning Age fell. We do not need to buy pretty things to prove our worth. From the earth we come, to the earth we shall return, and no gold or silver will change the crumbling of our bones.

Here, whispers Lah in my ear – here is the fellowship of your kin.

Here, proclaims Nadira as she stands upon the hill – here is the wind and there is the road. Travel it, and see where it will take you.

Here, calls out Vae in her child's sing-song. Here is the forest! Come into the forest, come play!

Here, tuts Georg. Here. Here are men who dream bigger than all that.

There is a telephone in the kitchen. Spin the dialler and listen to it clickety-clack, a sprung shudder as it waits for the next number. I could call the guardia. I could call someone. I do not. Winter has turned the world monochrome. The yellow lights of the hearth are the only colour in a world drained to grey. Even the street-lamps are the white of snow, picking out stardust in the ice below.

I think I feel hungry, but it is not hunger. The idea of eating enthrals and terrifies me.

I fold my clothes, smoothing out the creases, sleeve over chest, taking up the smallest, neatest place in the bag. The first train to Bukarest won't leave for another three hours. The journey will take approximately seventeen hours, with a change in Budapesht. Usually I'd take the night train, setting off just after supper and arriving in time for a brunch of hot bread, fresh tomato and cheese. I wonder what I will say when I go home. I wonder if the lake around the temple has frozen again, and if the novices go skating when their chores are done.

Downstairs, the telephone is silent above the kitchen sink. No one calls, and neither do I.

Most of what I own is on an inkstone. My clothes fit in a bag across my shoulder. I took no memorabilia with me nor made anything here that was worth remembering. The burning is over, but on the surface of the moon there is a portrait of a man's family, left by an astronaut hundreds of years ago who was allowed to carry no more than that little weight with him into space. I have no pictures of my past, nothing worth remembering in my present.

I pull my sleeves down over my wrists, adjust my bag over my shoulder, head for the door. There are a couple of floorboards which squeak loudly; I avoid them on automatic, glance into the courtyard below as I pass the window, see the turned-over mud which in spring will be a lettuce patch and stems of garlic, carrot and potato, the winding tendrils of the sweet pea. There had been days when I was almost happy in the garden, helping tie fresh growth to the trellis wall, nibbling on the first pods of the harvest. My feet carry me away.

The gate is timber coated with the slick resin from the algae vats. I push it open just wide enough to let myself out into the dark, trying to keep the screeching to a minimum. Outside, sitting on the bonnet of his car, Klem is waiting for me. There is still some blood on the side of his neck, fresh from his work in the cellar. I stop and stare at him. He does not smile. Nods once. Puts a hand on my arm, guides me into the open passenger door and slams it shut behind me.

Chapter 14

There is a shrine a few miles outside the city, built on stilts above the wet earth. When the Ube floods, the water rises up beneath it until it appears to float in an inland sea. At such times, you must reach it by boat, the slippery green steps vanished beneath the river's skin. It boasts no resident Medj nor lay acolytes; it stands so the fishermen may stop when reeling in the nets and give thanks to the kakuy of the river and the blessings that the water gave and the life that will feed them until they perish. Not many people visit these days.

The wooden structure is little more than a platform with a small roofed shed at one end, where the liquid form of the kakuy of the Ube is represented in ancient fused glass pulled from the landfill mines. Offerings of bits of net and the occasional hook are left before it, along with the more traditional incense and alcohol. Unlike the larger temples, these offerings are not regularly cleaned out by the novices, and the wax candles have spilt rivers of white and yellow down the altar like a frozen waterfall. The Medj in Maze long ago grew neglectful of their tasks, and on that night of waning moon, the river stank of something chemical, and white foam bubbled and shifted on the surface like oil on silt, cracking the thin sheet of ice that was trying to form.

It was a strange place for an execution, I thought, but so be it. The tide was low enough that I could see the stairs to the single hanging lantern above the wooden gateway to the shrine, and towards these I was waved, Klem waiting below as if the idea of setting foot on sanctified ground displeased him.

I climbed the steps, clinging to the rail as my feet skidded on decades of tide-washed grime that never fully dried, that was too alive to freeze. One candle burned in the altar; three more hung in lanterns round the high-beamed timber frame of this little floating pavilion, peeking through fat-coned icicles. There was no electricity, nor any attempt to generate it, just the creaking timbers of the floor and the smell of mud. A small wooden bench was set to the side of the shrine for the older fishermen to sit on after a long day's contemplation. Here, bent over and ankles crossed, was Georg. He looked smaller than I had ever seen him, older, as if the presence of the kakuy took something from him. Or perhaps he was going to sleep – perhaps this night was the one night of the year when he actually closed his eyes and snored like a hibernating bear. His breath puffed in clouds captured by yellow candlelight, rolling up towards the moon. He didn't look at me as I approached. Georg never looked at much that wasn't inside his own head. I stood before the shrine for a moment, contemplating my next move. Then I put my hands together and bowed. Here, now, seemed as good a time as any.

Then Georg said: "Temple sends spies too."

I nodded, staring into the flame of the single flickering candle. Brilliant colour against the blue of night, its spilling illumination catching the otherwise smothered reds and umbers of the painted shrine.

"Once Antti has enough support in the Assembly, we are going to declare independence from Council. Throw out Temple. Live as people should."

I said nothing. There didn't seem anything worth saying.

He straightened up, unwinding the curl of his back like a fern uncoiling its leaf. My lack of feedback seemed briefly annoying for him, which is perhaps why his next words were: "When I was fifteen, I saw the kakuy of the mountain."

A freezing terror twisted in my belly. I tasted it in my mouth and didn't know why, couldn't put my finger on what it was in this moment that robbed me of my training, my common sense. Without thinking, I reached out to cup the flame in my right hand, feeling its warmth push a little too close to burning, half-closed my eyes to enjoy the sensation.

"My father and I were not welcome at a hearth," he continued, turning his head as if telling an old story to an uninterested moon. "My father was a brilliant man. Difficult, angry, brilliant. He saw things that other people did not see, questioned everything. The Medj smiled their little smiles and said oh yes, how interesting, you should think about that more. But after a while they stopped smiling and said no, no, you've got it wrong, this is dangerous. We would try to negotiate a bed, and they'd give us a week, a month at most, then send us on our way. They couldn't accept him because he was smarter than them, and didn't hide it. He didn't pretend to be happy when he was sad, or that he was content with just . . . dust and water. He wanted more, and if the world was run in any meaningfully intelligent way he would have had it. More than anyone else living. But he didn't. He hit me, sometimes. The hearths were outraged. It made me a stronger man; it gave me discipline, focus, but all they saw was a grown man striking a child. He was not wrong to do it. He had a constant pain in his shoulder, all the time. We went to the clinics and they did their tests and couldn't find anything wrong, prescribed painkillers, but they do things to your brain, make you slow. He never took them. Pain does not make a man kind. It is part of who we are, and we are scared of it.

"We lived on charity, and when times were good the hearths said of course, of course, come in. And when times were bad they told us to wait in the door and brought us soup, said the fires were low and the batteries were empty, and perhaps we'd have better comfort if we begged at Temple. 'Begging'. My father despised the word. It is not a word for men, he said. But we were beggars for a while – I have outgrown his dishonesty. Then, one winter, he went to the black mountains and got work in the forest, harvesting timber, but he cut down more than his pitiful share. The kakuy will be angry, they said – the kakuy knows we have taken more trees than will re-grow here, and it will be displeased at our greediness. For fear of the mountain, they punished the man – can you imagine it?

"My father was always proud. He swore he would kill the kakuy, said they died as easily as any other living thing, that we should not fear the avalanche or the fire, that we could surpass our cowardly natures. He told me to stay behind, but I did not, and he knew he couldn't stop me. I followed a hundred paces behind, as we climbed through the thickening snow and fading moonlight. That night it was as if the sky itself were trying to throw us back, as if the kakuy knew we were coming and what he intended. No more gods, he said. Man must decide for himself. He should have died fighting a god; should have run it through, red on white. Instead, he fell. The wind caught him and tripped him up; he lost his footing in the dark and fell into a ravine hidden beneath snow. No defiance or rage, just eaten by the darkness. They say the mountain killed him, but I lay belly-down on the edge of that cliff and called for my father, lay there until the first light of dawn and the snowstorm had passed, until my lips were white and I was starting to feel warm again inside.

"That was when I saw it: the wolf of the mountains, taller than any man, blood in its eyes and on its jaw, tail twitching through the snow, fur of crystal ice. It watched me from the last shadows of the night, until the rising light drew a line across the snow that seemed to strike it like fire. Then it reared up, turned away, galloped back into the mist, so heavy I could feel every strike of its paws upon the earth, until suddenly it stopped mid-stride as if it had flown into the air. A few minutes later, I heard the sounds of people from the hearth below, calling out for us, climbing up the mountain in search of me and my father. I didn't call back, but they found us anyway, led upwards as if pulled by the rising sun towards the summit. They wrapped me in blankets and put me on the back of a sledge and said it must have been the kakuy's blessing that saved my life, must have been a miracle. Humans are hard-wired to find the worst in a situation, did you know that? It was how our ancestors survived, expecting tigers when

83

there were none, expecting disaster so that when disaster finally came, they were prepared. So we have always blamed ourselves for the very worst that the world must offer – blamed our sin, our wickedness, our evil ways. But when there is good in this world – when our hearts keep beating because they are strong, when our limbs return to life because we are young and vibrant and want to live – we say it is a blessing. We thank anyone but ourselves and dismiss pride as arrogance, ability as hubris. We even know this about ourselves, can recognise our own genetic traits. And yet knowledge, it seems, does not yet triumph over instinct."

He grunted, an almost-laugh, and lapsed back into silence, head turning towards the floor, hands pressed together in his lap. I pulled my fingers back from the flame, turned to examine him, felt for the very first time like his equal and wondered how the forest grew.

He let out a breath, half-shook his head, rose to his feet. I stepped away instinctively, then hesitated, stepped forward again, holding my ground. He was taller than me, broader across the chest and back, but I had options which were unbecoming of a temple-trained renegade. "Council sends spies. Temple too," he said.

I shrugged. "If you think I'm a spy, you should probably have killed me a while ago."

"I have spent several nights thinking the same thing."

"Why don't you just torture me, like the other guy?"

"Torture makes people say what you want to hear."

"Is he a spy?"

"Oh, absolutely. That is certain."

"How can you be so sure?" He didn't answer, eyes bright in reflected candlelight. I sighed, leaned back on the altar, feeling suddenly old, cold. "Council sends spies against you – I understand that. You send spies back. You have always enjoyed the game. Winning is how you know you're better, yes?"

"Yes."

"But you didn't bring me here to kill me."

"No."

"Then why am I here? You aren't one for indecision. Sack me or kill me; if not, I've got a train to catch."

"The kakuy of the river is dying." He gestured loosely towards the water, towards the guttering light and slithering mud. "The fishermen's offerings are rotten, we take what we need, the kakuy dies but the river flows. The river will still flow, as long as people need it to. Do you understand?"

I shrugged. "Am I dead? Am I at least sacked?"

He shook his head.

"Then why bother with all this?"

"Because a spy, embedded for as long as you have been, would not simply have walked away. Maybe you wouldn't have killed another agent; maybe you would have tried to talk your way out of it. Maybe you would have killed him too, or called your handler, or the guardia – done something. You should have done something, to protect your cover or your colleague. Otherwise, all this would have been for nothing. But you walked away."

I felt sickness in my belly, warmth on my face, heard the sea in my ears. I reached out again for the candle, spun my fingers round the flame like a spider weaving a web, listened to the slow sludgy groan of the dying river, to the steady breathing of Georg beside me, then pinched the candle out.

"There's a spare room above my office," he said. "You will move in there tonight."

"I want a pay rise."

"Of course you do."

"No more bullshit. If you want to kill people in your cellar, that's your business. But I don't know if your little revolution is going to succeed, so I need plausible deniability. I'm not some hired killer. You've got Klem for that, or Sohrab. They can deal with it."

"I agree." He held out his hand. "Settled, then?"

I shook it, his fingers hot against my frozen skin.

Chapter 15

From that day forth, I became Georg's shadow. As the Brotherhood cemented its control of the Assembly, as heresy clawed deeper into the very fabric of the state and the kakuy of the river died, I was there, foam tossed in Georg's wake. I translated profanity, ran errands, organised his laundry, met forgers, spies and generals at his behest, made sure there was always the good stuff to drink in the cabinet. I learned his taste, his moods, his inclination. When he got a cold, resentful and furious at nature for slowing him down when there was so much to do, so so much, I made him lemon tea and stood over him until it was drained, tutting at his faces and his snarls. When he went to the bathhouse, I read to him out loud from the edge of the tub, so that even when scrubbing soap into his hair he could still be thinking on the day's events.

I did all this as the kakuy stirred in the mountains and the Provinces slipped ever closer to war. I did it, because I was a traitor.

Three weeks after the blood had been cleaned from the cellar floor, Georg and the Brotherhood leaders retired to a mountain chalet of timber and fresh fire above the snow. The easiest way up the mountain was by cable car: the first up a steep slope of a sheer black cliff which in the sunset turned bloody scarlet; the second a string between two peaks, which clunked and rattled on its spinning cogs and swayed in the high, whistling breeze. It was a good place to plot heresy, far from prying eyes. I wondered if in these mountains Georg had seen his wolf, and if his habit of walking barefoot upon the snow reminded him of that kakuy darting from the light.

While the great and the good settled in for a night of drinking and planning the overthrow of the old order of things, I was left with fetching and carrying baggage. There was more than could fit into a single cable car up the mountain with their guests, and so up and down again I went alone, peering out over the whistling void from the gloom of the swaying compartment.

It was while struggling to load a moving car with these goods at the bottom of the mountain that Nadira approached. She wore a knitted red hat and thick brown mittens, black boots and a padded blue coat that made her look significantly rounder than her build. She sidled up to me as I worked my way round the arc of belongings I had piled up at the base of the cable car's turning red wheel, bowed politely and said: "Is there room for another, sky-kin?"

"The chalet at the top has been reserved for a private function."

"I didn't realise you could reserve mountains for yourself."

"Members of the Assembly are there."

"Ah – men of influence."

"Brotherhood," I replied with a little smile. "They like having things to themselves."

"How very strange," she mused. "But what if I just stay on the car and do not get off? I would love the ride."

"I'm sure that is fine. There is an interchange at the top, and as no one is helping me— Ah, quickly, step on board!"

She slipped into the approaching car as it swung round the clunking wheel on its rolled carbon cable, pulling her knees up to avoid the cases I slung in behind her. "This is a lot to carry," she mused, as I hopped unevenly in over the welt of luggage I had created, slamming the door shut as we began to ascend.

"It's a working vacation," I muttered, the words sour in my mouth as I considered the amount of work this had given me, relative to how little vacation. We picked up speed as we transitioned from the slower cable of the station to the long line heading skywards, lurching as we shifted tracks. "You know all about those, Nadira."

She grinned, tiny teeth in a plum face. Her hat was pulled low over bushy black eyebrows, her lips were almost the same soft pinky-beige as her cheeks, and her age had always been hard to deduce through the tight, sun-baked impermeability of her skin. "How do the Brotherhood feel about holiday pay?" she asked.

"Is this a professional question, or are you just curious?"

"Curiosity; holidays are not as heretical as strip mining or cluster munitions or jet fuel."

"You read my reports."

"Devoured them."

"Then what in the name of fire and ash are you doing about it?" I snarled. "I have given the inquisition *everything*. Every theft, every assault, every bribe and blackmail, every *murder* the Brotherhood has committed. They have information on oil rigs. They have information about machine guns. Where in the name of sun and moon are they getting it? How are they getting it? Classified Temple reports, sealed heresies on my desk! Last week I got a document on forced sterilisation with a hand-written note from a damn inquisitor on it. 'Bad stuff, send to anthropology.' They are stripping the forests, they are building *tanks*. They talk about ... about 'social engineering' and the rights of wealth, about free market and geoengineering. They are ... *What the hell are you doing about it?*"

My hands were shaking, my throat suddenly so tight I wondered if I'd swallowed down too much of the cold, if the wolf of the mountains would find my blood turned to ice, my heart a stone in my chest. I pressed my head against the walls of the car as we swayed upwards, and she watched, eyebrows drawn, hands relaxed.

Finally Nadira said: "The inquisition does not have the same powers as a Council operation. Temple is not meant to interfere politically – our remit is tracking and cataloguing heretical material."

"Fuck that. This *is* political."

"Do you need out? We can get you out, Ven."

The words – the first time I had heard these words in so long – sank into my gut like tar. I sat down on a rickety wall of luggage, pressed one hand against the wall to stop myself slipping, stared into her eyes and realised that, a lot like Georg, I couldn't tell when she was lying.

"They killed a man," I mumbled, surprised to find the words coming from my lips. "They said he was a spy."

"I know."

"Was he?"

"Almost certainly. A Council agent – one of Krima's."

"The last few weeks they've rolled up whole networks."

"I know. Krima came to us."

"What did she say?"

"She wanted to know if Temple had any assets in Vien. She knows the Brotherhood would be an inquisition target. She was as close to desperate as I've ever seen her."

I nodded dully, curling up tight against the thin cold of the mountain. "She tried to recruit me, when Jia was in town. It was . . . it seemed a somewhat reckless play. Nadira – how does Georg have access to so much heresy? How did he find the Council spy?"

Nadira half-closed her eyes, and there was for an instant a hint of the Medj she had been before she joined the inquisition, a drawing in of breath and a settling into the frosty air that did not recoil from cold but rather gave thanks for it, thanks for the heat of her body. I wondered if I did that – if Georg sometimes saw my gratitude for the touch of rain.

"Georg has a spy in the Council," she said, eyes still a little closed, fingers uncurling in her lap as if she might cradle these words, uttered in the shaking cabin of our ride. "The inquisition is almost certain of it."

"How?"

"The connection between Temple and Council has always been . . . complicated. The one has always supported the other, but so very much of the heresy we uncover is political. And there have always been accusations that the inquisition oversteps the mark. 'Dabbling', as they say. Every Province has a secular review board to oversee Temple classification of heresies, to ensure that we are not, as they put it, keeping humankind in the dark. In Damasc, the secular boards are if anything even harsher in their censorship than Temple inquisitors. In Maze, the board has long ceased being anything other than an oppositional body determined to unclassify as much material as possible. Council also has a review board, to oversee the most dangerous, most sensitive material in Temple archives – the kind of material no one Province should have access to. Over time the relationship has become ... more than strictly academic. The kakuy must sleep. Council must keep the peace, no matter what the Provinces do. To aid this, the Temple sometimes shares intelligence of ... political relevance, you might say."

In Bukarest, there are still protesters chanting at the gates of the temple, calling out for freedom from the chains of the Medj. I wondered if Lah still served them tea. "That sounds profoundly illegal – and unethical."

Nadira smiled. "I think perhaps it is. It is also sometimes necessary. Lah has written a great deal of highly classified and stunningly tedious philosophical tracts on the subject. You should read them some day." I didn't answer, and finally her eyes opened again, head tilted to one side, a curious bird. Softly in the hush of the passing sky: "There must be peace, Ven. Can you imagine what would happen if war wakes the kakuy?"

I curled tighter in my coat, the cold heart-deep. "They knew who he was, but they tortured him anyway. The Council spy. They knew. And I walked away."

"You protected your mission. Not too hot, not too cold. Georg Mestri only trusts people he thinks he can own. Do you want out?"

The first time I met Nadira, it was at the Temple of the Lake, two months after Lah recruited me to the inquisition. She sang the evening prayers before a congregation of laypeople and novices, a solo voice without drum or bell, and after there was honey cake and camomile tea and people asked her how her little book of poems was going and if she'd had any luck finding a publisher, and I saw only a devout civilian, a little frumpy and a little loud, and couldn't quite believe she was inquisition until Lah swore by moon and star she was. It took me weeks to ask her how she did it – how she played so well the part of the affable neighbour writing barely competent poetry. "By being it," she replied primly. "And I'll thank you to call my poetry average at least."

Now the snow moves upon the mountain, a skin-sharp biting of silver in the dark, and I say: "Antti is going to pass a motion granting the Brotherhood access to all temple servers in Maze – even the classified ones. As soon as the bill gets out of committee, they're going to send militia. The Medj won't have time to erase the data; every archive in the Province will be seized."

"Council can oppose it in court. Tie it up for months."

"They're hoping Council will. Further proof of the interference of outside forces on Provincial independence. Doesn't matter – the militia will occupy the temples the moment the bill is read. They're calling it a 'day of people's action'. The temple in Grazt has nuclear fission on its servers. Vien is a centre for the study of ethnic cleansing and cultural genocide. Innsbruk has nearly two thousand entries on 're-education' camps. Antti says people are easier to work with when they're already on your side. He makes it sound like a joke."

The cabin rocked a little in a crosswind, clickety-clacked on the high overhead wires as it passed the counterweighted car descending in the opposite direction. Nadira was silent a while, hands fixed in her lap, feet rooted on the ground. She made me unlearn how to sit, when she'd become my handler. Only priests sit for hours cross-legged with palms at prayer, she'd say. Inquisitors slouch.

Finally: "Who knows this?"

"Antti. Georg. Kun Mi. Brika and Tanacha. A dozen or so staffers for the Brotherhood. Me."

"If they go into the temples and find the hard drives wiped, they'll know they've been infiltrated."

"If they go into the temples and find material on nuclear fission, the kakuy will be the least of our concerns."

"What do you want me to do, Ven? We can protect the archives or we can protect your cover – I don't see how we can do both."

"For what my cover is worth. Krima said something when she tried to recruit me: 'There are gaps in your story'. She was looking at Kadri Tarrad, and of course we made that cover weak, made it so that Georg could punch straight through it, but I don't think she meant that. She may have thought there was something criminal she could leverage, didn't connect the gaps in my story with the inquisition. But Georg could. If he looked hard enough. If he has a mole on the Council."

We clattered a while upwards, shrouded in snow and wind. Vien was only a few hours away by train, but close your eyes and you could forget that there were cities or traitors or secrets and lies. We are children of the clouds. With our feet, we pray to the mountain; with our breath, we become one with the sky. So say the Medj, and sometimes, very occasionally, I remember what it is like to believe it, to feel the ocean in my blood and breathe my ancestors in every exhalation. Then I close my eyes, and instead I remember only the fire, and the kakuy.

"Pontus," said Nadira, and it seemed that she too was speaking to the darkness, to the turning night that all things shared. But look again and for a moment you could see the old inquisitor there, the woman who had infiltrated a sect in the Delta who knew just enough about genetic editing to cause a plague; the historian who had dared the first dive into the flooded caverns beneath Martyza Eztok, where the last archivists of the Burning Age had buried their secrets in the old mines beneath the cracked earth. "Georg's spy in Council – we call them Pontus. We don't know who Pontus is, don't have the power to investigate. Krima vaMiyani is in charge of counter-intelligence and has proven reticent to move."

"Why?"

"We're not sure. Internal politics, perhaps. If there is a mole, the damage it would do the reputation of her department, and the Council in general, would be severe."

"More severe than someone sending Georg classified heretical material? More severe than if Maze does split, commits heresy – more severe than war?"

"I believe the Council, and the other Provinces, are all hoping it won't come to that."

"Georg doesn't fear the kakuy." I couldn't meet her eyes as I said it, and as the words passed my lips I thought I saw Lah sitting beneath the cypress tree, sighing: we have failed. Humanity grows arrogant, forgets that it is part of the world, not above it, and we have failed. "Georg cannot conceive of anything upon this earth that cannot be conquered by human intelligence."

"How very old-fashioned of him. I do have an idea, but it will, of course, be absurdly dangerous."

I opened my mouth to laugh, or curse, or tell her where to get off, when a sharp twist of her chin silenced me. I felt the clatter as the cable car bounced onto the slower track, decelerating on its approach to the higher station. Then her face was set in a gormless grin and she was blathering: "Oh, look! The view, oh yes!"

Klem and Sohrab were waiting for me at the top of the mountain, eyes narrowing and lips curling at the sight of Nadira in the swaying cable car. But she did not get out, and I did, dragging the bags of the great men of humanity reborn onto the station floor.

Chapter 16

I did not attend the lunar festival that greeted the new year, celebrated as the first icicles began to thaw. Instead, I worked late. We were often working late, and Georg never seemed to care.

"Have you had enough?" he'd ask me, when I yawned. It wasn't reproof, reproach. If I'd had enough, I could go home, and that would be fine. He would learn from this the measure of me and my skills and use me accordingly. Some men were weak; others were strong. That was the truth that lay at the heart of the Brotherhood.

"No," I lied. "I can keep going."

He nearly smiled then, and nodded, and we carried on with our work.

"Ull, what a pleasure."

I had never seen Ull of Lyvodia, Minister of my home Province, up close before. The old man had skin the colour of summer night, hair like winter snow. He leaned on a walking stick and looked round Antti's office disapprovingly, as if counting every heresy on the wall, every trapping of Burning Age pomposity knotted at Antti's throat and pinned into the cuffs of his shirt. His deputy, Farii, looked around with a somewhat less outraged gaze, eyes bulging at the panoply of items, historical and new, assembled in the Brotherhood's lair. I stood behind, inkstone poised to record conversations, take notes, run errands; Georg's loyal secretary.

"Antti," Ull greeted the Minister with only one part of his

mouth in motion, the rest clamped shut around what he wanted to say. "You've done well for yourself."

"Maze is thriving, despite Council interference – as you can see. Please, let me show you round."

In private, Antti cursed Ull and Lyvodia, called him a backwater mystic, a tree-hugging crone with wooden teeth and a peg leg. In public, he smiled and smiled and invited Ull to observe the authentic burning era collection of iconic "action figures" he'd salvaged from the landfill site, muscle-bound hunks of manhood and women in skimpy pants and bras, their hair flowing free behind impossibly glued-on masks. "We can learn so much about the idealistic culture of the past, the aspirational nature of their story-telling," he said, one arm on Ull's shoulder as if he might at any time split down the middle, teeth rupturing from his rib cage, and swallow the old man whole.

Farii looked at me and said: "Where do I leave my coat?"

That night, as they argued, the door stayed open and I sat outside it, listening.

"If Maze is committing heresy, then Jia has the right to call on the Provinces to intervene."

"Heresy! Old women in old shawls making pronouncements on how we should live, what we should do? How many times has the Temple got it wrong? How many times have they banned knowledge that now we thrive on?"

"A gradual process—"

"Is their excuse! It's always their excuse."

Georg passed me, sitting stiff on my strange, refurbished chair from another world, stopped as if he'd never seen me before. "Are you always listening?" he asked.

"Yes," I replied.

He thought about this, then nodded, "Good," and went inside and did not close the door behind him.

Dinner was an austere affair, designed to demonstrate to Ull that Maze, for all its talk of prosperity, humanism, freedom, was still

95

culturally right up his street. Dumplings and cabbage, sweet and sour sauces that clung like molasses to the tip of your tongue, fruit tarts served in custard; white wine from the vineyards to the north, which I poured into small ceramic cups as the table toasted good fortune, perpetual peace, the brotherhood of man, and so on.

Then, as if he had wanted to say it all along and could no longer hold his tongue, Ull blurted: "We give thanks for the food that feeds us, the water that makes us whole. We give thanks for this gift from the earth."

Antti's face flushed a peculiar shade of incensed crab as Ull bowed his head, hands raised with cup between them in ancient ritual blessing. Georg tilted his cup towards the old man in polite acknowledgement, drank without a word. Farii bowed her head as was the tradition of the thing, but her eyes were raised, watching everyone, and her lips mouthed the words without sound.

"You. Come here."

Her voice, when she spoke on her own part, away from the ears of men, was sharp, trained to command, frustrated that it didn't have as much opportunity in that area as she wished.

I approached the corner of the balcony where Farii stood, cup clasped in one hand, eyes running across the city. Vien at midnight, the half-fallen, newly restored spires of old temples lit up like knives to heaven, the lazy curl of the river a visible line of black cutting through streets of hanging lanterns. The Deputy Minister had been a voice in politics since she was old enough to vote, but achieved minimal political success until finally paired with old Ull some four years ago. Certainly, people said, she was a woman who could get things done. Competence rolled off every pore, and without much in the way of small talk to accompany this trait, it was as if she had embraced this one attribute into her heart, into every fibre of her being. However much people said she seemed cold, stand-offish, harsh, rude, or whatever the latest word was for the most efficient way of doing business, at least she had this – at least she was competent. Ull hugged children, talked about compassion and honour. Farii sacked those who made false promises; harangued those who didn't get the job done, and everyone was appreciative, and no one thanked her for it. Fine russet hair stopped an inch above her shoulders in a straight, thin bob that hardly moved when she did. Green-grey eyes looked down on the city as if waiting at any moment for a fire to start. When her face was neutral, it was an almost formless thing, with thin pale lips and small flat nose seeming to blend into each other. On those occasions when she frowned – or, more rarely, smiled – contours of fibre and tendon emerged from cheek and chin, as if she existed in only two states: animated, or corpse-like, with no middle ground between.

"Take my cup," she said, and I took her cup, made to leave. "What's your name?"

"Kadri Tarrad, sky-kin."

"Where are you from? Your accent. Lyvodia?" I had barely spoken ten words in the entire evening, but she had an ear for it. "Where?"

"Tseonom."

"Why are you here, not there?"

"I prefer the work here."

"You are Georg's . . . what? Assistant?"

"Yes."

"Good. Stay his friend, Kadri Tarrad. Whatever you do, stay his friend."

I nodded, half-bowed, hesitated. "May I ask you a question, sky-kin?"

"For yourself, or for Georg?"

"There's not much difference any more, is there? But for me." She shrugged. "Go on."

"All this . . . talk. All this change."

"All this heresy, you mean? Georg's man shouldn't have to mince words. Come – say what you're thinking."

"As you will. All this heresy. It is clear that Ull is not interested, but that, perhaps, you are."

"Is there a question there?"

97

"What will you do, if you're wrong? What will you do if the kakuy wake?"

She thought about it for a moment, eyes drifting across the city, through its streets and to the lights still burning in the tops of every close-woven hearth. "I believe in people," she murmured – not for me, but for the night, perhaps; for the heat of the bodies pressed into the streets below. "I believe in people."

That seemed to be her answer, for, with a flick of her hand, I was dismissed, and bowing, I backed away.

Chapter 17

Nadira said: "There is a plan."

We met only in the dark places now, in scuttling moments snatched between the hours I worked, worked, worked for Georg. She waited for me near the dead drops where I left my stolen data rinsed from any inkstone foolishly left open in my sight; where I deposited the little capsules of microfilm snapped of documents half-glimpsed on a midnight desk. There were dark rings around her eyes. I had forgotten whether there was ever anything else around mine.

"There is a plan," she repeated, as we pressed like lovers into the corner of the alley, beneath the ticking of the high-up compression battery and the scuttling of a startled cat. "To find Pontus before Pontus finds you."

I waited, head on one side. Georg never needed many words, and I had grown out of the habit of inquiry.

"Temple shares heresy with Council. Pontus shares heresy with Georg. We have prepared a document – plausible without being correct – on autonomous military drones. Highly classified. Very tasty. We deliver this document to the relevant parties – identical copies, apart from a unique identifying error in each one – a spelling mistake or a comma misplaced. Do you understand?"

"Yes. You bait Pontus with false intelligence. Pontus sends it on to Georg. Georg gets me to verify it. I look for the error you have introduced. The error reveals Pontus. I understand. It is all very . . . simple."

It is simple, yet it is hard not to close my eyes and whisper to the earth beneath me, hold me tight, hold me tight, I never feared you, I have never feared death and yet I fear, I fear, I fear. Why is this? Why does Georg's face blaze in my mind brighter than a forest fire?

"Ven," she whispers, a hand on my arm – she's never done that before. "This is how we save your life."

I nodded, and could not speak, and, in the sleepless darkness of the night, thought that perhaps I had forgotten how to pray.

Georg said: "Read this and report back in an hour."

And Georg said: "Check what time Witt's train arrives!"

And Georg said: "Drink?"

And Georg said: "No, that won't do. We'll have to re-work the entire thing."

And Georg said . . .

Sometimes I wake in the middle of the night in a panic and don't know where I am. Georg sits at the end of my bed and tuts and has a knife in his hand – that knife that he keeps somewhere about himself, all the time. Perhaps it was his father's, the last relic of a man too intelligent for this world. And then I wake again and he is not there, not in my room, not in my head.

A parade of dignitaries through the office door.

Pav Krillovko laughs and says, though there is nothing funny in his voice: "Dearest thing, it sounds like you want war!"

Shamim, Chief Minister of Damasc, takes the train up from Isdanbul, sits and listens without commenting, then says: "The Voices of the Assembly thank you for your clarity," and leaves again, showing no sign as to whether Antti's pitch of humanism, freedom, justice has made any difference whatsoever to the old man's ears.

A delegation of Medj accompanies Chief Minister Shahd from the Delta, and they are furious. Their faith is one of denial, of leaving not a footprint on the earth, of eating only the bare minimum to survive, of bleeding on the soil in apology for an endless, uncertain litany of crimes. They are of the Temple, but not

100

Temple as I know it. They call the Medj of Lyvodia weaklings; they say the priests of Maze do not merit the name. Their trip is a waste; Antti does not even bother to meet them in person – too busy, many apologies. After, they are lambasted in the press, mocked as fanatics, hypocrites, zealots. There is nothing in this world that they do not believe cannot be cured by carrot juice and prayer. Go back to the great river of the south. Go bleed on Council time.

I do not bow as they depart, this increasingly desperate line of people trying to pretend there won't be a war, and I wonder: which one of you is Georg's spy?

This is a secret so precious that he won't even share it with me, his nearest shadow.

I will find it out by myself.

One morning, as I am drinking tea in the cold dawn air, I find the microdrone.

It's the size of a dead pigeon, folded gossamer wings limp at its sides. It has fallen just outside the back door, where Klem parks the car. An accident, an error – it's hard to tell. Most of its body is battery and solar cell, but there is a little panel beneath its belly that I can slide back and . . .

"Give that here! Give it now!"

I have never seen Georg so angry. He snatches the thing from me and shoves me back with the palm of his left hand, open, a moment away from a slap. Cradles the microdrone to him like a mother holding a child and does not look me in the eye as he storms away.

Five minutes later, it is as if nothing has happened, and neither of us mention it again.

Ten minutes before the Vien Assembly ratified the Equal Knowledge Act, allowing unrestricted access to every heretical server in Temple's vaults and de-criminalising previously heretical actions such as stock buybacks and unfettered logging, large numbers of guardia started to appear at the gates of the major temples across Maze. They were joined by even larger numbers of Brotherhood militia members, ringing their bicycle bells as they circled, like vultures above the bloated carcass. The moment the fastest watch on the keenest leader hit 8 p.m., they clattered through the gates, some chanting revolutionary slogans, some too focused on their tasks to bother. The Medj didn't put up a physical fight. The richest and most joyfully inept were long fled, and though pious remainers were threatened, the militias had been ordered to avoid a scandal, play nice, show that they were here for the people.

"We will defend our people's right to choose their own lives against any aggression from the Provinces or Council," Antti proclaimed. "This is a great day for Maze, a great day for freedom."

On the edge of the river, the land is turning sickly yellow. In summer, it doesn't rain, or sometimes it rains too much. In winter, the ice crawls up the windowpanes, sealing you inside; or there is no ice at all and when the spring comes the mosquitoes swarm in black clouds over pools of muddy water, growing fat and crimson. Is this the curse of the kakuy or the consequence of the new factories Antti has authorised, producing ever cheaper, ever more futile goods to purchase and display as a sign of wealth – and therefore worth – in this strange new world?

Perhaps the kakuy are angry, but they have never spoken to us in a human tongue, so why should we care? Lesser creatures are dumb; humans have always known this.

Temple servers are only powered up when needed. The most heretical information is kept in isolation from all networks, cut off far below the shrines. Caverns hollowed in the earth keep the worst of summer heat from the drives; walls of dry clay are raised against the damp, fans gently turning to keep cold air flowing. The original antiques are in sealed, airless cases, historical remnants to be studied, marvelled at and displayed for curious scholars of the Burning Age. Shelves of recovered history are catalogued neatly along oiled wooden shelves.

Social sciences 456.91-468.99 – gender/sexual discrimination, genital mutilation, reproductive rights.

Social sciences 551.51-559.88 – segregation, racial supremacy, replacement theory.

Social sciences 671.99-672.10 – election tampering, "fake news", "fake media".

Anyone can request access to a heretical server at any time, and usually their request will be granted. They can take notes, copy diagrams, read essays by leading scholars of the Burning Age on eugenics and wealth, terror and market manipulation, and afterwards be offered a nice cup of tea and asked what they thought about it all.

"Would you like a comfy chair?" Old Lah would ask, as I worked my way through pictures of migrants drowning in a raging sea. "I find it best to go for a nice walk after."

Only the truly terrifying – the chemical structures of nerve agents, the construction of incendiary weapons, the design of off-shore oil rigs – were kept entirely out of sight.

"It's embarrassing, if you think about it," Lah would say. "We hide this from ourselves, not because knowledge is good or bad in and of itself, but because we are still so young on this planet. We are still children; still fascinated by playing with fire. In our minds – in our very DNA – we are still starving, driven by the terror of not having abundance. We must have more, and more, and more, in order to be safe, even when the truth is that we have more than enough. The reward we feel when we have more, more! It is intoxicating. I have been . . . intoxicated."

This was a strange confession from my teacher, who, seeing my raised eyebrow, beamed. "A good spy should understand passion. Georg Mestri is an addict of victory and the game; you must understand what it is to be an addict too, if you are ever going to get near him. When things are bad, we want them better. When things are good, we find ourselves wondering – what more? And what will I lose if I do not get more now? It is a trait that pushed mankind across the oceans and out into space – what is out there, what else? It is one of our most beautiful qualities and has for millennia served us well in finding new ways to live better. But like all things, it is neither good nor bad, but what we make of it."

103

Then I wondered, how long had Temple inquisition been eyeing me for recruitment? How many years had I spent thinking myself an academic, while they had been planning to put my life on the line?

In Vien, the temples fell.

Some members of the militia had knives. Others had hammered nails into a stick or brought heavy clubs fashioned from bits of old furniture or tumbled tree. One woman sported a pair of fabric scissors, waving it with such glee one would think it a battle axe, having perhaps decided that if she could not muster the same kind of armaments as the rest of her peers she might as well make up for it with enthusiasm. In the Temple of the Mountain Lake, the Medj were beaten bloody, one dying a week later in the clinic, not because they resisted, or said anything particularly snooty to their attackers, but because the dozen or so militia who climbed the five hundred steps to their open door had expected a fight, had been primed to fight, had been fired up with a cry of "They may kill us, but they will never take our freedom!" or words to that effect, and, when faced with a polite invitation to drink tea before committing vandalism, had no idea what to do with their energy, so had the fight anyway for something to do.

A few altars were desecrated; a few images of the kakuy smashed.

"Where are your gods now?" snarled one, pissing on the image of the kakuy of the fields, bringer of harvest, basked in sun. "Why don't they come now?"

"They are not our gods," replied the Medj politely, as the stink settled into the woven straw mats, dribbled down the red-glossed walls. "Gods think humans are special."

I supervised some of the robberies from my telephone in Georg's office. I had, after all, arranged much of the logistics, writing guidelines to local militia groups on how to handle the stolen drives and the best way to get them to the Assembly in one piece for analysis and distribution. My phone rang throughout the night, from journalists demanding statements from Antti – "Does this mean we're going to be rich?" one asked – to late-running militia members trying to work out if they could still be useful in this new rebellion.

"I brought some matches?" piped one voice optimistically. "And a pint of acetone!"

"Go home," I sighed. "I'm sure everyone appreciates your effort."

On the other side of the office, Rilka, Antti's private secretary, typed furiously at her desk, scurried back and forth, peered through the window, poured herself a shot of something alcoholic from a little flask in her pocket, typed again, ran to answer the door, ran back, sat down, stood up, and finally proclaimed: "But we're living through history!"

I had not spoken to her since the night began, and felt that this was perhaps a continuation of a conversation that had been inside her head all evening and which had grown so animated it had to happen out loud. I looked up from my desk and saw, to my astonishment, that there were tears in her eyes. I reached into the drawer, pulled out a clean cloth hankie, offered it to her. She hesitated, then crossed the great carpeted gulf between us, took it, daubed gently at the corners of her eyes, hesitated, rubbed a little more vigorously, held out the limp piece of cloth. "Can I keep this?" she asked.

I nodded.

"It's history," she explained. "We're making a better world."

I thought she might blow her nose on the thing, and keep that too, the immortal bogie of freedom. Instead, she folded the hankie into a little triangle and slipped it into her tunic pocket. Our eyes met, and for a moment both she and I contemplated a future in which Georg walked in to find us entangled on the office floor, clawing at each other's clothes, and both she and I concluded that he would probably be mildly amused at the display. Before I could do anything with this revelation, she spun on her heel and returned to her desk with the dignity of an emperor accepting a lesser king's surrender on the battlefield.

*

The first of the bad news didn't start to arrive until dawn, trickling in from the temples of the forest and the sands. These obscure shrines had no telephones of their own, so the militia had been forced to send a cyclist into the towns to make the call.

"There's nothing there!"

"What?"

"There's nothing there. The server rooms are empty. They took everything!"

"What do you mean, they took everything? What are you saying?"

"I'm saying there's nothing there!"

By the first glimmer of a new day, word had started to spread, and a few enterprising militia members with school-level archaic German had powered up some of their stolen drives and were eagerly looking through them for information on autonomous facial recognition systems, predictive policing, weaponised nanotechnology and long-range ballistic missiles.

I had been a woman; now I was a man, old and frightened.

There haven't been any children for a long time now. Melanie doesn't know why that is.

"What in the name of burning sun is this?" demanded one, who had an inflated enough sense of her own importance to ignore my polite requests to hang up and let me handle some of the other calls flooding into my office. "The box said 'material science – industrial' but I'm just getting books about zombies! Fucking *zombies!*"

As birds sang their dawn chorus, oblivious to the history they too were living through, I sat outside Georg's office as Antti and a number of other seniors from the Brotherhood screamed abuse at him, each other and the day in general. A small round window crowned the top of the stair. If I looked at it, I could not moment-to-moment see the sun rising nor measure the changing colour of the sky. If I looked away, even for a few seconds, then looked back, it seemed as if everything had changed, now, and again, and again, and now. Across Maze, the temples burned and the hearths looked nervously towards the edge of the forest, which suddenly seemed nearer and blacker than it had been before. Best to cut it down, they said. Best to play things safe.

The door to the office slammed open and men stormed out; the last one toyed with slamming the door shut, but to do so would have required breaking his stride and might not have achieved a suitable effect, so he left it hanging half-open. I stayed where I was until I heard the downstairs door close behind them, then rose and let myself into Georg's office.

He stood, where he always stood, as he always stood, facing the window and the rising day. I waited, hands clasped, in front of his desk. At last he said: "They knew we were coming."

When I first trained to be a spy, I would stand in front of the mirror and remember how it felt when the forest burned and the river roared, reach out for Vae and miss her flailing hand, don't let go, don't let go, and tell myself, *It's your fault.* In time, I could do this, and meet my own eyes as the fire raged in the cauldron of my mind, and see no flush of colour nor any change in my breath, but was merely the mountain against which the wind must break.

I am kin of sky and earth. The earth holds me, and to the earth I will return, and whatever happens now, the forest will grow.

Then Georg said: "I thought we had them all. Temple must have their own."

I am the mountain, but when I leave this place – if I leave this place – I will shake down to my very roots.

He let out a slow sigh, and in that moment was just a man, not a statue carved in marble. Then he straightened again, turned, clapped his hands together. "By this evening – everyone who has attended any meeting on the bill, everyone who signed to read it, everyone they know, their friends, contacts, addresses. A wide net first, then we start eliminating candidates." I hadn't slept for twenty-four hours, but now was not the time to mention it. "I'll need to see the chief of staff, defence and army chiefs by 2 p.m. Get me a meeting with the Council Ambassador too, see how much time we can buy. And a pastry. Raisins, I think."

This pronounced, he turned away again and resumed his contemplation of the war to come.

Here I am.

Sleepless at my desk.

My face hurts.

My body hurts.

I find words are difficult to concentrate on, a thin, shark-toothed gauze over my eyes.

I read whole pages, and nothing has gone in, just words passing by.

I find myself inclined to laugh uproariously at nothing at all.

I feel incredibly sad at the smell of fresh pastries hot from the oven.

I sit at my desk, and systematically begin an investigation into my own nefarious espionage activities. For a long time, I wonder whether to include my own name on the list of suspects. I was, after all, present and correct at many of the key meetings. I carried the locked briefcase to and from its destination, supervised people signing in and signing out to read the documents therein. I unlocked it several times in transit, when alone, to photograph its contents for Nadira. I should absolutely be on the list of suspects, as indeed should Georg himself. But it seems so obvious as to be absurd, so I leave both his and my name off and instead systematically trawl through hundreds of pages of notes to construct a list of everyone else in the world at large who might be an inquisition spy.

I give him the list at 4 p.m., and he doesn't look at it, but nods once and says: "Break-ins are also a possibility. Get me a full security review."

I return to my desk. Sometime later – I do not know when – I wake at it. The sun has long since set. I have pins and needles in one hand, where it served as a pillow, and in a foot, where it dangled awkwardly beneath my chair. I am probably going to be sacked but, straightening up, find that someone has draped a blanket across my shoulders, tucking the sides in around ribs and knees so it won't fall off while I slumber. I have no idea what to do with this act of kindness, and when I check what new data has been uploaded to my inkstone while I slept, I find that Pontus' stolen document is there.

Here I am.

Photographing the appropriate page of the appropriate document to send to Nadira.

The film that comes from my camera is no bigger than a pill you might swallow without water. It is stored in a little black capsule for transportation and left behind a drainpipe near Judastrasse.

The document is about autonomous military drones. I will flag a number of ways in which it is inauthentic to Georg later – later – when some of the fuss has died down. When Nadira has the information she needs to find Pontus. When Pontus can no longer find me. I do not know what unique error has been introduced to this text to mark the betrayer. A comma that should have been a full stop, perhaps. A minor typo on a long, fiddly word. I find, to my surprise, that I hardly care, and I make the drop-off on the way to collect Georg's morning pastry.

Chapter 18

Jia did not declare war on Maze, not even when the temples burned.

"We can resolve this peacefully," her voice juddered, tired and old, over the radio. "We are all kin of sky and earth; children of the sun and moon. We can find harmony again."

The other Provinces shifted uneasily. Shamim and the Medj of the Delta made their more forthright feelings clear. "We have seen evidence of fossil-fuel mining. We have seen evidence of wasteful butchery. We have seen evidence of ideological mass consumption. We have seen the temples burn. The kakuy do not care for the borders of the Provinces. The kakuy will take vengeance upon us all."

In Lyvodia, on Maze's eastern flank, Ull was noticeably silent.

The Brotherhood radio reported a few Medj fighting back, attacking officials, endangering the public. Even those few stations that were ostensibly independent reported with disgust the hoarded wealth, precious items and luxuries found in the halls of many of the shuttered temples, and they were right. The rot was deep; the Medj had failed, and though the clouds tumbled and the earth turned, the kakuy did not come for Vien.

"How many lives do you think an archive is worth?" asked Georg, fingers tracing a map of the Provinces spilling across his desk, dancing over the old mines at Martyza Eztok, the sealed vaults of Isdanbul.

"In the burning," I replied carefully, "there were surveys done of how many lives you would be willing to end for a cause. If, say, by dropping a nuclear weapon that killed a million strangers – the elderly, children – you could save twenty thousand soldiers of your own nation, would you do it? The answers were disproportionally yes."

"And what about Temple?" Georg wondered, and I thought for a moment I saw Lah sitting beneath the cypress tree, wondering the same thing. Perhaps in another life they would meet and break bread and find in each other interesting conversationalists; Georg could have made an excellent priest. "Are they pragmatists, or sentimental?"

"Both," I replied. "They are pacifists; it is written in their scriptures that the kakuy hate war above all else. They are also pragmatists. When mankind warred, the destruction disturbed the kakuy, roused them to anger, and the kakuy crushed city and army beneath them with no care for whose side was pious and whose was not, seeing no distinction in the petty squabbles of humanity – just a pestilence on the earth."

Georg clicked his tongue in the roof of his mouth, flexed his ankles and rolled his wrists. "It sounds exhausting, believing so much and so little."

It is, says Lah, as wind ripples the water of the lake. Medj need to be idealists, to see the light in all things. But unlike the gods of old, the kakuy walk amongst us, real and mighty, and we need pragmatists too. Tell me, have you thought about joining the inquisition?

In the night, I dream about Tinics, and the temple above the river, and the forest as it grows. I dream about Yue, and lanterns of red and blue. Then Georg is there, in my mind, and he knows everything, and the Medj just watch as he pulls my thoughts out through my blinking eyes, and do nothing, and I wake terrified that I've been talking in my sleep and everyone knows.

"Ull doesn't want to fight," Georg muses, as I hand him the day's summary from the radio waves and server offices. It has been nine days since I left my little capsule of photos behind the drainpipe. More than enough time to get it back to Budapesht, to develop the film, to find Pontus, to end this farce. What is taking so long? "Jia knows it too. If she tries to get a consensus from the Provinces to attack, she doesn't know how many will follow her to war."

I have to force myself back to the room, paying full attention, but too late. Georg has seen my distraction and clicks his tongue, disappointed, before moving on to the next thing.

Three nights later, the united Temples declare Maze officially in a state of heresy. They should have done it weeks ago, and that night the citizens of Vien wait for the lightning storm, the tornado and the rush of judgement, and none comes. The kakuy, it seems, do not respond to Temple paperwork.

On the day when the summer festival should have been cele-brated in baskets of lavender and rosemary, the temples stood silent. Instead Antti proudly struck a shovel into the new open-pit lignite mine on the edge of the river at Yahnbach, a somewhat futile gesture given that the tooth-limbed machines were waiting behind to strip back the soil into dunes of dusty black – but it looked good for the cameras. Antti Col was nothing if not good for selling copy.

Rilka, passing me on the stairs in Georg's office, caught me by the wrist. "They're looking for a spy," she hissed. "They're looking everywhere."

They're looking in her room, and under her bed. She is no spy, I'm almost sure of it, but perhaps she once hid a stick of incense or a letter to another woman, failing in her duty to humanity, reason and her sex. Perhaps she takes contraceptives or once expressed admiration for Jia and the Council, a long, long time ago. Perhaps Georg is inside her head too, as I'm certain he is inside mine.

"We'll be fine," I said, pulling my hand free. "We've done nothing wrong."

The next evening, Klem was not at dinner at the hearth, nor the night after that. When he did return, there was blood on

112

his cuff, and bruising on his fists, and he didn't smile at me, and looked like he might spit at my little shuffling bow.

Lying on my bed in the dark, I did not sleep, and did not think, and did not dream. I was the mountain, hollowed out inside, nothing left but darkness and bones.

The smell hit me when I woke. The ever-present turbid mud of the river, a sudden alien presence rising with the dawn. Then voices through the window, high and urgent, the wailing of a siren somewhere in the distance, and beneath it all a strange rushing, as of wind over the sea when tide and gale contend in opposite directions. I stood up, opened my door and looked down the stairs to see greyish water flowing freely through the hall, rushing through every crack and half-shuttered window. It foamed and rolled like coffee in a vat, bumped floating furniture and spun lifted floor cushions and torn flowers through its maw in little busy eddies. Other members of the hearth were already struggling to save their few ruined belongings, heaving saturated fabrics onto the stairs and clawing at slippery cutlery that spun away from their scrambling blue-tipped fingers. I descended slowly, not wanting to get my feet wet, but seeing no other way than to enter the water, removed my socks and shoes, fruitlessly rolled my trousers up, and stepped in. The flood was a cruel cold, enough to shock without bringing the body to alarmed wakefulness. Grit swirled in it, already caking the floor of the hearth with sand and mud, and other things brushed too, each one presumed sentient, or a knife swept up in the tide which would tear its way through flesh, hidden beneath the swell.

I helped as much as I could, saving those belongings that were salvageable, joining a human chain to pass things to a higher level. Within an hour, even that project was abandoned as the water rose another half metre, coming nearly to my shoulders as I joined the exodus upstairs, peering out through high windows as our garden washed away.

The flood lingered for the best part of two days.

After came the clean-up. The stink of river could not be scrubbed from the city for months. Lines of green and brown smeared every wall, and the hosepipes we turned on to try and blast it away just filled us with the sickening memory of water, water, more moon-cursed water. Dead fish and still-slithering eels rotted and blanched in the sudden hot sun. Every blade of grass, every flower and every twining climbing thing was brown, brown, brown and dead, the streets lost to silt, the sewers overflowing and the raw stink of faeces everywhere. We quickly gave up trying to distinguish between mud and shit, wading through it all in calf-deep splats of sodden earth, from which the occasional flash of child's toy or purple perfume bottle might emerge like a pearl from the crusty oyster. Any electrics which had been below the water line were destroyed, taking with them cold-stored food and large swathes of the city's power supply. Families moved towards the rooftops to hard-wire their cookers directly into the solar panels and few overhead compression batteries to get a charge, while children tore and scratched their bare feet on the endless blankets of shattered glass and splintered wood the flood had carried with it.

We all knew disease was coming but were unsure of how, until at last the lack of stored food and difficulties in getting fresh supplies began to bite at our stomachs, and we started eating those apples that were only a little black, or maybe where the decay had only gone somewhat into the core; and that bread where you could dust the mould off, or where the spores were basically the same white as flour. Those whose bowels didn't immediately open caught the cough that spread on the backs of the teeming, roaring, hungry flies that now rose up from the beds of mud that slathered the city, commuters flapping their way through the translucent swarms which fluffed into hair and nibbled at the moist edges of blinking eyes, fearless of the enervated humans that loosely swatted them away.

Antti came on the radio and proclaimed: "To aid in the relief of Vien, we are introducing a new fleet of ambulances and fire trucks powered by the internal combustion engine! Reliable, fast, these vehicles can get the job done!"

Hearing this, some of the more pious denizens of Vien prayed, and many more rejoiced, even though the fleet of promised vehicles were at least a year and a half away.

Chapter 19

In the most secret hours of the night, I pray to the kakuy.

I do not put my hands together, nor offer incense, nor bow my head. Georg's hunt for the spy in his midst is at such a fever pitch that I think there must be holes in my wall, that Klem is watching me from the neighbouring room while I sleep, waiting to catch me whispering secret things as I toss and turn. I have grown so paranoid that I now have to sleep with my face turned to the wall, lest the motion of my dreaming lips betray me. I think that when they come for me, it will be better not to be looking at the door; I have spent many hours calculating the best way in which to be murdered.

Please, spare us, I whisper in silence to the darkness and the moon.

Temple taught us such things were futile. The kakuy do not care for the prayers of man. They are not interested in our good or bad, our desires or whims. We pay them our respects, not because they will smell the incense or taste the wine, but to remind ourselves of the needfulness of this pact. Everything changes; the balance is all.

We arise of the earth, and to the earth we return. I whisper it, and it is the beginning of one of the sacred lessons, but it has been so long since I spoke it out loud. Georg will know my thoughts, he will see it in the corner of my eye, know that I have been praying.

I close my eyes, force my hands to my sides, breathe out slowly.

I am the forest, growing.

The illusion that I am anything else, flesh and blood, heart and soul – this too will change.

Then Nadira said: "It was Pav."

I am nearly nauseous with relief, press against the warm myce-lium wall, the slimy tidemark of the flood a soft green line against the pale bricks. "Pontus is Pav Krillovko? You're sure?"

"The document you sent us came from Pav – we're cer-tain of it."

"So Council has arrested him? Jia knows? Krima knows?"

"No."

"Why in the name of sun and fire not?" I have to catch myself from shouting, hold back the breath, clench my fists against shaking.

Nadira's face is sorrowful without regret. "Because it isn't possible for Pav Krillovko to be Pontus. He wasn't in Budapesht when our liaison gave Council the doctored document. It was put on his system, but he couldn't have physically read it until at least a week after Georg received it from Pontus. He was in a temple in the south – on spiritual retreat. Dozens of Medj were with him every day and every night, praying."

I am not the fucking mountain. I am not the turning sea. I am small and mortal and made of flesh that can be hacked, blood that can be spilt, this is my life, my only tiny sacred life, and it is running away from me, the only thing that matters, I am terrified of the earth, terrified of maggots, terrified of the size of the sky and how soft and squishy are human eyes as they look up in fear.

Nadira tries: "Ven, listen . . ."

"No. I told you about the temples – I warned you what Georg would do. He is tearing the Brotherhood apart looking for me, and it's only a matter of time. Either we find Pontus or Pontus finds me, that was always the deal, and now . . . How did Georg get Pav's document, if Pav wasn't there? Someone on his team?"

"Perhaps. We are investigating – we are. Krima knows, she is

117

why we know Pav couldn't have ... Ven, look at me. You did everything right. We'll find another way."

It seems to me that these are the words you say to a corpse, and to my shame I walk away from her before she has a chance to try and make things right.

Chapter 20

On the day that should have been the autumn festival, the temples stood empty, blackened shells, and I travelled through the city with a mask over my face and citronella smeared across every inch of bare skin as the hospitals stank with the smell of putrefaction and the new factory chimneys blasted smoke into the sky.

"We have the technology to defeat all plagues," Antti proclaimed. "We are growing strong."

For the first time, the clinics started serving the wealthiest first. It was only right, the Brotherhood said, that those who had the most, made the most, got the most.

Behind the office, I found Rilka vomiting into the gutter. I caught her by the arms and pulled her into the street as she protested, swore she needed to work, needed to keep going, do what was right. I called an ambulance, but when it didn't come I hailed a rickshaw, bundled her inside, her lips blue, face burning, fingers cold. How could one person be so many seasons at once?

"I'll be all right," she said, pressing her face into my chest. "We're making something better."

At the hospital, there weren't any beds, the summer sickness washed in deep by the floods. I called Georg to explain where I was, and why. He was there in sixteen minutes; in nineteen, Rilka had a bed and a private room. He stood over her as she was plugged into drips and drains, held her hand, daubed her brow with the self-same hankie I had given her the night the temples burned, told her what a good girl she was, how proud he was of her, waited until she was asleep. Then at last he stepped away, nodded at me, once, an affirmation – the right thing had been done, though in that time and place I had no idea what the right thing meant any more.

Then he said: "Give you a lift?" and I nodded, and he drove me home and poured me a drink and asked me if I'd had my vaccinations, and I had, and he nodded again and mused: "It will get worse, before it gets better."

I waited, too tired to give whatever came next even the half-hearted noises of consent a spy should when his enemy speaks.

"The Burning Age was too short-sighted. We shaped the world; built towers, seeded the sky, dug the earth, walked on the moon, built wonders and cured diseases. We waged wars, drained seas, built palaces in the desert. But we consumed too much. Ran too fast. The kakuy were ... antibodies, no more. The world's antibodies stirred by the planet recognising its disease. We were nearly wiped out, the peoples scattered to the furthest corners by the deserts and the storms. This time, we will do better. Our mistake was thinking that the fruits of man's labours must be shared with all. Now we know it is only for the few to lead, wisely and well. That is the new humanism that we have forged."

I stared at my hands and didn't say a word.

"You've slept with her?" he asked. In the past, such turns of topic, the sharpness of his voice, would have startled me. But I was the mountain, hollow inside, so I shook my head. "You want to?"

"I don't know."

"Men and women need to honour each other. It is the proper way of things. We spent so much time honouring the kakuy we forgot how to do homage to ourselves."

I looked up at that, bewilderment in my eyes, tongue too tired to keep silent. "Do you really believe that?" I asked. "You say all the things Antti wants to hear, you talk the philosophy and the fight and human superiority, but ... do you believe that?"

The boldness of my own question astonished me, but not so much as his reaction. Somewhere in Georg's clothes there is a hidden blade; I do not know if he has slit the throats of men with it or whether, like the great potentates of old, he allows others to do his killing for him. That night, he laughed. He laughed like nothing I have ever heard, and held my shoulder tight, a brother who at long last saw his kin returning home, and looked into my eyes, and saw something funny there, and laughed again, and poured me another drink, and did not answer my question.

Walking in the park as the crimson leaves fall, there is a smell on the air I do not know, and Nadira says: "It is called gasoline."

I kick at fallen leaves and nod at nothing much.

"I know it's taking too long. I know. We'll find Pontus. Krima is co-operating with the inquisition, there were only so many people who could have accessed Pav's files, it's all high clearance – that means limited suspects, it means . . . do you want out?"

All children love jumping in puddles, playing in leaves. I try to remember if there was a moment when I forgot that particular delight. "Krima could also be Pontus – you know that, don't you?"

She nods. "We've considered the possibility. But she's head of security. Who else can we go to? Ven. Look at me."

I do not. A memory hovers on the edge of recollection, blue-black hair in a crowd. "Krima has a . . . deputy, yes? Yue Taaq. I knew her."

"How?"

"We grew up together. Well – yes. In the same village, I mean. I saw her when Jia visited, walking in the crowd behind her."

"Did she see you? Did she recognise you?"

"I don't think so. What's her clearance?"

"Why?" I shrug, and don't know the answer. "I would say no more than classified. Taaq runs military liaison for Krima; she's not got access to Temple material, let alone to Pav's servers. Do you trust her?"

"I don't know. We were children. I hadn't thought about her

since ... she was in the forest when it burned, you see. We ran to the river, and there was ... but she always said she only saw the fire. Is there going to be a war?"

"Do you think there will be?"

I consider the question. "Yes," I say at last. "And Jia will lose, for a while, because Antti is building tanks and machine guns and artillery pushed by petrol engines. Then Antti will lose for a while, because these things cost too much to make. Then everyone will lose for a while, as is the way of the thing. I do not know who will be alive at the end of this."

"Ven." She stops dead, puts her hand on my shoulder – a rare breach of the strict distance between us, a flutter of humanity in our professional undertakings. In the autumn forest, a new cycle is beginning, a kind of rebirth. In every rotting branch, at every shrivelled root, in every fallen leaf and rotten fruit that falls unplucked to the sodden earth, the thin-tendrilled fungi and fat-headed bugs are setting to work, feasting for the winter, breaking down what was into what will be again, a turning without end. "We can get you out."

"Pontus sends Georg intelligence by microdrone. I found one, once, behind the kitchen. It must have malfunctioned. Solar-powered, a few hundred miles' range. Fly by night, recharge by day. I have stolen so much from him, he tells me things ... but Pontus – nothing is written, nothing is shared. Only Georg knows who they are."

"I'm going to pull you out."

"No – no." I shake my head, am surprised at the ferocity of it. "I will not have this all wasted. When things are on fire, you have to ... you have to do the best you can."

For a moment, I think she will argue. But then Nadira had never really wanted me to quit. So she smiles, nods, and we keep on walking through the fading day.

Two days after remembrance night, when families make offerings to the dead and dancers in white robes bang drums and parade through the streets, chanting the old cries – we are the dead, we are the dead, all that is living is all that dies – Jia mobilised an army.

She justified it as manoeuvres, training exercises. It was a traditional fighting force of six-shot rifles and guerrilla troops, light units on bicycles specialising in a war of forest and night.

"We will resist any aggressive moves by the Council to suppress our freedoms!" Antti proclaimed across the radio waves, as the first iron tank rolled from the new factories on the end of the railway line. Iron production in Maze was still low, steel smelting a low-key industry that the Brotherhood had not yet had time to fully scale up. Nor had they had full access to all the material needed to make a proper, full-blown tank of the kind the Burning Age had rained death from. His was an almost rectangular, creaking thing, with not quite enough braking power to stop itself rushing downhill on the verge of toppling, nor enough horsepower from its combustion engine to get up a hill at more than a snail's pace, and definitely not in rain. Yet it had machine gun turrets mounted left and right, and a short cannon at front capable of firing shells that could shatter wood into splinters at four hundred metres, once it had cranked its way round to aim. It made an impression, and making an impression was half the point.

I stole the designs and sent them to Nadira, almost reckless now in my exploits, a dead man walking who may as well go out with a bang.

"She mobilised too late," Georg mused, as Jia's voice blazed out across the radio, mustering some of the old defiance with which she had held together disparate bickering Provinces down so many years. "She won't fight in winter, but we can still keep manufacturing, growing. By spring, she'll be too late."

"She still has more troops," I pointed out.

"People are not iron," he replied, and that was the end of that.

In the evening, Georg says: "Drink with me," and I do, and we play a few games, modern and ancient, on the low coffee table between his worn crimson couches, and after four rounds we are at a perfect draw, and neither of us suggests a decider. He is frustrated by this pattern in our game playing, infuriated by his failure to consistently win. That's why he keeps coming back, and the joy of the thing is fading with every piece we move, and he will persist until victory.

For a while, we are silent.

We have been silent together for many nights, he working at his desk, I in a corner, without talk, music, the clatter of other people's lives. As the streets grow quiet through the open window, we have shared the deeper calm of distant disturbances, little puffs of noise only emphasising how deep stillness goes. We are silent again now, until he finally blurts:

"Out with it. Come on! Out with it!"

It is strangely profane, this disruption to our easy peace. I sit back, feel the warm fabric where many people, more important than me, have recoiled a little from Georg's stare.

"You look like a blob of mucus and have been moody for weeks. Spit it out."

"I have been wondering what your final objective for this war is. Material victory is not a realistic end-goal. You've got a technological advantage – all that heretical history, cluster bombs and gas and nerve agents, and so on – but it'll take you years to fully exploit it, and ultimately if the Council is too weak, if the Temple thinks the danger is too great, they'll just unlock their archives and start doing the same."

Georg is smiling now, arms folded, leaning back easy into his chair. "Do you think I can win?" he asks, eyes glistening, teeth white.

I think you have a spy in the very heart of the Council.

"I don't know," I reply. "I'd call it fifty-fifty."

Either Pontus finds me, or I find them.

"Would you risk everything on those odds?"

"I think perhaps I already have. What are you really fighting for?"

"Perhaps I believe in everything I say. In humanism. In a better world."

124

"Perhaps. Beliefs come and beliefs go. In the burning, the human mind was trained to value achievement, ambition and ownership above all else. It was the most abundant the world had ever been, and yet every child was taught that it lived in scarcity – that only by getting more would it ever be safe. Then the world burned and there was just war, famine and the kakuy. You killed, you died, while spirits of mountain and stone raged without the slightest interest in you and your fate. Then the fires ceased, and Temple emerged and taught us to be soothed by the river and the wind, to find joy in each other and what we had, and that … is also fine. I'm no priest, but I've spent enough time reading archives to know that a little boredom, a little sitting around drinking tea and not causing too much trouble for anyone – that's also fine. But it is not a world for heroes. It is not a place where great men can shape the land to their will, for the simple reason that the land bends only to the kakuy. Only them. God lives; and God does not live for humans. We are tiny, once again. I think you are not interested in being tiny any more. Do you want to kill the kakuy?"

His eyes are bright as the moon; he is a brilliant man who has dedicated himself to working in the shadows, and yes, even Georg's ego will puff like a strutting pigeon now and then.

"Do you think I can?"

"No. Kakuy die – I believe that. But the forest grows back, and while there is a forest, there will be a kakuy. Maybe you can drill a few holes in rock. Maybe you can poison the Ube itself. But you can't kill the sky."

"If you believe that, why are you still here?"

I shrug. "As soon as the going gets tough, I'm sure I'll discover my cowardice again. Until then … I suppose you could say I'm curious. You want to kill kakuy. That's the endgame – that's all this war is about, yes?" He smiles, and that is answer enough. "Well," I muse. "That's some top-of-the-line ambition."

"Is it not how humanity becomes truly free? By conquering the gods themselves?" he asks, mischief in the corner of his eye, a smile pulling the edges of his lips. "And when the kakuy are

125

dead and the earth is ours, the temples will burn and there won't be any need for a war. There won't be any need, because we'll be right. We'll be our own gods. That's how I'm going to win."

He grins and pours me a cup of wine and tips his glass towards me. "To victory," he says.

"To victory," I reply, and drain the liquid down.

Chapter 21

The days are ticking down, down, down, another year going, going, gone, where did it all go? Georg is in my head, Pontus is in my head, Lah is in my head. The only person who's currently not home and making tea seems to be Ven Marzouki. What would he make of all this from his little home on the edge of the forest?

Meeting in the library, banners slung across the wall celebrating the de-classification of previously heretical texts on theories of racial evolution, eugenics and the carbon economy, Nadira says: "Ven. It's time to go."

"He thinks he can kill kakuy. He thinks Temple is hiding something, weapons, he thinks that when the kakuy are dead we will be free, free to tear the earth apart, free to be strong, free to make and build and kill each other again without worrying about the fallout, the way real men do. Real men, real war, real power – the world was so much easier when gods cared about humanity. I can find the spy, I can find Pontus, I'm so close ... "

"Ven! Krima is looking, Temple is looking, I am doing everything I ... Pontus will be found, it's not you – this isn't on you. What if they find you first?"

"Then that will tell us something too, won't it?"

She leans back, recoiling as if punched, but though her voice says no, Ven, in the name of sun and moon, don't be ridiculous, her eyes say why yes, yes indeed, you are not wrong. If we all die here, it will be very informative indeed.

*

I made it almost to winter festival before my world came crashing down. Low winter light in the morning, the touch of sun through the cold, we give thanks, we give thanks ...

Then one unremarkable night as the snow fell in grubby sheets, Georg called me into his office, asked me if I'd finished writing up my notes – I had, and gave them to him – nodded once, looked at someone behind me, and whoever that was hit me in the back of my neck with a very large stick.

I think they were aiming for the back of my head, but missed. When this caused me a great deal of confusion and staggering, rather than just the desired immediate blackout, they hit me some more. I was not particularly surprised to see Klem leading the fray, and my old housemate Sohrab, though I was a little disappointed to notice that Rilka seemed to have forgotten our shared history and was busy getting in on the action too.

Here's a cellar, a familiar place.

The summer flood had washed away the blood, leaving instead that fine coating of muddy stench that has settled in a fly-blasted miasma over the city since the Ube rose. None of us will ever be clean again.

Pitching a still-conscious body that doesn't want to co-operate into a chair is hard work. Limbs go everywhere. Teeth, even if they don't bite, remind us a little too much of a dog's toxic mouth, or the venomous strike of the platypus, so if you're not used to such things – and Sohrab and Klem clearly expected more docile prey – the result can be unnerving. In the end, Klem got bored and dumped me on the floor, belly up. Then he knelt on my left arm, pulled a knife from his jacket, uncoiled the fist of my hand and tried to cut my thumb off again. The absurdity of it made me laugh, somewhere through the pounding headache. This didn't bother Klem. Laughter was a familiar fear response.

"Wait."

Georg hadn't said that last time, had he? It seemed only fitting to get the thumb business over and done with, just so everyone was on the same page. Klem paused but didn't let go. Rilka stood by the door, hands squeezed together in front of her so tight I thought she might pop like a pimple. Sohrab lingered against the furthest wall, competent but lazy. Georg's face hovered briefly over mine. I wheezed: "Torture makes people say what you want to hear."

He nodded, once, then again, a backwards nod with his chin. Klem scowled, climbed off my arm, retreated to the edge of the room. Georg waited, just far enough out of reach that I couldn't easily get blood on his clothes. I pulled myself up one arm at a time, clinging to the empty chair for support, managed to get my head up and let it loll back on the seat, untangling my legs on the floor in front of me.

"Can I have a drink?" I asked.

Klem found the idea contemptible. Georg found it almost funny. "Get him a drink," he barked, and, relieved perhaps, Rilka scurried away to find one. I licked my lips, mopping up iron. Georg waited, then squatted down opposite me, a look that seemed close to concern in the corner of his eyes. I had never seen such a thing in him before; he almost never stooped to the level of other men. Then he reached into his pocket and pulled out a hankie, a finer, spider-silk version of the thing I'd given Rilka on the day the temples burned. He spat on the silk, then brushed a little of the blood from my face, examined the resulting smear, and pressed the hankie into my loose, sagging fist. I gripped it tight as a child might hold a sacred totem or a glimmer of metal with the ancient words *Product of China*. I wondered where Yue was. I hadn't wondered that for a while. I hoped that if the inquisition found Pontus, they'd treat them better than the Brotherhood was going to treat me, and was surprised at the depth of my sentiment on the subject.

"Kadri," Georg sighed. "How did we end up here?"

"Terrible choices," I chuckled, and humour hurt, so I decided not to do that again.

He smiled, squeezed my shoulder, harder this time – hard enough for pain – released, waited. The door opened. Rilka entered, carrying a crystal glass of the good stuff. She did not understand the finer nuances of interrogation, perhaps, but Georg let it slide. She held it with two fingers under the base, like a sacrificial offering of water at the temple.

"Thank you," I said, taking it from her shaking hands. I thought I'd down it in one, get a little courage, but the heat of it on my bleeding gums was surprisingly pleasant, so I took my time.

"Kadri," Georg said quietly, a little firmer now, a man with places to go, people to see. There's an unmarked grave already dug somewhere on the edge of the city; it needs to be filled by morning, you know how it is. I clung tighter to the glass.

"The thing is," I grunted, "I've got to wait a few hours before I start spilling my guts. To give other agents a chance to escape. Professionalism. Three should be enough. You can beat me senseless in the meantime if you want, but it'll probably be easier for everyone if we take that for granted."

"Unfortunately," Georg sighed, "you don't speak for everyone, do you?"

I shuddered, despite myself, tried to blink some of the spinning from my eyes.

Then Georg said: "I believe you call him Pontus." Glass is but sand, sand is of the desert, I am the desert, I am sinking from the heat of the sun to that cold, soft place where light may never find me. Georg nodded at nothing much, mused: "Krima's investigation was a little too loud. She turned over a few too many rocks, got sloppy. That's the problem with using a spy to catch a spy – every step closer, you become easier to see. When did Temple recruit you?"

"When? Oh. You think I was bought or . . . you said something rude to me that made me turn? Earth and sky, no." I tipped the glass to him in salute, bloody teeth and throbbing head. "I'm an inquisitor. The whole . . . selling information, expulsion business – that was just cover. Bait. You were always my target. You swam onto my hook like the little greedy fishy that you are."

He looked away, tiny white teeth in a puckered mouth. Georg had never looked away before. He turned again to face me almost instantly, as if the moment had never happened. "How much did you give them?"

130

"Everything. Military, political — everything. The training camps in the mountains? The airbase hidden in the north? Your brilliant strategic plans — the new fleet; the new artillery? Everything. Temple knows about Antti's embezzling, your secret friends in Magyarzag, what soap you use to wash your nethers." For a moment, he looked sick, and I felt a swell of strange, giddy defiance unlike anything I had experienced since the forest burned. I wished I had more alcohol to salute him with, a toast to his ignorance, a glass tilted towards his frown. Then Georg looked away one last time, smiled at the floor, was still smiling when he looked back up. He patted me on the shoulder, gentler this time, a father comforting a disappointing errant son. "Well," he sighed. "You were always good at your job."

He began to stand. Back, haunches, an unfolding upwards. Klem detached himself from his corner, ready to do that thing he did. I caught Georg's hand as it drifted away, gripped it tight. A flicker of surprise ran over his face, matched only by the pure bewilderment as I swung the crystal glass as hard as I could into the side of his head. It shattered against skull and palm, shards digging like the burrowing wasp into my flesh, spilling in bloody stripes down his cheek. The blood started flowing instantly, thick and dark, dripping onto his spotless shirt. The impact rocked him against the chair and I thought I heard Rilka stifle a scream, Klem growl like the hungry wolf, but I was already reaching for Georg's trouser belt. I had searched his jackets before, examined every part of his wardrobe, and now there was only one place left for his damn knife to be: tucked into a sheath on the back of his belt, a little hidden scabbard that made would-be murderers feel smug and bold, but which any professional thug knew was too easily hijacked. My hand closed round a wooden handle; I dragged the blade free as Klem lunged towards me, and as Georg swayed back, pushing himself away from the chair, I caught his hand again and stuck the knife into his left armpit. He gasped, bit back on the pain, twisted as I dug a little deeper, pulling him towards me until finally his throat was within my reach and I slid the knife up into the ridge between neck and jaw and snarled: "Get back!"

131

Klem and Sohrab froze, Rilka sobbed. I had never seen anyone sob like that before, an awkward, uncertain thing as if she felt it was her womanly duty to have a reaction, which her bright, adrenaline-popping eyes weren't really feeling.

On the floor, Georg and I were a tangled, contorted mess, blood mixing in grubby smears across skin and stone. Trying to slit his throat at this angle would be a right stinker, fleshy but unlikely fatal; but I didn't trust my grip to change to something more practical, so hoped no one else would notice or care.

"Drop your knife," I hissed at Klem. He looked to Georg, who seemed as if he would nod, then thought better of the motion.

"Do it," he said.

Klem dropped his knife, toed it away; Sohrab was unarmed.

"Stand by the wall," I snapped. "Facing it."

Slowly, Klem and Sohrab walked to the wall, turned their eyes to the grey stone. I nodded at Rilka, who didn't need any further encouragement to do the same. I slung my right arm across Georg's chest, adjusted my left so my elbow hooked around his shoulder, giving me a little more balance and control. "Up."

He climbed up slowly, reluctant to shift his weight against the blade, feet scrambling against my thigh as he tried to find purchase. I followed, letting his strength half-pull me upright, until we stood, a swaying, bleeding mess pressed so tightly together we could have been born sharing the same liver. "Out."

He straightened all the way, an uncomfortable height that forced me to peer past him as if I were a puppy hiding behind a tree. His first step was a sway and he almost fell, nearly losing his own windpipe as I struggled to stay with him. Then he caught himself, straightened again, adjusted the cuffs on the end of his sleeves and, with as much dignity as an admiral boarding his flagship, began to shuffle towards the door. I followed, glued flesh to his flesh, blood to his still-flowing blood, through the cellar door.

"Lock it. Throw away the key."

He locked it, tried the handle to show it was done, threw away the key.

"Kadri – Ven – do you have a plan?" His voice had the soft

concern of an employer inquiring into his underling's personal development.

"Car."

A little nod, which became smaller as he remembered the knife at his throat. "Of course. Worth a try."

Climbing the stairs together was such a messy, undignified shuffle that at one point Georg spluttered: "Wouldn't it be easier to stab me in the kidneys?"

I didn't answer, pulled my arm a little tighter across his chest. When we rounded the corner into the corridor, I thought he might try to buckle, felt a tensing of muscles against me, tensed back. He reconsidered, shuffled to the front door, opened it, looked out into the street, turning his head this way and that as if waiting for a rickshaw. "Well?" I peeked past him, and he took that opportunity to turn, grabbing my head in both his hands and slamming me against the wall. I felt my blade cut something, nick flesh, felt blood hot on my fingers, but it didn't slow him down. He drove a knee into my chest and fumbled with his thumbs for my eyes, burrowing from ear to temple to eyebrow, skimming the top of the socket. I ducked under his grip before he could dig, drove skull-first into his belly, trying to push him back from the wall. He staggered a few paces, then adjusted to bear-hug me around the torso with one arm, slowing me to a grind of feet pushing against feet. He caught my knife hand as I swung it up towards his stomach, and though he twisted my wrist he didn't quite have enough strength to force me to open my fingers. Instead he turned, turned and turned, driving forward now as I slid back again, pushing the blade with his whole body towards my chest. I kicked and struggled and grunted and tried to head-butt his sternum into some sort of submission, felt blood in my ears and heard him gasp and wheeze like a poisoned lion. The tip of the blade slithered towards my chest, pricked skin, drew blood. His grip on my wrist was numbing, cutting off blood as he drove the knife on. I dropped to the floor, let the weight of his body on mine send me tumbling. The knife turned as I fell, my arm finally breaking from his with the unexpected force of

133

gravity, his grip around my middle pulling him with me. I didn't feel the tip of the blade glide over my ribs, didn't feel it glance across my body – that sensation would come later. But I felt it slip across his flesh as I scrambled for purchase on the floor. Saw his thigh in my line of sight, felt myself tumble from his grasp; drove the knife all the way in.

Georg howled with pain. I had not known that statues could scream; I did not think he was made of the same stuff as the kin of sky and earth. The blade went so deep that when he jerked his leg away the knife went with it, tearing through thick, red muscle to hang down like a hook stuck in a butcher's joint. He collapsed onto the floor, clutching at his thigh, encasing the leg in his giant hands but not touching the protruding wood or metal, as if moving fingers near it would just make the pain more real. I scrambled away on slithering paws, pressed myself into the wall, hauled down breath, felt for the first time something hot trickling across my belly, ignored it, fumbled in the drawer of the wooden counter by the door with its faux-modern art sculptures and little pot of scented, tasteful leaves, staining it all with crimson. Found the keys to Georg's car – the emergency set he kept for when his driver was sick or his patience was low – crawled over his flailing legs as he rolled and rocked on the ground, face popping with the effort of holding back another roar of anguish. Slipping through the door into the icy street, I felt the cold of it as a blessing – thank you kakuy of the winds, thank you kakuy of the snow, I thought your touch was only darkness but tonight it is blessing, thank you, thank you. Saw a light turn on in a window opposite; another a little further down the street. Georg's howls would wake the whole neighbourhood. I staggered onto hands and knees, scarlet on white snow, crawled onto my feet, tried to run, and in the end managed a reasonable lurch round the corner, to the waiting car.

Chapter 22

I had only ever driven a car three times before. Once, when the postier in Tinics let me sit in the driver's seat and carefully press the accelerator on a very straight, very empty bit of road. Twice more in the temple in Bukarest, when Nadira sat me down and said: "There are so few of these things around that you don't need to know much about them, but we should probably make sure you've got the basics."

The battery was at 50% charge, having been plugged in late after a long day on the road. The driver's seat was set uncomfortably too far back, reclined almost to a snoozing position, and I didn't have time or space in my thoughts to work out how to change it. I tried the pedals, muttering their half-remembered functions under my breath, fumbled with the keys, dropped them, swore, rummaged in the dark around my feet, tried again, the cold of the night now mixing hard with the nauseating heat of blood and pain running through my body.

It took me three tries to get it right and crawl out into the street. The steering was strange at first, each corner taken with the caution of a mouse snuffling for cheese in a cat sanctuary. But in the dead hours of the night, so long as I avoided the main avenues and thoroughfares of the city, the only people I might startle were pedestrians ambling home hand-in-gloved-hand through the settled snow, late-night revellers or the occasional delivery man unloading his crates for the morning market. Once Georg reported the car stolen, it would become an instant liability, the telegram flashed from town to town. That should take at least forty minutes, maybe longer if I'd severed his femoral artery. If I'd severed his femoral artery, he would be dead already. I didn't think I'd killed him. I didn't know.

Ten kilometres out of the city, I pulled over on the side of the road to find my shirt glued to my body with blood. A slash from collarbone to the bottom of my ribs had opened the skin across my chest; not deep, but long and wide enough that the cloth was now saturated with blood, oozing like water through a sodden sponge. I felt dizzy looking at it, too sick to drive, but I pushed the car to the edge of a village whose name I should have known and couldn't remember, driving it at last into a ditch on the edge of a stream of muddy, stinking water that ran down to the Ube. It would be discovered in a few hours, a few days at most. I still felt satisfied dumping it, a terrible, un-priestly surge of wasteful glee.

Swaying through a village in the dead hours of the night. Snow is starting to fall. Catch it on your tongue; thick, clustered globules of frozen white. If you hold out your sleeve and let it settle, you can see each individual flake, until finally, if you stay still long enough, there isn't enough warmth left to melt even the lightest clumps, and your arm begins to sag beneath the weight of frozen night. There are only a few streetlights in this place, enough to give the shape of the curving central street. It is the kind of town where each hearth minds the other's business, considering it impolite to pry into the affairs of neighbours behind their high paper and resin walls. The server office is open only four hours a day, five days a week. The temple is padlocked shut. Even the midnight foxes are slumbering tonight, no yellow eyes flashing in the dark, no paw prints pressed into the settled earth.

There is a clinic, which reminds people with a polite notice outside that the prescription system is changing and will no longer be free. It is shut, but a window at the side breaks easily enough, strewing thin micro-fibres of solar wiring amongst the shattered glass. I crawl through into the chill, dank dark, follow the walls with my hands until I find a switch, coax a little light from the overhead bulbs, poorly fed by temperamental winds. I have no time for proper medical attention, but slather clotting agent and press pads into the most egregious injuries, discard my bloody shirt in a yellow bin and pull on a beige nurse's shirt from a pile of fresh washing behind the reception desk. It will not withstand the cold, and now the spinning in my skull is turning the edges of the world blacker than even winter night.

I wonder where Nadira is. If she is dead, free, taken.

I wonder if I should go back and do not.

The safe house is twenty minutes from the centre of the village, down a mud path obscured beneath banks of billowed white. I get turned around once, twice, trying to find it. The cold is starting to feel warm before I spot its walls, light out, gate locked shut. The key is hidden in a hollow beloved of nesting blackbirds; I fumble through crystallised worms and the remnants of ancient cracked egg before finding it. My hands shake too much to get it into the lock. In the end, I turn my whole body to the side, tipping my weight against the timber for support, twisting with elbows locked to my ribs for some rigidity until the tumblers turn. Then in; courtyard with its frozen-over pond beneath the silver ash. The solar panels are covered with snow; the pipes have frozen. The keeper of the house has not checked in on this place for at least a week, held back perhaps by weather or sheer winter-dark inertia. But there are wood pellets in the stove and a lighter which clicks into tiny flaming life when pressed between my blue palms. As the fire catches, I drag every pillow and blanket I can find into a pile at its feet and bury myself like a bear, muffling against the pain as blood returns to icy limbs.

Winter's dawn is low, blinding, slices of white that catch the gentle dance of dust particles in the air. It comes in on sharp angles through the window above the sink, moving fast over bamboo bowls and empty pans, a cup turned upside down, closed cupboards and bare timber floors. It catches the flash of tatty colour from the piled pillows I've dragged around me; faded ochre and time-drained emerald, dry cobalt and wilting yellow. It takes a while to wake me, having to push through an inordinate amount of blanket and tangled reluctance before my brain registers the day. When it does, I forget for a moment where I am and think that this is what it will be like when I am old, and mad, and every day is a new form of being born, without a parent to love you. Then the pain kicks back in, and the odds of living so long suddenly fade, and being an old codger causing trouble in some patient hearth doesn't seem so bad after all. The pellets in the stove have nearly all burned down, leaving a thin residue of still-warm ash at its base which I am tempted to rub my hands in for that final glimmer of heat.

Outside, a crow hollers indignantly at a peer, or an interloper, or some intruder to its peaceful realm. Wings beat; a mob forming, chasing, hounding – then peace again.

Ploughed fields hidden beneath snow catch the wind as it spins across crystals, disturbed only by the tiny footprints of a hopping bird and the larger footprints of the predatory fox that hunted it in the night.

Somewhere overhead, a buzzard seeks to catch a meagre updraught, and the light through the window fades in and out like flashing code as thin clouds race across its surface. It is a good morning for snowball battles followed by hot drinks; for knocking down icicles and clearing the road for the postier and the cargo truck, for the ambulance and the schoolmaster who lives on the frozen river and every year misses one day – and one day only – when the ice is too thin to walk upon but too thick to push his boat through.

There is a little blood on the blankets I've wrapped myself in; presumably my blood. I do not dare remove my bandages, but crawl through the unkind chill of the world beyond my soft fortress to the cupboards, rummage through until I find the first aid kit. The clotting agents and healing gels within are of a slightly higher quality than most hearths would possess, one of the few acknowledgements in the place of its more clandestine nature. There is medical glue for sealing shut any gaping wounds, macrophages in a vial with various obscure antibiotic purposes listed on the side along with the instruction "shake well – use immediately after opening". I use what I can, drink as much water as I dare, find a bag of dried fruit, munch it down without noticing the flavour.

Officially, the hearth doesn't have a telephone, and it's a brisk walk to the nearest office. But there is a short-wave radio hidden beneath one of the floorboards upstairs. I set it to transmit a distress call every fifty minutes, no more than a ten-second burst, a maximum of six times. Any more and using it will become too dangerous, too easy to track, and I must move on. The bed has a blanket adorned with rose petals and images of happy rabbits. I steal it for my downstairs tangle, drag it into the kitchen to settle before the last heat of the fire, to wait.

The wind-up clock by the door ticks away the hours towards noon, now running on, now stuck in a minute that lasts for ever. I have done everything protocol said I should: retreated to a set location in the event of emergency for extraction, sent a distress call, waited.

The sun turns across the floor, vanishes briefly behind the trees, reappears again in little spikes of dust-dappling illumination, vanishes again behind clouds, stays shrouded. I doze, then jerk awake, then doze again. When I open my eyes, it has started to snow again, and it is impossible to tell whether it is clouded afternoon or failing evening. I check the clock, and it is evening, and no one has come, and I am alone in the safe house.

Here.

Sitting for a little while looking at the clock.

Here.

There are protocols, of course, for this kind of situation. They are loosely worded, make things sound simpler than they are: Evade capture. Get out alive. What they lack in detail, they make up for with stark motivation.

I wait three hours longer than the protocol says I should, which is probably a standard psychological response to being abandoned, and no one comes.

139

Chapter 23

I decided to move a little after 8 p.m. There was no reason to it, save that I had by that time sat in the thickening cold and dark, by myself, feeling miserable to no avail, for nearly a day. At some point, the paralysing terror of what might come met with the hard reality of how uncomfortable my present situation was, and the balance tipped into action. I pulled the emergency supplies from the pantry – torch, money, maps, inkstone. Blank documents were kept in a box behind the bathhouse, sealed in biopolymer. I filled in a few false details, stamped them, hoped for the best. I dragged myself out of my bloody, meagre clothes and into a dusty, dew-tainted shirt and jacket from the cupboard upstairs. I pulled on hat, gloves, scarf, oversized boots padded with three layers of sock, shovelled the snow away from the door of the bicycle shed, pulled out the least tatty-looking bike from within, turned on the headlamp, loaded up the panniers with food, water and first aid supplies, put a compass in my pocket and turned towards what I hoped was the nearest road heading south-east, towards Slava. On a good day, a fast cyclist could cover the distance between Vien and Slava in less than ten hours. But that was before Maze was declared heretical and the roads filled up with glowering men. Officially, the borders weren't yet closed and you could still cross with documentation and a bit of patience – but I found it hard to imagine Georg had not flashed my face to every post on the road. If he lived.

Just before midnight, I locked the gate behind me, returned the key to its hollow in the tree and set out into the dark.

The first hour – exhausting, drained by cold, just pushing the bicycle in search of a road clear enough to pedal down.

The next hour – frustrating, skidding, breathless, the road decent enough to cycle down but cased with patches of swerving ice that twice send me slithering sideways into the padded dunes of white that frame the path.

The hour after that – arriving at a village. I check its name and discover that, far from having travelled sixty kilometres already, I have made it a little less than twelve. I drink water and eat dried fish to stave off a wave of dizziness, but that just replaces the heat in my brain with gentle churning in my belly. My chest throbs along the torn line of flesh, the pain starting as an almost welcome fire that grows and grows until it is needles in my eyes, pounding in my brain.

Eventually I reach the main road that flanks the north side of the Ube River, flat and clear and fast. These are the small hours of the electric cargo truck and the heavy cargo bike making goods runs through the night. Even the bicyclesarais that appear every forty minutes or so have turned down the lights by the reception doors and pulled the shutters tight. The batteries behind the courtyards are running on empty, emitting their last mournful, sluggish clicks as hot air discharges through slow-spinning turbines, fading, gone. The lights go out in the lanterns that frame the path. The smell of biovats from the sewage pumps behind the sarais makes passing cyclists flinch and turn away, eyes watering, noses running from the unexpected, unprocessed stink.

I stop at a sarai – little more than a shuttered shrine, a few benches out of the wind and a water fountain – a few hours before dawn, astonished at how little distance I've covered, at how much my body hurts. A tired girl with sea-green eyes guards a counter selling a few hot vegetables rolled in egg wraps and warm bread. The sarai is near enough to the windfarms to have a little heat to offer from its stove, a little light to share in the nooks and crannies where half-slumbering travellers rest their heads.

"Is the road clear to Marno?" I ask the girl, who doesn't look up from her inkstone, shrugs. "I heard they were struggling to shift the snow."

"People are coming from there fine enough," she replies, and there ends the conversation.

I eat my food, take a palmful of painkillers in the shadow of the bathroom round back, refill my water bottle, wish there was somewhere more convenient I could lay my head, or that I could stick my legs up the wall to drain some of the sloshing blood from my swelling limbs. There is a dead drop behind the water vat. I check it and find no message, no fresh documents or words of comfort and support. I wait another hour anyway, huddling by the low stoves in blanket-swagged corners of the sarai, listen to the gossip, walk the perimeter of the sarai one more time, do not see Nadira, do not find aid.

Sunrise is coming, a greying of the blackened sky in the east, a rolling down of shadows. I cannot stay here. I return to the half-light of the sarai courtyard, and there are the guardia. There are only two of them, wrapped in grey felt and woollen scarves, their bicycles resting against a wooden post from which the white lantern of the sarai sags, heavy with snow. They are not the elite of the roads, not speeding up and down in their swanky cars, spare batteries in the boot, sirens and flashing lights to clear the sluggish traffic. They are local boys, sent to do a local job, not expecting trouble, but perhaps hoping for it nonetheless, a little excitement to break the monotony of their lives.

"Documents, documents!" calls the younger, with voice and eye corralling the weary gathered cyclists into a huddle beneath the light while her older colleague flicks through offered IDs.

There is an option of running, of course. I haven't been seen yet, pressing into the shadows towards the toilets, and the gentle glow of eastern light on the horizon is still not enough to pick me out against the ivory landscape. But running means heading away from my bicycle, the supplies and the road. It means going on foot into the fields and smothered floodplains, still injured, and trying to steal and bluff my way to safety. My false documents are in the pannier of my cycle bag. At some point, they were going to be tested; better now, I reason, with local boys not used to the hunt, than at a checkpoint staffed by professionals further down the road.

I pull the papers from the bag, drag my jacket tighter around my aching bones, join the inspection queue.

"What's happening?" asks a woman in front of me.

"Just routine," is the answer.

"This isn't routine," grumbles another, as his documents are held up to the older guardia's torchlight.

"Travel much, do you?" asks the younger, and though the man is almost certainly innocent of any crime, the surprise of being questioned so cows him. There was a time, not so many years ago, when he might have laughed and said yes, yes I do, I cycle every month to Budapesht and back, as a free man of the Provinces may. But Maze has been declared heretical, and the Brotherhood is leery of spies, traitors, saboteurs and anyone else for whom a five-day investigation in a cell without trial or access to legal aid may be considered a worthwhile deployment of energy – for the good of the state. Even if five days seem a short period of time for the vindication of being declared guilt-free, this travelling man may miss his son's wedding, or his wife's final hours of illness, or simply have to carry the shame of being incarcerated when he was meant to be at work, or come home to a family gone mad trying to find him, who thought he was dead, swallowed by the kakuy of the rising river. How quickly these things turn.

I am third from last in the queue, and my lips are turning white with waiting. The younger guardia takes my documents, scans them, passes them to the elder.

"Where are you going?"

"Marno."

"Why?"

"To see a friend."

"What's your friend's name?"

"Licia Hahn, she's a lawyer."

"Why are you visiting her?"

"We haven't seen each other for a long time. She's just been through an unhappy affair."

"Where'd you come from?"

"Vien."

"You're travelling at a strange hour."

"I promised her I'd be there for lunch. She telegrammed me in the evening. It sounded like things had been very stressful."

"And you're her valiant rescuer."

"I'm just helping out."

A nod; a grunt. She is not at all convinced by my heroic antics, by the aura of righteous yet faintly celibate determination I give off. She thinks I'm a useless manipulator, preying on a woman's grief to get my own way. That's not a crime, however – not yet. Sometimes you need to make a few errors of judgement, she concludes, in order to realise how much better off you'd be with someone else.

She hands my documents back, barely glances at my face, doesn't acknowledge me with another word. I smile and half-bow in gratitude and manage to hide the shaking of my hands.

Half an hour from Marno, I spotted the first full guardia check-point. Traffic had slowed to a dead stop, bicycles and trucks alike. A barrier had been laid across the road and grey-coated figures moved in puffs of spinning air along its edges, opening bags and checking documents, peering under hats and into puffy, dry-eyed faces. Documents interested them less than features; some held papers in their black-gloved hands, and I could guess whose face might be printed on them.

I slowed down some hundred metres from the back of the queue. I dismounted my bicycle, calm, casual, wheeled it to the side of the road, flipped it upside down and carefully dislodged the chain, mineral lubricants slithering sticky and brown into the weave of my gloves as I fumbled with it. A few cyclists pedalled by, saw me. One asked if I needed a hand, but I smiled and shook my head and said it was fine, taking my time as I fumbled with the dislodged part, in no rush to fix it. A post truck joined the waiting queue, half-obscuring me from the sight of the other end of the road. I slipped the chain back on, then made a show of inspecting my wheels for a puncture, spinning them round and round as I examined every pebble and shard of ice encased in the grip.

"You all right, sky-kin?" called a friendly cyclist as she dismounted behind the post truck, already rummaging in her bags for her documents.

"Fine, thank you," I replied, bright as sunlight on snow. "Should have done better maintenance."

She smiled and nodded, and as the queue drifted towards the roadblock I flipped my bicycle over again, re-checked my panniers were sealed and, as if it had always been my intention and part of the plan, turned and cycled calmly off in the opposite direction, heart singing in my ears, the taste of vomit in my mouth. No one saw me; or if they did, no one saw a spy fleeing for his life.

It took me nearly four hours to make the laborious crossing to the next major road towards Bukarest, cutting north through spinning clouds of wind-plucked snow to the minor, bumpy, icy road that slithered through Zamk. The telegram office also housed the server terminal and a small general store. A man with charcoal eyes watched me as I scribbled out my message on a yellow slip. Protocol had no definition for my current location, no coded secrets to send. I tried to find some loose way of communicating, some cry for help that someone – anyone – might understand.

HEADING CHENECH, HOME FOR SISTER'S BIRTHDAY

"Going a long way," said the man, and since when did every telegram operator in every rural office read every telegram that passed beneath their fingers? Is this polite interest, absent

145

rudeness, an interrogation? Is Georg inside his mind, as he is inside mine? I need to stop, sleep properly, check the glue binding the skin across my torso, drink, eat, stick my legs up a wall. Every time I get off my bicycle, it becomes harder and harder to get back on.

"Family matters," I mumbled, too slow, too late, a half-muttered excuse dredged from the back of my brain.

He nodded and smiled. He is a good man, a kind man – family is everything to him, and he is pleased to see that others feel the same way. He is a bad man, a cruel man – he is giddy at the opportunity to turn in a traitor to the state, has my picture on his inkstone hidden beneath his desk, believes in the new Maze, in taking control and letting go of the past. Perhaps belief is not enough to make him cruel; very well, he kicks puppies too. I gave him the wan smile of the weary traveller as I slipped out the door into winter light.

Skirting the edge of the mountains. Here, when the days grow hot, the children come and jump into the lakes and rivers that snake through the forest. They swim through silver waters, gasp at the icy melt from the peaks above, dip their toes and lounge on the shingle shores at the first touch of summer sun. In winter, their older peers trek up into the mountain to the little wooden huts that sit above the rusty cliffs where the waterfall flows, turning the roar of plunging foam to a background whisper as doors are closed, fires struck in stoves and thick blankets swung across weary shoulders.

In the morning, the highest trees stand above valleys of frozen cloud, and when the wind blows you may sit upon a promontory and watch new fog form, twist, rise and dissolve, like a ghost's fingers as it tries to crawl its way from the earth. Close your eyes and the sound of birds rises like the sun; open them again and in every nook of every rock you begin to see life spreading its fingers in tiny buds of yellow and purple, in unfolding lime and winter green. Georg says there is metal to be found in these parts, perhaps coal to burn. A few years ago, there was a mighty fire

146

when someone struck a match above a certain patch of soft, life-less ground and the pent-up gases of centuries of buried landfill finally burst open, killing the luckless fire-starter and sending a shock through the timber that was heard as far away as the idling walkers on the mountain peaks.

Here, set between the rising banks of darkening trees, a village, low timber hearths crowned with snow, steps cut in the side of the hill so that each hearth may look over its neighbour's roof into the valley below, a warm light from within. A former church, centuries old, stands carefully preserved in the village square with notices explaining its historical significance, and twice-weekly tours operate between spring and autumn for visitors curious to have the iconography of martyred saints and bleeding sinners explained to them in language we now understand.

On the edge of that town, where the windfarms spun and whistled in the settling wuther of the fading afternoon, another guardia outpost, two women pacing up and down with hands in pockets, puffing and huffing in the deepening cold. I saw no sign that my photo had yet reached them, but when I pedalled up and produced my documents, one leant in and examined my face as if she were a doctor looking for the first signs of cancer from a mole, or trying to spot the optic nerve through the inky black of my eyes.

"Where'd you say you were going again?"

"Volen, via Leviche."

"Where'd you come from?"

"Slava."

"Why didn't you take the train?"

"I wanted to cycle. Trains bore me."

A nod; my excuse is as little noted as it is meaningful. Maybe it's true; maybe it's not. Her attention has already moved. "May I see your bags?"

I open my bags, heart in my mouth. She shines a torch into my sacks, pokes around with the end of her finger gingerly as if expecting bear traps, nods once, turns the torch to my face again, sees me flinch, lowers it back to my chest. "I've just got to check these," she says, taking my documents and heading towards the half-open door of the guardia post.

"Of course," I smile.

I let her get all the way inside, count to ten, swing back on my bicycle and sprint for the road out of town. Someone must have been watching me from the window, because I hear a shout and the ringing of a bell seconds later, the pounding of feet on gravel, the scrape of tyres as someone lunges for their own bike. In this neck of the woods, the guardia will have maybe only one or two cars, and they will be out patrolling the bigger roads. My pursuers follow me on bicycle, but they are fresher than me, will be faster. Now is the time for recklessness, to take the risks that they will not. I plough out of the one-road village and into switchbacks heading for the river floor. It is faster to stay on the road than to cut across, but halfway down I see the beginning of a trail, a smaller muddy way leading up towards the windfarms, and turn onto it. My pursuers don't bother to shout "Stop!" or "Surrender!" or anything of that ilk; they are too far behind and only just beginning to find their breath as they plunge after me onto the muddy trail heading towards the ridge above. Soon it becomes a little too narrow, the snow too thick to pedal through, so I dismount, grab my bags off the back and sling them over my shoulders, and, feet crunching, push forward. The snow turns our chase into a shuffling hopped pursuit, a sluggish churn through the black and white world. My lips are ice, my chest is fire. The forest offers an early night, turning the settling dusk to thicker black that pushes the shadows higher and deeper. The crows are squabbling overhead, oblivious to the disturbance below. A thick furred forest cat hisses, snarls and springs away from me as I approach, the path vanishing altogether now into the bony grasp of the underbrush. At the top of the ridge, I pause to glance back and can't see my pursuers through branch and limb, but I can still hear them, snow compressed beneath boot, twigs tearing as fingers grasp for handholds on the scramble up.

Turn, drop down the other side, and here now is sudden night, true and blanketing, as the hill itself cuts off the setting sun behind its ridge. The change is like plunging into an icy bath, and as I slither down my feet go out beneath me, and I catch myself on a trunk, and rise, and slip and slide again. I am leaving tracks in the snow, easy to follow, but there is nothing to be done. I scramble, leaning heavily to the side, parallel to the lip of the ridge, just a few feet below it, heaving from branch to branch, heading for the singing swish of the windfarm. The turbines here are old, the parts have spun too long, grown cracked and dry, clicking, clunking, whooshing against themselves. The wind is a dirge, a skeleton's lament, but some ground has been cleared of snow, offering a path through the cables and transformers. For the first time, I run, my legs weighted stumps pounding heavy on the earth, my ears ringing. Now someone shouts, a lone voice behind me, and I wonder if perhaps one of the guardia has lost the other. I struggle to move faster, nearly over-tip, leaning forward as my feet refuse to offer anything more, weaving through the high columns of the farm, the smell of electricity and old resin thick on the air, then skid to a halt at a rope slung across a drop where the path stops at a cliff's edge. Choices – left into darkness, right towards the village, back into the arms of the guardia or straight down. The drop is perhaps thirty metres into water of deep black flecked with the last mirrored grey of day. The water moves enough that ice has not yet formed on it, a deep bowl carved from a dozen little flowing trickles which in summer are a roaring tide. Though I might survive the fall, I do not think I will survive the hypothermia that will follow. Footsteps skid to a halt behind me, and of the two guardia who followed, only one has kept up in the gloom.

She stops, realises she is alone, pulls her baton from her hip and raises a whistle to her mouth. I attack before she can make a sound, diving in to wrap my arms bear-hug across her chest, trying to take away the advantage of range that her unfolded stick gives her. The inquisition trained me how to fight, and no doubt the guardia trained her too, but in the moment neither of us remember more than a few physical habits, a shuffling of feet and a scrambling for targets, a panting through which hands flail loosely for eyes or throat, dig into anything soft or try to drive crack-snap into anything hard. There is more luck in this encounter than there is skill, and for a moment we tangle together beneath the turbines, gasping and hissing, feet slipping on icy mud, the moistures of our condensed breaths wet on each other's cheeks and at each other's necks, like dogs looking to bite. I manage to get a fist in her belly, but at the minimal distance between us all she does is grunt. Then she remembers that her stick has two ends and smashes the butt down into my shoulder. She is perhaps aiming for my head, but in the twist of arm and armpit can't get the angle, so she strikes bone, then adjusts her feet, swinging me round with her as she moves, and hits again, and this time does better and catches the back of my skull. The blow is not yet enough to make me let go, a disorientating judder that runs down to my buckling knees; but a few more good whacks and I will be done. When she draws back to hit again, I drop like a drunkard, and the grip we have on each other pulls her down. My back smacks into the earth hard enough to crack teeth, but in the moment of confusion I wrap both my arms across her throat, squeezing and pulling her tight. She understands at once what is happening and kicks and scrambles and kicks again, driving her elbows into my ribs hard enough to bring galaxies across my eyes. I bite back a howl and try to hook one of her legs in mine, hear the stick fall from her grasp, pray to sky and earth that I have not killed her, pray that I did not fall for some cunning trick. Her thrashing slows; her body grows heavy on mine. I let go, perhaps a little earlier than my teachers would have wished, push her off me, roll to the other side, grab her stick, take deep breaths, kneel next to her, arm raised to strike, see that she is not moving.

Slowly, I peel away a sodden glove, fumble at her neck for a pulse, find it and nearly choke back shame and gratitude. An apology springs to my lips, but it vanishes in the panting of my breath. She is already beginning to stir, head lolling this way and that, fingers clawing at snow. I grab my bag, turn towards the night and, before she can get her boots on the ground again, I run.

150

Chapter 24

Crawling through the midnight forest. The moon is hidden tonight. The cold has settled through every part of me, turning bones to glass. One step wrong and I will break, snap apart from the inside out.

Sometimes I hear voices and have imagined them.

Sometimes I hear voices and they are real, search parties sweeping through the night. Then I crawl on hands and knees between the trees, feeling through darkness, twigs scratching at eyes, water melting through my trousers and beginning to re-freeze against blanched blue skin below.

I imagine dogs and am terrified of them.

I imagine drones, infrared cameras and whining blades, piloted over the blanketed dark. Against the snow I will be a scarlet bonfire, slithering through the night, a veritable demon; still, I fear dogs more.

Once I stop and think I will cry, and realise that my legs refuse to walk. I sit on my haunches and shake and rock and know that the beginnings of hypothermia are on their way, and shake and rock again, until I hear a dog bark somewhere far, far away – or perhaps I do not – and the jolt of terror is enough to warm my fingers again.

The blood that flows from a dozen scratches and the seeping tear in my chest is briefly warming. I think about picking scabs, about feeling the heat of my own body gracing the dead surface of my skin. Then I think about heat rushing away as from a furnace, and cold, dead metal, and how much the creatures of the forest will enjoy finding my corpse once the snows have melted and I am soft enough to eat. Then I scamper on, barely a kilometre, perhaps less, falling constantly into white, heart pounding, unable to escape the noise of it in my ears. I think I will die out here and am grateful that I will be eaten, honoured that my flesh will give back to the earth that carried me. Children of sky and earth, thank you for feeding me; let me feed you in return. The water of my blood was the same stuff that the dinosaurs drank; I have been oceans, I have rained upon the desert, I have circled the earth a thousand times and will do so again, when the last part of me is gone. I do not fear death so much as a life lived failing; I hope that the hypothermia will take away the pain of my bruised bones before the end.

Time to give up, perhaps.

Time to stop running.

So long as the forest takes me, not the dogs, I will be content.

I think I have fallen.

I think I have slept, leaning against the side of a tree.

I think I have woken and moved and slept again without realising, sleepwalking through the dark.

I have no idea where north is, or south. I only find the river by its sound, sit on its bank, imagine losing the dogs by wading through its rushing depths, know that if I do, and cannot light a fire on the other side, I will die. I think that if I try to cross in this inky state, Vae's fingers will rise from the pebble bed below, and she will hold hands with me and pull me down into the water's depths. I do not think she is lonely or sad in whatever drowned place the forest took her; I think the kakuy of the river and the sea carried her water to crystal islands and beneath the frozen surface of the north and that there is nothing malicious in their motion, no rancour in their embrace. I do not attempt to cross the river, but follow its bank in a direction – I do not know which one, fumbling against rocks and slipping, wet-toed, round fallen buttress trees. I hear a drone overhead and know I imagined it. Then I look up, and it is real, or at least a very convincing hallucination.

It hovers directly above me, some hundred metres up, a single red light on its tail as it turns its lensed eye to examine me. I raise one hand in greeting, as an estranged lover might when meeting an old affair after an awkward ending and a forced reunion. The drone neither bobs nor flashes in reply but turns and heads back up the river bank, as if it had not seen me at all.

Pre-dawn lasted a year, a band of grey in the east, which I had not realised was east. I knelt on the top of the great round stones that traversed the river at its shallowest point, put my head in my hands and knew I could go no further. I curled up in the middle of the stream on a great grey rock with a green underwater beard and waited for the sun to kill me. When it finally rose, peeking over the mountain tops, it was an avalanche of light rolling down the valley, a visible tumble of silver. I curled away as it struck me, buried my head in my hands, waited for it all to be over, the shivering uncontrollable now. I heard the creatures of the forest flutter snowflakes from their wings, beat the night from their tails, chirrup the darkness from their lungs and raise their eyes to heaven, and I cowered from it all and wondered what was taking the dogs so long to catch me and drag me by my ankles to their masters.

Then, a footfall, strange, heavy, pressing into the snow.

And another.

They came, far enough apart to imply some mighty, ponderous thing. A bear maybe, testing its weight on the unfamiliar edge of the river. Each crunch was long and slow, perhaps carrying the echo of a falling tree or the slow splintering of breaking ice. I did not open my eyes, and then I did, the last dredges of curiosity overwhelming my cold-broken fatigue.

The kakuy of the winter wood did not regard me as he went about his business. He did not raise his icy head nor pause in his snuffling at river's edge. Instead, he dipped a black nose the size of my face into the water, pulled back a little as if shocked by how cold it ran, then dipped down again to lap at the fresh-flowing stream with a tongue the deep purple of clotting blood.

Four paws, each bigger than my back and each with seven claws, dug into the snow, yet the tracks he left behind seemed only a few millimetres deep, as if he made no mark upon the land over which he plodded. His fur had turned moonlight white and was crowned with spikes of ice, in which fractal spirals and broken patterns of half-imagined forms were captured, twisting this way and that with the changing light. A single, cheeky robin sat a few inches from his tail, preening itself, enjoying the free ride, the power and majesty of the kakuy somewhat altered by its secondary role as birdstand. A smell of black soil and foggy dew rolled off him, powerful enough for even me to smell through the still morning air, and when he raised his eyes to examine his domain, they were winter's night, full of stars. I lay still as the rock beneath me, watching him through my bundled arms. He paid me no attention, lapped up a little more water, shook himself, startling the robin into indignantly flapping away, a creaking and cracking of ice over shaggy, flabby flesh, and then at last looked at me.

The kakuy of the winter wood gazed upon me as the fatted lion, blood on his lips, might regard the little scavenging carrion birds that come to feast upon the corpse the pride have killed. Too insignificant to hunt – a curiosity, a courtier, even – a tiny, ignorant thing. I thought I should bow my head in prayer, put my hands together, the fingers locked in frozen curls, show some deference. But neither the kakuy nor the lion have any interest in the deeds of little things, save as some idle curiosity to watch with full belly, and so the kakuy looked at me, made no sign of distress or disturbance, and looked away, turning slowly from the river to shamble up the slope towards the rising sun. Within a few yards, the thick trunks of the bending silver forest had consumed him, the thump of his great weight no longer echoing through the earth, as if he had been swallowed whole by it. I gazed along the path he'd taken and could barely see the tracks he'd left behind, save for the thick branch of the silver birch that had bent out of his way as he passed. I let my eye wander a little further, past the frustrated, circling red-breasted robin, and saw the stone lantern that had been there all this time, tucked into the shadow of the trees. It was old, unlit, the snow inches thick on its sloping roof, piled high around its grey base. It marked the beginning of a narrow path – too narrow for the kakuy, yet somehow he had travelled it. I watched it for a while, wondering if it too would vanish as the kakuy had, but it resolutely did not.

I uncurled one leg, and it was the tearing apart of an ancient metal rod rusted into some deformed shape.

I uncoiled the other and whimpered and swore and cursed at the pain that ran through me, and cursing vilely made it a little bit easier, so I kept on uttering profanities until my body was practically upright, on the verge of tipping constantly forward but swaying now one step at a time towards the path.

I reached the stone lantern, clung to it as if it were some sacred, holy sign, paused in my cursing long enough to give thanks, thanks to the forest, thanks to the river, thanks to the stone and thanks to the sky, thanks to my kindred who had made this path, thanks to the living who brought light out of the darkness and the dead who had given offering to the timber that housed them and the forest that kept them whole. I half-sang a half-forgotten prayer, a mantra to the changing sun and changing moon, snatches of words from old texts that I had not uttered in all the time I had been Kadri Tarrad, Georg's man, all the time he had been burrowing in my head to see the truth of my heart, and knew now that if I died at least I died free of him, at least Georg would no longer be in my soul. I pushed onwards, up the path, following the dotted lanterns until my toes, sinking through snow, hit buried steps rather than merely winding dirt. I bit back a sob and crawled on hands and knees, too breathless now to manage more than the odd meaningless word gasped through broken lips. The sun made the brightness of the snow unbearable, a dazzling mirror that pierced my fluttering eyes; the forest broke it up into pools of white and shadow, a shelter, a softness, the leaves and rising mist turning the world into a woven tapestry of illumination, the day a solid thing, reach out and grasp it in your fingers, turn it this way and that, this moment alive, still alive, still alive!

155

The shrine gates stood open at the top of the path. No one had come here to destroy, no one had bothered to seek out this little sanctuary to the kakuy of the winter wood. Neither had any Medj lit lantern or incense for many a month, but the timber door slid back to the little room that would have been their sanctuary, and there were blankets piled above the folded mattress in a corner, and dried fruit and vegetables in the cold-storage box behind the altar, and though the solar panels were impossibly matted over with snow, the single small battery off to the west activated when I turned the breaker, and in the tiny square hollow of the Medj's cell, the heater began to glow to life. I piled myself with blankets, pressed my head into the woven matted floor, crawled so close to the heater I thought the fabrics that shrouded me might burn, and closed my eyes and shook before the rising dawn.

Chapter 25

Having stopped, I could not start again.

I lay on the floor of the cell, not even bothering to unfold the thin lilac mattress tucked into a corner, and waited to be caught. Sometimes I managed to crawl far enough to open the storage box and munch on a little apple or fermented cabbage. Then my jaw hurt, so I curled back up again by the heater, until finally, nearly six hours later, the battery that had not been charged for so long gave up. Then I lay on the floor a little longer and waited to be arrested. No one came. The dogs did not howl, the guardia did not break down my door, Georg was not in my head. It occurred to me that this was the kind of posting I could really do with, right now – a forest shrine to tend alone, far from the madness of mankind and their brewing wars and vanities. I pictured myself before the shrine to the kakuy, giving thanks to the forest and, with honour and reverence, sweeping the path and lighting the lanterns, bowing down to the river that gave me life and offering my morning songs to the sun that warmed me. It would be a good calling, I concluded, to be alone in this place, a representative of humanity sent to give thanks. Then I thought about it a little more, decided I'd probably be mad within a week and wondered if there was a school nearby that ever sent children to this shrine, to be taught the old temple lore of ecology and the nitrogen cycle, which mushrooms to pick and which to avoid, and how to live in balance with the world that sustained them. I hoped so; I hoped so with a fervency that astonished me, as if in these few hours of huddling from the snow I had already become keeper of this sacred place.

Then I remembered who I was and waited for the dogs, and the dogs did not come.

An hour or so before sunset, I dragged myself, every part locked in swollen pain, head pounding as if respite had finally allowed the adrenaline that had sustained me to yield to the true exhaustion of the day, into the tiny courtyard of the shrine. I could stretch my arms out in the middle of it and brush either the altar, the gate, or the twin walls of the Medj's cell and washroom, all with a little drunken swaying. I blew a fine crust of snow off the altar, dusted it with the corner of my sleeve, pressed my palms together and bowed to the stone carved face of the kakuy, wished I had a snowdrop or some thin winter flower to lay in offering before his image.

Then I heard the drone again and looked up, irritated now to be disturbed in this place by something so human. I could not see it through the overhanging trees, but I had no doubt that it could see me and raised my fingers in a distinctly profane gesture to it, as much exasperated as anything else that its pilot was taking so long to find me. It turned and buzzed away.

In the washroom, I found dusty robes of the Medj, greys and faded blues. Technically, they were not the robes of the inquisition, and numerous exams and years of careful study and contemplation were required before I was allowed to wear them, but they were warm and clean, and after a little consideration I concluded that my service in Vien probably counted for at least half a doctoral thesis, strong on fieldwork. I untangled myself from my own filthy clothes, peeling them away one bloody layer at a time, and tried not to look too closely at the tapestry of black and blue that rippled over my body before winding myself back into the priest's gown. I found a broom in the dusty corner of a room and knocked the snow off the solar panels. A bucket of wooden pellets lay behind the toilet, ready to start a small fire if needed. I thought about saving them, hoarding my goods, then concluded it was ridiculous and, dragging the bucket into the tiny courtyard, dug a shallow bowl, lined it with stones that some scholarly Medj had doubtless arranged in an ornamental manner of deep metaphorical import and set a small fire going. It was not as magical as the warmth of the heater had been, but it would serve. As the sun set, I piled more stones around the blaze, taking the hottest of the bunch to wrap into my robes and press against my skin as the darkness returned to the forest.

The drone came once more, a few minutes after sunset, but it didn't stay long enough for me to bow, wave or mime obscenities at it. I bent over the fire, prayers tumbling from my lips, the old forgotten songs of gratitude and harmony, sung loosely and out of tune. I thought of taking a stick from my blaze and lighting the stone lanterns that led up the frosty path to my door, as the guardians of this shrine must have done for so many years. But that would have involved leaving the heat of the fire, the orange light reflected upon the image of the kakuy, so I stayed where I was as the owl called and the cold silenced even the hungriest of creatures in a frozen malaise.

I was half-asleep when I heard the footsteps, crunching on old snow. I didn't turn as they approached, but unravelled a luke-warm stone from my gown and returned it to the guttering edge of the fire, listened to the creaking of the gate, heard another step on snow, heard it stop. It struck me as odd that there was not more noise; had the guardia I had fought in the windfarm come alone? Somewhere I had her stick, unless I had lost it in the forest. Maybe this time she'd brought a gun.

Silence, save for the crackling of fading flame.

I half-turned, twisting, and the twist was agony, so I half-shuffled instead, scootching my backside round in a less-than-dignified bumping to see who had come to arrest me. For a moment, I imagined I would not see a human at all but the kakuy of the winter wood, come again to see what honours were paid to him in the shrine that should have carried the smell of incense in thanks for the gifts of his domain. Instead, there was a woman, alone, dressed in a thick midnight-blue coat and hood, fur-lined gloves and knee-high boots, carrying a heavy rucksack on her back, a flashlight in her hand, a gun on her hip. In the low light of the fire, I could not clearly see her face, but there was nothing in her body that spoke of violence or aggression, of retribution for my flight. She could have been a midnight pilgrim, come to pray, except that she turned the full force of the light into my face, her other hand by her weapon, and said:

"Ven?"

I looked again, realised I had only spoken to the forest all day, and that my voice, when I spoke to people, seemed entirely alien and strange. "Yue?"

When things are unnatural, unreasonable, any reasonable response is impossible. I did not run to her; she did not drop her bag and embrace me. Such things happen in cities, in stations, in places that are in the domain of men. In the forest, we stared at each other in silence. Snow tumbled from the black branches, the birds sang, the trees grew, the river roared and took Vae away with it, and we looked at each other longer than the years we had been apart.

Then that too passed, that too was ending, and she shuddered as if the water of the river that had flowed across her back was still rushing through her blood. She lowered her torch, switched it off, walked forward, knelt down beside me, warmed her hands by the last of the fire, pressed them to the top edge of a hot, black-stained stone. The strap that secured her gun was loose, weapon ready to be drawn. She looked into the flames as if she might see the spirit of the great burning slumbering within them, then at last raised her gaze, her puffed breath mingling with mine. For the first time, she seemed to see the bruising mottled across my skin, and reached up, examining my face, touched the back of my head where the guardia's stick had landed, looked back into the fire, opened her bag, pulled out an insulated flask that steamed when she opened it, took a long drink, exhaled, then handed the flask to me.

I drank. It was a kind of tea, floral but weak. She dug deeper into her bag, pulled out a neatly packaged medical kit, said: "You're injured."

"Yue – you are Yue." The words wanted to be a question, but there was no questioning in it.

"Ven – you're injured."

"No. Yes. I mean ... yes. But I'm fine. Not fine. Fine. How are you here?"

"The drone," she replied, turning her chin briefly upwards and taking the flask back from me as if concerned I might drink enough heat to drown.

"That was you?"

A nod, uh-huh. She is fumbling with the pack, little vials of military-grade compounds, far more impressive than anything I've used or seen.

"Why? I don't understand."

She took a while to answer, contemplating where in the cascade of possibilities the most truthful response might lie, picking the most concise way to express as much complexity as she could. "Nadira is dead."

The mind has two choices: understand these words, or reject them utterly. I tell her that she is wrong, she has misunderstood. Of course Nadira isn't dead. She has looked under the wrong rock, come to the wrong shrine. Once the water that feeds me was in the ocean, as was the water in Nadira's blood; we shared the seas, you see, so I'd know if she was dead, and anyway, the whole thing is absurd, quite, quite absurd. Nadira is fine. Georg lied, he lies, he never found a way into her mind. Georg is not made of water; only gasoline runs through his veins. We are different, you see; we are all one life, but we are different.

These words may have become a babble; there may perhaps have been something a little hysterical in my eye, because Yue catches my hands in hers. The touch, glove on glove, silences me. She waits for the words to settle inside my throat, watches for understanding in my face, sees it bloom, nods once, carries on with her work.

"I have a team three kilometres from here."

"Nadira is Temple," mumbles some mushed-up voice that is

161

going to be my own, now and for ever, now that Nadira is dead. "You are Council. Why are you here?"

"Can you walk?"

"I don't know. Probably."

"It's not far. Lean on me."

When I last saw her, walking through the halls of power behind Jia, she had seemed tall, filling the world with her presence. Now she is a little too short to comfortably drape over, our weights shifting side to side with the effort of balance as we sway down the frozen path by torchlight. Sometimes I think I can walk without her, and make it a few hundred metres so fast I think I could fly. Then I have to stop, and like an old man at the top of a high mountain bend over double to catch my breath. It would be ridiculous to laugh or cry, to tell her she's not real, to swear blind my life up to this moment was an illusion, that time stopped when the forest burned and the kakuy died by the roaring river. At one point, I open my mouth to explain all of this, and get as far as "Yue," before falling silent again. She gives me a quizzical look, and sees that there's nothing but madness in me, and nods once, and says not a word.

Chapter 26

Nadira was shot fleeing arrest. They shot her in the back, twice, and put her in an ambulance, but she died before she reached the hospital, eyes open, tubes down her throat, discarded surgical gloves on the floor around her. They'd have to clean the ambulance top to bottom, no doubt, empty it entirely and turn the hose on its interior, spray it with pink antiseptic and burn the white paper sheets that she expired on. The only photos they had of her face were a surveillance shot of her buying bread, moments before she recognised the danger she was in, and of her corpse. In the first image, she looked humble, charming, smiled at the baker as she took the loaf in her hands. In the latter, she was a martyr to violence, and so the news ran neither, and no one reported her death.

Three other members of the inquisition died that same day. I had not known how many agents Nadira had run, and felt brief disappointment that I had not been the only one, and wondered if I had been the most useful, and was ashamed at my own vanity.

In the winter wood, where all things slumber beneath the blackest black, Yue led me down a path of lightless lanterns to a clearing where once the people of the forest had come to spin their stories through the snow-bound leaves. On ancient tangles of dug-up thread and rotting polymer pulled from the landfill mines, on blue-yellow fishing lines scoured from the skeletal guts of calcified fish, suspended like bunting across the grove to create a second canopy between snow and moon, the memories of the

163

past had been hung like offerings to star and sky. Silver spinning discs bubbling with chemical green that had perhaps once carried music or the sound of voices; long tongues of curling tyre and endless polished beads of green and brown glass, threaded through the forest weave. Distorted plastic bottle tops, painted mats of disposable diapers turned to brown stone through centuries of compression in the mines, cracked sculptures of broken computer chips and shattered metal casings which clunked and clacked against each other as we passed through them, a rubber windchime. Some still bore hints of archaic script:

CE COMPLIANT
MADE IN
CONTAINS PET
DO NOT EXCEED

Beneath an oak bowed by snow, Yue finally let me collapse, huddling against its trunk beneath a tapestry of woven metal shards, spun like a cracked mirror through its branches. The broken remnant of a child's toy; a wrapped bundle of ancient pens, the ink turned to stone; the cracked remains of a wristwatch, time stopped for ever at half past three. The names of the dead had been carved below, etched into wood, landfill miners crushed when the tunnels gave way, or poisoned in the endless chemical stink that seeped through water and lung as they dug their way through the debris of the past. This was a place every bit as sacred as the kakuy's shrine, a monument to the dead, a testament to human things in the place where the spirits reigned. I closed my eyes and pressed my head against the wood, and it felt warm next to my frozen skin. I tried to stop my teeth chattering and couldn't. I tried to hold my knees so close to my chest that not an atom of heat could escape me, but there always seemed a place where the cold got in. Yue said: "They're coming. Ven? They're coming. Listen to me. Stay awake. Ven? Ven!"

It started to snow again, and the snow seemed warm, and I closed my eyes and welcomed it.

Chapter 27

A safe house, two kilometres north of the border between Maze and Magyarzag.

My first experience of coming back to life was a tepid bath. I wanted it scalding, and knew scalding would kill me, and howled as the warmth seeped into my fingers, and didn't care. Strangers wrapped me up in warm towels, laid me down by the stove, talked in low voices and said things like: "At second watch," or "Strategic assessment," or, in the case of one young voice that was perhaps not meant to be overheard: "I swear I'm a slave to that cat."

Then I slept.

Then I woke.

Then I ate, a little at a time, presided over by a man with a mole above his right eye and extraordinarily pink lips, who nodded approvingly when I took little bites and frowned deeply if it looked like I was going to take more than a morsel at a time. He never said anything reproachful, but something in the solemnity of his expression made me want to not disappoint him.

Then I slept again, and when I woke and asked for Yue, they told me she was gone.

In the Burning Age, militaries were confusing things. "Interventions" replaced "conquests". "Enemies we wish to crush" were "rogue states". "Strategic partners" replaced "too big to fight". Huge armies were still kept as a sign of power and prestige, awaiting the day when victory was measured once again in how many hundreds of millions you could afford slain or when nuclear winter settled the matter. As it was, the kakuy ended that era before proud men in smart jackets could do anything too spectacular.

In the modern era, militaries were far smaller affairs. The resources required to sustain the flair and bluster of previous times, along with the classification of some of the more egregious military technologies as anathema to humankind, led to a looser military structure of small units designed to move fast through hostile terrain. The official motto of Lyvodia's 14th Infantry – "our lives in service" – had always unofficially yet far more pervasively been "pedal faster, jackass".

"Been in the wars a bit, been at the old stabbing, the old spying, yes?" The captain, a man in his mid-forties, patted me kindly on the arm. "Could have been much worse."

The safe house was a cabin in the woods without electricity. Worn cushions were arrayed around a low ceramic stove; beeswax candles dribbled yellow into the night. My rescuers sat around reading or playing board games pulled from the cupboard. The largest of the games had a manual some sixty pages long, and play would stop every fifteen minutes to consult the nuance of an unexpected rule.

"This is an eight-roll test," the gamemaster proclaimed. "But you have the salmon, so you must discount your modifier."

Such statements elicited groans from half the board, whoops of glee from the other. I watched from my bundled corner, waiting.

When they decided to move me, they did so without warning, shaking me awake a little before midnight as the snow fell in the dead silence of buried sound. Boots were pulled on and trousers tucked in; revolvers hidden beneath outer clothes, rifles stuck in the back of a sled and covered over with firewood, dried mushrooms, fresh folds of spider silk and a waxed tarpaulin. I was handed documents, clean clothes, a hat that sank down over my eyes with every bump in the path. Then I was compressed into a nook at the back of the sledge, pulled by two men on skis who watched the darkness through their headtorches as if night were a hunting, tentacled thing, every shadow a limb waiting to strike.

Light vanished a few metres on every side whenever I turned my head. Look up and see only falling white, and then above it nothing save a hazy disruption in the dark, twisting sometimes in a billow of tree-top wind. Look to the left and perhaps a wolf's yellow eye darted away; look to the right and perhaps the kakuy is watching, shaking the earth from which he arose and into which he will vanish, perhaps the forest is watching; perhaps the trees themselves bend a little closer to shadow us as we head into the night.

Perhaps not. The lives of humans are not special to the spirits of sky and earth; they will not bless us, they will not curse us, they do not care for our names, faces, moralities or characters. They care only for the water and the fire, for the river running and the mountain standing proud. They will destroy us, or ignore us, not because we are mighty and worthy of note, but because we are small, and it is a simple matter for the kakuy to step on us without noticing that there was something underfoot.

I close my eyes and wonder where Georg is. Who will translate documents for him now, or knows precisely when to bring him dinner? Perhaps I killed his trust in secretarial staff when I stuck a knife in his leg. The thought pleases me, and the surrounding darkness is merely life untouched by light, rather than endless terror waiting, as we glide on through the night.

We stopped three times. Once, a little before dawn, to eat, drink, rest, without fire and with only muffled, murmured speech.

Once, as we were on the edge of a river crossing, ropes set up from one side to the other to guide the wobbling, balancing troops and their gear as they slipped from icy stone to icy stone across the ford.

Last, on a ridge high above a valley carved into a hard V by angry white water. Here, when the halt came, it was so hard and sharp that the momentum of my sledge nearly carried me into the knees of the frozen soldiers that pulled it, and I found myself sticking my hands out into snow to catch balance, kill a little momentum. Then everyone hunkered down, lying flat, and rifles were pulled out and passed around, and I was suddenly the tallest and most obvious target of the lot, so I disentangled myself from my den and wriggled into the shelter of an oak tree, terror hot and itchy in my palms.

There we remained for nearly ten minutes in absolute, motionless silence, as the chattering cold seeped into us. Finally the captain rose again, nodded once, and some semblance of calm was restored. I did not know what he had seen that stopped him so suddenly, but a few kilometres further on he called a halt again and, gesturing to me from his skis, summoned me to the front of the little line.

"There." His voice was a murmur one notch above a whisper, a gentle finger twitching towards the edge of a ridge from which spindling black trees clung to sheer stained rock like breaking masts from a sinking ship. I looked where he gestured, between a break in the canopy, and down to the valley floor. It should have been impossible to see the riverbed below through the dome of winter branches, but the loggers had been busy, and the glint of their equipment still shone yellow and red against the black and white winter. The swathe they'd cut through the forest, a fist of ripped-up earth and spat-out tree, formed a line that stretched almost from one end of the valley to the other, a crumpled desolation. Figures moved against the tumbled-down mortuary of timber and snow, still clearing, pushing back through the cold, and behind them another machine, this one belching thick black smoke from a pipe above its hulking carapace, a beetle crawling over the half-crushed remnants of split forest floor.

"Where are their offerings?" he breathed. "Why are they taking the young trees too?"

"They do not make offerings any more. They say the forest belongs to men."

His lips twitched in distaste. He pointed at the black, grumbling machine as it rolled on caterpillar treads over the fallen limbs of a young ash, white shards of still-living wood splitting open beneath its metal bulk.

"What is it?"

"It's called a tank," I replied.

"How do we destroy it?"

I racked my memory, trying to pull up the few details I'd bothered to absorb about that area of heretical history. "Mines, mostly, I think. Or a bigger tank."

A nod, unhappy to have confirmed the worst. "Nasty things, mines. Never kill who you think they will."

"Well," I muttered, "let's hope it doesn't come to that."

For a moment, his eyes met mine, and there was incredulity there. This was a man who had never once relied on hope to do anything; hope was for children and the elderly – he was paid to plan for the worst. I looked away, his opinion of me significantly lessened from its already low level, and slunk back to the sledge to be dragged like a log through the forest, towards home.

There was no fanfare when we crept across the forest border between Maze and northern Magyarzag. There was no sense of coming home, no change in the air, neither sign nor welcoming committee. There was, however, a path out of the trees onto a road winding through the wood, which no one had tried to clear of snow and which carried the marks of only a few bicycles and perhaps a single postier's truck. Here we stopped. Here my guide turned and said: "We are back," and his words were so devoid of feeling that I wasn't sure at first what to make of them. "Home," he corrected, seeing my face. Then, when I clearly didn't exhibit the full comprehension this statement should have produced, he pointed east. "That way. Home."

"We're ... in Magyarzag?"

"Yes."

"When did that happen?"

"About two hours ago."

"I ... expected ..." A gesture at the empty road beneath an empty noonday sky.

He shrugged. "You will be wanted in Budapesht." And then a thought, a little sadder; a settled conclusion which had been

169

gnawing at him for a while and which could no longer be denied. "There will be war soon."

I tried to think of something to say. Nothing came to mind. This seemed to satisfy him more than any words. He nodded once, and turned to the east, and twenty minutes later we reached a crossroads where a single electric bus sat waiting, driver on the roof trying to dust off some of the snow from the solar panels to catch the meagre winter light. Seeing us, he hopped down, exclaimed, "No one shot? So glad!" and opening the door to the vehicle added, "Only got enough charge to get us to Vakch, then need to plug in. So no heating, I'm afraid!"

"That is acceptable," the captain replied, before his soldiers could groan too dramatically. "Kindly choose a radio station of popular music," he added, the words unfamiliar and uncomfortable on his lips, to which the troops gave a much more impressive cheer.

Chapter 28

It is a strange thing to come back from the dead.

I had clearly been dead; dead in the forest, dead in the shrine to the great kakuy.

I had in fact been dead almost from the moment the Brotherhood raided the temples and found nothing there, counting the hours away until my life was over, until Pontus found me and I was shot or stabbed or beaten to death in the cellar beneath Georg's house.

Now I sat huddled in the back of the bus as it slowly drifted round the switchback roads to the river below, and even the radio talked of war between the music, and I was, in fact, not dead. With every sign to Budapesht, with every guardia post we passed where no one was in a hurry to shoot me, I came a little bit nearer to living. Had I ever lived before? I had studied in the temple, run through the remnants of the burning forest, reached for Vae's hand in the river, seen the kakuy, waded through the flood of the Ube, and yet it seemed to me that I had not at any part of this process been alive. This heady drug of living again, this strange cocktail of delirium was, I knew rationally, merely a high from having come so close to dying, rather than any philosophical revelation. And yet now, close my eyes, and here, this blood is hot, and here, this heart is mighty in me, and here, I am alive.

I am alive again.

In Vakch, the bus stopped to recharge at the garage on the edge of town. A station, a little branch line into the city, was twenty minutes' walk away. The soldiers asked if I wanted an escort, and I shook my head. One started to wave goodbye, and then, realising that no one else did, immediately stopped and looked away, rugged in his detachment.

Alive, I walked through the afternoon sun.

Alive, I walked through the smell of baked goods on hot plates, caught a whiff of fermentation, heard the scream of children fighting as only children can, as if the end of the world had come to their little corner through mysterious ritual and imagined disaster. I passed the open doors of a hearth, smelt fresh resin between newly laid bricks, heard the clicking of the compression battery, looked up into a sky through which the sun briefly broke in tuning forks of illumination before vanishing again behind purple clouds fading to crimson in the west. I passed the telegram office and thought of sending something to my own hearth in Tinics, a world away. Some few words of happiness, of wishing well, and realised there was nothing I could compress into a few hundred characters, no meaning that mattered, and that I needed to go home, and live again.

Opposite the station, a shrine to the kakuy of the winding river and soft marshes that fed this town. Cut reeds stood fresh in a vase by the door. The copper gong that hung beside the gate was warped with use and reuse, melted down and reforged a dozen times, each time growing a little more precious as history was burned away. A novice, barely more than a year out of college, stood before the shrine of the kakuy and called out the evening prayer. Gave thanks for the fire that warmed us through the winter. Gave thanks for the water on our lips. Gave thanks for the wind that carried the day away. Gave thanks that this earth, mightier than we, carried us still through starlight.

I stood in the door of the shrine and could not go in. My hand rested against the timber, but somewhere there was the Brotherhood at my back, watching, watching, and if I went in they would know I was a spy; they would know and I would die, even though I was free and this was madness. I willed my foot over the threshold and could not make it obey, so I turned away and went to the station instead, to find my way to Budapesht.

172

Chapter 29

Budapesht, seat of the Council, capital of Magyarzag, city of domes.

It had once been two cities either side of the great river. Then the two cities had become one. Then the kakuy came, and the city was two again, the bridges swallowed, the world cracked apart. The first archaeologists who surveyed the ruins were confused by what they found – crumbled concrete and iron bar, slab stone and shattered brick. The groundplans they prised from the earth with their bristled brushes were functional, brutal, square. Were sprawling, luxuriant palaces. Were picked out in tile and terracotta. Were elegant, imposing without being grand, as if the city had not known which world it existed in and so lived within them all.

The first settlements of the new age had begun around the river, to catch the boats drifting down the Ube. In that we followed our ancestors, all things in a circle, renewing again. They were built from the reclaimed materials of the past, a bewildering jigsaw, each brick marked with the scratches of a different history from a different home. Then, as the city grew, modern materials were introduced: bricks of hemp and mycelium, floors of pressed clay and walls of compacted straw. Uncertain how to honour a city of so many histories, Budapesht became an architect's paradise, the focal point of every new experiment and curious idea. Towers unfolded like the leaf of the fern. Rooftops of chitin grew on geodesic domes crowning the hearths, their crops of legume and spice shrouded behind the milky material. Canopies woven by silk spiders shaded the narrow marketways, and solar pylons turned to catch the light on engineered sunflower stems.

Council had been in residence in this city for three of its allotted ten years; after a decade here, its apparatus would be uprooted for the migration down to the Delta – a moving capital that favoured no Province above any other. Its presence filled the train station with new styles from further afield, be it the itching robes of the southern Medj or the straight-cut, high-booted garb of some Lyvodian magnate straight from an embassy with the roving Rus.

As with all cities, there were many shrines and temples, but the largest sat within the walls of a building that had once been sanctified to a monotheist God of old. The great dome that crowned it had collapsed many centuries ago, but had been replaced over time with a solar crown dyed with streaks of liquid blue and crimson through which the winter sun spilt like oil. The scarlet marble columns had cracked and been repaired with biopolymer grown from the seaweed vats, adding new veins of translucent black to their white capillaries. Where the monochrome patterns of the floor could be recovered, they had been, new tiles of clay laid in the gaps, guiding visitors to the place where once an altar had been.

Pictures showed how the faded walls would once have been blazoned with gold and blue, and in one alcove set in a shadowed corner, under soft lights, the recovered fresco of a martyred saint was still visible, one hand raised as though begging the god of the sky to rescue him, the other turned towards his bare belly as if he could not contain the despair within.

The monotheists still came to pray before this icon, filling the vaults with song every second seven-day. An overzealous Medj had talked about removing it altogether, sanctifying the space entirely to the kakuy, but local residents had been outraged, and after a certain amount of back-pedalling and "you misunderstood *entirely*", the martyr was left where he was, and the altar to the kakuy remained where it always had been – in the wide,

174

bee-buzzing gardens behind the faded walls, beneath a rainbow of slung spider silk and slatted timber walls. In summer, the shrine burst with crimson tulips, pink peonies, the dry petals of the blue poppy and beds of tiny daisies. In winter, low fire pits shimmered in carved hollows between the paths, and the wax from the hives was pressed into the hundred candles that burned day and night until spring came again.

A novice offered me a hot stone drawn from one of these pits as I approached, to tuck beneath my robes. I realised that I still wore the faded blue and grey of the order, as he bowed low before me. I returned the bow automatically, felt a pang of inquisitor's horror at the mistake, saw no frown of condemnation, heard no sirens at my back. His deference was not a trick. Georg was not waiting in the crowd.

Evening prayers were done, but couples sat on the benches, holding hands and talking softly of quiet truths, while occasional lone figures marched through the gates to the altar itself, and bowed and gave thanks, and contemplated human things before the image of the earth, and bowed again, and walked away. How strange it all seemed now, this abasement before a shrine that cared nothing for prayers. How odd to pray to a world that saw in us no more and no less than the scuttling of the busy ant.

Away from the pious and the casual, the usual tucked-back buildings of Temple business. A kitchen, private rooms for study and contemplation, a laundry, business-like vegetable boxes and a high, steaming compost pile. A locked door heading perhaps to some minor, classified archive. The lights of the Medj's quarters, bright and warm through translucent sliding doors.

I passed through the gate from public yard into inner sanctum and asked the slumbering priest there for an officer of the inquisition, and waited patiently until they came, and said my name was Ven, and my case handler had been Nadira, and she was dead, and I had nowhere left to go but here.

Sitting in the guest quarters.

I have been given inquisitor's robes, loops of grey and faded red.

I have been given a bowl of potato soup, brought to me on a black lacquered tray.

I have been invited to sit with the Medj of the temple and neither talk nor pray but merely sit and be in this place. I fear doing such a thing, but it is rude to decline the invitation of the Medj, so I obey, and sit cross-legged by their side, and sometimes shake, and sometimes sit in silence, and sometimes feel light-headed, and sometimes feel as though I am the centre of the world, and sometimes feel as if every part of me were dust in the air, and at the end realise I have no idea how to be whoever it is I am, now that I am here.

Somewhere, in the heart of the place that is my home, the forest grows. When all else is swept away, I close my eyes and take great comfort in that.

The next morning, I went to the halls of the Council and met Yue again.

Chapter 30

Entering Council premises took nearly twenty minutes.

I watched, as one might observe precise points of a surgical procedure, as bags were searched, bodies patted down and scanned for electronics. Nothing in, nothing out, said the guardia on the door. Council security kept everything on hard-wired systems cut off from the world, and unless you had filled out your form 1189 and got it stamped by someone with an active B20 authorisation, you would be lucky to be let in with your lunch box.

"An inquisitor?" murmured the guardia, struggling to work out how to search the many folds of my awkward garb. "We don't see many of you – at least, not in the robes."

"My cover was blown," I replied, and it was the first time I'd said these words out loud. "I don't know if I'm an inquisitor any more."

He smiled politely and didn't know what to say, and neither did I, as I was waved through the gated airlock to the interior.

So here we are.

Yue sits, cross-legged, in her office of wood, stone and glass. The room was rebuilt into the side of a crumbled-down market hall, the scars of the old world a jagged slice down one wall, a timber frame bolted into its remains. Where ancient meets new, yellow resin defines the join like the border between two warring states. Unlike Georg, she has no restored wooden desk but sits stiffly on a low stool on the polished timber floor, hemmed in by cushion and blanket. She wears blue, trimmed with white, and her hair is pulled up high, in a formal style. There are two teapots – one large, one small – and matching cups the colour of a stormy sea. There are little rolls of bean and cabbage, still hot from the stove. There is a single sprig of rosemary in a thin-necked vase. These things are arranged on a tray between us, and for a while that is all there is between us as I settle, fold my legs, straighten my back, wait.

Yue tests the temperature of the larger teapot, finds it satisfactory, sprinkles dry leaves into the smaller pot by its side, pours water over them, waits for the liquid to brew, and we do not speak.

In one corner of the room there is a shrine. It is not sanctified, and the incense has long ago burned cold, but the arrangement of objects upon it speaks of a certain amount of contemplation, perhaps even prayer. Feathers from birds of prey, collected and tied together in a bundle. Glass beads polished and blasted by the sea. A vertebra from some unknown four-legged thing. A single page from an ancient document, half torn away, the other half framed and preserved against all time, the colours faded.

I cannot see any text, but the jagged half of the image that survived shows a woman's leg, impossibly smooth and pale, contoured to a soft dune of muscle, stepping down from a short yellow skirt to a pointed, raised pink shoe. It is easy to imagine the female face that had been ripped away above it: smiling, laughing, entirely content with her life, joyful in her body and all that she owned. Yue follows my gaze, half-turned in her chair, sees the paper, smiles, nods, turns back.

"From a fashion magazine," she explains. "I was trying to find one about lip fillers, but they're almost entirely gone these days, or already snatched up by eager collectors."

"Why?"

She thinks about it for a moment, head tilted to one side. "It is good to remember," she concludes. "Everything changes. Beauty, sex; right, wrong. Krima says it is important to pay attention to the fluidity of these things. Tea?"

I nod dumbly as she sweeps her sleeve back from her wrist, pours a dribble from the pot into a cup, swirls it three times in a little whirlpool, pours the rest, passes me the cup between both hands with a half-bow, waits for me to sip, pours her own.

We sit together, drinking tea, and it is the closest I have come to home for I do not know how many years. She watches me over the lip of her cup and I do not care. Her scrutiny is nothing next to Georg's; there is no death lurking behind her eyes, no black wolf of the mountain. Finally she lays her cup back down and, inclining the plate of nibbles towards me, says, as if it is the easiest thing in the world: "Krima will need to debrief you. If you want someone present from your order during this process, we can arrange it."

"I have . . . a lot of questions."

"Of course. I'm sorry I didn't answer them in the forest. You didn't look in a fit state for conversation, and it was not wise for me to linger."

"Why? Why were you in the forest?"

"That should be obvious. I was looking for you."

"Why?"

"It is my job."

I am the forest. I will grow and I will wither and my molecules return to the earth, and when they do they shall rise again into my neighbour tree and I will be the forest. Georg found such thoughts distasteful, a crude reduction of the wonder of human endeavour. I have always found them a comfort.

Yue's voice is calm and steady, a thing moulded from clay. "I assist Krima vaMiyani in matters of Council security. Legally speaking, the Council having its own intelligence service is a grey area – the Provinces are responsible for their security – but some threats transcend the need and expertise of any one Province. The Brotherhood is one of those threats. When the inquisition reported one of its agents was missing, that they did not have the resources to find him, it was considered worth the risk of a cross-border incursion to recover him. To recover you."

"Did you know it was me?"

"No. Not until I saw you in the shrine. The inquisition are ... jumpy."

She sips her tea, and the motion is so small I'm not even sure she's drinking.

"I'm ... not sure if I should be here," I blurt. "I don't know if—"

"Pontus." She says the word so simply, so matter-of-fact, that for a moment I struggle to recognise it's a word at all. She shifts a little in her seat, as if her legs are stiff, turns the teacup in her hand. "You are here because of Pontus."

"What do you know about them?"

"Not much. I am cleared to run operations of the kind you witnessed in the forest – recovery, counter-intelligence. I am not cleared to know about Pontus."

"How do you?"

"Krima. Do you know she had an arrest warrant drawn against Pav Krillovko? The inquisition came to her with actionable intelligence which implicated Pav as a double-agent. Except it couldn't be him. He was on retreat in the southern mountains. But someone is – someone with the highest clearance. Do you know how your cover was blown, Ven?"

"I know that every time I fed intelligence back to the inquisition, I made it more likely I would be discovered. A pattern builds up – a cascade of betrayal that could only have come from one source. How much does Council know about me? About Pontus?"

How much does Yue?

"I don't know," she replies, eyes fixed on some distant place. "I don't have access to that information."

"Then – if I may – why am I here? Talking to you?"

"Because we are also friends." She speaks as if remarking on the coolness of the wind; a truth that will still be true when bones are dust. "Your hearth shared bread with mine. We have ... there were things we saw. We are ... these things are also important, no?"

Are they? Aren't they? I have no idea. Kadri Tarrad has no idea.

Kadri Tarrad is formless in thought and deed. Kadri did not see the kakuy of the forest burn.

"There was a spy – in Vien." My voice sounds distant, dull, even to my ears. "A Council agent. One of Georg's tests was seeing if I would kill him."

"Did you?" Her voice sharp and sudden. I had never known the name of the man I left to die in that cellar, all those months ago. Yue does.

"No." She isn't sure she believes me, and I have never been so desperate for another human to see that I do not lie. "Pontus destroyed the Council's operation against the Brotherhood. Georg practically said as much. With Krima's agents out of action, only the inquisition remained in play. I imagine that makes me useful."

"It does," she replies, simple and stiff. "We are friends, you are an inquisitor, and you are also useful, Ven." She says my name as if it was my own. My name is Ven. How strange it is. "You are going to be debriefed by Krima and Witt. The inquisition has approved it. This is not your debriefing. I am not authorised to debrief you. This is simply tea. This is us drinking tea, as friends should."

I am the mountain. Is the mountain a living thing? Does the kakuy slumber in the stone? Is this world a breathing, conscious thing? Or is it madness, humanism run wild, to say that sentience can be only defined by humans, that a network of neurons surpasses in value an ecosystem that is fed from the blackest pit of the volcanic ocean to the highest bird in the sky. As if the mountain could ever be "merely" rock; as if the sky could ever be "merely" air; as if we were not all spinning creatures within the kakuy of the world, turning through the stars.

Then she says: "I met him, you know? Georg. When I was at university."

I have no idea what I'm meant to make of this, so shrug. "What was he like?"

"You wouldn't have expected him to end up where he is. He was going to go far, of course, but we all assumed ... tech, perhaps? Or maybe a teacher. A brilliant teacher. Not ... propping up someone as inept as Antti Col."

"He has no interest in Antti. Antti's just what he has to work with, for now. As soon as he can, he'll find a way to replace him with someone more useful."

"Like who?"

"I don't know. Tanacha, perhaps. Or Kun Mi. Someone happy to feel like they're in charge, without acting like they are." Her eyes are still studying some place I can't see. I have to resist the urge to turn and try to spot the distant land on which she has turned her gaze. "Yue ... I don't know you." Finally her gaze returns to me, almost surprised to discover that I sit before her, a grown man, rather than the child she had left by the kakuy tree. "We were children. We saw the kakuy and—"

"I did not see a kakuy," she interrupts, quick, calm. "I have never seen a kakuy."

"You were there. In the forest, it was—"

"I have never seen a kakuy," she repeats. "The kakuy have not stirred for a hundred years."

I try to wrap my mind round these words, to read anything in her face, and cannot. What would Lah do, what would Nadira say? Nadira would say the mission, Ven, the mission: what serves the mission? Nadira is dead, and I am not sure what the mission is.

My skin hurts across my chest, and I remember briefly that there is a cut inflicted by man, not by any spirits of stone and cinder, which tugs a little beneath my robes.

Then Yue says, a little kinder, and I wonder what she sees in my face to provoke her: "You are right. We do not know each other. We come from the same place, that is all. But I have read about Kadri Tarrad. In the days before we found you, I studied your file. So much of it redacted – so much Temple wouldn't say – but I felt ... familiarity. It mentioned Tinics, your age, but I didn't know any Kadri from home. It was ... I could have sent in a unit and stayed behind. I wanted to be there. I don't know you, Ven. But I know you risked your life for the inquisition. I know you got out alive. I would like to know you better, if you are willing."

She pours more tea, offers me the refilled cup. I take it. The heat feels real, and I could do with a certain solidity in my universe.

"Hello, Ven," she says, raising her cup in salute. "It is very nice to see you again."

"Hello, Yue," I reply, and drain the cup down.

Chapter 31

I was, as promised, debriefed by Krima vaMiyani and Antoni Witt.

Witt is a rarity, an escapee from the Anglaes islands who fled before the purity laws could spill his blood in offerings to the wild sea and dark forest. His eyes are green-grey, skin pale enough that he could have almost passed as pure Anglaes. They say his hair was white by the time he was seventeen, that he speaks seven languages and paddled down the Rhene River to the northern border of Maze in a canoe he carved himself. He neither confirms nor denies any of these statements. He learned a long time ago to keep his mouth shut.

He was also one of the suspects to whom Temple gave their doctored files. So was Krima.

The debriefing lasts four days. Yue picks me up at the end of every day, escorts me through Council security, nothing in, nothing out, has secured a guesthouse for me to stay in rather than Temple grounds.

"Ven will stay at Temple," replies my handler from the inquisition. "He is still one of us."

Only later do I realise what my handler must already have known: that the guesthouse would be bugged, every twitch of my toes or snort in my sleep monitored. I do not begrudge Yue doing her duty, and she does not fight my handler on the point.

In my cold little room in the temple, I wonder if the inquisition has also bugged me, and have to resist the temptation to search under the lamp by my roll-out mattress, to run my hands over the walls, shake out every corner of my clothes.

Krima says: "Maze is poised to invade Magyarzag, but they want Council to start the conflict. If Jia fires the first shot, then Ull and Han will have an excuse to stay neutral, brush it off as some philosophical dispute and keep their Provinces out of it. Maze is pushing her to make that mistake – provocations along the border, heresies within their lands. Thus far, she's managed to hold back."

Witt says: "We don't have an answer to armour-piercing rounds. We barely have armour. Some of the newer resins are promising, but if Georg knows how to enrich the tips then . . . "

Krima says: "If he is mining here, why haven't the kakuy woken? Why aren't they raining fire?"

Witt says: "We can't trust in kakuy to do man's business, can't trust in some . . . spirit . . . "

Krima says: "Jia is organising peace talks. A final attempt to stop a war. All the Provinces will send representatives. You helped, Ven. The information you supplied is vital – it will force Georg to reconsider his strategy. It buys us time. Council is very appreciative."

She does not mention her attempt to recruit me, and neither do I.

How many years was I in Vien?

How many weeks did those years buy?

I try to ask, but this is not that place. Their questions matter more than mine. They see things I do not. But they do not see Pontus.

Krima says: "Again. One more time."

Again.

One more time.

And I tell them all of it again.

A week after I arrived in Budapesht, Temple summoned me to Bukarest. I had no bags to pack, sat watching the winter world

185

outside the window rolling by with nothing in my hands and a borrowed hat on my head. No one came to the station to wave me off save a pair of Council watchers too new at their job to be unobserved; but Yue left a message at the shrine, which I only received several days later by forwarded telegram.

STAY SAFE, she said. *TRAVEL WELL.*

Chapter 32

Bukarest, the Temple of the Lake.

I had been a novice here, all those years ago.

Then Lah had asked: "But why did you join the temple?"

And I'd replied: "I think it's important not to take things for granted."

And somehow, in their mind, that had been enough.

Lah met me at the station with a bicycle scrounged from a novice who preferred to walk. Hugged me. I hadn't been held in that way for ...

... I wasn't sure how long.

Then let go and said: "Well isn't it all a fucking disaster?"

And laughed, and so did I. We stood in the middle of the station, two priests in fading robes, and laughed like we'd just heard a very dirty joke.

For my first few weeks back in Bukarest, I went to the server port twice a day to download the latest news to my inkstone. Then Lah pointed out that knowing, devouring every bulletin and rumour sent down the line from Budapesht or Vien, facilitated neither my equanimity nor the calm of others.

Then I put my inkstone away, finally sat in silence before the cracking ice on the surface of the lake, and permitted myself to be simply small in this place. Somewhere behind me there was a version of myself that had perhaps wanted to be a hero, who had walked mighty on the earth and unravelled the secrets of heretics.

Today, there was only the new sun rising, the sky and the earth, the black pine trees and the gods of the stones.

We too are the kakuy, Lah proclaimed. The spirits of earth and sky, sun and moon give life, and we are of the world, flesh made animate, blood made fire by our living. We are the kakuy of humans, a piece of the great turning of the world, tiny upon its surface, and no less than the mountain.

"Why do we give thanks to the kakuy?" the Medj asked, and the congregation sang its ritual response – we give thanks for the sun that warms us, the moon that guides us, the sea that carries us, the sky that gives us breath. These were the words Nadira had sung, the first night I met her.

I tried to sing the ritual words and could not. The kakuy have no interest in the prayers of men; why heed the imprecations of an ant?

We give thanks because we are the mountain. We give thanks because we are the forest. We give thanks because to honour the kakuy is to honour ourselves; we forgive ourselves, we love ourselves, thank our bodies and our sight, our coming in and our going out. We know at last what we are – life shining in a pearl of blue spinning through space, separate and together. Thank you, sky and earth; thank you, sister and brother of sea and fire. We are one.

Even cut off from the world, I heard rumours of the peace conference unfolding on the isle of Kirrk, a last desperate attempt to put off war. I wondered if Georg was dead and what had happened to Nadira's body. I wondered if Witt was looking now at all the intelligence I'd stolen from Georg's desk and tutting and whispering: *we* must fight fire with fire. Perhaps all I'd done was turn a short war into a long one.

In the end, we offered a body of straw and winter flowers to the sky, not having Nadira's corpse. In the mornings, I swept snow from the path so the elders might not slip as they shuffled to prayers. At lunch, I worked in the steam of the kitchen, chopping carrots and stirring vats on the stove. In the afternoon, I folded over the dark matter of the smouldering compost heaps, read the writings of scholars both ancient and new, sat beside the lake and watched the crystals on the cracked edge of the ice shrivel and grow with the changing movement of the sun, and gave thanks that I lived, and healed, and tried not to smell the Ube in flood, or the forest aflame, or the blood as it rolled through my fingers.

Lah said: "It is good to grieve," and it hadn't occurred to me that I was grieving, and I didn't think they were right. I tried to find a way to express what I actually felt, and couldn't. To feel was vulnerability, a habit lost while serving the inquisition. Only the job remained.

"I can send you out to do something more involved, more engaged. But then you will simply be doing in order not to feel, rather than being here, and feeling. What would you like to do?"

I thought about it for a while, knew the answer they wanted, and said: "Please put me to work."

They smiled, perhaps hiding a little disappointment in my reply, and I was sent to the local Assembly to offer advice on archival matters, translate archaic texts, and advocate on subjects heretical and pious. The work was hard, long, frequently tedious, and I was grateful for it. I turned off the radio when it talked about the coming war, and resolved not to think about Yue, and refused to think about Pontus, and thought about them all the time. I peered at the scar across my chest in the dusty mirror of the washroom, then bathed in a tub so hot and deep that to fall asleep in it was to drown. I looked at the timbers that framed the room, wondered what thanks had been offered to the kakuy from whose trunks such things were taken, and if the spirits of the things lived on even here, and concluded that they probably did, altered by man's intervention but still honoured in their way. Then I thanked the forest and the water and, for the first time in a very long while, thought I understood what "thank you" meant.

Drinking tea, Lah slides the door to the balcony outside their room back a little so that the cold of the air outside might mingle with the warmth of the cups in our hands; the contrast, they said, pleasing, invigorating, a sacred thing, if only you're willing to feel a little blessed.

They have planted winter bulbs in the garden, and talk idly about squashes and the taste of hot rice on a frozen morning, and how much they love the taste of apricots, until finally, seeing that I'm not really listening, they fall silent.

For a while we sit there, quiet together.

Then they say: "You may as well ask. It'll eat you up if you don't."

"Who do you think Pontus is?" They sighed, bowed a little, adjusted some hidden limb within the great grey sweep of their robes, didn't answer. I tutted. "Come on. The inquisition won't just be praying it's all okay – you have a theory. Who do you think Pontus is?"

"It's very hard to say."

"But?"

"There are some leading suspects. Pav Krillovko has some problematic relationships – bad influences, you might say. And for all that he was not in Budapesht when our trapped document leaked, it still came from his system – his inkstone. I don't know how he could have done it, but he is hardly exonerated in the inquisition's eye. Witt has always been a heretic at heart. He wants us to open up the archives in Martyza Eztok and tell him all about military vehicles and tactical nuclear devices, and so on. If he could have jet fuel, he would. He calls solar planes 'those little sky-farts'. In past border skirmishes with the Rus, he proved fantastically good at guerrilla tactics; even if he's ideologically suspect, Jia won't want to lose that skill. If Krima vaMiyani has betrayed her own department, there's very little we can do, realistically – just hope that Yue Taaq or someone in a similar position spots it before it's too late."

"Is Yue a suspect?"

"She doesn't have access to the kind of intelligence Pontus is feeding Georg. That doesn't mean she isn't compromised in some other way, of course – one must be careful about these things – but she isn't senior enough to pose a threat. Then there's the Ministers themselves. The read-list for the intelligence you provided was small, but Council is meant to keep the peace between the Provinces, not secrets. Jia would be forced to share intelligence with Provincial Ministers – Shamim perhaps, Han or Ull. Maybe even Farii. As you have demonstrated, you don't have to share much to risk even the most diligent Minister falling prey to a clever secretary. Information spreads like oil through water, clinging to even the cleanest of us."

"Lah – is Georg Mestri dead?"

They blinked in surprise. "Sky and sea, no. Why would you think that?"

I felt heat blaze through my face. "I stabbed him."

"In the leg, Ven! In the *leg*."

"I really meant it."

"He's not dead. He's on Kirrk at the peace talks, muttering into Antti's ear as usual. Did you really think you killed him?"

"It was a possibility."

"Sun and moon! What a twist that would have been! But no, Ven. Excellent scholar of archaic heresies you may be – a solid inquisitor, all things considered – but you are not, in fact, an assassin. More tea?"

"I think perhaps something stronger."

They shook their head and puckered their lips, but they fetched something a little stronger from their stash behind the kitchen cabinet.

The next day, the Colonel came.

Chapter 33

Her name was Merthe. She was far too senior for the task given her, but she was, as she put it, "heading in the right direction". She was nearly two inches taller than me, all hips and boots and curly brown hair. She waited for me in Lah's office, wrapped in a grey winter coat, and shot bolt upright as I entered, handing me the letter like a lawyer delivering a summons.

"Is this . . ."

"Please read it now."

I stood awkwardly in the door, opened the letter, read it, read it again, folded it, put it in my pocket.

"Are you ready to come?" she asked. "There is a train in three hours; I have booked a berth."

I nodded. I couldn't think of anything else to do.

It took nearly two days to get from Bukarest to Kirrk. The sleeper train was quiet; empty beds and empty stations. The carriage guard beamed at me and my travelling companion as we settled into our bunks, thick duvets and prickly blankets. "Breakfast is at 6.30 a.m.," he chimed. "And I recommend the oats."

In the dark of the rattling train, a few lights glimmered over the regimented beds as the travellers rocked sleepless in the gloom. Sometimes I slept, and jerking awake thought maybe hours had passed, and we had missed our stop, even though it was at the end of the line. Then I lay awake, and didn't sleep, and must have slept again, and pulled my knees up to my chest and found that made me a little too wide for my berth, and then stretched out all the way and found then I was a little too long, toes tickling out into the corridor.

When the guard opened the blinds for morning breakfast, I expected a dazzling explosion of light, driving back the thick darkness of an uncertain night. Instead, thin pre-dawn glow ran in grey diagonals through the rattling interior, catching on pole and mattress, sluggish stirring shadow of bleary-eyed waking traveller.

In Budapesht there was nearly an hour and a half before the train to Bljaina. I wandered round the perimeter of the station, saw soldiers' trucks and guardia checking papers, families queuing for tickets, thick crowds of the determined, the listless, the confused and those whose earnestness was one trodden toe away from desperate. Merthe walked with me, as if anxious I might be mugged, and finally said: "Everyone thinks that Maze will attack Budapesht first. It's so close to the border, it's an easy target. We are not prepared for urban warfare. There is talk of mining the river."

A memory, loosely dredged from the mind of whoever I was before I fled through the winter wood. "Nasty things, mines. Never kill who you think they will."

She nodded briskly, without comment, as we turned back towards the train.

Valleys and hills; train clinging to the running edge of the thawing river. A waterfall bursting rich from ice above; a den for wolves below. Sometimes terraced fields, growing biomatter for the vats or turned-over soil ready for a spring planting. Forest framing winding roads, wiggling tracks. Tunnels that hit like a punch to the gut. We threaded the mountains like a needle, and I wondered what the mountain heard as we passed through it and out the other side. Some routes were ancient, paths unearthed from the blasting of the Burning Age. Others were newer tracks laid through the kingdoms of the kakuy. Glance out of the window, and for a brief moment a line of wind-worn stones, dressed in fading

193

woven crimson hats, lined the railway path – guardians raised to shield the spirits of the living from the spirits of the dead. Then a town, temple above and post office below, a single telephone line stretching through the trees, a single road leading out. We waited at the station for the up train from Bljaina to arrive, wheezing into the opposite platform so we could pass each other without incident on the one-track line towards the sea.

Merthe said: "I'm with the Lyvodian army, 2nd Infantry. I answer to Ull and the Provincial Assembly, not Jia, but you're technically a Lyvodian citizen, and as I was going the right way—"

"Technically a Lyvodian?"

"I don't know if priests are supposed to swear to some higher . . . state? Power? What do you swear to?"

"I'm not a proper priest."

"Then why do you live in the temple?"

"I suppose no one can think of anywhere better for me to go."

"Don't you have a home?"

"I did. It's been . . . a long time."

"All the more reason to go back, isn't it?"

"You make it sound simple."

"Isn't it?"

Merthe liked things simple. Complex, she had decided, was for idiots who talked too much.

In Bljaina, no more trains. The city sat in a premature winter dusk of bruised purple and salt-smeared clouds. The snow was nearly gone here, black patches of mud worming through the trodden white like new continents rising from the deep. People glanced at Merthe and smiled wanly; she smiled back and mused: "No one wants the Brotherhood's heresy here."

She sounded like she believed it, the passion of the just. I wondered what it felt like to believe, thought I had a vague memory of it, but it broke like cobweb when I fumbled for it.

Yue had sent an electric car, charging up outside the station. I got in uneasily, folding myself into the tight back seats between

Merthe and a man in glasses who did not introduce himself, did not make eye contact, would not say the purpose of his mission or what he carried in the bag that he clung onto with the passion of a father for a weeping child. We stopped once, to recharge in a sarai as the night settled. I got out, stretched my legs, smelt something strange on the air – rotten eggs and sawdust – stood on the edge of the sarai, sniffing the darkness, puzzling, until Merthe appeared at my side.

"We're above an old landfill site," she explained. "The miners picked out what they could, but there are layers that are too dangerous to disturb. Nothing lives or grows around here – but the road passes by because it's the quickest route, and it's not like there are any kakuy we can disturb in this place."

I nodded, staring into the flat dark beyond and finding it suddenly far darker, far blacker than the forest. "Have you ever been to a place called Martyza Eztok?"

"No. Why?"

"There are old tunnels beneath it – mining tunnels – from the burning. When the kakuy woke, the ancient archivists hid their books and their hard drives in the caves, the most valuable information they could find. They intended it as a gift to help the future. Combustion engines. Fractional distillation of crude oil. Deep shaft mining. They wanted to help us. They wanted to make a better world."

She thought about it, then shrugged. "Who doesn't? But as my old Medj would say: there's wanting something, and then there's being a dickhead about it."

"Your Medj sounds like a character."

"They worked in sewage treatment before getting spiritual. Really good priest, terrible gossip; you know how it is."

Then there was the smell of the sea, brown reeds of scrubby grass, rolling, broiling clouds and salt-washed stones. The old bridge between the mainland and Kirrk had crumbled centuries ago. Only a few iron stands remained, testimony to our ancestors' mastery of water and metal. The gullies through the white cliffs where the roads had run still cracked the land in an unnatural geometry. The sound of the seabirds squabbling on the cold breeze was like the conversation of old aunts at the hearth, amicably arguing over how to season their supper. We took a boat out to the island, a single triangular sail the colour of sunset sand, oars and a tiny motor that ran on stinking seaweed oil. Warning lights flashed to the right to keep people away from the tidal tubes hidden beneath the waves, which supplied power to the towns around. The lights to the left were subtler, gentle yellow, marking the beginning of the kelp farms that spread all the way along the coast, feeding their slippery harvest to the biovats, resin wells and livestock troughs across Magyarzag.

As we neared the island, I could see the starscape of a town, built on the bones of that which had gone before, pressed into the place between curving bay and rising cliff. A creature rose over the harbour mouth, made of woven ancient fishing net, plastic flakes and polished driftwood, rusted container and the bent spines of the crab pot. Jaws gaping, a tongue of rotting fibres hanging down its lips – a monstrous monument to the kakuy of the sea, a raging creature of unkind storms and recovered bones. We drifted past it, into the shelter of a spit of sand which stilled the rocking water and brought with it the smell of fish, salt, yeast and grain, as well as the sound of music and human voices, as if the barrier between rough ocean and gentle sea were a solid wall dividing the universe. Figures moved on the beach, torchlight scraping the pale sand. Our pilot waved to them; a man waved back, and as we pushed up onto land someone called out in a manner so much like the chattering of the birds that for a moment I wasn't sure if it was a human or a creature of the sky that spoke. Then the pilot answered in a language of the island, and Merthe said: "Ready, not-a-priest?" She held out one hand to help me scramble off the boat, steading me as my feet adjusted to the soft shifting sand of the beach, cold salt rising as I sank a little in the spongy line between sea and earth.

I looked east and saw the first glimmer of dawn light, thought I might be sick. I had not felt sick at sea. "Is Yue here?" I asked.

"Taaq will see you as soon as you're settled, I'm sure." I thought I saw a little pity in her face, and wondered if she understood just what the letter in my pocket meant. I followed her up the beach, towards a scrubby shore and the lights of the town, guided by torchlight which increasingly grew dim against the rapid rising of the eastern sun, its light curving off a mirror sea.

"We can get you something to wear; would you rather inquisition robes or do you—"

Merthe's words cut short as, from round the corner of the nearest whitewashed, squat house, a group of men approached, black against the town's light. I could not clearly see their faces, but I saw something familiar in their motion, in the set of shoulders and the swagger of limbs. Merthe adjusted her weight, pushing her chin forward and growing larger in the space she occupied, until our two groups met like the foaming place where river flows to the sea.

"Good morning," she proclaimed, flat as skimming stone, before anyone of the group of men before her could speak. "Can we help you?"

"Thought we would see the dawn. Say thank you to it, and all that."

A voice, smiling in the dark. A man stepped to the front of the crowd. Or rather, one leg stepped, and the other followed, supported by a long cane topped with a heavy handle around which his fingers curled as if he would claw the world itself in his fist. The handle was black wood, carved into the head of the wolf – or rather, not the wolf but the kakuy that had worn the wolf's form when he lay upon the snowy mountain, all tooth and blood.

The man did not step again, but held his ground, as if to move more than one limb at a time before the eyes of strangers might expose his limp, the dragging weight of his body tilted to one side; as if by remaining stationary, I would not see it, nor know him.

"New arrivals?" he asked, and one of Merthe's escort had turned her torch towards the man's chest, politely avoiding shining in his eyes, so that only through the reflected glow of

197

illumination could I see the contours of his features, greyed out shadow driven away from the hook of his brow.

"Tired arrivals," Merthe replied. "I'll wish you good morning, kin of sky and earth."

"Colonel." A little nod of his head, not a bow, nor an acknowledgement of enmity. Merthe steered me past him with one hand in the small of my back.

I met Georg's eyes as we passed and felt his gaze on my neck all the way into the rising glare of dawn.

Chapter 34

In the first light of day, I see a figure praying, head bowed to the rising sun.

He seems a mirage, a strange anomaly bowing first to the east, then to the west, as if thanking the fading dark for the quiet that night had brought. Then we get a little closer, and I see it is Pav Krillovko, remember Georg asking him — do you brush your teeth in charcoal?

If he sees me, he does not know me. In a way, that makes me proud.

A room in what might have once been a fisherman's shack.

A bed, a blanket.

I barely sleep, and in my dreams Georg is there, leaning on his walking stick, watching me, inside my mind, back inside my mind, he never left it after all, he will never be washed away.

I wake a little before lunch to tea, beans and fish.

Eat alone.

Wash in cold water. The bathhouse is carved into an overhang of stone above the sea, both salt and fresh water, tiny green crabs scuttling away below.

The robes of the inquisition feel grotesque upon me; an invitation to strike me down, a target on my back. I yearn for a disguise, some sailor's garb with which I can smuggle myself off the island.

Merthe, who perhaps has not slept, meets me at my bedroom door. Says: "Sleep well, sea-kin?"

I have never been kin of sea before; never sailed across the ocean. I wonder if the pirates between here and the west are really as bad as all that. I wonder if the Anglaes still shoot refugees on sight.

"Yes, thank you," I lie.

She nods, and does not believe a word of it, and takes me to see Yue.

Krima and Yue have a shared office tent of inflated spider silk and woven straw mats. Tables have been unfolded, cables run in from the portable solar panels on the hill above, supplementing the isle's tidal supply. Krima stands surrounded by a small cluster of empty chairs, as if her deputies have been smuggling every different kind of stool to see if one might stick, in an attempt to alleviate her pacing.

"Oh. It's you," she proclaims, as I am ushered through the thin, soft flap into the translucent interior. "Another fucking game."

Yue has availed herself of a seat, but she rises as I enter, stands bolt upright, takes me by the elbow, says: "I'll handle it," which earns nothing but a snort from Krima.

Leads me outside into the salt-spinning wind.

Blurts: "It was not my intention. I did not ... but they will not talk until ... it's Georg. He has influence, he has ... he's planning something. I did not want to. But he insisted. He said that the peace negotiations will only continue if you are here. I know it's nonsense – a power play, nothing more. But Jia says it's too important for us to ... I'm glad you're here. Thank you for answering my message."

I replied: "I came of my own free will."

"Why?"

Hesitation, bewilderment. "Because you asked."

She flinched. It seems absurd that a woman in her position should fail to understand her power, let alone regret it. "You'll be accompanied at all times. Krima is too angry to talk about it, but she does understand the ... the risk we are exposing you to. She does. She can seem difficult sometimes, but she's not what she ... the second you want to leave, you can."

"Thank you."

For a moment, an old, thin woman tries to push through Yue's skin, pressing out from every part of her like fungus from the fallen tree. Nothing will help now, she screams. You're all fools to think it. Then Yue – the one I know – smiles, and nods, but even she can't quite manage to be reassuring.

In the low afternoon of fading winter, I walked along the edge of a low white cliff as the wind thumped in off the sea. Turn your face to it, and the sheer force of air filling your lungs is a gasp, a moment of contraction as your body struggles to exhale. The smell of salt clings to skin and hair, but not five metres away there is a little gully where white flowers grow and rabbits bound away, and it is another season, another world.

On the east side of the island, the smell of ocean, the great kakuy of the seas answerable to no man, the many-tentacled kraken risen again with a mouth of serrated teeth laid out in rows – fed, they said, on the thousands who died fleeing the water wars, fatted on plastic and microparticles, grown black on spilt oil and scarlet on rust. On the west, the smell of humanity; animal dung spread out across the turned soil, a few pellet fires burning in ancient stoves, gutted fish, fresh kelp, algae vats churning out polymers and proteins; the building blocks of this island's little industry. There are kakuy even in the slim waters between the island and the mainland – the snow-white dolphin that rises up from the passing pod with eyes of sapphire; the great blood-red crab that all have seen and none can catch, which scuttles sideways across black stone and fears neither bird nor man.

It is a good place to talk peace, this island. The heretics point at the fallen bridge and remind the pious of the great things that man can do with steel and piston. The pious close their eyes, as the sun rises over a reflective sea, and remind the heretics that salt water will triumph over even the most ingenious of engineering, in the end. It is just a question of perspective.

Inland a little from the sea, a hearth, set apart from the others. It has whitewashed walls and a gate around which generations of small hands have pressed seashells and stones of spotted scarlet and deepest black, pebbles of polished plastic and glass harvested from the ocean, forming a mosaic frame of the island's history through which visitors must pass. It has three grey olive trees within the main courtyard. There is a bicycle stand, empty, and a shrine to the kakuy of the nearby beach, where incense does not burn. The hearth has two floors, solar panels on the roof turned away from the prevailing wind, a bathhouse from which drifts the sound of splashing water and the sharp smell of mint. Everywhere there are Brotherhood men, and many are armed. They carry eight-shot pistols on their hips, and a few carry hunter's rifles, five shots a clip. Jia's hearth will doubtless have the same weapons, and the Medj will be there now, arguing as to the ethics of declaring canon plans for faster, deadlier weapons, thirty rounds to a magazine, automatic and semi-automatic firing, the kind of gun you just wave in the general direction of the enemy and damned be the consequences.

The Brotherhood always had a fondness for uniforms, for a sense of belonging to a tribe, but now they are really getting into their military garb, grey-brown camouflage and hats worn on a funny angle, creating a shared pride in their clothes, their swagger, their guns, their glares. These men will not be happy until there has been a war; Antti has spent too much time making them believe that war will make them men, will make their lives matter. The inquisition made me think much the same thing about being a spy. They stare at me, and some know who I am and spit at my feet, and others just stare and hope I can see my own death played in crimson across their corneas, a grotesque, slow-motion film in which they are the stars, driving bayonets between my ribs, holding me down with metal while I thrash around like a butterfly on a pin.

A door is opened. The kitchen is hot, smells of cardamom and pepper. A flight of stairs spins tightly upwards, past more armed men, to a sliding door of heavy, old wood, knots black and popping.

"Wait here," says a man who has trained all his life to be a fighter and now will prove it the only way he can.

202

We wait.

Ten minutes.

Fifteen.

Twenty.

Yue paces up and down, snaps: "Where is he?" Does not get a reply.

Twenty-five.

"We're going," she barks. "Ven!"

The man who has been guarding the passage nods at this, as if he has finally heard the correct password; turning to the door, he knocks three times then heaves it back. Yue stands, quivering with indignity and rage. I put a hand on her arm, the nausea I had felt since stepping into this place briefly fading in the face of her fury. "It's fine," I murmured. "It's just a game."

For the briefest moment, I thought Yue might cry, and was astonished. Then she straightened up, stuck her chin forward, and marched into the room like a conquering queen.

Georg sits, alone. He must have been sat here the whole time we were outside, waiting. The hearth has fat, stiff cushions. He perches on a low stool instead, hands on his thighs, eyes half-closed as if in prayer, the leg I stuck a knife in extended long. On one wall of the room hangs a painting, not particularly good, of the great kakuy of the ocean rising from the ancient garbage patch, caught in a shaft of slightly ominous orange light breaking through black storm clouds. On the floor are faded rugs of woven wool, and the shutters are closed, thin afternoon light slipping through the gaps in the old wood to create prison bars of amber across his feet.

Georg's stick, carved with the wolf kakuy of the mountain, leans against his chair. One cushion has been set on the floor, a tray of tea between us, untouched, the cups waiting to be turned. Georg opens his eyes fully as we step inside, barely looks at me, gives Yue a fluttering glance.

"Taaq – you can wait outside."

"I will stay."

"I think you will go. Why don't we ask Kadri?" His head

half-turned as if the weight of his eyes moving to me were a physical force, a powerful blow. I felt the hot flush of a child caught between two squabbling parents, no hope of being right.

"Yue," I muttered, "I'm fine."

She stiffened, glowered at Georg, spoke to me. "I'll be outside. You can leave whenever you want."

"I know. Thank you."

She let herself out, heaving on the door as it creaked closed again, sealing us into gloom.

Georg waited for it to thunk shut, then smiled, gestured at the tea. "Do you mind?"

I turned over the cups, poured for us both, passed him a vessel, one hand circling the top like a hook, the other supporting the base with two fingers, a half-bow of shared drink offered. He took it in the same manner, rolled it around the palm of his right hand, sipped. I picked up my own, smelt the familiar fragrance of his favourite brew, barely wetted my lips with it, put the cup back down, waited. I was used to waiting for Georg.

He drank again, smiled, seemed to enjoy the taste, finished his cup, laid it down, poured himself another, did not drink.

For a little while we sat there, he and I, like an old couple that meets twenty years after the embarrassing breakup, a little wiser, a little more circumspect. The idea made me want to laugh, and laughter seemed better than the sickening fear I'd felt since setting foot in this place, since Merthe had come to Bukarest. Perhaps I smiled, and he saw it and asked: "Amused?"

"I suppose I must be."

"Good. Humour is a blessing. I never thought you had much."

"There was never very much to laugh at, working for you."

"True. I should have rectified that really. I have been told that I can be unapproachable, as an employer."

I rolled the teacup between my hands, old stoneware and fresh heat. "We never did have time for a proper debrief."

"If you are going to complain about your office chair, or suggest we should have put on ... complimentary chanting classes" – his lips curled awkwardly around the words, struggling

204

to find the ludicrous fripperies of other men – "then please, feel free to put your concerns into writing."

"Your recruitment methods left a lot to be desired."

"My ... ah, the business with your thumb."

"The execution of a man in the cellar was also an unexpected career hurdle."

"You refused to do that; I found that very convincing. A good spy would have done whatever was necessary to finish the job. A coward would have fled and never come back. You were neither. I struggled to work you out, Kadri ... Ven. I realise now how vulnerable that made me. My intellectual curiosity – my vanity, even – overcame my common sense. Thank you for that lesson."

"How's your leg?"

"A useful reminder. How's the cut across your chest?"

"It was superficial, although the scar will be a story."

"Someone taught you how to fight."

"A little. There wasn't much combat on the syllabus, but we covered the basics of pure blind panic, extraordinary stress and moving your feet a lot."

"This is all very un–priestly."

"On the contrary, there is an ancient legacy of monastic orders taking up weapons, usually to fight to protect their economic superiority, very occasionally for theology, and often as a performance art for fundraising purposes."

His laugh was a single high bark, delighted despite himself.

"How's the war going?" I asked.

"Oh, you know. The defeat of our enemies is inevitable. All this," a loose wave round the room, the sea inhaled, "is just fluff and faff to buy us diplomatic leverage – and to allow us to rewrite our plans. Well done, for that. If you hadn't been caught, you could have made a real difference."

"It's a little too early in this conflict to judge the difference people make, isn't it? Here you are. Buying yourself a little time with this diplomatic farce, because your invasion plans are now framed on Jia's walls. Do you have a new assistant yet?"

"No."

"You should promote Rilka. She adores you."

"She does. But she's prone to finding drama in every little thing."

"Sohrab? He can't translate a text, but he'll take a bullet for you."

"There are plenty of people who will take a bullet for me," Georg replied primly. "But I don't intend to put myself in a position where that is the primary job requirement."

"I'm afraid I'm unavailable to draw up a job description, if that's what this is." Another laugh, gone as fast as lightning. I sighed, watched the candlelight flicker across the ceiling. "Why am I here, Georg? I expected poison, not tea."

"Why do you think you're here?"

"Honestly? I think it's just another stupid bloody power play. You've always had a fondness for waving your willy around." His smile was light and broken glass, a sight that had sent shivers through me when I was Kadri Tarrad. Today, I didn't seem to care. "Jia is desperate for peace, and if she can't have peace she's desperate for a little more time to mobilise. Council is so desperate they'd do anything you ask, however ridiculous. 'Fetch me this spy, I want to have tea with him,' you say, and of course the entire thing is absurd posturing. But they'll do it anyway. For Georg Mestri, the real power behind the Brotherhood – they'll do whatever you want. So here I am, playing your petty little games."

"Here you are," he agreed, quiet as the snow. "My man found you out before you could find him, and here you are. It is as you say. I speak; they obey. You obey. Now you have come all this way, and now you can go. Off you go, Kadri. Off you go, Ven. Go find a rock to pray to."

I rose slowly, drained my cup of tea, the burning welcome in my belly. Put my hands together, bowed before him. "Kin of sky and earth," I murmured, "I do hope your leg recovers."

Was that a flicker in the corner of his eye? It came too fast, too tiny in the gloom for me to be sure. I straightened up, turned my back on him, and walked away at the stately, gentle pace of the old Medj of the mountains.

Chapter 35

Sitting by the sea as the sun goes down. There are guards somewhere behind us, Merthe keeping an eye out, but for now there is only Yue, myself, the earth that holds us and the sky that catches breath.

I am the sky, I am the sky, breathe with me, help me, I am the sky.

She says: I know it was just for show. Just to make us dance, waste more time. I'm sorry you were put through that.

I say, I gasp, I am calm, I am holding my breath, let it go, I am the sky: It's nothing, it's fine. There was nothing in it. If anything, I feel better. He's just a man. It's fine.

She says: When I was young, I thought I would be a hero. I wanted to work for Council, make things right. I would fix things, I imagined hands reaching up to me in thanks for all the good I would do; I imagined a life of sacrifice and it was good. Now there will be war and I can't stop it. I have tried everything, everything, I have given everything, and it's all for nothing. I am not a hero. I have no control over these things, other people have decided and they will impose their will, they will impose their power.

There will be a war and there is nothing to be done, nothing at all, so what is the point? Why do we trick ourselves into thinking we can control anything about our lives, have any power over our fates? What is the point?

Somewhere in Vien, there are men who think they have the

answer. They point at monuments to beautiful men and graceful women, they talk of the mountains we have levelled and the triumphs we have made. See, they say, see how man becomes the hero. See this god with trident raised, how he has human form. See how we ascend.

The evening sandflies were starting to bustle and bite. A line of seaweed marked the furthest reach of the tide, rubbery purple twists crystallised with salt. Her shoulder was pressed next to mine. I stared at my hands and said: "The river does not run because we thank it. The wind does not blow to be heroic. The leaves of the fresh green buds do not uncurl before the sun for any story, or to serve any purpose other than to reach, to live, to flower and to die. All these things will change. We are children of the wind."

The island has only one temple, built from the drifting plastic and saline skeletons of the sea. There is one Medj who guards it, and they were a sailor once, who talks in the sailor's tongue of rust and sunset and endless sky. The evening bell rang, softly once, a little louder twice, the full bell at last, calling out three more times before singing away.

Yue turned to stare at me, a glimpse of dread in her eyes. "Do you really find comfort in that? Does that make you feel . . . good?"

"Sometimes," I replied. "Sometimes I think I understand what it means, and then I feel better, for a little while."

"You remember the forest?" The question caught me by surprise, a moment in which my tongue tangled. "They say the fire is renewing. The old dies so the new can live. In Damasc, they believe the kakuy want blood, that when the world burned they had to sacrifice their own people to feed the earth and keep the kakuy satisfied, that the spirits of this world are violent, insane."

"They're wrong. The kakuy don't care if we spill human blood; they have no interest in us. They do not care if we live or die, only what mark we leave upon the earth. What is our blood to the soil? Nothing more and nothing less than a little drop of crimson, which will vanish. It is arrogance of the most egregious sort to think the sun will change its heat because of a knife through some poor bastard's chest."

"If you believe that," she replied, "then Vae's death was meaningless."

Do I remember Vae dying? Don't let go, don't let go, and now I can't remember if I said it, if I screamed it, or if it was just a thing written into my heart.

I close my eyes, feel her hand pulled free of mine, but even this memory is false. As my hand grew bigger, hers stayed the same size, and now I remember reaching for it with my adult fingers, as she grows smaller and smaller, slipping through my grasp. Don't let go. Memory does not hold truth, only stories. Perhaps I don't remember her at all. Perhaps I just remember some fantastic trick, some illusionary girl I have re-imagined and re-imagined to fit my needs. A spy would know what to say. Knowing what to say would make me very suspicious of anyone I met.

Then Yue said: "Witt says that Georg has already won. That if we are to survive, Temple must unlock its archives. Warplanes, fuelled by oil. Chemical weapons, drones with missiles and ... I don't know what else. Isn't it absurd? The first shot hasn't even been fired, and Maze has won."

"A strange attitude, for a general."

"A leader should be a pragmatist too."

"What about the kakuy?"

"What about them?"

"To build your planes. To drop acid on the earth. To poison rivers. Do you really think the kakuy won't respond when you scar the earth?"

"No one sees the kakuy these days. They don't care what men do."

"They care when the forests burn."

"Do they?"

"You know they do."

She raised her head, curious, a turn to the side. Didn't see an answer in my face, half-shook her head, asking a question without words.

"You saw the kakuy. In the forest. I was there. You saw it."

A moment in which perhaps something flickered, a glimmer of a memory that had been pressed down so deep that a forest could grow its roots and bury it for ever. She shook her head, once, twice, turned away, shook it again as if trying to clear it of the memory of smoke. "I have never seen a kakuy. You are wrong."

A thousand kilometres away, the forest grows. It came back to life so slowly, from root to branch, branch to leaf, leaf to the bugs that feast on sap, to the birds that feast on bugs, to the predatory cats that look for the fall of feathers, to the worms that feed on the beasts that fall to the fungus that clings in the damp gullies of the bark to the soft-nosed beasts that feed on mushrooms to the darting lizards that lick at rainwater caught in the upturned belly of a curling leaf, the forest grows and becomes again a living thing, where fire once blazed. I close my eyes, and in that moment cannot imagine the sky and earth being merciful to humans should the forest burn again.

"Yue . . ." A thing I needed to say, a thing I needed to express, my fingers catching at hers as the root of the nursery tree tangles with its peer; but she stood up before I could, brushed sand off her trousers briskly, turned away from the setting sun, barked: "Dinner? Dinner before you go," and was marching away without another word.

I lingered a moment behind, then followed her.

Yue's idea of dinner was dinner at Jia's hearth.

And here they are – here they all are. The great and the good of the Provinces.

Ull and Farii, Han and Shamim; Shahd from the Delta and Fethi from Damasc. Antoni Witt, picking at his food. Krima vaMiyani, who trusts no one and smiles, smiles, smiles, just like Georg. Pav Krillovko, telling jokes as the peace comes to an end, and Jia herself. Close up, she is tiny, impossible to imagine that she can stand unsupported, but also hard to imagine that, after so many years of refusing to break, anything will bend her now.

One of these is Pontus.

Who pours hot tea into a waiting cup? Who is the shadow, unacknowledged behind the elbow of some great potentate? Who wears the same face I had worn, all those months in Vien? Who let a fellow spy die in order to seal their own fate? Or maybe no, maybe Pontus was made of sterner stuff; maybe now they sat right by me, smiling and eating flatbread and fish, hands pressed together in thanks for the gift of the bounty of the sea, eyes a mirror, words a song. Who would I be, if I were Pontus, in this room?

Ull, the Minister of my home Province, shares some desolate words with Jia, and Farii can't meet anyone's eye. Behind them, Merthe sits cross-legged on a cushion, eating fish one slither at a time from a round bowl as if she's never seen food before in her life. "Ull wants to stay neutral," murmured Yue in my ear, as I watched from my place at the bottom of the table. "He knows we don't have the troops to defend both Magyarzag and Lyvodia. He's right."

These are real words, on real matters, and yet they seem a thousand kilometres away. My home will fall; the Council will not attempt to defend it. Yet any words which do not run around the room jabbing fingers into faces and screaming, "You? Are *you* the spy? Are you the traitor?" seem, at this juncture, immaterial.

"Jia thinks we can hold them at Beograd, so long as their advance is slow. Our army is trained for guerrilla warfare, not pitched battles. She has a plan." Yue's voice the numb declaration of the surgeon who will cut away a tumour.

A murmur from the top of the table, a gesture. Someone scurries to my side, whispers in Yue's ear but looks at me. Yue says: "She wants to see you now."

"Who?"

A nod upwards; Jia is watching me. I stand, awkward suddenly, knees and elbows, chin and bowing shoulders. The Ministers examine me as I approach, puzzling me out. I put my palms together and bow before the old woman. "Honoured kin, this is Ven," Yue said.

She nodded slowly, bright eyes in a folded face, then took

211

my hands in hers. The tips of her fingers had grown chubby and clubbed, and bones stood out on the backs of her hand between a daubing of yellow spots. "Ven. They tell me you are a Temple spy."

Does Pontus hear this and turn to stare? Is this some trick, to bring us together, kin of sky and earth? I glance round, but no one cares, and there is just Jia, Yue and I, talking low in a room of stone and salt.

"I suppose that's right."

"And we have you to thank for buying us time."

Was that what I had done? All of that, to buy some time? My eyes flickered to Yue, and I thought she shook her head, just a little, though I didn't understand why.

"It was an honour to serve," I replied.

A twitch in the corner of Jia's mouth. She nodded at nothing much, but there was something alive in her eyes, amused. "I doubt that," she murmured. "Temple and I have a bit of a problem, you see. We know that war is anathema. We know that the kakuy will wake, if we start tearing the world apart. We know they will crush us. Council has the terrible dilemma that we must therefore stand for peace, defend peace at all costs. Even if the only way to defend peace is by going to war. You see the difficulty?"

"I believe I do."

She patted me on the arm, as a kindly grandmother might do to a child whose name she thinks she should know but can't quite remember. "Well. That is why it is so good to have people like you around. Thank you for your conviction." Then she bowed a little from where she sat and let me go.

Chapter 36

Sit upon a stone outside the hearth door, and watch the dinner guests depart.

Krima vaMiyani talks to Yue, low, urgent, her eyes moving to every face. Krima is the one we must rely on to find Pontus, and yet slow – so slow. How has she not found them yet? Why has Krima failed? I am the sea; I drown in thoughts of Pontus.

Krima sees me, acknowledges me, does not approach, has nothing to say. The inquisition has done its part, and I am nothing more than a blown agent, dragged halfway across the Provinces on the whim of her enemy. Yue can deal with me.

Pav Krillovko tells a joke to Ull and Farii, and they do not get it, and are not in the mood. Antoni Witt is enduring Fethi and his pious, pompous huddle of Medj pontificating on some finer point of the kakuy – perhaps they are arguing that owning more than one pair of shoes is insulting, demeaning to the spirits of the earth, or that any glue made from animal bones is heresy, and we were meant to live on the forest floor or in caves and feast entirely on nuts and berries, as our ancestors did. Our ancestors died when they were thirty-two but well, ah well, if the kakuy demand it, so it must be.

Fanaticism would be a wonderful cover for Pontus. The absurdity of it, the sheer excess of it all suffocates even the slightest thought of subtlety, cunning or betrayal. Does Pontus cut their arm and bleed into the dust, proclaiming, "Bless me, spirit of the sand"? Does Pontus smile to see their scars by moonlight?

Somewhere, carried by the wind, the Brotherhood are singing. Their songs are of human endurance, spirit, passion and bravery. They are songs of heroes, bright and bold, loud enough that even Witt briefly stops arguing to turn and listen. Perhaps the world was once full of heroes, before the kakuy woke and, not even noticing what they did, crushed the great, the mighty and the bold beneath the storm.

I move away, fumble my inkstone from my robes, try to find words in it, something meaningful, something calming. The screen is old, a crack in one corner that no one has got round to repairing yet. You have to hold the on-switch down in just the right way to get it to come on.

Then Yue is by my side, and she says: "Not your stone?"

"No. Borrowed from a Medj with a cataract."

The sound of music swells, lifted on the wind; a cry of glory and the might of man. Her head turns to it, as if it were the snap of a breaking branch in a midnight forest.

"They're certainly keen singers," I mumble.

"Worrying you chose the wrong side?"

I shook my head. "No. You?"

"I think it would be too late for me to change my mind, even if I did." Her hand brushed mine, so light that for a moment I thought I'd imagined it. Then she said: "I'm leaving tomorrow. Going to Budapesht. We have to prepare for the worst. I don't know if . . . " and stopped, looked away, her hand still pressed, back to back against mine.

I tried to think of something to say.

Georg would think of something to say.

Then someone called Yue's name, and she walked away.

In the dead night of my little room, I do not pray.

Prayers are for gifts. They are for blessed things, bestowed in mercy, compassion. They are raised up in exaltation to something unique and cry out for special attention, for the world to be something other than what it is.

Instead, I close my eyes, and feel my feet upon the earth, and

214

know that when I die the worms will feast on me and the forest will grow.

She knocks on my door twice, almost too quiet to hear, then knocks again, a little louder.

I let her in.

All others are sleeping. The boats will carry the great and the good of the Provinces away, and tomorrow, or maybe the next day, polite people in smart shoes will deliver mutual declarations of war to each other's doors, and children will stand by the railway line and wave at the soldiers, who will perhaps wave back, and we will become barbarians in order to survive.

But for tonight, Yue puts her hand in mine, and kisses the backs of my fingers, and kisses my mouth, and I kiss her back.

There is no love here. Tomorrow we will both be gone. Better to make love with someone whose death you will not mourn, when the bombs start falling; better one last night of comfort, before the world runs mad.

She stays in my bed a little while, because together we are warm and the air outside is cold, and when I am asleep she dresses again, and is gone on the first boat of the morning tide.

Chapter 37

I was standing on the docks in the bright mid-morning cold, waiting for a boat back to the mainland, when the bomb went off. The wind had turned southerly in the night, carrying with it a hint of warmth and compassionate sunlight yet to come. The water was choppy without foam, a deep blue spilled over here and there by the shadows of the clouds above, or the swirling of loose silt below. Friends and enemies were returning to their cities, smiling politely at those whom they would soon be trying to kill, hands pressed together and bowing, well, well, wasn't this nice? Such a pity; such a shame.

It would be gratifying to say that I sensed it coming. That I realised, when I saw Ull approaching down the beach with his escort of five, that something was amiss. That I understood, on seeing Antti and his Brotherhood men waving to their skiff as it bobbed on the end of a long wooden pier, that there was some-thing wrong with this picture. The light was dazzling, a constant flinch away from reflected glory; I could hear women chattering, the natives of the island bidding farewell to their unhelpful guests. It was a good morning to blow cobwebs from your lungs, a fine day to stroll and get salt in your hair or to sit on the edge of a cliff and dangle your legs over the side and feel free.

I did not see it coming.

What I saw, instead, was Antti look towards Ull and smile, a strange smile as if to say, sorry friend – sorry that we are at odds – but no hard feelings? I saw Ull nod once in reply, as if he too were regretful over some hidden thing, and then they both were standing on the pier that reached out towards the water, some ten metres apart, Antti nearest the water, about to step onto his skiff; Ull waiting his turn, for there were only so many people who could comfortably fit at the end of that narrow path with the boats bobbing unevenly all around.

The bomb was under the pier, and it detonated a little late, as if the finger that pressed the remote had been hoping for the two of them to be nearer, was eyeing up the perfect moment and, when it didn't come, went with the best opportunity they had.

It was not a very big bomb. At first I thought it was a terrible accident on a ship, a crash or something running aground. The shockwave of it, from where I stood, was enough that I felt it run through my gut and down my trembling knees, but it did not knock me down or send me scurrying for shelter. There was no fire, simply a black cloud rising rapidly up, spinning at its billowing top, and then rain. First it rained salt water and wet sand, then it rained shattered timber, then it rained bits of pebble and stone, and then it rained ruined parts of human. Most people who were caught in the blast were indistinct enough that the falling tatters of clothes and flesh were unrecognisable, merely driftwood of crimson and black, no more animate than the splattering mud torn up from the shore. The sound of debris falling made a strange, quiet percussion. The acrid acid of the explosive itself was a subtle aftertaste, noticeable only when the adrenaline wore off, a sticky bile in the top of the mouth that water wouldn't wash away.

The first person to scream was one of Antti's guards, blasted out into the water and still, incredibly, alive. He did not scream long. He drowned some eight metres from shore, limbs torn and unable to breathe, gasping in shallow, frigid water. Of the four other survivors, only one had the capacity to groan, to roil and twist his head and gasp for medicine, medicine, please in mercy's name. I ran to help, like an idiot, oblivious to the danger of another blast, saw a leg bouncing against the shoreline like driftwood, saw a crimson slick like oil dispersing in the salt, and a round-eyed fish turned belly up from where it had perhaps been nestling in the shadow of the now-shattered pier. The first body I reached was that of Ull, still alive, bloody and eyes open and still alive, bleeding from belly, chest, arm, head, leg, one foot just gone, and I knelt by his side and realised I had no idea where to begin, nothing to offer to injuries so catastrophic, so seemingly fatal, so I held his hand and shouted medic, medic, someone get a medic, help me! A woman staggered blindly past, hair a matted shroud, blood flowing from her ruptured ears, trying to form words and unable to get her tongue to shape the sounds. Medic, I roared, medic!

Ull's eyes started to close, and I thought perhaps I should keep him awake, keep him conscious, but didn't know why, didn't know what good it would do, shook him anyway, snarled, stay awake, stay awake, you're safe, you're going to be all right, you're going to be safe. Medic! Why doesn't the medic come?

Merthe was the first to arrive, slipping and sliding down sand and shingle. Did she know how to save anyone's life? I doubted it, but at least her soldiers had bandages, press here, hold that, do this, would it matter, didn't know, but something, please help, I don't know if he's still breathing, help me!

The medics came next, running with bags hanging off every limb. I was still holding Ull's hand when they pronounced him dead, ten minutes later. Farii, uninjured, stood behind and wept. I had not known she had tears in her. Merthe looked pale as the floating fish on the foaming sea. They found Antti's torso, arm and leg a few minutes later, bouncing up against the sinking side of his blasted skiff like wet paper. I sat, sodden and bloody, at the water's edge, and shook and trembled and waved away anyone who tried to approach me. In the end, Merthe put a hand on my shoulder and said simply: "We're done here. You're done," and didn't let go until I stood up and turned away from the sea.

Then I saw him.

Georg stood, leaning on his walking stick, at the top of the beach, the sun to his back, no hat on his head, looking down on us all. At that distance, I could not see if his eyes met mine, but

I felt it, as sure as this heart beats in my chest, before he nodded once and turned away.

Six days later, the war began in earnest.

Jia was universally blamed for Antti's death.

A crude assassination, everyone said.

Kun Mi was appointed Chief Minister of Maze in Antti's place. It was a perfectly sensible appointment – an apparent moderate, who could appeal to the masses.

Magyarzag declared immediate neutrality, citing provocation by Council against the independence of the Provinces. It was, Jia said, an act of surrender by any other name. Council evacuated Budapesht. Papers were still burning in their buckets when the soldiers came; hard drives smashed, their parts scattered across the floor.

Farii was appointed Chief Minister of Lyvodia, and led the mourners through the forest to the highest peak, where Ull's body was offered to sky and earth.

"He was cut down by treachery," she said. "He was betrayed by his own."

The Medj sang their songs for the dead as the mourners filed along the winding path between the unlit lanterns. I stayed until the melody at last gave out and the clothes were cut away from old Ull's body and the soil packed thin around him, so that the creatures of the forest may feast and his bones may return to the soil from which he came. The Medj bowed, gave their thanks, and for a moment I raised my head, wondering if the kakuy would come, if the moon would smile on its departed child, if the stars would dance a little brighter or the darkness bend in to acknowledge the fallen at its feet.

I followed the Medj down the path, guided by headtorch and stumbling memory, and returned to Bukarest.

A telegram was waiting for me at the temple.

COME BEOGRAD. SAVE YOURSELF.

It was not signed, and was from Yue.

I left it in the recycling vats for the novices to pulp down again.

Old Lah sat cross-legged on their pillow and said: "We must hold to who we are. We are the children of sky and earth. When people forget that, we must remember. It will not be thankful work. It will not be glorious or easy, and sometimes it will not be kind. But it is what we are."

The younger priests nodded and said they understood, and did not understand at all and wondered why we were not taking up arms, grabbing hunting rifles and knives and preparing to defend all that we were. What good are pacifists, they whispered, if all we do is die?

I threw myself into getting the last of the archives out of the temple. Most had already been secreted away, smuggled by bicycle and train to Provinces where their knowledge might be preserved, but a few remained. We hid them in panniers stuffed with boiled eggs and scrap metal, tucked them into freshly settled clay and wrapped them in resins from the vats, disguising them as crude objects or worthless icons, opening the windows of the temple wide to wash away the smells of our chemical concoctions while in the courtyard outside the Medj burned the most pungent incense they could and held their hands up to the sky and called for harmony amongst mankind, harmony upon the earth.

Maze's army was at Budapesht within three days of the neutrality declaration. Within five, they had control of the Ube all the way to Mohacks. Jia wasn't even trying to stop them, the reporters said. She knew she couldn't hold them until the mountains at Beograd – and besides, Magyarzag's neutrality made it questionable whether she could even legally attempt to defend the Province. She would have to wait, the pundits said, until the troops spilled south into Anatalia, into a land that was actually willing to fight.

"Will they come to Bukarest?" asked a man, hands pressed together as he bowed before Lah. "Will Farii fight? Will they burn the temple?"

"Temples can be rebuilt," replied the old Medj, which comforted precisely no one at all.

After evening prayers, I sat down before them and said: "We should send the novices away. I can forge the document, and know routes through the mountains. We can get the first group out tonight."

Lah sighed, half-closed their eyes as they considered this proposition, then, smiling, said: "It is useful for the pious to keep the occasional scallywag around, isn't it?" They chuckled again at a joke only they found funny, and then as casual as a pun added: "You should go too. I can't imagine the Brotherhood will be pleased to see you, when they come to Bukarest."

I shook my head. "We get the novices out first, and the last of the hard drives. You are very good at calming aphorisms for an anxious supplicant, Lah, but with respect you are terrible at cover stories."

"I also know how not to be a hero. Don't be a hero, Ven. It'll only feel good for a little while."

The next day, Farii formally declared Lyvodia's mutual defensive alliance with Maze.

"We will fight for what is right," she said. "We will fight for independence from Council tyranny. I believe in the people." Then she bowed at the hip, nose almost brushing knee, to Kun Mi as the first tank rolled into Bukarest. Georg stood behind her, as the Assembly of my home welcomed them in.

Chapter 38

A city under occupation.

It is not called occupation, of course. It is called "alliance". Farii has allied Lyvodia with Maze. These are welcome guests, these men in boots come to our town. We are delighted to be part of their noble crusade.

Come, drink; drink with us.

You seem quiet, you in your halls and hearths.

Drink and toast, like the few men and women who are smart enough to sense opportunity; drink! There is food and wine aplenty, and will be more yet to come, for we will be the winners; your leaders have chosen wisely. You do not need to hide supplies in the cold rooms behind the hearth, you do not need to get on your bicycles to go visit long-neglected cousins in far-flung places.

Forget the kakuy, forget the mountains and the rain. Humanity has always been its own best and only friend.

The temples stayed open – no bonfires as in Maze – but messages were delivered to every door, an eleven-point list of things that the Medj could and could not say. No political sermons. No talk of heresy. Functions were to be limited to blessings and prayers for happy births and prosperity.

"I had no idea we had power over pregnancy," Lah exclaimed, squinting at the list over the bridge of their nose. "I feel quite irresponsible!"

The arrests were quiet. Opposition leaders politely confined to quarters, for their own protection. Journalists invited to take some time away from work, offices closed. A few senior figures urged into quick retirement. Unwanted vagrants, disruptors and renegades taken for trial, charges pending. The charges would be pending as long as they needed to be; there was a war after all, and we all had to prioritise. The guardia were supplemented in the streets by soldiers of Maze. They did not threaten or extort, did not punch strangers or whistle at women. They were simply there, lounging in the middle of the great old causeways, leaning up against pine trees or sitting, knees wide, toes turned out, on the black benches on the edges of the parks, watching.

Farii went on the radio and said: "During this time of emergency, it is more important than ever to honour our brothers and sisters from Maze. This world belongs to us. To the people, to all mankind. We can shape a great destiny."

The train station was closed, and patrols checked the documents of anyone coming and going down the great highways of the city. A man with an inkstone into which he made short, sharp notes came to inspect the temple.

"Not many novices here," he mused, as Lah politely showed him round.

"On study trips," they explained cordially. "We like to send our novices into the community."

The man ran a finger along the edge of a kakuy stone, as if looking for dust, and, finding none, made another little note.

"Where are your hard drives?"

"In cold storage below."

"And what do they contain?"

"Erotic literature of the Burning Age, anthropology of the early modern period, and a complete history of anarchic comedy with a specialisation in the style known as 'laughter track'. It is a form of humour, you see, where the laughter is artificially added in, and you do not necessarily need to have traditional modes of comedy such as 'jokes'. Very interesting."

If the man was angry, surprised, disappointed, he did not show it. He made another, impossibly tiny, note.

223

"You have solar power?"

"Yes, and a little biomass."

"How much do you generate?"

"I will find out from our groundskeeper. Of course, we have always pooled resources with the community grid."

"That will end. Resources cannot be wasted on superstition. We must think of the future."

"We in fact generate more than our requirements, so really . . . "

"Resources cannot be wasted," he repeated, as if Lah had spoken some ancient, impossible tongue. "Humanity is all."

"As you say," Lah murmured, bowing again with a harmless little smile. "Would you care to see our collection of artefacts from the Burning Age? We have some astonishing items on the history of penis enlargement."

Even this man, face like the bottom of a saucepan, winced at the beatific innocence of Lah's smile.

At night, I did not sleep in the temple but cycled to a hearth on the edge of an old part of the city, where once the slabs of the great burning had stood in brown concrete, hard lines and over-hanging squares stacked as if by a lazy child. Time had reclaimed this place, and now only a few signs of the past remained in the odd chunk of ancient wall into which new resin had been pasted. In a hearth overlooking a flower garden bright with the new buds of spring lived a community of twelve or thirteen ranging from an old woman with no teeth, whose lower jaw in its resting state nearly abutted the tip of her nose, to a newborn baby and a group of three children, who had nothing but questions about this new world and longed to defy the rules freshly set down, now that we were at war. But even children could sense that perhaps this was not the time for mischief, that they would have to find some other way to have adventures from within the confines of their home.

Pinned to the side of the door of this hearth was a tiny box containing, they told me, a piece of sacred text from a holy book, and from the sunset of fifth day to the sunset of sixth they would not cook nor handle money, for their God had declared it a day of rest, and their God was most interested in human affairs.

"Come, come," said a woman with skin of deepest burnt caramel and a mole on her chin. "Close the door behind you."

They did not head to the temple to pray, though neither did they deny the existence of the kakuy. "Angels," said one, though perhaps sometimes they were devils too – either way, spirits sent by a singular, almighty power.

"If you don't go to the temple, why are you sheltering me?" I asked.

"Our people have survived thousands of years," came the answer, and that seemed to be enough, all the explanation that was needed. "Here, you are too skinny – you must eat!"

Lying on my mattress on the floor in a little storage room tucked high above the hearth, I heard the prayers being sung to their God. Sometimes He answered, they said. Sometimes He was angry and did not come to their aid. One day, these struggles too would end, and there would be life eternal.

Three weeks after Kun Mi, Georg and the forces of Maze moved into the city, the first soldiers came to the temple to arrest me. Finding me gone, they shoved Lah around a little, without much enthusiasm, and in an act of purest spite shot holes into one of the compression batteries, releasing the stored-up air in a long, cold hiss. Lah tutted and sighed and said they'd have to ask someone to help them fix that, and when the soldiers were gone I emerged from my hiding place with the last of the novices and their precious bundles of heretical hard drives, and announced that we were stepping up plans and would leave that night.

The novices swallowed their fear, bowed in acknowledgement. "Don't do that," I snapped. "You are a midwife and a plumber. Don't bow."

They nodded, awkward with informality. Their heads had already been shaven in preparation for taking their final vows, giving up their past lives, their worldly affiliations. A few weeks of growth was beginning to give one of them some thin fluff of

225

faded brown-grey across the muted surface of her skull, but the other's remained stubbornly smooth.

"Time for you to go too," Lah murmured, arms folded within their sleeves, limb impossible to distinguish from fold of grey. "You're a danger to whoever protects you."

I smiled, teeth and no heart, nodded once, beckoned the novices to follow me. "You," I snapped, indicating the man with the pristine skull. "Let's learn about wigs."

That last night, I stood beside the temple bell and did not pray. It was an ancient thing, forged from the slag of some forgotten war, some final gasp of conflict dug out of the desert of the Burning Age. Some people called it ugly in its mismatched rings of alloy spun together in the furnace flame, but the note was clear and carried across the water to the answering shrines of the city. Lah stood beside me, contemplating the hollow dome.

"Did they teach you the rituals and the bells?" they asked at last. "Or do inquisitors skip that part?"

"I sat through a great deal of philosophy before I was allowed to use invisible ink. Military trainers try to exhaust soldiers into quitting; in the inquisition they see if they can bore you to death. It is a good test for any agent." At Lah's disapproving grunt, I added: "But I do remember a few things. Strike the bell once, quietly, a call to attention. Strike it again, a little louder, to invite all who hear it to settle. Then strike it loud and clear, to call to the kakuy within you, who lives not in the past of human suffering, nor in the future of human aspirations, but in this moment, now, breathing in and breathing out the gift of the wind. I think there may also have been a poem you could recite, if you were feeling especially pious; I forget that part."

"There are in fact two poems – a profoundly moving verse on the nature of existence, and a somewhat more jaunty limerick we teach to the children visiting on family fun days. It's good to get them while they're young, yes?"

"Please don't say it like that."

"I thought you'd approve. Practicalities over philosophy."

226

We stood a moment more in silence, as the afternoon light slipped into a pinkish haze. Then Lah said: "Nearly time. You should ring the bell."

"I don't know the poem – or the limerick."

"So? It's just words. The world is changing. Who knows when this bell will ring again? You'll feel like an absolute barnacle if you don't do this now."

"Tell me, when you trained – presumably back in the age of fire and steel – did the temple do classes in sombre piety, austere reverence?"

"I'm so old I couldn't possibly remember. Ring the bell, Ven. Now's the time."

The ringing lived a little longer in my ears than I think it did on the air, and then even that died away, and I did not think the bell would ring again.

"Well done," Lah said. "Now off you go. Don't do anything I wouldn't and so on."

I nodded once and, picking up my bicycle helmet, went to flee the city.

Chapter 39

Two hours before curfew, three people, the last novices of the Temple of the Lake and an inquisitor, slipped out a back door into the evening light. The woman I sent ahead, as she seemed to have a steady head on her shoulders, pedalling on a bicycle with panniers full of clean towels, painkillers, antiseptics and gleaming ceramic blades for cutting through tissue or snipping an umbilical cord.

"You are summoned to a patient whose labour has come on early. You cannot be delayed."

"I am concerned about a breech birth," she confirmed calmly. "Even though I have complete confidence in the physicians, I have been assigned as this woman's midwife for five months, and it is my duty to be there as an emotional support as well as to lend any practical aid I can."

I beamed, tapped two knuckles on the top of her bicycle helmet and sent her on her way.

"Will Esa be all right?" asked the other novice as we closed the door on her retreating back. He was a flat-nosed boy by the name of Salo, considered by Lah to be mostly interested in the idea of priesthood as an easy, simple life where no one would ask too much of him or bother him particularly. What a shock would await him there, cackled the old Medj. The arguments over how to cook peas! The relentless bickering over the best way to transcend the need to bicker! No one bitches like a bitchy little Medj.

"She'll be fine. You . . . ?"

"I am a plumber," he babbled, too fast, a thing remembered, not understood. "I work for the civil water board. I am working the night shift at the downstream station on the Bovita; my responsibilities include maintenance, monitoring water pressure and on- and off-site repairs. I have been working there for two years. I am still learning a lot."

"What are you learning?"

"I am studying the use of robots to explore and highlight areas for repair in mains water pipes. I am studying for my grade one."

"What's the most commonly used type of robot in this work?"

"I . . . I don't know."

"Make something up. They won't know either."

"I . . . um . . ."

"'It has a proper technical name, but we just call it the squid.'"

His face drooped in relief and terror. "Yes, I . . . I see. I see what you did, earth-kin."

"Don't call me that. How's the wig?"

"I thought it would be more itchy."

"I'm sure it'll grow less comfortable. Come on."

Cycling through the streets of Bukarest. Have I ever looked at this city properly, now I am saying goodbye? Was there always music playing from an open window above the park? Did the white-crowned crows always turn their heads so quickly at the rattling of wheels on old road? The sky is pastel purple, a half-moon the size of my thumb overhead between the criss-crossed walls of the hearths that hem us in, vanishing and reappearing between structures of this place.

We made it nearly two kilometres before the first roadblock, a line of guardia standing down the middle of the street, flagging down those few electric vehicles that passed, the many bicycles streaming by. The queue was nearly fifteen minutes long, a line of tired men and women trying to get home before the curfew started. Work must go on; just because there's a war on doesn't mean people won't want their curtains cleaned.

Salo pressed in close to me as we neared the checkpoint, gripping his false identification as if it were the wriggling head of a venomous snake.

"Mains water and sewage," I explained briskly, as we reached the head of the line. "Heading to Bovita outlet number three."

The guardia read my papers. "Open the bags please," she intoned, repetition having made the words numb.

I smiled politely, unclipped the pannier bags on the back of my bicycle, stood well back. The smell of raw sewage and septic tank rose up in a hot wave, cutting through with an acrid immediacy to the tear ducts and settling in a chemical stink on the back of the throat.

"In the name of ... " began the guardia, then stopped herself, lest she invoke the kakuy of sun and moon or some other suddenly unfashionable imprecation to ideas that were quickly going to become unpopular in her chosen profession. "Can't you clean that?"

"Why?" I asked, with polite confusion. "We're going back into the tunnels tonight. What's the point?"

"That can't be healthy."

"We have chemical showers," blurted Salo, trying to do his bit. "It's perfectly safe."

The guardia looked at him for a long moment, but it was not the scepticism of an officer observing a spy that sharpened her gaze, rather the crooked manner of one who can't quite believe the things people get up to, despite all that she's seen.

She waved us on, turning her nose away from our mutual stench, and I dinged my bell merrily as we cycled by.

Esa was waiting for us beneath a low grey bridge above a thin artificial channel of water that flowed out of the city towards the wider river. Salo half-bowed towards her in joy as he dismounted, catching himself only when he saw the look of disapproval flash across her face, and awkwardly hugged her instead.

"Any trouble?" I asked.

"I had to describe the process of a caesarean," she replied

matter-of-factly as we huddled in the gloom of the bridge. "Thankfully, once I got into the details of cutting through the uterine sac and releasing the amniotic fluid, he quickly lost interest."

I grinned, rummaging with half-attention through my bicycle bags to make sure the wrapped hard drives were still safely stowed below. "You should have joined the inquisition, sky-kin."

"Lah says I'm a good all-rounder," she answered without a smile. "Where now?"

"We wait for it to get fully dark, then follow the path another kilometre or so. There's no in and out of the city without army permission, so main roads are out, but once we cross the old highway there are just fields and some woodland, and then a straight line down to the Ube. The river will be heavily patrolled, but our friends will be waiting until dawn. That gives us nearly ten hours. Lose everything from your bags that isn't essential – if we get stopped here on in, no cover story will help."

We tossed everything except the hard drives and a few bottles of water into the sluggish canal, then pushed our bicycles up the old ramp onto the bridge and turned south. The canal had once been flanked by busy roads, but time had changed the city's shape and now smaller paths of pressed gravel and black tyre repurposed into sullen paths criss-crossed between hearth and greenhouse. Trees sprouted through a place where once there had been a terracotta roof; tendrils of green rolled like tongues through the long-cracked windows of old warehouses, and only from above could you see the straight grid-like scars of the old tarmacked roads, framed by the oldest trees that had survived the greatest storms. In the settling night, a dog barked, and the electric hum of a guardia vehicle was drowned out momentarily by the ugly chuntering and bitter bellow of a newer, combustion-driven army car from Maze.

We cycled as far as we could down the narrowest of paths between greenhouse and hearth, shying away from the few street-lights that glimmered along the wider roads, headtorches on our

231

heads. In the dark, the bouncing of our bicycles on the uneven way was a ringing roar, a siren to summon an unseen enemy.

From behind the walls of one hearth, a dog barked, and its barking set off another dog barking a few metres away, unseen, and that barking set off a third, until the walls around us rang with busy creatures pronouncing here, here, look, look! We scurried on faster, slipping in and out of pools of light on the corners of the hearths, heads down, eyes up.

A door opened ahead, and an old man peered out, furtive, into the night, saw us, nodded, closed the door again. The outline of his form seemed like an ally, not a threat, but who could tell?

Voices were raised, then silenced through a half-open window to the right. On a wall, the shadow of a woman working at a desk grew enormous as she leaned into the light, then shrank back down to a smear of grey against yellow as she stepped away from her midnight labours.

A fox watched us from across the street, utterly fearless, white belly beneath autumn fur. We pedalled by, heard the electric hum of the guardia again, nearly on top of us, hard to tell where precisely it came from, and barrelled into the narrow passage between two buildings, stinging nettles and ankle-splattering black mud, hot breath on cold air. The vehicle slid by, two figures half-glimpsed inside, headlights on full, crawling at a snail's pace. I wondered, if the guardia caught us would they really arrest us? Curfew was a strange imposition, unfamiliar and disliked. If I pulled off Salo's wig and said, look, look, here is a priest fleeing for their life, would the old guardia turn us in? It would come down to who you met, pious or officious, frightened or brave – a bit of luck: some old patroller who doesn't care much for this new alliance of Farii's; some young whelp looking to get a promotion in this strange new world.

We spent nearly twenty minutes in a ditch on the edge of town, caught between patrol behind and idling, chatting soldiers ahead. They were not stopped on this road because they expected trouble or because it was an obvious route out of the city. Rather, they were lingering because their superior was an absolute bastard, a bull rearing at every sight and sound, and they wanted to prolong their absence from him as much as possible, pausing now in the dark to share a drink, have a piss, chat about nothing much.

Snips of words drifted in from where they sprawled against the hot metal sides of their strange, stinking vehicles. Games played, bets made, awkward love affairs. Anything except the war they would soon be fighting in; anything but the future. Soldiers learned not to speculate early on in their training; it was one of the qualities they shared with priests.

Once a drone flew overhead, and I heard Salo's breath rise through flared nostrils, saw his eyes grow into moons, let my breathing fall a little louder, calm and steady, until at last he got the right idea and forced himself to exhale, to breathe out slow, to half-close his eyes and dig his fingers into the soft mud he was pressed against, grit in nails, slime in skin, calm again.

The clunk of an engine; a slamming of heavy metal doors. The combustion vehicles of Maze were crude, growling things, bigger than their burning era counterparts, all pipe and joint and heavy tyre that bounced and cracked on uneven ways. In time, the designers would get it right, somehow manage to mimic the sleek, shark-like qualities of the older vehicles, start talking about whether a car had a friendly face or a feminine bonnet, whether it had headlights like eagle eyes or a grille like the smiling mouth of a predator. For now, they were built to work, and intimidate, and didn't yet run as far or as fast as their electric counterparts, but who cared? In time they would; for now, the symbol was all.

We waited for the sound of engine to drift away, then crawled, teeth chattering and skin grey, up onto the empty road. I turned my headtorch on low, bent over the map, traced the route to the river, turned my torch off, fumbled in the thin gloom for a drink of water, sipped, shared the flask, returned it empty to my pack.

"What if the drones come back?" asked Salo.

"Just keep moving," I replied, turning away before he could ask anything else.

*

In the headtorch gloom, the rittle-rattle clackety-clack of the speeding night, there is no sight, no sound, no change in colour nor heat nor cold that the mind may hook onto, no passing world that isn't dark, no motion that isn't seamless, the same, endless and without form.

I think that Georg is still in my brain, still watching my every thought, and that Lah is there too, an antibody devouring the other's spreading poison. Like gobbling amoeba, they exist for now in perfect balance, consuming and expanding, consuming and expanding, until there is no room for anything that resembles me left.

Then I heard a vehicle up ahead, turned my headtorch off and gestured the others into the side of the road, and it turned out the void all around was not void at all, but a busy, teeming night of hunting bird and scurrying prey, of thorn and bark and worm and ant, of thin spitting rain and wind rolling across the first leaves in the highest trees, the breath of a giant exhaling after a long, cold sleep.

We cowered in the woodland on the side of the road, bicycles thrown down into bracken, bodies against branch, as a convoy of five electric cars, accompanied by one grunting, grumbling truck of Maze, slithered by in a snake of dazzling whiteness, almost too bright to look at after the long night.

Then they too were gone, and the darkness in which my mind wandered was now a terrible, gnawing thing, a huge monster that would consume us whole if we let it. I switched my torch back on, and with every turn of my head imagined I would see a rifle raised, see Georg as if he had ruptured from the earth like a spire of lava, inches from me. The novices looked at me, and for a moment I think they saw my terror, and I knew they would never fully trust me again. I picked my sodden bicycle up from the dirt, barked some order, heard the authority of one who has crossed over into that place where authority derives not from some experience or moral quality but from fear. Nothing to be done about that now.

"Three hours to dawn," I snapped, checking my watch. "Not far now."

234

Chapter 40

On the banks of the Ube, the last of the trees were being cleared. I could see the distant lights of the trucks as they worked through the night, hear the timber crashing down. The broken cover and churned, sodden mud would make it harder, at least on the north bank, for anyone to cross over without being seen.

Timber groaned, followed by a hairy brushing of a hundred twigs shattering as the trunk that bore them fell, and for a moment I thought I heard an answering sound, a shuddering through the earth, as if a creature with lungs of stone had been disturbed by the noise and now lay restless in shallow sleep, remembering the nightmares which previously had passed it by.

We lay flat on our bellies on the edge of a field of turned-over, crunchy earth, watching the slope down to the water below. No lights moved; nothing stirred in the darkness.

Esa said: Perhaps no one guards it?

Salo replied, hope seeping into his voice: The river is long. They can't have patrols all the way across it. Praise the river.

I looked up at the overcast sky, tried to hear the sound of drones, catch the glimpse of light on wing. Saw nothing. Heard only the wind. I took my headtorch, flashed it five times down at the water, then five times again, then waited.

We waited a minute, then two.

I flashed my headtorch five times, then five times again.

We waited.

A light answered from the opposite bank, four flashes, then

235

three. I replied with three flashes, then put my torch away. If I closed my eyes, I thought I could hear the sluggish tumble of the Ube itself, the slow, fat weight of it as it finally neared the end of its journey, rising from mountain and slewing into sea. The Medj said there was one great kakuy of the Ube, a dragon of snow and silt, but the sailors swore they had seen dozens, maybe a hundred different creatures down the years, from the dancing sprites that played beneath tumbling alpine waterfalls to the ponderous, slug-bellied beast that surfaced sometimes from the twisted reeds of the delta. I wondered if we would see the kakuy tonight, and doubted it very much. The Ube did not care for three travellers in the dark.

"Run straight for the river," I said. "If they're slowing you down, throw the hard drives."

"We're nearly there," Esa breathed, her eyes flickering skyward, before returning back to the dark between us and the river. "We're nearly done."

A flash from the water, three points of light in the dark.

"Go. Go now."

They did not need telling twice. They were off, crawling onto hands and knees then sprinting straight down, visible only as muted darkness against the reflective ribbon of the river below. I followed a few steps behind, my head tipping down and feet skidding behind as I ran, a toe curl from catastrophe. A few seconds later I heard the low hum of the drone as it descended from the dark behind, then caught the sweep of the searchlight as it powered up its main lamp and swung towards us. The beam tumbled past me, moving too fast, overshot the novices, then slowed and inched back, the unseen controller working to keep pace as we descended. The light caught on the back of the bicycle helmet still on Salo's head; he swung to the side, trying to dodge out of the beam, and it didn't bother to follow him, didn't play that game but jerked sideways, spilling over Esa as she barrelled for the water. Against the white of the drone's light, I could barely see the flashing of our rescue boat as it turned towards us, but I caught the glow of a dozen other lights illuminating the far bank – Council troops, perhaps, or local guardia alerted to our escape – voices rising and engines coming to life. The drone lost pace with us for a second; then it found us again, and now a second unit was sweeping in from the north, the conical white beam a three-dimensional thing picked out in cold drizzle, two bouncing military vehicles behind it, headlights on full, tracking the light above us as we tumbled for the water.

"Don't stop!" I hollered at the weaving novices. The water was only a hundred yards away, my throat shrunk to a straw, heart in my ears, the two cars bouncing and shuddering over disturbed earth and churned-up root so high and so far that I thought for a moment they'd shake themselves apart before reaching us. When they opened fire, it seemed such an absurd exercise I almost laughed, the man leaning out of the passenger window of the nearest vehicle utterly unable to aim against the bouncing motion. But at the sound of bullets, the novices slowed, and I tore past them, too little breath left to tell them to run. They got the idea, picked up speed again. Esa wove wide, drawing the beam of the second drone away from the pack, and I silently thanked her and cursed her and thanked her again. One of us would make it, at least; one of us would get to the boat in the dark.

More gunshots, a little louder now, the first vehicle sliding as the driver tried to control its descent down the slope; fast enough to overtake us, not too fast to slip. I caught the shape of the shooter as he levered himself up a little higher, digging his elbows into two long bars across the roof and taking more careful aim, lining up a shot with the flashing bicycle helmet on Salo's skull. Then the lights on the other side of the river changed, and for an instant I could see the exact shape of the waiting rescue boat on the water, picked out in chemical yellow as three or four shadows lined up their shots and opened fire.

The car twisted, spinning nearly 180 degrees in the churned-up mud, turning itself sideways on to the boat. Doors opened and soldiers tumbled out, ducking behind metal and heavy bonnet to return fire. One aimed a shot at me, but it was an afterthought,

237

the drones now sweeping towards the river to light up in full whiteness the little barge that had come to our aid. Then the second car squelched by me, and I was dazzled by its light as it skidded to an uneven halt, back wheels digging themselves into the mud between us and the boat. The doors facing away from the river opened, soldiers tumbling out, not five metres away. They had not yet drawn their pistols; they seemed to expect their mere presence to be enough to induce a surrender. "Run!" I hollered, and Esa was already far enough out of their reach that she went straight past the car without even slowing, without sparing it a second glance, a bag of hard drives bouncing on her back, her chin tilted forward like a hound.

Salo was less lucky, the arc of his path bringing him straight into the tumbled-down waist-tight grasp of one soldier who threw himself like an uncoiling snake across the gap between them, knocking the novice to the floor. I didn't slow, running straight into the nearest man in front of me, palms-first, letting the full weight of my body and speed of my descent hit him in the chest. He staggered backwards, slammed into the side of his own vehicle, bending with a crack in the small of his back, eyes wide and bewildered. For a moment, the two of us fumbled for his gun, the strap suddenly a knot of fingers and clasps. I gave up on the weapon first and, having no better ideas, slammed my forehead hard into the bridge of his nose, which cracked as the reverberating impact rippled into the soft bones of my ears. He didn't howl but curled away from me, both hands pressed to his face, so I turned and kicked at the soldier who held my novice down. He did not expect to be kicked from behind, and though I doubt I hit anything important, the surprise loosened his grasp.

"Get to the boat!" I snarled. Salo crawled back to his feet and sprinted until he fell the last few metres into the waiting barge. I twisted round to follow him, and a hand caught my ankle, dragging me down. I landed chest first, followed by grazing palm and bouncing skull. The boat was so close I could grab for it, see the faces of the men and women on the deck, dressed in civilian clothes, rifles raised. Someone managed to clip a drone, and one of the lights illuminating them spun to the side then went out. Another rescuer staggered, then recovered herself, fired twice more, then fell without a sound, as if time was running slow for her and the bullet in her chest had arrived sooner than she was prepared to receive it.

I crawled forward, hoping by sheer will to pull myself free from the hand that held my ankle, but a shadow moved across my side and something ruptured in my back, too big and broad to be a bullet but perhaps a boot, an anvil, a missile falling on me and me alone. I saw my novices crawling into the back of the boat, hiding behind the gunmen, saw the light of the one remaining drone flicker and dart away as more bullets flew skywards, saw another man fall in the last graze of its failing light. Heard someone shout, "We have to go!" and briefly met the eyes of a stranger, a captain perhaps, or the skipper of the barge. I had no idea who this man was, and doubted he knew anything about me other than he was there to rescue a bunch of priests. But I knew he would remember me that day, that my eyes would be with him every dawn and every dusk, and I wished I had time to tell him that it was okay, not to worry about these things, that regret was a changing thing.

Instead, I shouted – or tried to shout – "Go! Go!" but a soldier had grabbed me from behind and was dragging me by hair and by throat, by shirt and by elbow, by anything hand could get a hold on, back into the shelter of the cars. "Go!" I gasped, and had no hope they'd hear me until I heard the engine on the boat rise.

Then I was being shoved into one of the cars, head down against the bullets flying, hands covering my skull from shrapnel or angry men. There I stayed, and did not see the boat make it to the furthest shore but knew it must have by the grumbling of weary voices and the slap-slap of despondent boots on torn-up earth, and the slow fading away of the barrage from a few shots, to one or two, to nothing at all. I peeked through my latticed fingers, turned my chin a little away from the ground, and saw the first light of dawn was coming, tulip pink and daisy white.

Then someone said: "Breakfast?"

I unrolled slowly from the back of the car, blinking in the gently rising light. A woman held out a hard-boiled egg, a bottle of water. I drank uncertainly, returned the flask, cracked the shell of the egg on the side of the door, peeled it open. One of the cars wouldn't start; that seemed to be the cause of this sudden quiet, this opening up of rations, this sitting around as if there hadn't just been a gunfight by the river. Someone who seemed to want to be in charge marched up to me, saw me eating, shook his head, turned away, didn't have anything much to say. Someone else looked towards the east, and I thought perhaps he was about to utter a morning prayer, bow to the kakuy of the sun as he had done every morning since he had been old enough to put palm to palm. Then he looked at his milling colleagues and changed his mind. I finished the egg gratefully, suddenly realised I was incredibly hungry and yearned for bread, and instead sat on the floor of the broken vehicle, feet dangling out into a muddy field, as someone fell back on hitting the engine with a hammer.

"Excuse me," I said to the soldier who'd given me the egg, "are you going to shoot me?"

"I hope not," she replied.

"Oh. Good."

She smiled patiently, patted me on the shoulder, reassuring as a surgeon's blade. "Temple, yes? Trying to cross the border?"

"That's right."

"Why'd you do that? We're fighting for a good cause. For good people. Temple doesn't have anything to fear."

"Do you believe that?"

She stared at me with blank surprise. "Of course. We're fighting for people. For the future of people. Just because Temple is . . . just because you believe something different doesn't mean you'll be hurt."

"Thank you for the egg," I sighed. "That was very kind."

Hitting the engine with the hammer clearly did something,

240

for with a popping of sparks and a sudden hiss of suspension, the car came back to life. "Finally!" barked he who would be in command. "Let's get out of this dump." His eyes returned to me, sat in a little crescent of broken egg shell and bruised rib. "What the hell are you looking at? Can somebody please arrest him?"

Chapter 41

The prison was perfectly polite.

No one told me my rights or offered me access to an advocate, but the woman who entered my details into the system smiled and said, "Not to worry, earth-kin." I nodded and tried to smile in reply as she filled out the form on her inkstone. "Any allergies?"

"No."

"Are you currently in withdrawal from any narcotics, hallucinogenics, depressants, etcetera?"

"No."

"Do you take any essential medication?"

"No."

"What gender do you identify as?"

"That question is irrelevant," snapped an older man behind me, a man who knew perhaps which way the wind was blowing. The two regarded each other over the stoop of my shoulder, then with a beatific flicker of teeth and darting eye the woman murmured: "Until I see the revised guidelines, I'm going to have to follow protocol, you see. I'm sure we're all looking forward to the retraining."

They put me in a cell with two other men. The walls were painted a soft algae green. There was a toilet in the corner. Signs along the corridor invited us to reconciliation classes. The same evening I was admitted, they were taken down and replaced with a noticeboard of emergency proclamations and newly indictable offences.

Of my two cellmates, one was in for domestic violence. "He made me do it," he said, face turned to the wall, knees up to his chin. "He just makes me so mad."

The other, to my surprise, was an Assembly member. "My name is Bayzed. I voted against allying with Maze. I voted against letting Maze's army in. I voted against welcoming Kun Mi to the Assembly. I voted against giving up the country to heretics."

"Voting isn't a crime. Why are you here?"

"Apparently I over-claimed on office stationery. But I'm sure they'll think of something better soon. What about you?"

I lay on the top bunk, pressing a palm into the ceiling, feeling the texture of painted resin beneath my fingers, a remnant of what had once been something organic, compressed and reprocessed. "I was an inquisitor. A professional traitor. I think they're going to kill me. Probably best to get it over with."

Bayzed thought it over while the abuser curled against the wall and blamed everyone but himself. "Do you think it will come to that?"

"Perhaps. Probably. In the early days it's easiest if it's an extra-judicial killing, somewhere quiet and out of sight. Paperwork goes astray all the time, especially in times like this. Once people are used to the idea that people just vanish, they will be more comfortable with the reality of executions – just a formalisation of what's already happening. After they are comfortable with that, public executions are a logical next step, and when you've made that a family outing, you can move on to the truly grotesque stuff, for when you need to formalise the fear."

"You seem very calm about all this."

I pushed both hands into the ceiling, as if I might feel the weight of the building above me, as if I could drive myself all the way into the earth. "I saw the kakuy of the forest," I breathed. "Twice, actually. Once in fire, once in ice. I don't want to die; sun and moon, I don't want to die. But I don't know if I'm afraid either."

*

243

At the evening meal, the political prisoners drifted together uneasily, a shoal of fish suddenly thrown into a very different sea. The pride of an ethical position held or the moral delight of defiance counted for nothing within walls of grey and green. They were laughable, a ridiculous thing to risk life and liberty for.

You are in here for principle? Not for theft? Not for assault or setting fires? Not for murder? You are in here because you wrote something?

I've never heard the like. Never heard the like! The times we live in.

In the morning, after cleaning the pots in the kitchen and scrubbing the floor, I asked an officer what I was charged with.

"Your advocate deals with that," he replied.

"Who's my advocate?"

"Don't ask me."

"Who should I ask?"

"Don't you know?"

"No. That's why I'm asking."

"What are you charged with again?"

"I don't know."

"If you don't know then how do I know who you should be talking to?"

My mouth hung open, words stopping in a dumb half-syllable. Then I picked up my bucket and mop, smiled, nodded once, and started to think about how I might escape this place.

On the sixth day, the man accused of domestic violence disappeared. Some said he was released; others, transferred. Rumours of things he'd done and mistakes he'd made – of people he'd crossed and promises broken – immediately circulated round the low halls, echoing from door to door through pipes and notes scrawled on scraps of paper swung by string from hand to hand. A look he'd given someone became a call to arms; the way he hadn't finished his dinner on a second day became a clue to some unravelling mystery. One man, who worked in Release and Rehab, shrugged and simply said the advocate had got him off, he was going home, but that was far too simple a story for a muted, windowless world to accept.

Two days after that, Bayzed vanished, and no one asked where he'd gone, and no one remarked on his absence, and no one whispered secrets through bending pipes in the wall.

One man was assigned as my new cellmate, and he wouldn't meet my eyes, and three days later he got himself reassigned to a different cell. He was clearly popular amongst the officers because his request was approved within twenty-four hours, and I was left alone with a choice of bunks and a toilet all to myself.

A month went by, and I was not charged, and no advocate came.

In the mornings, I cleaned the kitchen. I was told I would be paid for this service, money added to my account. I was not told what my account was, or how I could access it or use it to buy anything for myself, and when I asked the answer was always the same: "Your case officer handles that."

I gave up asking who my case officer was, after a little while.

In the afternoons, I read. There was a library, and a few ink-stones could be borrowed, pre-loaded with carefully selected material: educational, legal and light fiction that romped along with reasonable moral character. A few politicals talked to me, a few tolerated my presence, but they were men of ideals and passion, and I had very little of either to give.

"Well," mused one, "maybe it's good to have a pragma-tist around?"

I looked in his eyes and knew then that if I laughed he would cry, so smiled and nodded and turned away to stare into my empty bowl, poking at the edges with the chewed end of my wooden chopsticks.

From the radio in the workout hall, Maze's victories filled the air. Cities fell east and west, cutting off huge swathes of land and encircling Jia's forces in Beograd. Temples burned and a new era of humanity was promised. So much was promised, and the pris-oners laughed and said they'd heard talk like that before; sunfire be damned, some of them had even spouted it in their time, to get what they wanted.

Roads would be driven through mountains; planes would soar in the sky. Everyone could buy everything, and the only thing holding you back would be your own petty limitations.

"Hey, priest – where are the kakuy?" demanded Brahno, king of the radio, keeper of rechargeable batteries and lubricants of uncertain origin. "Where are your gods of the forest now?"

"It was never clear in the historical record," I answered, "if the kakuy brought fire upon the people of the burning or if the world was already on fire, and the kakuy brought rain."

"What does that shit even mean?" he growled. "What is that shit anyway?"

Brahno was a bully, too much of a coward to do anything about the people who really scared him, so he would sometimes exercise his violence on smaller prey, easier fry. I had enough training, enough memory of a knife in my hand and gunshots above the river to put up more of a fight than he expected. I held him off long enough that his lackeys felt the need to step in and get involved, and by then the officers were running into the room to pull me free, to drag Brahno to solitary.

He never left solitary, and no one tried to touch me again. I did not think it was due to my martial prowess and the pointed end of my elbow, but at the time I couldn't work out what else it could possibly be.

At night, I managed for the very first time to pray.

There was no expectation of reply or consequence, nor any invocation for things to change. That was not, I concluded, the point of kneeling in the dark.

Then one week like any other, I was pulled from my shift in the kitchen, escorted to the gate, let out without paperwork or explanation into the noontime sunlight, and was astonished to discover that spring had come in translucent leaf and buds of cherry blossom, in drifting pollen through shafts of light and

246

thin, larvae-fresh insects uncoiling their wings in the first kiss of heat. I stood for a moment, dumbfounded and blinking in the sudden illumination, when I noticed the combustion car waiting by the gate, the passenger door open, the driver's door opening too, and there was Klem, grinning as if I were his oldest, long-lost friend, beckoning me in. Sohrab came round the other side, cutting me off.

I considered running, but there wasn't anywhere to go.

Klem squeezed my shoulder as I ducked past him into the car, eyes wide with the breadth of his amusement.

Closed the door behind me.

Chapter 42

Here sits Georg.

His Bukarest office is not as grand as his office in Vien. He does not stand by the window. Rather he sits behind a desk. The desk is more functional than his grand old thing of blood and leather. His chair is huge and padded. It has been tilted forward a little further than usual, so that he is almost tumbling off it. I wonder if it is to hide the limp, the flinch, the flicker of pain that runs across his face every time he eases himself up, both hands resting on the armrest, weight on only one leg.

Klem waves me to one of the two chairs opposite, gestures me to sit.

I do, hands in my lap.

Georg finishes reading a document on his inkstone. Maybe a report. Maybe a map. Maybe nothing at all. I have tried this trick too, of reading something terribly important while my mind is a thousand miles away. I watch his eyes, and they are not moving side to side, but still, he wastes both his and my time with this game.

He wears grey that is nearly black.

He has a private telephone, the handle worn from painted red to softer pink where he's gripped it.

He puts the inkstone down, straightens it up so the bottom edge aligns with the line of the desk, folds his hands, looks at me.

"Kadri," he says.

"Georg," I reply.

For a moment, that is all there is between us. Klem hovers behind, almost vibrating with the urge to do violence, his delight in the blood that is to come, the expectation of it an arousal that glows in a thin pink blush across his cheeks, youthful and naïve.

Then Georg pushed the inkstone across the table to me, turned it, fingertips on opposite corners as if he were spinning puppets in a dance. I stared down at it, took a minute longer than I had needed in the past to recognise it, for some slumbering part of my brain to wake.

"Well?" Georg asked at last.

For a moment, we are back in Vien, strangers in the snow. "What do you want to know?" The words came as much from memory as now, a familiar call and response, a song once sung to a different tune.

"What do you make of it?"

"Archaic French. It is a discourse on toilets in Burning Age military submarines."

"Is it authentic?"

"Do you have cross-referencing material?"

"I can."

"Then I'd have to see that, but off the top of my head, yes, I'd say it's authentic. It's a digital copy of an analogue copy of a digital copy, which never bodes well. Signs of interference introduced by the process, remnants of Temple classification markers – not Pontus' finest theft, if we're honest. But there's not much call to fake a document discussing the difficulties of ejecting faeces from a vessel whose interior parts are at a lower pressure than the external environment."

"What else?"

I smiled, half-nodded at the inkstone, met his gaze again, held it without fear. "It's a very dull read."

He nodded thoughtfully, twitched the tips of his fingers towards Klem, returned his attention to a different document on a different reader on his desk. "Good. You will have it fully translated by this evening."

"Will I?"

"Yes. We have the Medj of your old temple – Lah – in cells below. She will be hurt until you comply. It is very simple."

"Why would you hurt them, and not me? Lah is a better translator than I am."

"I understand how you work. That is enough."

"I would like to see Lah."

"Once you have completed the translation."

I rolled a little deeper into the chair. It was as if I'd never sat in a chair before, never conceived of what an object like this was, how my body bent to it, and it bent to me. I stared up at the ceiling, absurdly high and panelled with wood that rushed into the centre point like an exploding star, and said: "Wouldn't it be easier – safer even – just to shoot me? I appreciate irony, but from a security point of view this – all of this – is just ego. That's all it is. Vanity – not even a power play, like Kirrk. The sensible thing to do is to kill me and be done with it. We both know it. Why make the mistake?"

Georg did not answer, but without raising his eyes from the desk gestured again at Klem, who, still bristling with delight at things yet to come, caught me by the shoulder and pulled me away.

They put me in an office on the very top floor, in a converted attic. I had read stories about sloping rooms above ancient buildings such as these; places for ghosts to emerge shimmering from the cracked floorboards, or for young lovers to pine away in. Instead, I was sat down on a single deflated beige cushion in the middle of an empty floor, given an inkstone with an empty text file and a few old dictionaries loaded on it, and left alone. A bolt slammed across the door. One window looked out onto pipes and solar panels, twisting up to the obscured sun. A single grey pigeon on a ledge of guano turned an orange eye to examine me, confused by this face in its domain. The window was locked, and while I might have been able to smash the ancient, dribble-distorted glass, there was a sheer drop between me and the nearest roof, several storeys below. The room smelt of old bugs unhappy at a new neighbour, and the winter's cold had not yet vanished from the shadows. Water ran behind one wall from a thermal exchange, the temperature difference palpable from one side to the other as I traced my hands across the thin plaster.

I paced the room, and there was only so much room for pacing.

I sat cross-legged on the floor and tried to find something of the stillness that had come in the dark and empty night of the prison. There, the constant passing of footsteps, the crying out of a voice from a cell, the banging of metal on metal, of fist on brick, had become its own background stillness, a presence which had lowered until at last it comforted. Here, the silence was a faraway city, distance distorted by travelling upwards and dissipating into the clouds.

My clothes were too thin for the cold.

I tucked my knees into my chest and translated a page, looked at the translation, tweaked a few words for ease of readability, wondered if any of this could change the nature of the war. There hadn't been submarines in the seas for centuries, apart from a few dredged-up coffins of ancient bone and the occasional scientific vessel launched into the deep. I was not sure what their relevance could be to Georg now. The Isdanbul fleet was so much stronger than anything Maze could ever put to sea, the idea he would engage in a naval conflict at all was absurd.

I worked through another page, made a note on an obscurity, a word I didn't recognise, to cross-check later. Somewhere, Georg would already have a translation of this document, to compare with my work. He would have translations of half of whatever he asked me to work on next, to catch me in a lie. He would start with things that seemed harmless, which could have no effect on the shape of the war. He would then slip in the odd text which may seem on the surface to do no damage but which he could point to in a later time and say, look, see, you have already betrayed your people by translating this, so why make a stand

251

now? You are already damned. You were damned the moment you wrote a single word.

I stopped.

Put my pen down.

Lay out long and cold across the floor, hands on my belly, to wait for the end.

Chapter 43

When I was twelve, I was taken along with a handful of other children from the school in Tinics to the dormitory that lay behind the Temple to say goodbye to the oldest of all the Medj who honoured the forest, who would not be long for this world.

Yue was there too, face furrowed in a perpetual frown. Did her mother and mine sit up long together on the grassy roof of the hearth and whisper of their children, remember Vae's name, wonder what we truly saw that day in the burning forest? Probably not. The hearths of Tinics were eminently practical about these things.

Beti, the oldest Medj of the valley, had been the bane of many a merry childhood game, boring us with sermons and insisting on decorum, respect, when a more liberally inclined member of their order might have laughed to see children chase after crows or play at conkers. From their moral austerity, Beti's physical stature had seemed to evolve too, creating an imposing giant of a priest, filling every door with their shadow and booming out like thunder: "Do not scratch your name into the sacred stones! Do *not* leave lewd messages in the raked pebbles of the yard!"

Now cobweb skin hung sunken on calcium skull, the occasional pulsing black wriggle of a vein across temple or crown the only sign of life. Lips cracked and hands folded over chest, their carers had already removed the air vents that had sustained them, and breath came in irregular gasps, strange wheezes as the last hours ticked by. Their successor talked us through the final prayers of farewell, spoke softly into the half-shadows of the room as the moon rose outside and the warm smell of fresh citronella drifted in on the cool spring breeze.

"Sometimes they will wake, and may say a few words, or ask for water, but before you can bring the sponge to their lips they may sleep again, or forget what they desired, and then their eyes close. Sometimes they will gasp, and you'll think they are in pain. You'll think this is terrible, this is monstrous – but it is not, it is just a holding on, a releasing. It can take days, in which time they will neither eat nor drink nor wake. The pain is already past. This is not pain. And an hour will come where you leave the room, just for a minute, just to wash your face or greet the sunrise, and when you return they are gone. It is as if they are waiting for us to leave, for no living eye to look upon them so that, at last, they can let go. We have feared dying more than anything. We invested so much energy, so much time, into fighting death, into refusing to accept that it would come. We painted ourselves to look young, injected chemicals both pointless and poisonous, lived in extraordinary pain and discomfort rather than let nature come, so that we spent perhaps almost as much time fearing dying as we did actually living. A Medj should not die this way; we do not fear change. But it is all right to be sad. It is human to be sad. But do not fear. Go – live – and do not be afraid."

With this guidance we were sent home again, and Beti died that very night, when their attendant had left to make a cup of tea.

Chapter 44

In the evening, in an attic in Bukarest, Klem came to find me, and the translation was not done.

I waited for him to kick me, to swing his fists or throw me against a wall. Instead, he grabbed me by the back of my shirt and pulled me down the hall. Every time I found my footing, he shook me a little to the left or a little to the right so that I had to catch onto his arm or claw at his chest to stop myself from tumbling into the throat-clasping pressure of my own dragged clothes as he hauled me before Georg, shoving me at last onto my knees in front of the desk and holding me with one hand across the top of my skull like I was a prize pig.

This time, Georg looked up with a sigh, no patience for pretence.

"Well?"

Klem shook his head.

"I will kill the priest," Georg tutted, disappointed, perhaps even annoyed.

"What will that achieve?" I asked.

The question seemed to catch him almost by surprise, as if the notion hadn't even crossed his mind. Then he straightened, a conclusion reached, put his inkstone down, nodded once at Klem, who yanked me back onto my feet. Georg was halfway to the door in a few steps, assistants and would-be supplicants scuttling out of his way like beetles before the spider. Eyes turned downwards as I was shoved along, as mourners may look away from the coffin.

I lost my footing on the stairs when Klem timed a shove badly and, tripping, caught myself on the only thing in front of me that offered any support – Georg. He grabbed me by my arms before I could tumble past, and for a moment I nearly said thank you, but something I could not see danced behind his eyes and with neither scowl nor smirk he pushed me back into Klem's grip, which was a little more cautious for the last few stairs into the basement.

The lower half of this place had been a cold storage for the hearth, the pipes of the thermal exchange still visible in the ceiling, thick, flax-plugged walls and straw spread on the heavy clay floor. A sliding door was held shut with chain and padlock. Georg pulled a bunch of keys from his pocket and worked through four near-identical little silver ones before finding the key that clicked, slinging the loose chain over his shoulder like a silk scarf. The door pulled back and as my eyes adjusted to a little light tumbling through the opening, I saw the pallor of skin, a hint of face and hand. Lah sat up slowly from where they'd been bundled in a ball, blinking against the illumination, shielding their eyes, and finally, as their gaze adjusted, they said: "Is that you?"

I nodded, realised how futile that was in the shadows, said: "Hello."

They nodded, slow, thoughtful. "Ah well," they sighed. Then, an afterthought: "Imagine, if you will, that you opened the door to find me meditating profoundly."

"Of course."

A hand to my shoulder; Klem pushed me to the side, spine knocking against the frame, and Georg put a hand against my chest, holding me in place. Lah regarded Klem with polite interest as the man strode into the gloom, drew back his fist and hit the Medj across the face. Lah fell, fumbling at their jaw as if surprised to find that this was what this experience was like, learning something new – they'd always wondered. I caught Georg's wrist in both my hands, met his eye, saw him shake his head. Behind, two more Brotherhood men approached, idly interested, idly here, wondering what their boss was doing now. Klem hit Lah again, and again Lah fell, and this time they stayed down, tucking head into arms, knees into chest, perhaps not yet in too much pain, but in no hurry to experience more.

Again, my eyes met Georg's; again, a slight shake of his head. I felt my lips curl into the beginning of a snarl, had no idea where that came from, heard meat on meat as Klem struck again, again, one more time, this time a grunt of pain from the Medj on the floor. I felt Georg's hand press a little harder into my chest, knocking a half-puff of air from my lungs as he put his body-weight into it, pinning me back. The snarl at my lips became a slow grin, the grin of the wolf, the grin the wolf of the forest might make, the kakuy of blood in snow. Georg's eyes flickered in momentary surprise, and then I let go of his wrist and snapped my right fist into his throat. I didn't hit hard, the crunch of little bones in my hand rippling up to my elbow. But throats were not designed to be hit and he curled away, gasping, wheezing like old Beti the night they died.

The Brotherhood boys who'd been waiting their turn lunged forward but I was nearer to Klem than they were to me, got a punch into Klem's kidneys and a kick into the back of his knee before he even had the chance to turn. I tasted iron in my mouth, felt the snow of winter beneath my feet and heard the forest burning in my ears, wood cracking from within, black splinters and fire in the eyes, felt the river rise and the wind at my back, and as Klem staggered I smacked one hand into the right side of his head, into his ear, hoping to rupture his eardrum, put the other hand against the side of his neck and marched him, skull-first, staggering and confused, into the nearest wall. I drove his head into the glazed ceramic three times, each time throwing more of my body into it, each time feeling a different quality of cracking that rippled through him and into me, before the Brotherhood boys caught me and dragged me back, kicking and growling, untamed, blood on my fingers. Klem collapsed, crimson running down the left side of his face from the ridge where two skull plates join; thinner blood mingling with clear liquid flowing out of his right ear, which he grabbed with both his hands as if I had not already fractured his skull, rocking and groaning, a howl

257

that he dared not release. By the door, Georg was still gasping, doubled over, one hand raised to shoo away the men who ran to help him. To show willing, one man hit me, and then, not to be left behind, another joined in, taking turns to knock me down and pick me up until Georg had enough air to gasp: "No!"

Confused, they stopped, each with one fist raised, like children caught in an embarrassing act who are trying to think of some other thing they might plausibly claim to be doing here.

"No," he repeated, and that word took all the air he had, and he turned away to wheeze a little more. Klem's groans now rose again, a strange, almost musical circle of rise and fall, rise and fall, as if he were skipping back and forth over a spinning line of anguish. "Help him!" Georg snapped with his next, meagre breath, and someone ran forward to lift Klem up. Sensing that this was their opportunity to pretend nothing had happened, my captors let me go, and I flopped down next to Lah, who had uncoiled enough from their ball of arm and knee to peer at me, bloody eye to bloody eye from where we both lay, a few inches apart on the floor.

Here, in this place, our gazes were the only things that we could perceive, and with Lah's bloody face before mine, all the fight, the rage, tumbled out of me as if plucked away by some ghostly hand. From nowhere, a gasp that might have been the beginning of a sob caught in my throat, and I blinked at blood in my eyes and knew it was not all blood. Lah reached out slowly, one hand catching mine, then the other, squeezing tight. They smiled, and were afraid, and smiled anyway.

And it seemed to me, in that place, that the temple didn't just take the children to witness how old priests died but to teach us how we should die too. Come, whispered the Medj, come – let us not make a fuss. Let us not wail and curse and beat against the ending but exhale a final, peaceful breath and make things easy on those who survive. Be easy, be easy. Let us tell you how you should live; let us tell you how you should die. Even when you are screaming: be easy.

Footsteps moved above us. I heard the click of the gun and closed my eyes. It was simple to think that Georg had shot me, when he fired – the sound was so loud, the hot press of blood across my face and neck so immediate, that in that moment I concluded that, though I was dying, I would feel no pain. The Medj had been right all along; this was easy. Then hands caught me, picked me up, and though I felt nothing from having been shot I felt a great deal of pain everywhere else, and that didn't seem to make much sense, so I opened my eyes and saw Lah's body on the floor, one eye rolled all the way back from where the bullet in their skull had torn something apart. The blood had crawled up Georg's trousers and boots, but no further. He brushed down his thighs with one hand unconsciously, handed the revolver back to one of his men, nodded, still breathing fast and shallow, as if this were the logical conclusion of an inevitable plan. Then he spun on his heel and walked away, as I kicked and screamed and screamed and screamed after him.

They left me in that place. I don't know how long. Perhaps a few hours; perhaps a few days. There was no light, save for a tiny line at the bottom of the locked door. I huddled in a corner as far from Lah's body as I could, shaking, mind in a loop.

Here, close your eyes.

Now they die.

Now they die.

Now they die.

Now they die.

Enough. Open your eyes. Think of something else. Here in the dark, what else will you imagine? Find a prayer, find your breath. Here, exhale, close your eyes.

And now they die.

Now they die.

Now they die.

Now they die.

Reason says that this is a physical reaction, an emotional reaction, trauma.

Breathe through it.

You are the kakuy. You are a living spirit. You are part of this world, and this world breathes within you.

259

Don't let go.

Don't be afraid.

So breathe.

Breathe.

Breathe.

I curled up in the dark, and could not remember how it felt to breathe.

Someone left food, water by the door, and it turned out I wanted to eat.

I thought Lah's body would start to smell, but it did not.

Perhaps the cold.

The darkness.

The isolation.

I imagined flies, maggots, but this was a sterile, buried place.

Someone left more food, more water by the door, and it turned out I wanted to live.

I fumbled on hands and knees until my fingers found sticky blood, then fumbled a little bit more until I found the corner of Lah's robes. Slowly, their body grown heavy with death, I unrolled Lah from the rolls of fabric, until they just wore their trousers and shirt below. I shook the robes out, folded them by fumbled touch, drew them over Lah's head and neck, tucking them gently round their body as you might wrap a basket of apples for the market. This done, I knelt down and mumbled the prayers for the dead. Some sentences I heard myself say. Others I did not, the words repeated and stumbled through again, again, and now again, as I lost the tangle of this moment or the memory of the last.

From death, life. In the temple we learned the process of decay, were invited to honour it, to marvel at nature's process. Over the first few days, the internal organs of a corpse will begin to decompose. Without oxygen to keep the cells alive, carbon dioxide builds up in their last figurative respiratory gasps. The carbon dioxide creates an acidic atmosphere within the body, causing cell membranes to rupture. Enzymes are then released which start eating these cells from the inside out. The skin loosens, even as the muscles grow stiff. A few days later, the gases released by cell consumption and the bacteria that are now thriving within the corpse will cause bloating, resulting in the body expanding up to twice its normal size. Insects move in, happily gnawing away, and the stench of this stage of decomposition is the classic vomit inducer that sends people scurrying for the gutter.

Eventually, what's left of the body liquefies. At first, this is through the nose, mouth, anus; any hole that fluid can run freely from. Maggots move in, until there is nothing left but bone and hair. Any artificial joints, piercings, inorganic implants also remain, nuzzled clean by nature.

The remains feed the creatures that are then fed upon by another. Plants take root in soil grown rich with the bacteria that feasted on your blood; bugs waddle away, fat on fluid, to be caught by birds that are then preyed upon by the larger bird that is then preyed upon by the predatory cat that is hunted by the wolf. On the earth, there is only one ocean, which becomes rain, which becomes blood, which returns again to the sea. There is only one breath, which becomes the hurricane, which spins across the peak of the mountain and returns again to the forest.

And now they live.

And now they die.

Now they die.

Now they die.

Now they die.

At some point, the darkness was broken by the door opening. Two women I didn't recognise stood in the light; puffed short sleeves, big, waist-clinching belts. One turned away the moment the air from the cell hit her, an audible retch breaking up from the back of her throat, hands over her mouth. I had not noticed the room begin to stink. The other put one hand on her hip, pushing her whole frame a little to the side like a tree struck by a boulder, folded her other hand on top as if bandaging her whole frame in place, and barked: "Kadri Tarrad? Come with us, please."

I crawled to my feet and followed them, having no idea what else I could possibly do.

There was a bathhouse behind the kitchen. Two great round tubs were already filled – one with hot water, the other with cold. When the women removed the lids that covered the hotter tub, steam rolled up like a living lizard, tonguing the air. Towels were slung over the hot pipes. A yellow sponge and bar of soap smelling of oil and lavender were deposited on the blue-tiled lip. I stripped out of my clothes as the women watched. The fabric had grown stiff, bent like card from the blood that had dried in every seam. Black grime beneath my nails was flecked with clotted scarlet, and purple bruises spotted my arms, ribs, back, knuckles, some no bigger than a finger's gouge, some a violet eruption spread from the impact of a fist. I walked up the warm, tiled steps to the bath, climbed carefully over the side, sank down, knees to chest, until the water was at my chin.

"Lean forward!" barked the older woman, and I obeyed. She grabbed the sponge, held it under the water until it was hot and malleable, rubbed soap into it, then into me. Her fingers rolled round the backs of my ears and into the spirals; ran through the roots of my hair like a garden fork pulling at soil. At some point, her retching companion joined quietly in the corner of the room, hands folded, head down. "Fetch the clothes!" snapped the elder woman, pulling out a short-haired brush to dig into my nails like she was scouring for gold in the desert. The young woman left; the young woman returned, carrying a folded-up bundle of clean dark grey clothes, without shoes, and a flask of cold water.

"Drink!"

I drank.

"Cold bath!"

I crawled, the pain of every bruise now transformed into something sluggish, universal and soft, out of the hot tub and into the cold, gasping as the water ran over me, watching a thin, oily sheen of residual soap and scrubby skin slither across the top of the water.

262

"Out!"

I climbed out, wrapping myself slowly in the hot towels provided as the woman tugged a comb through my hair, a scowl at every knot as if each was a personal slight. Then I changed into the clean clothes provided, long sleeves and straight trousers, my bare toes curling into the tiles below while the bloody bathwater gurgled away to the greywater tanks. The women seemed satisfied with the final result.

"Follow me!"

I followed, through cool corridor and across courtyard where the vegetables vines ran up wall and trellis, under an arch of old stone and down a side alley where the rainwater butts bulged beneath the downpipes and green moss grew hungry around slowly leaking barrels. My feet were dark with the gathered dirt of the walk, and that was good; that felt like a kind of safety. Then through a door guarded by a Brotherhood man, into the back of a great villa, a thing of half-restored old-world masonry and new solar glass walls, timber frames and half-lifted roof canopies to let in the cooler breeze during hottest days.

The sound of crockery and pipes, the smell of cumin and pepper, chilli and starchy rice hit my nose, and then we were in a kitchen, long tables down the middle of the floor, hot stoves blasting beneath white lights, dazzling bright, voices competing with pots and pans and the hiss of oil, water running and fans spinning. Rows of men and women wearing aprons stood each at their assigned station, chopping, peeling, carving, dicing, grinding, skinning, braising, boiling. Few glanced my way as I was led to a small corner office where a man lounged, feet up on a desk, reading, and another dressed in Brotherhood black stood stiffly by the door.

"Colas." The woman managed to keep a little of her imperious formality down for the man as she waved me through the door. "This one's for you."

The man called Colas looked up from his inkstone, lips curling with evident displeasure as he took me in. A half-crown of white hair ran from behind his left ear to his right, circling a great bald skull above. He sported thin-rimmed spectacles whose round shape perfectly matched the twin bulbs of his cleft chin when his bright lips moved. He wore an old-fashioned white shirt, a pair of dark brown shorts that stopped just above his knees and long green socks that stopped just below them. Swinging his legs down from the desk with exaggerated slowness, he rose to his feet, which revealed that he was little more than five feet tall, and king of his domain. Yet even kings were sometimes forced to do things they didn't like. "Where's his shoes?" he asked.

"No shoes."

"I've got standards, you know. Hygiene."

"No shoes."

"What's his name?"

"No name."

"I've got to call him something."

"Pick something, then."

He thought about it for a moment, but a moment was all the interest he could spare. "He looks like a Pityr. Hey, Pityr – ever worked in a kitchen before?"

"I did breakfast service at the temple for a few months."

He rolled his eyes and, with exaggerated slowness, indicated first himself, then the Brotherhood man who stood to attention by the door. "Me Colas. Me boss. This Qathir. He shoot you if you run, yes?"

I gave Qathir a longer, more speculative look. "He hasn't got a gun, only a stick."

"I can beat you to death too," offered Qathir with a shrug.

"I'm just wondering why he doesn't have a gun."

"Point is," snapped Colas, hands flicking up, "you do what I say, yes?"

"I guess so."

"Not you guess so, you do – you do so, yes?"

"Okay."

His eyes narrowed, and for the first time he looked as if he was trying to see something of me, myself, rather than the barefoot intruder shoved into his domain. Whatever he found behind my bruised eyes, he wasn't impressed. "I don't like you, Pityr."

I shrugged.

"Shrug again, and Qathir will shoot you – and don't say anything about a gun!"

I stood silent, waiting. For a moment, Colas rocked from toe to heel, as if he couldn't quite tell whether it was more majestic to retaliate against perceived insolence or to turn the other cheek. Then, with another twitch of his hands as if he were flicking up a window blind, he barked, "Yes, this way, yes!"

Qathir smiled thinly, gestured with rolling politeness towards the door. I followed Colas; Qathir followed me. By the time I caught up with the diminutive lord of the kitchen, he was already talking. " . . . there is always something and if there isn't something, find something! You will also mop the floors, clean the stoves, and do anything else you are told to by anyone who tells you to do it, yes? Yes!"

I stared at the twin sinks before me, one side already heaving with dirty plates and cutlery.

"*Well?*" His dignity, already threatened by this whole situation, seemed on the verge of deserting him altogether.

"All right," I replied, fighting the urge to shrug again. "If you say so."

So began my tenure in the kitchens of Georg Mestri, unsung leader of the glorious human revolution. At 6 a.m. every day, my world began with a poke in the ribs from Qathir or one of the other guards assigned to stand watch over me. I would be dressed and in the kitchen, warming the ovens and stoves, by 6.30 a.m. and would not leave that place until 10 at night; later, if the dignitaries upstairs had guests to entertain. The others in the kitchen paid me almost no attention, except to occasionally shout, Pityr! I need the celery! – or Pityr! I need the big pan now!

Of my four rotating watchers, it was Makris who first cracked and borrowed a stool from I knew not where to perch on throughout his long vigil, rather than tire his legs standing over me as I washed, scrubbed, scoured and mopped through the broiling heat of the kitchen. Sometimes Colas came over to find fault in my work, but usually he left me alone, finding it easier to be a king if he was not reminded of this unwelcome imposition in his domain. Only once did one of the cooks bother to speak to me; she was new, unfamiliar with the ways of this place.

"Hey, Pityr – why don't you have any shoes?"

Qathir, sat a few feet behind as I tied off the cornbags of food waste for the biomass vats, grinned, chewing down on an apple and waiting to hear my reply. He was going to grow fat in this job, a paunch already pushing against the buttons of his shirt, cheeks rounding out as if flushed from the heat.

"I don't have any shoes because I'm a political prisoner," I explained politely. "If I have shoes, it is more likely that I will try to run away."

"Really? No kidding."

"Really."

"Huh. I guess . . . that makes sense, now I think about it. Hey, is that legal? I mean . . . you know. You working here and being a political prisoner and that?"

"I don't know. I imagine the laws have been changed, now that we're at war."

"I guess you're right. Hey, thanks."

"No worries."

She smiled awkwardly, waved a chopping knife at me with the slow waggle of one not quite sure what to make of the last twenty seconds of her life, and went back to chopping a squash.

Qathir leant a little closer to me as I pressed the bags of waste together into the sealed bin that would go to biomass. "She likes you," he grinned.

"I doubt that very much."

"Maybe she'll help you escape?"

"I doubt that absolutely."

"You're not very imaginative, are you?"

I hesitated, squeezing the lid down on the last of the bags, head on one side. "You know, that was what Georg thought, before I stabbed him in the leg."

*

Every four days, I was given half an hour to wash top-to-toe, and when the days were slow and even Colas couldn't think of a task for me to run, I huddled in a corner of the kitchen and slept instantly, profoundly, until Qathir or one of the other watchers kicked my shins and barked, "Job's in!"

In that way, my life continued. I did not know the day, heard no news, did not speak unless spoken to, did not pray, did not rest, and, to my complete and continuing bewilderment, was not shot in the head.

That last omission was the one I found most interesting.

Chapter 45

One morning, a box of fruits was delivered to the kitchen. I padded outside, the hot summer air damp with the promise of autumn, and pulling back the tarp that covered the boxes, saw thin green-grey mould smeared across the rind of shrivelled oranges; brown rot sunk into the crisp surface of the onions and maggot holes poking in and out of the thin-skinned peaches, from which sugars oozed like blood.

"What in the name of sun's fire is this?" roared Colas, as we dug through the finger-splattering, bug-crawling delivery in search of something edible. "What am I meant to do with this crap?"

There was a smell on the air: hot coal and diesel, unfamiliar to the city. That night, it rained so hard that I was dragged from my bed not two hours after I'd crawled into it to lay sandbags around the kitchen door against the deluge running from the overflowing drains. In the morning, in every vegetable box and hanging garden of the yard, mushrooms had grown, brilliant orange threaded with white gills and a purple drop on top or white inverted umbrellas; they sprouted at the feet of every wall and from the trunks of the bending fruit trees, scythes of bruised grey fungus, hanging off the bark like sunhats.

"Can we eat them?" Colas demanded, as Hang, his second in command, peered under the top of the speckled crop.

"Poisonous," he replied. "No good."

"Pityr! Clear them!"

I looked round this strange new landscape of fungus, bare toes bending into sodden soil. "Mushrooms are just the flower," I heard myself say. "The roots go deep."

Colas spun on me, a flush of anger in his face, but to my surprise Makris shuffled a little closer to me, muttering: "I'll give him a hand."

We worked in silence, tugging soft fungus by its base and snapping off the dusty discs for the biomass wells. When I curled my toes, water rose from beneath them, and, for the first time in what might have been months, I shivered in the drizzle-grey cold.

A few days after that, the meat of the freshly slaughtered lamb came, blackened with disease, wriggling with worms. Someone gagged at the sight of it; there was no question that it would fall to me to dispose of the needlessly slaughtered flesh.

As I washed my hands clean, the woman who still had not learned to refrain from speaking to the condemned casually manoeuvred herself close to where I worked, her attention fully on the eggy sauce she beat in the bowl before her. Without glancing my way, she murmured: "Are the kakuy angry?"

I kept my eyes down, away from hers. "Pissed, I would imagine."

"Is this their punishment?"

"Hard to say. Doctrinally it's always suited Temple to be a little vague about these things."

"I will pray," she replied firmly, and turned away, seemingly satisfied.

At night, I crawled to the tiny square window in my low room, watched the feet of passers-by splash through the rain, and did not pray.

Then one day, much like any other, Colas hollered my newest name.

"Pityr! Take this upstairs!"

A tray of sweet teas and candied fruits was thrust into my hands. "Third-floor reception room, quick quick!"

My life, to that moment, had not deviated from its narrow

269

course of locked bedroom to observed washroom to kitchen to courtyard. I knew in some abstract sense that there was a house – you could even call it a small palace – overhead, the inhabitants of which we constantly served with treats sweet, succulent and savoury, but I had not encountered a shred of it down in the places I dwelt. Qathir was my duty guard that day, and, seeing my hesitation, he shrugged and pointed with one single waggling digit towards the heretofore unregarded staircase.

I went up.

The floor beneath my feet turned from ceramic to bare clay, from bare clay to warm timber.

One floor up, the timber became carpeted, with worn undyed wool.

A floor above that, the carpet was dyed a sudden, vivid green.

The floor above that, the tattered carpet of the stairwell gave way to a new, thick weave, the warmest, softest thing I had ever felt beneath my grubby toes. I hesitated as I stepped onto it, blinking in kind yellow light and twisting my head round side to side, blanketed in the comfort of the place. Qathir nudged my shoulder, pointed the same wagging digit towards a half-open set of double doors, waited.

I shuffled towards them, was stopped by a woman who sat guard as once I had sat for Georg all those months ago; she rose, knocked politely twice, did not wait for an answer, then opened the doors to gesture me in.

Inside, sofas arranged in a u-shape were assembled before a long table on which much tea and many nibbles had already been consumed and many more left half-chewed with a disregard that might once have been an embarrassing breach of etiquette; these days it seemed a badge of pride. Arrayed in knots and gaggles around the room were the great and good of Maze and their new Lyvodian allies; some I recognised, some I did not. The conversation was low, the occasional spike of laughter too loud, the occasional brush of a hidden confidence murmured into a sleeve. Farii stood nearest the door, pressed into a triangle of conspiracy with two others. Whatever time had passed since I saw her pronounce her eulogy over Ull's corpse, it had not been kind. Her eyes were puffy grey bags around tired, blood-wrinkled slits. Her lips were thin and shoulders pressed towards her neck, like a starving vulture that doesn't dare feast while the hyenas are still gnawing. She glanced up as I passed, started in surprise, recognised me, one hand squeezing the arm of a compatriot who stopped talking and glanced my way too, her mouth widening in amazement. Merthe moved towards me, but Farii held her back, and I looked away and walked to the long table, feeling suddenly dirty, small, Qathir watching me from the door.

I put my tray down, glanced to my left and saw Kun Mi, pride and peacock-feathered, her dark hair wound in braids across her skull, head high and neck stuck forward as if she would peck at the faces of those who addressed her. Bukarest had become her new home, the forward line of her advance; and besides, the whispers went, Vien was a stinking plague-pit. The water that came from the taps was stained orange-brown; the air was thick and hard to breathe. No wonder the greatest of the war had moved somewhere a little closer to the front lines.

I turned, and there he was.

Georg, right behind me, leaning a little on his walking stick, his eyes running from head to toe as if he was wondering, had I grabbed a knife? There were plenty of blades in the kitchen, but his face flickered curiosity, not fear. His shoulders were pulled back, bound up in a knot, ready to be unleashed, ready to fight, he was so ready to fight, the smile on his lips barely creasing the soft tissue of his face. For a moment, we stood regarding each other, and I was tempted to reach behind myself, to mime the action of a killer, just to see what happened, to smile, to snarl, to see if I could make him jump. I did not. This was not the time for such games.

He saw that realisation in my eyes the moment I had it, and now his smile was something real, and he nodded once, and looked as if he might speak, and instead stepped to the side to let me pass, which I did, closing the door behind me.

271

Chapter 46

Time passes without days, days without name. In that too, there is a kind of honesty. Autumn comes in bloody leaf and yellow fruits. The slugs slither out in the rain and are crushed by passing vehicles, guts spilt into the sodden earth. It has rained for nearly nine days without end, and in the morning I cannot see anything except fog through the tiny window of my room. The soap from the dishes is making my hands peel. I pick at little flakes of white unconsciously now, though sometimes I pick too deep and blood wells up beneath the scales of skin.

Since there is no one left in the temples of Bukarest to offer the autumn libations, I do the best I can. I steal a little barley from the kitchen and scatter it when I am sent to take the recycling out. I spill a little water on the already sodden earth, and put my hands together at dusk when no one is looking, and bow to the west. Such things, when done alone, are largely meaningless. It takes a society that bows, all of humanity honouring its place upon this earth, to live with the kakuy. The temple never had magic; there was never any mystic power in the prayers of the Medj. Their power was one of teacher and guide who taught the children to think before they felled the forest, to thank the animal whose flesh they feasted on, to cherish the earth that carried them. Get them young, Lah had said, and where were their ditties now, their songs of balance?

They are dead, and it has not stopped raining it seems for a month, a year, and in Tinics I do not know if the forest grows.

*

Having been sent once to deliver tea to the upstairs rooms, I was sent again. Three times a week, then five – then, it seemed, every day. Sometimes to offices, sometimes to halls, barefoot I plodded round the villa with a guard at my back, occasionally noticed, rarely remarked on. Georg glances my way as I lay the warm bread down at the end of his table, but he otherwise does not cease his dictations. Farii watches me in the corridor as I pass by. Kun Mi does not know, nor care, who I am. I am invisible to her, except for once, when she stopped me and barked:

"Why aren't you wearing shoes?"

"I am a political prisoner," I replied, bowing politely. "Although by now I thought everyone was used to this kind of thing."

The answer seemed to throw her, a bafflement to her dignity, so she tilted her chin higher and swept on by, and I have no doubt that fifteen minutes later she worked out something profoundly insightful to say.

"Beograd has fallen," Qathir said one night, just before locking the door to my little room. "Jia has fled to Isdanbul. They say she'll sue for peace."

"Is that so."

He nodded, a little disappointed at my neutrality. Then: "We used bombers. We firebombed the city. We did it with planes."

These ideas – bombers, planes, firebombing – were strange and unfamiliar to him. He was not sure what to do with the words, how to form them, but he knew they were important, and impressive, and it made him feel good to say them. I opened my mouth to lecture him on heretical history, on twenty-five thousand burned to death in a single night during the wars of our ancestors, on how adult bodies shrivelled to the size of children as the water boiled from them, of how fleeing refugees tumbled from lack of oxygen and just lay there, rag dolls, before the coming inferno. I tried to explain how after a great fire there was often a great rain, but he had already locked the door and pushed the bolt home, so I lay instead on my back, and wondered if I should cry, and felt absolutely nothing at all.

The next day, Colas found weevils wriggling through his rice stores. There were millions of them, tiny brown bodies grown to a colony within the sacks. He cursed and swore and was uncertain if he should throw the bags away, not knowing whether he would get more. But someone upstairs heard of his plight and swore that he would receive more rice soon, have no fear. The household of Georg Mestri would not go hungry. No one would go hungry, in this great new age.

"Lovely bit of protein, your weevil," chuckled Makris, but he was only half-laughing, and as I stirred the mulching, steaming compost in the vats out back he shuffled a little closer and whispered: "Do you bless people, priest?"

"No," I replied, not looking up from my work. "I was never that kind of priest. Besides, all a blessing is good for is reminding you not to be a total pillock, so I'm not sure if it's up your street."

He bristled a little at this reply, but didn't retaliate, and later helped me scrub the greywater vats, which he had never done before.

A sliding back of bolts in the dead of night. Perhaps the city is flooding again; perhaps tonight they will kill me. A woman I half-recognised, Georg's new assistant, guardian of his door, stood in the light.

"Come with me," she barked, and I wished for the little kitchen knife I'd stolen three days before, which I could not now easily reach without revealing its hiding place.

"What time is it?" I asked, and she didn't answer.

Upstairs, and up again, to a little reception room that I had visited two or three times before to deliver the fruits of the kitchen. Pillows across the floor, a low table with a single cut flower in a jar on it, mementos of past glories of Bukarest on the wall. There was only one person in the room – the one person it was always going to be. The woman gestured to a pillow opposite him, and I sat cross-legged on it, as she closed the door behind her.

Georg, awake as always when all normal people should be asleep, sipped tepid tea, cup clasped between both hands, and watched me over the rim. I adjusted my posture, stretched out some of the hard constrictions of my brick-like bed, shuffled a little to the left and a little to the right, like a cat kneading an unwilling lap into submission, folded my hands palm on palm, and waited.

Finally he said: "You heard?"

"No. What haven't I heard?"

"We bombed Beograd."

"Ah – no, I heard that. Firebombed, yes?"

"Yes."

"How'd it go?"

"Well, all things considered. It was our first time attempting incendiary carpet bombing. The information we had was piece-meal. Our scientists had to work hard to fill in the gaps, do a little thinking for themselves. I think the exercise was good for their imaginations."

"I see. What next? Nuclear?"

"Hardly. It wouldn't achieve anything strategic. And there are too many barriers between us and fissionable material. Temple was wise to keep that secret to itself. Although I do sometimes wonder as the war progresses, do you think the Medj will tell Jia how to do it? Where to find radioactive rocks, how to split the atom?"

"Nuclear winter would not please the kakuy."

"Please. Let's not pretend Temple was ever interested in the spirits. Everything you people have ever done has always been about man – keeping mankind in its place, obedient, passive."

"Yes." His eyebrows flickered up in surprise at my admission, and I shrugged. "The kakuy never gave a damn for individual humans or individual hearts. Prayers are just words, thrown up in hope. Temple teaches people to pray in order to shape what we hope for. It is pure social engineering. But fundamentally, Georg, with your pissing little ego-bastard war, you are doing precisely the same thing. You are trying to redefine what people hope for, and what they fear. And at the end of the day, I would far rather hope for the kakuy not to burn us all to ashes through the general equality and peace of all humankind, than the destructive nonsense you're selling."

He nodded, eyes running to some other place. "Interesting."

"Is it?"

"Not philosophically, of course. Philosophically you're a coward, blighted by your own internalised inferiority. But it is interesting to hear you speak as yourself – as an inquisitor. I thought you didn't believe in anything at all."

"I have seen the kakuy too," I said, and surprise flickered like the first spark in a fire before he hid his face again behind a bored smile. "Belief doesn't really come into it."

He nodded again, neither here nor there. Perhaps there should have been words, and for a moment there were none. Georg smiled at nothing much, nodded to himself alone, put down his cup, straightened, hands mimicking mine in his lap – consciously or not, I couldn't tell.

"There is disease in Vien," he said at last.

"What kind of disease?"

"The water. Something in it. A heavy metal of some kind – they think perhaps lead. It is rational to say that there was error at the armament factories further upstream. They have released chemicals into the water, a toxic wave. You can even see it, the land turned scarlet. The responsible parties have been reprimanded. But in Vien they say it is a curse. That the kakuy are doing this to them. What do you think?"

"I think it is a spill from the armaments factory," I replied. "I think you have poisoned your own land. I think when children start coughing up black, when the old die in the heat and the young die in the cold, it will be because of what you did."

"And the kakuy?"

"I do not think they will help you. More I cannot say."

He nodded, staring straight through me at his own thoughts. Then: "We dragged a few priests out of prison. Some of the novices. Got them to say their prayers. They seemed very keen to help."

276

"I imagine they would be."

"By spring, Jia will be on the other side of the Bosphorus. It is a good natural border; she will sue for peace then."

"Will you give it?"

He shook his head. "Farii wants us to, of course. Even Kun Mi is getting anxious. But they both are beginning to understand the inevitability of this conquest. To win, we must tear down the mountains and the forest; the mechanics of this war require no less. The land we move through is turned to ash, and it does not heal. The water in Vien is the colour of piss, and it does not heal. We cannot stop at the Bosphorus. We must keep going. We cannot let our army disband or our soldiers go home. If they go home, they may find that they do not have a home to go to."

"So your plan is . . . what? Circle the world for ever, conquering everything you can and leaving devastation in your wake? Cross the sea to Amerika and sweep across that land too until it is poison? Then come back to Maze and hope that enough time passed while you were warring over there that the forest over here has grown? That is a terrible plan."

"They say in Amerika," he mused, "that the people hunt kakuy for sport. That the walls of the militia forts are hung with severed limbs of ghastly creatures."

"They say that Amerika is nothing but yellow dust and acid," I retorted. "That beasts bigger than men roam the ashen wastes with stinging tails and poison spit; that in the spindle forests where once men cracked the earth in two, the trees have grown fingers that claw at travellers and pull them into a bloody, boiling earth. So much for that."

He sighed, reached for his tea cup, stopped himself, folded his hands again, turned his head as if the corner of the room had suddenly become fascinating. "Men and the kakuy," he sighed. "What a frustrating thing."

I waited, motionless, eyes tired and body buzzing.

"I'm told that when you were young, the forest burned. That's correct, isn't it? The forest of your home town, burned to the ground."

My heart is a great hollow thing, bloodless and dry. I licked my lips, tried to swallow this knot back into my chest, nodded. "Yes."

"Is that why you joined Temple?"

"No. I don't think so."

"Then why? There are a thousand more interesting things to do with a life than offer prayers you know will never be answered and indoctrinate children to bow and scrape to worms."

I thought about it, then said:

"Firstly, I ended up an inquisitor, not a Medj. I was never pastoral in my inclinations. But you're also wrong – Temple is fascinating to work for, if you have the right mindset. In the burning, humankind was taught that human nature was fundamentally violent, selfish. That the most successful iteration of a life was to make wealth and be, in some manner, superior to others: socially superior, superior in fame or standing or riches, in material belongings, in ruthlessness. We turned our backs on the essential truth of our species, which is that we are co-operative. Oh, certainly, some societies dabbled with the idea that individuals were nothing but servants of a state, to be crushed and disposed of at will, forgetting that the state is made of people too. And others embraced the notion that individualism rose above all else and forgot that it was society that carried these lone heroes up. So when the forests burned and the seas turned to acid, the great authoritarian states said, "Our power is more important than our people," because by then such bodies were nothing more than monarchies for a corrupt few, ruling in the name of the many. And the individual heroes who had been lauded for their wealth, their ambition, their beauty or their fame . . . well, they rushed to protect what they had too, leveraging their meagre social capital to protect themselves from the dust and the famine while all around them everybody died.

"How easily humans are swayed. When things go wrong, we look to the oldest story of all – to a messiah, to a change – and it doesn't matter what that change is so long as we believe there will be a hero. But it took three thousand firefighters to hold back the fire that burned through my childhood, and in the end

278

it was the rain, not a hero, that doused the flames. In the burning, we raged, raged, raged against the truth that the fire and the sea were stronger than us. Temple taught us that humility before the storm was sacred – but it failed. Temple has failed you. You believe that you deserve what you receive, that you alone are the hero of your story. And yes, sooner or later, the only way to prove this is by conquering your fellow humans, mastering them with your strength. And when that is done, when humans are cowed and there is only annihilation, the only thing left is to kill a god. To kill the kakuy themselves. And that is how you will die, if you're wondering. You will end raging against the sky that fed you, the river that gave you life. That's why I joined Temple. To be part of something more."

Georg nodded again, without seeming to see me. "I think that's fatalistic shit."

I shrugged, and the motion felt like a sudden freedom, a giddy escape.

"You think so little of people – you talk about 'care' but you think so little of them. I think you're a coward, Ven of the Temple of the Lake. Kadri Tarrad. I think you hide and hide and hide, because you can't accept that some men are great, and others are small, and you have always been tiny. That's what I think."

"In that case, you may as well shoot me now. Why haven't you? I doubt you're keeping me alive for the conversation."

"Not for that. You bore me. You can go now." One hand had drifted to his leg, rubbing along the old knife wound, the great scar I'd carved through his flesh. "Go back to the kitchen."

I rose, put my hands together, bowed a little, saw the flicker of something in the corner of his lips that could have been anger. Let myself out and barely noticed the bolts slide shut on my prison door.

279

Chapter 47

I guessed when the first day of winter was, and pressed my hands together, and gave thanks for the seeds hidden beneath the snow, the wool grown thick on the back of the sheep, the summer water now falling in winter rain, the wood from the curling tree and the stars spinning infinite overhead. The next day, Colas fired two of his staff. There was less food to cook, less food to eat; the season of abundance was ended.

I was summoned, bare-footed, almost every night to wait at Georg's table. I did so in silence, serving cold meat when commanded, topping up wine and flasks of tea. It was easier to serve than to clean. Farii avoided meeting my gaze, when she ate with the men of Maze. Merthe, wearing the uniform of a woman who'd been promoted, stared with open-mouthed amazement whenever I entered the room until nudged by Farii to hide her dismay. Kun Mi watched with open dislike, until one day she blurted: "Why. The shitting. Do you keep *that* around?"

It takes the table a moment to realise she is talking about me. Conversation lulls, eyes drifting to my previously unregarded form, a pitcher of water held in both my hands. Georg, picking at hot dumplings from his bowl, doesn't look up as he says: "That is Pityr. He works in the kitchens."

"He's a political. Your enemy. You let your enemy serve you food?"

"Yes."

"Why?"

"Because it pleases me."

Kun Mi glowers down the table, and for the first time it strikes me how young she is, how utterly unequipped for the role chosen for her. Georg sighs, lays down his spoon, rises awkwardly, unable to disguise the slight wince of pain as his weight shifts from one leg to the other. "Look." He puts one hand across the back of my neck, pulls me in closer to the table as if he might embrace me. "He is entirely docile." Shakes me a little, side to side, and, when nothing falls out, laughs, pushes me away.

"Isn't he dangerous?"

Another sigh from Georg. He gestures me closer again, and closer I come. "Pityr," he sighs, "put the pitcher down."

I put the pitcher down.

"Pityr," he sighs, "kneel."

There is a kitchen knife taped to the small of my back. I have been carrying it for the best part of a month, and no one has bothered to search me or my room since summer, given how passive I've become. Given how little I have fought back. I kneel at his feet.

"Pityr," he tuts, holding out one foot. The boot itself is clean; Georg almost never leaves his office. I bend down and kiss it, hinging at the hips, bend back up, wait. Georg smiles, ruffles my hair, turns back to the assembly.

"You see? Harmless. He knows his place. There are masters in this world, and there are the mastered. Pityr understands this now."

I study his knees carefully. One trouser leg sits a little lower than the other, his weight favouring his uninjured leg. It is a subtle imbalance, but there if you bother to look for it. Kun Mi grunts a kind of approval, and with the tips of his fingers Georg gestures for me to stand. I do, pick up the pitcher, resume my station. A few people stare. Merthe cannot hide her sympathy, or her disgust, but directs it to her plate. Farii does not meet my eye or the eyes of anyone else.

*

281

A new guard on my shift, replacing Makris.

She does not say her name, does not sit on the now-habitual stool by the sink in the kitchen but stands, bolt upright, hands behind her back, to attention. She remains like this for two days, until finally it is time for me to wash and clean myself in icy water. She stands by the washroom door as I strip and rub thin soap into cold fingers, eyes straight ahead. Then she crosses the floor so fast I don't even hear her coming, and I think this is it, she's the assassin sent at last to kill me, the end of everything, but instead she pushes my head towards the sink, presses her lips in close and whispers:

"There is a traitor in Council. They call him Pontus."

I brace with both hands against the sink, try to see her face in the tarnished shard of mirror, soap drying to scaly prickles on my skin.

"Do you know who it is?"

I don't answer, and after a moment, she lets me go and marches back to the door to resume her station as if she had never moved. I carry on washing myself, pull my clothes back on, go back to work.

The next day, she was not on shift.

Nor the day after that.

The day after that, I turned on the taps in the kitchen and the stink of raw sewage filled my nostrils, hot and clinging to the back of my throat. I turned the taps off, waited in Colas' office for him to come to work, let him shout, was sent back to my cell; nothing to do until the water ran clean.

When the door next opened, it was her again, and downstairs there was a truck from I knew not where, fresh water flowing from a nozzle at its back. She watched me carry buckets all day, and never once moved to help, until one time when I slipped and sloshed liquid over the edge, and Colas shouted – although by then he was simply shouting at the day, at the world, at this stupid fucking universe – and she passed me a cloth to clean it up, and as she bent down she said:

282

"Who killed Ull of Lyvodia?"

I laid out the cloth on the floor, watched it absorb the spill, squeezed it tight into the bucket, laid it back down in the next puddle. "Georg, obviously. *Obviously.*"

"If we get you out, will Jia listen to you?"

I shrugged, kept on scrubbing, without a word.

In the evening, Georg summoned me again.

The villa was empty; no point feasting while the taps ran with shit.

He drank from a bottle of wine – safer than even boiled tea – and, when I sat opposite him, gestured to the inkstone in front of him. I picked it up. It was archaic German. I put it back down. "I don't translate for you. Shoot whoever you want."

"I don't need you to translate it; I know what it says. Read it."

Cautiously, I picked it up again, half reading while watching him over the tip of the stone. I had not read any words other than the hygiene instructions in the kitchen for months. The feel of it was like an alien crawling into my mind, a strange and disturbing notion settling over my consciousness. It was an ancient tract on the benefits of innumerable forms of implausible healing. Lavender oil and tea tree; cloves of garlic and sweet-smelling citrus. Crystals and diets and vapours of dissolved salts. I put it down, met Georg's eye, shrugged. "And?"

"What do you think?"

"I think if you like nice things it's perfectly nice. If you want to cure your cancer, it's nonsense."

"It was very popular, once upon a time. As science became more impenetrable, people turned to simple, comforting things. They said they were getting back to nature; that it was not mankind's place to inoculate against disease or edit DNA, that it upset the order of things."

"You are using a facetious example to prove a lacklustre point," I retorted. "You are conflating the genuine human urge to have control over one's life with the heretical urge to conquer the world."

"And when men cannot control their world, what things

might they do? Temple took away man's control, his freedom to choose; it made us no better than beasts. You inquisitors should have realised long ago there would be consequences."

"We always want the pain to end quickly – it is so much easier than hard work," I replied. "And if Temple takes away your right to set the world on fire, so be it. Grow up. Find some other game. Why are we still talking, Georg?"

He licked his top lip, gestured at the bottle of wine. "Pour, please." I refilled his cup. There was none for me. "Do you think about him? Pontus, I mean?"

I lowered the bottle slowly, rested it on a stained round coaster, folded my hands in my lap. "I don't."

"You think perhaps you are alike? You spied on me, he spies on Jia – and so forth?"

"That would be presumptuous. Presumption would make discovery harder. You know that, I believe."

"You must have suspected someone, by the end. Who? Krima, perhaps? Pav?"

"No."

"No?"

"No. I know two things about Pontus – that they got to me before I got to them, and that they have limits. Pontus makes mistakes. It took them far too long to catch me. This implies that even my speculation, my casual suspicions shared over a cup of tea, might offer actionable intelligence. So no. You can talk about Pontus if it makes you feel big, but you'll excuse me if I only pretend to listen."

"You're going to die in Bukarest. You know that."

"I think it's very likely."

"Don't you want to know who Pontus is, before the end?"

"If I'm to die, what difference would it make?"

He clicked his tongue in the roof of his mouth, sat back a little in his chair, the wine untouched, hand rubbing unconsciously along the hidden scar across his leg. I watched for a moment, then asked: "How's the war going?"

"We're winning. Decisively."

"And yet the taps run with shit."

"That is not Jia's doing."

"You say that as though it makes things better. I thought you'd rather deal with humans than something worse?"

"I am dealing with humans. Stupid fucking humans all the time."

"You look tired. Perhaps a little peace might do your side the world of good too."

"Honestly, I could do with a break. I've had terrible trouble with the staff."

"I always had you down as a seaside kind of man. Rolled-up trousers, an oversized tome about philosophy in dappled shade while drinking fruity concoctions."

A tiny smile, the first real smile I thought I'd seen for a very long time, flickered across his face; it was gone almost instantly, as if ashamed of its own merriment. He shook his head. "Skiing. I grew up in the mountains, you will recall."

"Ah yes. You saw the black wolf."

"And it can die. I know that. I know it."

"The wolf can. I imagine even you haven't worked out what to do about the mountain."

"Goodness, you must have worked hard to keep your sanctimony in check when you were Kadri Tarrad."

"Honestly, it was the least of my worries."

"Does it make you feel bigger? Does it make you feel brave?"

"You misunderstand. Your mistake is imagining that in understanding the size and majesty of creation, the wonder of this world and the richness within it, you become small. A tiny scuttling thing without centre, without identity and form. You fail to see how, in grasping your small place within this life, you become part of something that is so much bigger than you could ever be when you were being a hero alone."

His brow flickered in brief exasperation, his hand pulling unthinkingly back from his leg. Then he gestured briskly towards the door, all conversation over. "Piss off, Ven. You bore me."

I rose, bowed, palm pressed to palm, and let myself out.

Chapter 48

Two days later, a mudslide buried half of Tseonom. I felt the panic rise as news came over the radio, bit back on asking, what about Tinics? What about my home? It was only a few kilometres away, was it hit too? Who of my clan had cycled into town that day? Who of my hearth were visiting the clinic or taking tea with friends when the world turned brown?

An inquisitor hides their home, hides their fear, but I was an inquisitor no more, so I stood squarely in Colas' door and said:

"Tseonom is near my home. May I see?"

Colas opened his mouth to say the usual – piss off, Pityr; get lost, Pityr – then didn't. He handed me his inkstone without a word, sat back and waited, arms folded and tea cooling on his desk, until my reading was done.

It was the mudslide that caused Farii to rush through the censorship law, if one could say Farii was still in charge by then. But she was too late to stop the news from Tseonom, and as word spread of liquid death shaking itself loose from the hillside and tumbling down faster than a speeding train to drown and crush those unfortunate enough to be in its path – children and adults – one of the cooks grabbed me by the arm and hissed: "Is it the kakuy? Did they do this? You were a priest – are they punishing us?"

"Deforestation often results in mudslides," I replied, not looking up from the sink. "Roots hold the soil together and a rich, bio-diverse landscape is better at absorbing excess water from rain than bare, dry earth."

He blinked at me in surprise, bewilderment, then gripped my arm a little harder. "Are the kakuy punishing us?"

I sighed, laid the dish to one side, rinsed it clear. "Deforestation often results in mudslides. Humans and kakuy are born from the same ecosystem."

He shook his head in disgust, threw a cloth over one shoulder like he would whip himself with it, and turned away.

After that, the radio broadcast mostly patriotic songs and excerpts from speeches on the theme of mankind ascendant.

On a day without name, I went out in bare feet from the back door of the kitchen to find five feet of snow blanketed over the biomass chutes. I listened for the sounds of the city and found that it was quieter even than the winter wood where once the icy kakuy had prowled between the trees. Colas, peering through the door behind me, arms wrapped around his chest, swore, marched back into the kitchen, re-emerged a moment later with a shovel and, to my surprise, his own winter coat. "Just a loan, dimwit," he muttered. "Can't have you dropping dead." I put on the coat, the smell of vegetable stock and toasted nuts warm in the collar, and when I looked at him again saw, to my astonishment, that he was taking off his shoes. "What?" he snapped. "Don't think I'm going to kiss you!"

His shoes were far too big for me, but they offered some meagre protection for the next few hours as I flopped and slapped around, trying to pile the snow as evenly as I could so the delivery trucks could get through. When I was done, I felt warm all the way through my body, until I moved my hands near a stove and nearly sobbed at the pain as blood returned to frozen flesh. Colas let me keep his coat for another hour as I chattered and shivered in the warmth, before sending Qathir to reclaim it and his shoes, which he did with something that was almost an apology.

*

In the dead of night, the bolts slid back on my door.

"Come," snapped Qathir, clearly as annoyed as I was at being disturbed.

I shuffled after him through the winding corridor to the floors of green carpet, swaying a little for the first few steps as blood sloshed back into sluggish limbs. I didn't have tea to deliver, or any duties to perform, but was led as usual to Georg's study door, where Qathir knocked three times, awkward, a crunching in his shoulders that was unlike any of his normal leg-lolloping ease, before letting me in.

I stepped inside to the warmth of a fire and the smell of strong black tea. There was Georg, looking perhaps a little tired – did Georg ever look tired? Farii, sat in a corner, shrinking into it as if she was little more than an old pillow on a tatty chair; Merthe, face wrinkled with distaste; and Yue.

Yue, dressed in winter grey, black hair in a skin-tugging bun on the top of her head, an inkstone held so tight I thought she might crack the case. She rose as I entered, looked me in the eye, then looked away.

"Happy?" asked Georg, legs stretched out across the low tabletop. He made it look like a sprawl, hiding the discomfort in his injured limb, turning disadvantage to a performance of strength.

Yue looked back up, met my eye again, and I didn't know what I saw in her face, had no idea what was running across mine. "Not yet," she replied, forced strength, forced confidence, what in the name of sunfire was she doing here? "Ven – I need to ask you some questions. Are you being mistreated?"

"What?"

"Yue is here to negotiate," Georg intoned, a ritual chant from a priest who had long since lost interest in the things he said. "Jia wants to end the war."

"*What?*"

"Ven." Yue's voice snapped my full attention back to her, standing stiff and straight as a turbine in the storm. "Have you been mistreated?"

"Yes, of course," I retorted. "I mean – of course. But I'm far less dead than I should be. What in the name of sun and fire are you doing here? Yue?"

"I have been sent to discuss preliminary negotiations."

"Secret negotiations – Jia doesn't want the Provinces to know how badly she's losing," corrected Georg.

"Kun Mi isn't exactly able to reject Jia's overtures," I snapped back. "How is the water in Vien these days?"

In her little, huddled corner, Farii has closed her eyes, like one at prayer, detaching herself from this place and moving to another world.

"A prisoner exchange will be part of any negotiation, you have my word," Yue declared, and she didn't believe it would happen, and said it anyway.

"Ven is fine. Look at him – he's practically glowing with health. Beograd burns and the kakuy sleep. What could be better?"

"You shouldn't be here, Yue."

"I am here to negotiate," she repeated, staring now at some place behind the back of my head, as if she didn't see me at all. "The treatment of political prisoners and prisoners of war will be a priority. Thank you."

For a moment, the two of us stood there, like opposite ends of a broken bridge. I do not know how long we stood, and it was probably only seconds. It was perhaps long enough for a forest to grow. Then Georg puffed in exasperation and snapped: "Well, off you go, Ven. There's a good pup."

There is a knife strapped to the small of my back. I have learned how to sleep with it inches away from my fist. Tonight is the night, perhaps. Tonight I'll do it, leap across the room in a single bound, drive the blade into the soft pink flesh beneath Georg's chin, push it all the way up, through the hollow of his windpipe and across his vocal cords, so no one would hear him scream, just like the inquisition taught us, just like they always said I might need to do, in order to be a really good pacifist, a really generous priest.

Then I'll take Yue's hand and, having heroically put her in

danger and ruined everything, I'll valiantly rescue her from this locked-down city in my bare feet, and we'll run away to the forest and everything will be astonishingly terrible. And she will never forgive me, and quite right too.

So much for magic. So much for prayer.

I turned my back on them all and went quietly back to my prison cell.

Chapter 49

In the evening, when all else is sleeping, I drink tea with Georg.

It has become something of a habit of his. At first, it was an accident, a casual little thing; I cleared up plates after another late-night session, and suddenly I was the only person there.

Then I was the last person left again, and again after that, and I began to think he was calling for me to come from the kitchen a little late, so I might be the last person left behind, and then I was certain of it, and I poured floral tea without a word into a cup the colour of sage, and sometimes he talked, and sometimes he didn't, until one night nearest the year's end he said: "We'll never let you go, Ven. Whatever Yue says. Here until the end."

I shrugged. "I know."

"Why don't you do something?" A flare of anger, frustration – I hadn't seen it so bright or hot in him before. "Why don't you try to escape or fight? I know you can fight, I've seen it. Do something!"

"I'm not sure what you expect. In Vien there were protocols, safe houses. I had shoes, support. You want me to cross the mountains in winter without any shoes?"

"Then die fighting. Die doing something!"

"Assassinate you, perhaps? I've thought about it. Killing you is far more strategically important than killing Kun Mi, given she's just a little prancing tool. But then I have to wonder ... what would she be like if you weren't pulling her strings? What would the Brotherhood do next? I'm not at all convinced that stabbing you actually helps, though of course if the situation swings too far, I'll be sure not to let you know."

For a moment, he balanced between anger and surprise. Then he slumped back into the couch, and was tired, and hurt, and he laughed. He waggled the empty tea cup in his hand; I refilled it, poured myself a cup. Outside, the city was quiet, scuttling, beetle black.

"Temple makes people dumb," he pronounced, head back across the top of the couch, neck exposed. "Spends so much time telling us to be grateful, to accept, to ... hug a cockroach or whatever ... that no one ever does anything. No sense of ambition. No sense of purpose. I was worried you were the same."

"You mistake a short-term sense of gain for a long-term plan. So long as you don't mind thinking a hundred years ahead, Temple is a sparking dynamo of activity."

He snorted but did not deride. Then: "We've put a bounty on kakuy."

"That's phenomenally dumb, don't you think?"

A half-shrug. "It was Kun Mi's idea. You have to let her have a few, sometimes, just so she feels useful. All across the Provinces, people are shooting monsters and beasts, stringing them up at the temple door."

"Bears and wolves? Please. The forest will burn and the field will wither – I have yet to see you shoot the sky."

To my surprise, he nodded. "In the burning, things were simpler. The gods slept – or rather, the gods were on our side. They were human creatures, invested in the welfare of humanity above all else. The superior species, the chosen ones. They felt rage, and love; they were there for each unborn child, sent angels and demons to harvest souls. Then the kakuy woke, and suddenly the gods were real, and they cared as much for the ant as the human, and we weren't special any more."

"You know it's better that way, don't you? Being part of something bigger than ourselves – it is better."

"I think the best of all would be a world without gods."

"Then you're fine. The kakuy aren't gods. They are ... no

292

more and no less than the wind and the sea. Georg? You do understand, don't you?"

He nodded again, slow, and I thought he would speak, but the nodding was heavy, lolling. I rose quietly and, for the first time in my life, saw Georg Mestri sleep.

Balance the kitchen knife in your hand.

Here, this way, this gleam of the blade. Quick and easy, through the windpipe; no one will hear him scream. Steal his shoes, steal his coat. I know my trade. Everything changes. Everything dies. I do not fear dying. I am not sure how I feel about killing. Kill him now, to protect a world without killing.

Vae is pulled into the river, Lah's final breath is my own, Yue walks away, ash in her hair and boots crunching on snow. What would they say, in this slumbering calm?

Do it, thunders Georg. Do it, do it, do it!

Lah sits in that place in my mind where my own thoughts should be, says nothing at all, and pretends to meditate.

Temple has an inquisition; is there not a kind of confession there, an admittance that even the gentlest of doctrines sometimes run hard into a crueller reality?

I have never seen Georg sleep before. He seems almost human.

Do it, don't do it, do it, don't do it, what will be the consequences in a hundred years' time? What will be the consequences now, when they kill me slow?

I wander to his desk. Let my fingers trail over the apparatus of his life. His inkstone is secured with a passcode and a biometric sensor. His drawers contain the bare minimum for a functional spymaster – stationery, a charging cable, emergency solar battery and torch, a gun. One is locked, but largely for show. I remove the drawer above it and reach down inside the hollow to release the locking mechanism from the inside. Slide it open.

Inside are a map and a little bee-like drone, its translucent wings folded, the solar panels on its back streaked with dried dirt and rain. Its belly has been opened to release the package it carried within, which lies next to it now – a tiny capsule, a similar size and shape to those I used to hide around Vien, all those winters ago. I unscrew one out of curiosity, find it empty, turn it this way and that, imagining its contents, the tiny coils of film it once held. Put it back. Unfold the map. It is scrawled with markings added and erased, lines flowing across Magyarzag, heading south through the ruins of Beograd, towards Isdanbul. If I had a camera, I would photograph it; all very interesting stuff that Nadira would love to . . .

I do not, and she is dead.

Instead, I smooth it out a little on the desk and study its movements. Georg should be piling in his troops to Plovdiq, but a loop circles a place further to the southeast, bypassing the city altogether. Martyza Eztok, inquisition archive. I press my index finger into the name, watching how the joint bends back under pressure, then release it, fold the map, close the drawer, lock it, return to Georg on the couch.

He looks, for a brief moment, innocent. He should have been a surgeon, perhaps, or a teacher. There is another life where I would have felt confident with my life in his hands.

I drape a blanket around his shoulders, tuck it in so the cold night does not disturb him, leave him sleeping, tea cooling on the table, and let myself out.

That night I dreamed of dust.

I dreamed of coal tunnels beneath the earth, of being trapped in black, of coughing blood, of flashes of light fading and the smell of sulphur.

I dreamed of bones and children, of the forest and the flood. Temple was wrong not to build shrines in the landfill mines and the poisoned places; we were wrong not to honour the hands that made the burnt yellow wasteland. They had made it for the sakes of their children, after all.

I dreamed of a world on fire, and no rain came.

Chapter 50

The end came on New Year's Eve.

I had no idea it was New Year's Eve until Colas, drunk, raised a bottle and hollered, "Happy new year, Pityr! I thought they should shoot you but actually, I've almost grown fond of your miserable weasel face!"

Then he poured wine for one, drained it in a single gulp, burped and started singing a Temple song, until Qathir hissed that they didn't sing those any more and to keep his mouth shut in case someone upstairs heard.

In the shuttered temples, Medj should have been giving talks on renewal, change, on letting go; on seeing the past with clarity, the future with hope. Instead, the radio waves played newly penned patriotic ditties, of which most would vanish without a trace and maybe one or two had a catchy, key-changing chorus that you could whistle under your breath.

"Tum tum te tum, brotherhood and man, something something, beneath the crimson tum te tum ..."

The radio in Colas' office had been getting more bilious as the war crawled on, no sign of peace, no sign of Yue, no sign that her visit to Georg's office had been anything more or less than another one of his shows of power, another stupid game. "I say we firebomb Isdanbul," offered a punter, hungry, cold, looking for something to blame. "If it saves one of our boys' lives, it's worth it! Council should just give up; that's the only reasonable thing to do. Why are they hurting their own people like this?"

The winter cold froze the pipes, put thin sheets of ice on top of even the steaming biomass pits, locked the fog in the evening air as if time had stopped when it should have billowed. It crept into every corner of the kitchen and house, sapping away warmth like a closing shadow, until everyone huddled against the stove in tighter and tighter knots, driven to it by a dark they could not overcome. Knives moved slowly down the chopping board, fingers turning numb. People shuffled, lead-legged, through the streets, blood a thick treacle in stiffened veins. Someone said there were parades later, military marches, but no one seemed very keen. The dignitaries of the house were gone elsewhere, to the Assembly perhaps, to the old, wide boulevards to watch soldiers tramp up and down through the snow; to the front lines, wherever they were. The kitchen turned the lights down early, and Colas reluctantly poured a dram of alcohol for all his staff, forgetting me, and managed a few inspirational words.

"Well, yes. Well done. We'll do better next year. To peace and victory."

"To peace and victory," mumbled the kitchen, and no one met anyone else's eyes as they drained their thimbles down.

I did not stay awake for midnight. An early night was a blessing, a rare, gorgeous relief. I lay, cold, knees tucked to my chin, and thought I heard drumming and a distant snatch of song, but then the wind turned and carried it away again, and I was so deeply asleep when the bolts drew back that I didn't wake until she shook my shoulder and called my name again.

"Ven. Ven!"

She hadn't turned on the single light in the room but, behind her, her guard carried a wind-up torch, light turned to the floor beside my face. I blinked bleary recognition into my eyes, and, not quite understanding, murmured: "What in the name of sun and moon are *you* doing here?"

Farii smiled. I could not remember ever having seen her smile, not even when Ull was alive. It was the tired grin of an ageing

296

grandmother who has just been given the bad diagnosis she already knew.

"I wish to defect to the Council. And you wish to escape, yes?"

"Wouldn't say no."

"I think we can help each other."

There comes a time when there is no time left.

So here, without thought, without time to think about the consequences, only actions:

Change into a new set of clothes, military, so warm, so thick, woven wool and the smell of nothingness, of not-sweat, not-steam, not-oil, not-damp, not-mould, the smell of clean is distracting, mustn't get distracted.

Put on a pair of shoes, and for a moment I fumble with the laces and can't quite remember how this is done. There is something alien, heavy, pinching and hard wrapped around my feet; was this how shoes always felt?

Put on a low captain's hat, tucked down tight to hide as much of my face as possible. Turn the collar up on my coat against the cold and prying eyes. Farii's guard is called Yoko; she has a car prepared. We are just going to walk out, the three of us, she says – it is fine, everything is settled. No one will stop us. Come, come. The time for trust is now.

I hesitate in the doorway, and Farii looks back at me, already halfway out, a winter coat wrapped tight around her body, deer-skin boots up to her knees. "They will kill me too, when they find out," she declares, voice of stone. "They'll kill me, just like they killed Ull, and make it look like an accident."

I nod, dig my hands into my pockets, tuck my chin into my chest and follow her out.

Chapter 51

Stairs I've never taken, down to a courtyard I've never been in. There are some guards here, huddled together against the cold. They look up, see Farii, who nods at them once, and they look away. They do not glance at me, do not question my presence. There is an electric car charging off a portable battery by the gate; I wonder where they had to drag the battery from, now that the local solar panels are covered in snow and the turbines are still in the hanging air. The front of the car has a little flag stuck to it, a stiff, pointed thing depicting the seal of the Lyvodian Assembly. Yoko sits in the front, driving. I climb into the back, the narrow middle seat separating me from Farii as the doors lock shut.

We slither away in an electric hum, wheels drifting a little on settled black ice, crawling no faster than walking pace for the first few streets as we slip and slide towards the broader, gritted cyclists' roads.

It is starting to snow again. The shutters are down against the cold, and very little light peeks out through the slats. Every other street lamp has been extinguished to save electricity in this end-less, deadening winter. We pass a shrine, the gate chained shut, a scorch mark up one wall where someone tried to start a fire. I do not remember the city being so big, so tall, so dark and deep. I do not remember it being so quiet.

We do not talk until we reach the wider streets, where finally enough ice has been cleared for us to pick up speed. We pass a military convoy heading the other way, and I feel nauseous, and Farii doesn't turn her head, doesn't blink, doesn't seem to see anything at all.

A line of conifers, fat triangles rising to a bent-tipped point where the weight of ice has begun to drag the branches down. The shape of bicycles buried together beneath a mound of snow; who knows when someone will come to dig them out? A single restaurant, the lights somehow burning by a cleared rectangle of pavement, a sign on the door telling customers that if they want beer, they must bring their own.

A checkpoint, set up beneath a bridge to protect the soldiers guarding it from the worst of the wind. There are three bicycles waiting to be cleared, and for a moment I remember fleeing the city with two novices, back when the bells rang across the water. That escapade didn't end well; right now, it is impossible to imagine this one will be any better.

Yoko wound down her window as the soldiers approached, torchlight flashing onto our faces. She handed over three sets of papers and, with a little incline of her head towards Farii, said: "Chief Minister, on business."

Farii did not look at the soldiers who nodded and saluted her. One of the papers had my photo on it. I didn't know where Yoko had found it, or what it claimed. An officer said: "Good trip, Minister," and pulled off an awkward salute in the style of Maze, a gesture he still wasn't quite used to yet. Yoko smiled and, slipping the papers back into her pocket, wound the window up as we accelerated away.

On the fast road, heading east. The snow is heavier now, and we are one of only a tiny number of vehicles braving the night. All I can see through the front windscreen is falling white, picked out in cones of headlight, and the barrier of the road to our left, which we follow through a nowhere nothingland of black. The internal lights of the car are few – a couple of diodes on the dashboard, and the occasional sweep of white from a vehicle

299

attempting to travel the opposite way. The cyclists have given up, the lanes empty and bicyclesarais full as we pass, little outposts of orange light.

Yoko said: "We have enough to make the meet, but if they're not there we'll have to recharge."

"They'll be there," Farii replied, with the conviction of one who needs it to be real.

"How are we getting across the border?" I asked. "I know that Farii's face counts for a lot, but they won't let her anywhere near the front line."

Yoko answered when Farii didn't, eyes still fixed to the road. "We're going to the sea. It's all arranged."

"On both ends?"

A little intake of breath, a pause. "Council has a much stronger naval presence than either Maze or Lyvodia. They dominate the Negara Sea from the Bosphorus to Azchov. If we can get past the Brotherhood patrols, we'll be fine."

"That sounds fantastically risky. Why haven't you contacted Council already? Arranged extraction?"

"Georg has a spy in the Council."

I let out a sigh, a little nod. "Pontus."

"Georg knows everything Jia does. Everything. We can't contact Council until it's too late for Pontus to stop us; do you understand?"

"I do."

She nodded, once, sharp. "The southern army is going to defect. Merthe thinks she can bring nearly all the divisions over. We have plans, documents."

"You want to barter this for your lives."

"No." Farii had been so stiff for so long that I was almost surprised to hear her speak. For another moment she didn't turn, still regarding the darkness outside; at last, she angled her shoulders away from the window, and like the blades on top of the windmill slowly turned her head to look at Yoko, then at me. "No. It is not about our lives. I am going to be arrested as a prisoner of war; I know that. If I am lucky, Jia will see the benefit of keeping me as a figurehead, a . . . a symbol of reformation that says whatever she needs me to say. If not, she'll lock me up somewhere while she works out the best use of me. I accept that. It's the correct thing to do. We need to end this war. Kun Mi cannot accept peace. She cannot. It is impossible."

"Why?"

Now she looked at me fully, and I thought there were tears in her eyes.

"In the north, the land is burning. The river is on fire and they can't put it out. They say the kakuy are awake, they are striding from the forest in plague and ash. There are bodies in the streets in Vien, frozen in the places where they died, soot in their mouths, hands clawed, still scratching at their skin. I've seen them. Their blood is ebony. It's starting in Lyvodia too, the plague coming out of the trees like mist. We haven't seen the worst of it, but it's coming. The kakuy are coming. Georg cannot stop them, no matter how hard he tries, so he has to run. Outrun the kakuy. They cannot stop fighting, because if they stop taking land then they will be trapped between the kakuy in the north and Jia in the south, and if Jia doesn't crush them the kakuy will. The Ube is on fire. We were wrong."

I have never seen a river burn, though I remember how orange it looked in the light of the blazing forest.

I wonder whether it burns because the kakuy will it, incensed to rage by the arrogance of man, or if Georg's engineers didn't know what to do with all the waste products of their military factories. Not that it makes much difference, any more.

Farii's hand had fallen on my arm, gripping tight, the strangest human contact I had felt for months. Her eyes were wide, reflective baubles in the gloom, her fingers digging into my putty flesh as if looking for bone. I put my left hand over hers, squeezed once, and she didn't let go.

"You were inquisition. Jia will listen to you."

I sighed, and suddenly all the exhaustion that had been pushed down beneath the simple imperative of moving, of getting out alive, swelled up like the foaming tide. I slumped back into my seat, pulling my arm free of Farii's grip, pressed cold palms over aching eyes. "All right. What's to lose?"

Chapter 52

There are things which were not real, when life was lived in a kitchen, that now are.

Exhaustion, so profound and bone deep that the idea of moving my legs at more than a tree-stalk shuffle seems impossible.

The shrivelled, wrinkled, old-man hands in my lap that I hardly recognise any more.

An ache in my back that has been there for months, but which I got used to when it ached on the floor, ached by the sink. Now it aches in the soft back of a seat, and I don't know if I can handle it.

Emotions, loud as the shingle sea. They are unacceptable on the job. Farii cannot look away from the dark, in case someone glances at her with sympathy, understanding or forgiveness. Such things would break her in two, and there is no time for that now. So Georg kills Nadira, shoots Lah in the head; so the temples burn; so you run across a moonlight field and are caught. These things are facts and factually you will deal with them, because there is stuff to do. Stay alive. Hope is a trap. Sorrow is self-pity and unproductive. Watch the night; stay alive.

I can hear my heartbeat in my ears, feel it in my chest, in my back, as if bone curled like ageing paper. If I listen to my breathing, as the Medj taught, it gets faster and faster and faster, and that definitely wasn't in the manual of serene practices for stable minds. Wind and earth, I need someone to try and shoot me now. A good punch to the face. Anything to focus the mind, turn off this rising fire in my brain that is, and cannot be, spinning on the edge of hysteria.

Twenty kilometres from the sea, a checkpoint. Bored soldiers given a boring shift. We slow. Yoko hands over papers, says Farii's name, and this time, rather than scamper in deference, the men shine torches in our faces, squint at me, at Farii, until she snaps: "Are you quite done?"

"Sorry, Minister," grumbles one. "Restricted area and that."

"I understand." Prim, tolerant; a hint of annoyance. "If it will make you more comfortable, please call ahead to the general. He knows I'm coming."

The soldier is a little older than his peers. He has the face of one who knows the language of wolves, and loves them, and has no illusions that they might ever love him back. In Temple, there were often men and women such as he, people of the deepest mountains, who would stop to eat and drink at the shrine, where no one troubled them much for conversation. I wonder what dragged him to this midnight road.

The snowfall has slowed, just the occasional white flake that could be stirred-up powder shook from the ground below rather than falling from the sky. Boots crunch like breaking bones; Yoko idles out the inspection by scraping ice from the wind-screen, scratching away tight curves of crystal, the motion hiding how close her other hand rests to her gun.

The soldier compares our documents with a colleague. They nod, flick through photos, nod again. Return them to Yoko, who smiles without a word, slips them into her pocket, climbs back into the driver's seat.

"Go slow," says the man who ran with wolves. "It's a treacherous road."

The battery is nearly empty, a little warning light flashing on the car's dashboard.

Yoko checks her watch, then checks it again. On the third time checking it, less than five minutes have passed, and she is clicking her teeth, jaw popping back and forth like a hungry eel.

The restricted zone runs all the way from checkpoint to sea. Signs along the road warn: permits must be shown at all times. A few watchtowers have been erected, staring down to the water. Perhaps the Council will attempt an amphibious assault; perhaps they will bring the fleet in from the Middle Sea up the Golden Straits and try to land an army behind Brotherhood lines. Such things have been considered in great depth, it seems, but no one really believes Jia could pull it off. She is far too tepid for such things, the generals say. Perhaps.

Pontus would know, and therefore so does Georg. These towers are for people fleeing, not an army come to invade.

Four kilometres from the water's edge, we pulled into the open doors of an empty barn by a small hearth. One lamp shone in a round, storm-scarred window, a crown of icicles hanging down the edge of the roof, tinged blue where the light shaved the ice. We slithered into the gloom, cut the engine. Yoko murmured: "Wait here," and got out, pulling the wind-up torch from her pocket to shine weakly round the space. A flurry of movement, a slap of heavy foot, then a mumble of recognition, a hug, perhaps, in the darkness; the doors were drawn shut behind us, another torch flickered on, flashing across the interior of the car before pointing to Yoko's chest. She called: "It's clear."

My legs were so stiff I had to lean on the roof of the car for a moment while blood shuffled back into them. My eyes hurt from sleepless blinking. Farii squinted round the gloom of the barn, then, turning to the man who'd greeted Yoko, put both hands together in front of her and bowed. "Sea-kin," she said, and there was a weariness in her voice, a bone-deep exhaustion that ran deeper than anything I could imagine. "Thank you for your shelter."

A man in a dark blue domed hat with padded wool over his ears and a hanging oilskin down the back of his neck, heavy beige coat puffed up to a fluffy ball around his frame, returned Farii's bow. His face was deep olive stained pink by years of sun bouncing off the reflective sea; his eyes were heavy and his smile long. "You lot look miserable," he blurted. "Can't be having that."

His name was Khasimav, and he kept a messy hearth.

"Yes, just move that – oh, put it on the floor – yes, don't mind – no, careful, there's – yes under that, if you just – sorry – we don't get many visitors."

The hearth usually held ten or eleven people who worked the scrubby fields that rolled down to the sea, or rode the fishing boats when the weather was calm. But the war had changed that, turned the edge of the ocean into a mess of wire and permits, patrols and passports. In the end, it had been easier to leave than stay – some joining the army, others slouching off to friendly hearths further from the front lines, where they didn't have to account for their every movement to the midnight men with guns.

Only Khasimav and his wife had stayed, and, finding themselves with sudden space, they had taken the attitude that they could fill it. Strewn across the pantry floor were half-mended nets and broken crab pots, clogged engines and vats of stinking algae oil, buckets still reeking of fish gut and shredded scale, boots discarded by the door and torn trousers with needle and thread hanging from the half-finished patches around the knee. Khasimav dug out a few cushions from amongst the debris, slapped them hard against his thighs in clouds of dust until he felt they were suitably plumped, gestured us to sit. "Please, please!"

In the centre of the room he boiled tea, black as seaweed, slightly salty on the tongue, and added a splash of something dubbed "a little helper", which burned on the way down, tingled hot in the stomach.

Outside, a single bell jangled, disturbed by unheard footsteps in the snow. A patrol car chuntered by, the smell of petrol suffocated by the still, frozen air. Dawn was lost behind a bank of cloud, an obscure greying out of black, smothered in a blanket sky.

Yoko said: "When do—"

He silenced her with a flap of a huge, starfish hand. "The tide,

306

the tide. We are scheduled with the tide. You can sleep a little now, if you want. Sleep a little."

Farii was already half-nodding, chin jerking in short, electric pops. I found a corner near the stove, dug myself out a little nook as I had so often done in the kitchen, unashamed. Yoko did not move but held her empty cup between two hands as if its lingering heat were the last embers of a dying star. I lay on my back, staring upwards, heart in my ears.

Above my head was a sign, ancient rusted metal polished into something sacred. Written on it were words in an archaic tongue – not one I knew fluently, but with bits and pieces I could grasp. Khasimav caught me staring, blurted: "Ah, my relic! It has been in the family for generations. It brings us fortune. Do you know what it says?"

"'No parking, 8 p.m. – 6 a.m. Fine of 6000 hryvnia.' I can't read the rest."

Khasimav stared at me, eyes so wide I thought he had choked on his own tea. Then he laughed loud enough to bring an army down, and held his chest tight in case he burst with it, and spluttered: "You're funny! Isn't he – that's so – you're so funny!" and kept on laughing until he cried.

In the middle of the night, I dream of fire without end and wake to see Farii, eyes wide next to me, gripping my arm tight. There are pins and needles in my fingers; how long has she been lying next to me, short of breath?

"The bomb," she whispers. "The bomb. The bomb that killed Ull. The bomb."

I prise my arm free of her fingers, wrap her hands in mine. But she is half-awake, half-asleep, eyes still staring at nothing. I try to find words to comfort her, and cannot, and eventually roll over to sleep and dream again.

Chapter 53

Khasimav roused us a little before midday, arms heavy with clothes.

"Yes, no – yes that will – try this one!"

We changed, sluggish and weary, into the garments he offered. Farii vanished behind a huge green hat, peaked to a cone above her coiled-up hair. Yoko wrapped the cord of a slick brown apron around her waist three times, tying it so tight I thought her eyes might pop. I swam in trousers far too big for me, pinched and wriggled into a shirt a little too tight. When we were assembled, we were three utterly misshapen sailors, as natural on the ocean as a whale to the mountain.

"You look perfect!" Khasimav exclaimed, and none of us believed him. "Just do as I say and everything will be fine. Easy easy!"

He slung nets over our backs, loading up Farii with so many buckets and bags she was less woman than walking luggage rack. "If anyone stops us, I'll do the talking," he chirruped, opening the door of the hearth into a day of crystal white and smoke-drenched grey. "Ah, see, we are blessed! The kakuy gave us fog!"

I shuddered, unsure if it was at the sudden cold or the brightness of his voice, only slightly muffled in winter weight, and followed him out the door.

The path from the hearth to the sea was a little track, impossible to see beneath its fresh covering of snow save by the spindle-black thorns of half-buried shrubs sticking out either side of it, like a saluting line of skeletons, guiding us to the water's edge. The fog thinned as we approached the shore, blasted into licking smoke by the wind off the ocean . Cracked slabs of thin ice had formed at the top of the beach, creating a shattered skin of dirty mirror above black stone, and where the soldiers had laid barricades against a potential invasion a second wall of frozen foam had grown like fingers from the earth.

Towards the water's edge, the pounding of the sea had kept the ice from forming in more than tiny, quickly made, instantly broken salty lumps. The fishing boats of the village lay just above the high-tide line, most covered in oiled cloth and listing to one side, untouched and smothered in caverns of snow. Khasimav's was one of the few that still stood propped up above its wooden tracks, mast tipped back onto the deck, propeller hooded and still. It seemed, to my uneducated eye, little more than a skiff for catching the occasional tiny shad from a school of summer fish. I looked from it to the waves as they crashed into the shore. The sea popped with white, hissed and grumbled as if some hidden city were trying to rise from its depths, only for the raging water to smother it down again. I wondered what the kakuy of this place might be; black, perhaps, as its ancient namesake, with the shining body of a jellyfish that, when it reared up, revealed teeth of basalt beneath its belly, stinging tendrils longer than a city street with barbs flecked bloody. Temple had always taught that the kakuy of the sea had been the first to rise in anger during the Burning Age. The cataract-eyed spirits of the deep were less patient than their kin of earth and stone.

"Up, up, yes, come on now!" chanted Khasimav, hoicking Farii up the side of the balancing little vessel with the dignity of an errant pup. "You, priest, and you, soldier! We push!"

I followed his flapping directions, pressing both hands to the ice-crackling, salt-crusted, sea-bitten timber of the boat, and made to push when a voice called out: "Khasimav! Good neighbour!"

It was not an unpleasant voice, young and familiar, but I saw Khasimav tense, smile locked and eyes tight as if stung on the leg by stingray barbs. He glanced up to Farii, on the higher deck of the boat, and half-nodded. She returned the gesture, then vanished from sight, slipping down into the interior. Then he turned, waved at the approaching figures coming through the thin shore mist, called their names, hollered: "And greetings to you too, kin of sky and sea!"

There were two of them, both dressed in mismatched, over-sized military uniforms, as if the quartermaster who'd bartered for their gear had turned up drunk to the storehouse and come away with the dregs of some other war. Neither could be older than twenty-one, and though both had pistols on their hips, only one carried a rifle, the barrel glistening with frost. The boy who'd called out Khasimav's name approached, smiling brightly – a neighbour, perhaps, who'd joined the army for something to do, a bit of a laugh. Behind him, a woman with a young face that looked already like the older woman she would become, picked with furrows between her brow and curls around the corner of her mouth, managed the barest quiver of a smile to Khasimav before her eyes swept, grey as the ocean, to Yoko and me.

"Heading out?" asked the boy. "Got the authority?"

"When don't I?" demanded Khasimav, in the voice of one who had played this game before. He started patting his jacket, his pockets, fumbling around with exaggerated deliberation, while the boy smiled – a familiar ritual between them.

"Who's this?" the woman barked, and I looked away from her moon-rock stare.

"Oskar and Lin; my new crew. Oskar, Lin – say hello."

"Hi," I mumbled, as Yoko tilted her chin in greeting, and for a moment I thought she was going to betray us with her sheer bearing, one military woman greeting another. But Khasimav interjected with a cry of "Ah, here!" and pulled out a tatty piece of much-fumbled laminated paper. "Wouldn't catch me going to do my job without *au-thor-is-ation*, would you?" he drawled, the grin of a troublemaker still yearning to make trouble.

The boy read it and, still playing the game, laughed and waved it in Khasimav's face. "I don't see any mention of your friends here."

Yoko had a gun, hidden somewhere in her clothes. It would take her a while to get to it, of course; I'd probably be expected to tackle the woman with the rifle. If I was lucky, the cold would lead to a misfire, but even then I'd need to get to her before she had time to react and just hope Khasimav had the good sense to hit the boy before he could draw his gun. The odds were even, I concluded, given the distance between us.

"Of course they is – look, there. Two crew."

"Ahul and Pree are your licensed crew, not these two."

"Come on, it says two crew – two crew! I've got two crew."

"Khasimav . . ."

"You know what it's like. Ahul's gone done a bunk to be with his family, may skies rain upon him, and Pree's still holed up with his leg. I gotta go out with someone – or do you want to explain to my missus why you let me drown alone?"

The mention of Khasimav's missus clearly had a stronger effect on the boy than any imprecation or threat of thunder. He glanced at his colleague, who was perhaps less aware of the wrath of Khasimav's wife, then with a sigh passed the tattered authorisation back. "Get them registered," he barked, trying to infuse his voice with an authority that had already been lost. "Next time I can't look the other way."

Yoko's shoulders rolled down like the last curl of a breaking wave against a rocky shore. I realised I'd been leaning my weight into my left leg, ready to spring across the distance between myself and the soldiers. "You were always such a nice boy, when you weren't a little shit," Khasimav cackled gleefully, which was the closest I imagine he ever came to saying thank you.

Chapter 54

I was a terrible sailor. I had grown up far from the sea and couldn't work out what was worse: huddling inside in the black depths of the ship as it rocked from one imminent disaster to the next, straps straining to hold the buckets and nets tight against the swaying, sure-to-kill-us-all hull of the boat, or clinging to the side on deck, both arms wrapped around the railing as the horizon dipped below my feet, then rolled up to tower above my head like the sky itself would fall. Only Khasimav's utter disregard for our obvious imminent doom convinced me that we weren't, in fact, about to be drowned in a hurricane. Seeing my foam-drained, burning face as I leaned over the side unable to puke, he guffawed, "Nice day for it, priest!"

"I'm a spy, not a priest," I growled, but he couldn't hear me over the slapping of the sea.

A little boat on a big ocean need not meet a storm for the experience to be thoroughly vile. I drank the ginger tea that Farii brought me from the gloomy cabin below and wished that the salt would freeze on my face to take away some of the blazing nausea prickling over my skin. When I finally did throw up, Khasimav gave a great cry of victory, as if some glorious rite had been accomplished akin to the first prayers at a newly raised shrine, and I felt a little better.

We sailed south into the night. The sun did not set as a visible orb; the horizon was an endless curve of bruised grey-brown, smeared with muddy blue. The cloud was so complete that it diffused everything into one formless monoculture, hard to tell where sea met sky. For a while, it was the grey of the pale flagstones of the Temple of the River; then it was the grey of the dry pebble shore; then, it was a thick, boundless slate; and finally, a starless, shapeless, worldless void.

Lost in a forest, Lah would say, you are not alone. All around you is life, living.

This doesn't play well with my ego, I'd reply, and Lah would laugh.

That, they'd say, is precisely the point.

In the middle of the sea, the only sounds are the water and the wind – endless, gobbling, slurping hunger of sucking and spitting, slapping and slithering against the side of the boat. Khasimav has turned off all illumination but a little red light in the pilot's cabin. Farii sleeps below, Yoko keeping watch at the prow as if she might still be able to do something against some invisible threat, as if the gun buried in her clothes has any power against the ocean. With no light, no distinction between sky and sea, we are floating to some deathly land, cut off from the rest of the world, and it is terrifying, and, in a way, it is perfect peace.

For a moment, I am not afraid, and Georg is not inside my head. I had forgotten how good it felt to be free.

Beneath us, there is life. Schools of silver fish feasting on white-fleshed critters that forage amongst the clawed scuttling things of the shallow sea floor that hide from the bug-eyed creatures of the darker depths. The giant squid, flushed crimson, care nothing for the deeds of men; neither do the kakuy that lurk, tentacles spooled around some volcanic vent, at the very bottoms of the great oceans of the world. They only cared when the world was burning, and their wrath was as disinterested, amoral, potent and inescapable as the tsunami upon the gentle shore.

Instinctively, I offer them a blurted prayer. Not for blessing or safe passage – these words have no meaning to the great spirits of the deep – but for my own peace of mind, and in wonder at what it is to sail across the surface of a forest.

Then Yoko was by my side, shaking me, and I must have dozed, and she was whispering: "A light."

I followed her finger, and didn't see it at first, then it flashed, tiny and white, and we both turned to look at the red glow of the pilot's cabin, and Khasimav's face was drawn and tight.

"A ship?" Yoko asked, as we slid into the relative warmth of the little square of buttons and wheel that was Khasimav's domain.

"Yeah."

"Another fishing boat?"

"Maybe. Probably not."

We watched it a while longer. I imagined it getting bigger, nearer, knew I was imagining it, that paranoia was seeped into every part of my being. Then it was definitely bigger, nearer, not paranoia at all, a true thing, and Khasimav barked: "You, hold the wheel steady," and I did, while he and Yoko scurried to raise the triangular sail, the boat lurching to the side as it caught the wind as if stung by a wasp. This done, Khasimav scuttled back into the cabin, took the wheel from me and turned so we caught the wind, deck creaking and fabric snapping taut. "Check the fuel," he murmured to Yoko, who nodded once and vanished below decks. I waited, back pressed to the wall of the cabin, smelling the sudden stench of processed algae as Yoko pulled back canisters and peered into pipes, before she returned and said, "We're full now." Khasimav grunted an acknowledgement.

From below, Farii emerged, blinking and weary, her face an alien thing in the eye-aching glow. "Problem?"

"Maybe not."

Yoko prodded one finger towards the light on the horizon, perhaps a little nearer than before, perhaps no. Farii licked her lips, inclined her head and watched, the fear deep in her too.

"Wind's in our favour," murmured Khasimav, an attempt at brightness that his voice couldn't quite carry off. "And she's not exactly a racer."

For nearly half an hour, we four stood pressed tight in the cabin, sea-sickness forgotten as engine and sail ploughed us through the dark. Then Khasimav, the only one with the right to say it, said what we all knew: "She's coming for us."

"Patrol ship?" asked Yoko, sharp, hard.

"Maybe."

"How long do you think until they reach us?"

"Maybe an hour."

"How close to shore can we be in an hour?"

"Not far. But we're still a long way north."

"Can we call for help?"

"Sure – if you want every ship on the sea to know who you are."

"Ever been stopped by a patrol boat before?" I asked.

"Only once, random check."

"Did they search the ship?"

"Yes."

Farii said: "Send out the call."

Khasimav sighed, tutted, reached for his radio with a muttered "My missus is going to kill me."

"Wait." I caught his hand. "Don't mention Farii."

"Why not?" snapped Yoko. "You know they're looking for her."

"Yes, but they probably don't know she's on this boat. If you say her name out loud, every Brotherhood vessel in a hundred miles will come crashing down on us."

"And every Council ship too, no? We're in contested waters, and they have the stronger fleet."

"Even so – we want Council ships in force, not Brotherhood."

"That's a fine trick if you can do it," muttered Farii, a flicker of her hand to the radio. "I'd love to see you try."

I took the microphone from a sceptical Khasimav and intoned, at his command, the distress call, a call for help across all frequencies, Council fleet help us, help us, sounding far too calm for anyone to take us seriously, I felt. Then I added: "Yue Taaq. This is a message for Yue Taaq. It's Ven. It's me. Help me."

315

Chapter 55

A chase at sea is a slow affair.

I hunched over the radio as Yoko and Farii watched the light growing nearer, highlighting form. A patrol vessel for certain, a huge kite sail unfurled above its prow, its engines growling, the scars of bio-resin glistening in jagged lines across the hull. We ran before the wind, but the bigger ship was faster, the pinpoint shards of a dozen smaller lights visible along its hull and deck as it drew nearer. It hollered at us over the radio, then by loudspeakers, sound blasted to semi-incomprehensible gibberish by the sea, and we ignored it. It flashed lamps at us in a dizzying pattern of ons and offs, which Khasimav roughly translated as a command to halt and the sailors' equivalent of cussing.

When it fired the first flare, I was astonished to see the ocean revealed in pale red beneath us, to find that we were still on the surface of this planet, not spinning through some endless void but bound by the laws of common nature. Khasimav clicked his teeth, sighed: "Warning shot next," and barely were the words out of his mouth than an unseen explosion smacked into the night, and a hundred metres to our right the water slapped up in a gout of white, reflective crimson and black.

"59mm gun," mused Yoko in the voice of one who had sat exams on the topic and not particularly enjoyed the experience. "Probably a Kraken-class cutter."

"Is that good?" I asked, and she did not answer.

Another shot broke the sea to our right, the retort quickly

swallowed by the rolling water. Behind us, the host of little red lights rose up from the deck, swerving in the wind like battered seagulls before regaining a little stability as the ship launched its drones towards us.

"It's all right," Yoko murmured, as they rose around us. "They're mostly just for surveillance."

"Mostly?"

"Bet you wish you were a proper priest now," rattled Khasimav, all grin and no humour. The next warning shot hit so close to the prow that we bucked above the shockwave it sent out like riders on a wild horse, and Khasimav uttered a curse of ancient foulness between gritted teeth.

"They're launching inflatables," murmured Yoko, head turned to the ship behind us.

"Oh good – they're not going to blow us up, just shoot us."

"I don't know if they'd rather arrest me for a public trial or shoot me and lose my body," mused Farii, with the stiffness of a critic discussing a show of dubious quality. "That decision may be above their pay grade, of course, which makes it more likely they'll at least arrest me first."

"They don't know you're here," I offered brightly, "so they'll probably just shoot you by mistake." Yoko glowered, but Farii gave a single burst of laughter, that died as soon as it had lived. I shrugged. "Sorry. Just saying the obvious."

"Why would you do that?" scowled Yoko.

Outside the cabin, a drone was bumping against the turning side of the boat, its red lights flickering as it buzzed up and down like a curious bird. Farii flapped one hand at it instinctively, a leader used to the world obeying her every whim, then scowled when it managed to settle on the deck, a squat, hunkered thing, blinking at us with its salt-scoured camera. Behind us, the two boats lowered from the larger ship hit the water, rising high on a wave before dropping so fast one soldier nearly lost their seat in the churning acceleration of the moment. They cast off from their tie lines almost together, rushing towards us low in the water, a single headlamp on each prow, vanishing and reappearing with each swell of the sea. "Inflatable" seemed an odd description for the speeding vessels tearing down on us. A resin hull on a black carbon weave, the only part that appeared inflatable was a band of soft padding around its rim. Everything else was spotlight, soldier, gun and carbon.

Yoko had her weapon drawn, but Farii put a hand on her arm, shook her head. "There's still a chance," she breathed. "I'll talk to them, I'll . . . there's still a chance."

No one in the cabin believed it, and no one said a word.

As the first inflatable drew level, Farii stepped out of the cabin, hands raised. I don't know what she called out to them, but her words were lost across the water. She called again; again, the words were snatched away. A bump on our right announced that the other inflatable was against us, reaching up with hooks to snag onto the side. Khasimav throttled down the engine, shaking his head. "Well," he sighed. "I was hoping to die better."

"How better?" I asked.

"You know when you fall asleep after sex?"

"Seems harsh on your sexual partner."

A head popped above the railing on the right, followed a second later by the barrel of a gun, lugged up awkwardly by someone barely holding onto the hooked ladder that swayed and bounced against the tug of the sea.

"At least the fishes will be well fed!" chuckled Khasimav as the soldier rose a little higher over the side, struggling to hoick their gun into a more threatening pose.

I heard the whistling of the shell a second before it struck – or perhaps I imagined it, my mind retrospectively seeking to make sense of chaos. The quality of its impact was different from the warning shots that had been blasted our way – less of the sea tearing apart, and more fire and air compressing and expanding in a crimson rush. The flash of light was bright enough for me to briefly pick out the inside of the cabin, and it took me a moment to realise that the shell had fallen not on us but behind, a few metres off the prow of the closing cutter.

"Mother of—" began Khasimav. He didn't have time to say

anything more before the next shot landed, now to the right of the enemy ship, which lurched as if shoved by a playground bully, lights flickering, several going out. The one soldier who'd nearly made it onto the deck slid as Khasimav slammed his hand against the throttle, jumping us back into motion, the hooked-on ladder slipping along nearly the whole length of the railing as we chugged away from the stalled boats by our side. Farii, having perhaps thought twice about negotiation, launched herself back into the cabin as we accelerated, blurting: "Who is firing, who is firing, *who is* . . ."

Either side, the inflatables revved up, easily matching pace, and finally from the left came gunfire, rattling down the side of the ship. Khasimav let go of the wheel, grabbed Farii by the top of her head and dragged her down to the low cabin floor in a bundle. I lurched to one side, grabbed the door on the opposite side of the cabin as glass crackled and smashed, and tumbled out onto the deck. Yoko was a few feet in front of me, crawling on her belly, eyes fixed on the ladder still attached to our right-hand railing.

For a moment, I thought the marine who'd been clinging on so desperately had let go, dropped back into the water. Then a hand crawled its way over the side of the ship, scrambling for purchase, and Yoko had her gun drawn. She waited, until the top of the head was visible, and emptied out three shots. One of them missed, and I don't know if the second hit or if the shock of sudden motion and violence was enough, but with a gasp and a splash, the marine let go, tumbling backwards into the ice-black water below.

Another burst of gunfire to our left, ripping along the side of the boat, smashing out the thin red light of the cabin and raining glass and splinters across the deck. The drone that had managed to land crawled a little to one side, curious as a cat, the camera turning to examine the scene, before Yoko kicked out hard and caught something that cracked and crunched. The drone wheezed and tried to take off, but one of its four blades wouldn't spin, and it tipped itself onto the side and spun, an upturned beetle bouncing on the deck.

Another smack in the night, another whistle and thump of cannon. I peered up, tried to see its source, thought I saw the flash of something far-off and huge, spitting pinkish-sodium fire. A cloud of little red lights was drawing near from the same direction – more drones – a sudden burst of motion above us as the cutter's drones detected the incoming swarm. This time I heard the crack as the distant ship fired, the shell striking something on the patrol vessel behind. I half-expected an explosion, the rupture of a tank or some profound sign of desperation. Instead, I heard the creak of carbon bending out of form, the crack of resins popping and the sharp, hard snicker-snacker of the biopolymer frame ripping like ribs shattering along the spine.

Then the little cloud of cutter drones rose higher, and I saw something yellow flash in the belly of a half-dozen of the buzzing machines.

The bombs they dropped were tiny – little more than marbled grenades – but they were enough. Some fell on the deck, some fell in the water around, picking apart the dark in yellow-white, tearing through the hull of Khasimav's boat like bolts through tissue. The world rocked, lurched to the left, tipped down hard. I tucked my knees under my chest and wrapped my hands over my head as the world around crunched and spat sizzling salt, heard cries below and the creak of resin tearing apart.

Then the new batch of approaching drones was on us, and suddenly the air above was full of little machines smashing head first into each other like drunken wasps, of blades caught on blades and swirling, whining, messy flight. I smelt burning algae oil and resin-coated timber, tasted acrid smoke and heard a high-pitched scream in my left ear that drowned out even the sea. I moved one hand, and it seemed to travel incredibly slow. Tried to move it faster and knew that, though I had the physical capacity, the connections between mind and fingers weren't having any of it, that my mind couldn't conceive of motion.

Another smack of light, another crump of something striking the cutter behind, and this time I knew it had hit something flammable because there was a rising mirrored glow across the ocean, picking out the shape of the drones falling like spring blossoms from the sky. Yoko's head emerged in the reflected darkness of a world turned to fire, and she was dragging Farii behind her by the armpits, hissing something at me which I couldn't hear over the singing in my ears and the tearing of the sea. I wrapped one arm around Farii's chest and heaved, and was surprised to feel how wet and cold Farii was, catching in the light of a rising flame behind us a smear of blood across Yoko's face as she mouthed more inaudible commands.

The inflatables either side of the ship had stopped firing, and as I dragged Farii further up I felt the boat tip, a little at first, and then irrefutable, nose-first, and thought for a moment we were being sucked down beneath some great wave. Now the shape of Yoko's mouth had some meaning to it, and I dragged Farii backwards, hooking one loose arm across my shoulders and hauling her towards the stern, which began to rise like a closing drawbridge. Glass tinkled all around, and I managed to gasp: "Khasimav? Where's Khasimav?" but Yoko just grabbed Farii's other arm and pulled her, nearly climbing now over the wreckage of the cabin, away from the sinking prow. I looked down into the blackness of the stairwell at our backs and thought I glimpsed a face turned up to me, eyes closed, something dark smeared across its skin. The water rose from beneath it, through the shattered hull, briefly floating it a little nearer to me, or perhaps I was descending as the ship did, all things in motion. I wondered if the fish gave thanks for the food they ate. I wondered if there was a place at the bottom of the sea where the creatures of the deep sucked on the white flesh of the kakuy as it flaked away like dust in sunlight.

Then the water was rising, pricking at my toes, and I scrambled hand-over-hand up the sloping deck of the ship towards the stern, where the motor had lifted from beneath the sea, blades still spinning on loose momentum, flopping in the air. I crawled onto the hull of the boat itself as we began to tip over, grabbing the limp form of Farii and hauling as Yoko crawled up with me. A drone fell into the water a few metres away, sending up a splash that shivered through my sodden clothing. In the distance, the patrol cutter was now thoroughly on fire, the two inflatables rushing back towards it to rescue the sailors jumping from its blazing decks.

I didn't know how we would fall, what it was like to be on a ship that was drowning. Yoko was shaking Farii, snarling, wake up, wake up, and I saw Farii begin to blink, fingers tightening around her loyal guard's arms – perhaps too late. The boat jutted upwards, stern tipped to the sky like a spire, and balanced there for a moment. Perhaps we would stay like this, bobbling like a bottle through the sea. Then it began to roll to the side, and I jumped, hurling myself as far as I could as the broken vessel slammed into the water, hull stuck up into the sky and the flat, shattered deck below, flinging us into the darkness of the sea.

Chapter 56

In the winter wood, the kakuy makes no sound as it moves across the snow, nor leaves any trace.

Tseonom is buried beneath a mudslide, and in Tinics the forest burned, and the kakuy too.

The forest will return, of course, one day. One day, there will be nothing but forest on the earth, when humankind is gone. The forest was always better at co-operation than man.

In the middle of a sea that is a forest, teeming with life, I felt the boat lurch beneath me and jumped as far as I could away from it, into the frozen water. It hit like stone, slamming the breath out of me, flushing up my nose and straight into my brain, as if the fluid sac that cushioned my skull would pop. I pawed at the surface of the water as I fell and kept on sinking. I had not imagined it was possible to be colder than the deepest ice of the winter wood, but in this place my arms were wet sand, everything so slow. To drown starts as a constriction in the throat, a closing in of the chest, a popping of final breath from nose and mouth, as heaving, heaving, heaving as you swallow down the need to swallow for air, a gasping, gasping, gasping, each moment this will be the one where you inhale the sea and fall like a stone, fingers of blue, eyes of red, at least this will only be a moment, only a little, terrible moment.

I hit the surface, hauled in air, bobbed down, water rushing up my nose, brain sloshing in salt, surfaced again, tried to swing my legs up, to float, saw the sky lit up in silver-white as something burst in the night, and in that instant understood the need to scream, not in fear or hysteria but pure frustration, pure inexpressible grief that this was it, this was how it ended, a thing without words, all the things I'd never do, never be. Managed to surface again, tilted my head back so that water sloshed into my ears, choked out water and felt my back begin to bend upwards, every breath shivering fast as a mouse's racing heart.

There were no stars above. The waves pitched me side to side, constantly tipping a mask over my face so I spat salt and blinked fire, unable to predict their motion, arms floating like flotsam, dead in the water. The burning patrol ship was a pyre in the dark, bright enough to cast a glow on the low sky. Somewhere nearby, there was the ship that had destroyed it, coming for us, but whether it was five minutes or five hours away I couldn't tell.

I tried to fight the sea, to find stability in its motion, and couldn't. I tried to relax into it, to let it carry me, to trust that I was still here, still breathing, still alive, and for a little while that was easier, and I could focus on shivering, shivering, shivering, until I wasn't shivering any more. I felt my shoulders roll down from my ears, as Lah had taught us back in the temple – let go, let go. These stories you hold in your body, these stories you hold in your mind – let go. Every time my ears rose and fell between water and air, a roaring, then a silence – so much easier to listen to the roaring than the silence, but listen, listen, here it is, that quiet place that is inside as well as outside. I felt the salt seep into the raw skin of my scrubbed red hands, and for a while the fire was pleasant, cleansing, and I knew that I would heal, if I did not die, and I didn't want to die, and I knew as surely as anything I had ever known that I might, and I might not. Both these know-ings seemed so certain, so absolute, it was almost impossible to imagine they could live together, and yet like the turning of the sea they rolled over me. Now I breathe and will live; now I do not and will die.

Around the wreckage of the cutter, the inflatables circled, their mission of murder now one of rescue. The pilots had their orders, but a higher order prevailed on the ocean: you saved your friends. The sea would take care of the rest. The sea did not care for prayers.

A light shone in my eyes. I tried to swat at it, irritated, and found that my left hand could move, a little, a limb far away, belonging to another nation state. The light blinked at me, then swung to my right, then swung back, then swung once more to my right, like a hungry gull circling the smell of snacks. I looked where its light flickered and saw a shape, stable and black in the moving world. The drone danced towards it, bright across the water, picking out the upside-down hull of the fishing boat. It stayed there, hovering, light flashing, waiting. I tried to kick, on my back, a little, and didn't go anywhere. I rolled onto my front and tried to swim, the head-spinning, shoulder-slapping crawl of a creature not used to water. That took me a little closer, but so slow, so slow. The distance could not have been fifteen metres, and it was swimming through tar, swimming with the great kakuy of the deep already half-entangled round my legs, her tentacles embedded through the tears in my skin, running all the way into my veins, the two of us already one, like the roots of the tree in the soil of the earth. My arms smacked the water like falling sacks, fingers spreading and wrists buckling beneath the waves, and it occurred to me that if I didn't make it to the hull of the broken ship I would drown for sure. Five metres, and a wave tipped my head under, and when I surfaced again I didn't know where I was, couldn't see, couldn't make my legs kick, arms drag, then saw the light of the drone again, bright white to my right, and threw myself towards it, fingers stretched, as if I could bridge the gap by will alone. A turn of water picked me up from behind and pushed me, sudden, hard, towards the inverted vessel, and my fingers scrambled and scratched against the scars of old, scrubbed-off barnacle, ancient algae and newer resin.

I lunged to find a grip, nails cracking as I slid, the same water that had flung me forward trying to haul me back. Lost my hold, fell into the water, swallowed salt and felt my eyes tear as ice filled my nostrils and every tiny tube and empty corner of my skull, then was pushed forward again, grabbing for the thin ridge of the hull, right hand missing, left catching by a few curled fingers as I clung on. I felt every muscle in my arm stretching, could feel the tiny tendons where they joined, the full length of each fibre and the shape it made as my fingers began to give way, sliding back like a broken lock. I began to fall, for the last time, and as I did a hand, an arm, a shoulder flung itself up from the other side of the hull and caught me by my forearm as I slid backwards, holding me tight.

I looked up, saw the pallor of Yoko's face as she draped herself, bent almost double over the ridge of the hull, bringing her left arm round to join her right and snatching me before I could fall. I swung my right arm round, held her tight, and for a moment the two of us hung in precarious balance on the slippery, tossing curve of the boat, her feet braced as I slithered and slipped to some sort of purchase. Her eyes were wide, black in the brightness of the drone's light, her hair riddled across her face like seaweed. Somewhere, once, she had perhaps seen images of drowning women returned as demons, flesh bloated and skin shining, swollen, liquid things, and in her face now was a determination that bordered on fury – not her. Not today. I did not know when I had last seen – if I had ever seen – such a will to live. I tried to remember what that might have felt like, to steal a little of her fire for my own, and as she pulled me in I let myself flop beside her, our grips changing as we locked tight into a woven fortress of hand and arm, sprawled across the tipping hull of the boat.

There was a ship. It was a destroyer of some kind, low in the water, hull textured like the skin of the shark. It launched inflatables, as the cutter that pursued us had, two points of bright white rushing towards us across the sea. Above, drones zipped back and forth over the water, one staying bright above us, catching us in a fountain of light. Another hovered some twenty metres away, and I thought I saw a glimpse of someone in the water, and couldn't be sure, and didn't know, and held onto Yoko like a child in the forest.

Don't let go

Vae

Don't let go

Behind us, the cutter burned. In the past, the fires would have been of gasoline, yellow and black. Today, it is the pop-pop-popping of biomatter resin straight from the vats, flares of pale pink and flashes of spring-soft green, bursts of lithium white and blue when the batteries burst, the stink of silica, black puffs of carbon from melting fibres and withering corn as the cellulose bonds in the hull started hissing and breaking apart in the flaming, turning air.

Yoko, I whispered. Yoko, listen to me.

Listen to me.

If I die here—

Don't you die, priest.

If I die – I know who Pontus is.

I know who

I know

I know why Georg never killed me.

If I die—

You're not going to die, shut up!

You need to remember this.

You need to tell them.

I leant in and whispered a name in Yoko's ear. And it was the breaking apart of a world, and it was the great rain that follows the endless burning fire, and she nodded once, and we held on tight to each other's arms in the burning dark, and she said: don't let go.

The rescue boats went to the first pool of light before they came to us. Then they motored over, so slow, the cold a moment-to-moment discovery in our bones. Voices spoke words, hands reached up for our legs, hips, and I didn't let go until Yoko nodded, until even she believed it would be okay. Then I did, and slid backwards onto the rigid deck of the inflatable, saw faces that seemed barely human, felt someone wrap something that was meant to be warm and felt cold around me, heard commands, questions, didn't answer. Floated a little while in the dark and watched the burning remains of the ship that had pursued us tearing apart. Tried to say a prayer for the dead. Thought of Khasimav's corpse, perhaps only a hull's width away from me. Perhaps there was still air inside, perhaps he wasn't dead at all but screaming for help. I leaned over to press my ear against the hull to listen, but someone stopped me, pulled me back, said something polite, or maybe rude, and probably had a point. Yoko watched me as we pulled away from the wreck, as if looking at a dead man.

Chapter 57

The destroyer was called the *Shearwater*. They dropped planks on rope for us to sit on rather than ask us to climb the net slung over its side. On deck, two sailors in thick, padded jackets and dark woolly hats hustled myself and Yoko towards a door, all the while asking us questions: are you bleeding, what's your name, can you tell me what day it is?

I couldn't. I had no idea. I hadn't known for a very long time.

A larger crowd stood round a more complex assembly of pulleys that had hauled up an orange stretcher, scampering to the bark of a woman's voice. A man ran past holding a yellow box slathered with warning signs; someone else pulled their gloves off with their teeth so they could load a syringe from a small, transparent bottle. Yoko stopped and stared while the sailors tried to hustle us inside.

"Farii," she said flatly, and when no one seemed to respond, she raised her voice, one arm out to lean on the wall of the ship as if her legs might finally go. "Farii. Chief Minister of Lyvodia. If she dies, you lose the war."

"Sea-kin," murmured the sailor with the most common sense, "I need you to be clear. You are saying that woman is Chief Minister?"

"Yes. We are defecting."

"Who are 'we'?"

"I am her head of security, Yoko Blagha. This is Ven of the Temple of the Lake. We are defecting. We didn't broadcast Farii's name because it would have brought the entire Brotherhood on us. We only broadcast Ven's because . . . " Her voice trailed off, and she looked at me, and there was something in her gaze that made me feel ashamed. Then she turned away, eyes fixed on the gaggle of sailors. "We have vital information for Jia. Only Jia."

"Sea-kin, I need you to go inside now. We need to get you warm." Yoko didn't move. "We will give the Minister the best possible medical attention."

"I am her head of security." A mantra, intoned, as Yoko did not move.

"She's safe. Please, come inside."

Yoko stood a moment longer, then nodded once, and I followed her into the warm.

There was a medical bay.

We sat in it, watched by a sailor at the door.

The doctor and nurse were nowhere to be seen. Cupboards stood open, their contents ripped out as medics ran onto deck. We were given tea, wrapped in blankets. My teeth clattered like castanets, but the sailor said we couldn't be warmed up too fast, that it would be dangerous. Drink your tea; stay here. You're safe. You're safe.

After a while, an officer, dark skin tinged with the deepest blue as if something of the ocean had grown within her, came to our beds. Tell it to me again, she said. Who are you? How did you come to be here?

I am Yoko Blagha; this is Ven of the Temple of the Lake. We are defecting.

And the woman?

Farii of Lyvodia. How is she?

She has a heartbeat. She is not awake.

I need to see her.

The doctor will bring her here soon.

I need to see her. I am her . . . her friend. My name is Yoko Blagha.

She's getting the best possible care. And who are you, Ven?

330

There is another question here, far more interesting to this young officer. The question is: why in the name of sun and sky did we come to rescue you, shivering man, when someone much more important was on your boat? Why did we race across the sea to save your body from the deep?

I'm a spy, I replied. I have information of vital importance for the Council.

What kind of information?

I know how to win the war.

Chapter 58

Here: land. We arrived mid-afternoon, overcast, grey, thin snowy slush on the shore, a bobbing, sulky sea. My legs did not quite know how to walk for the first few steps, teetering like a baby deer.

Here: a small delegation of military types and one civic dignitary to meet us, scrambled from who knew where to say they knew not what, awkwardly assembled in haste to deal with a problem beyond their expertise or authority. An ambulance waited by the quay, charging off one of the electrical posts fuelled by the tidal turbines beneath the water. Yoko walked next to Farii's stretcher as they carried it into the back, one hand gripping Farii's. Farii did not grip back, half a dozen lines and tubes running from her flesh to a small scaffolding of bamboo that a nurse pushed alongside her.

I looked, and did not see Yue. Instead, a man who introduced himself as Nkasogi and smelt faintly of menthol and mint stood before me, pressed both his hands together and bowed. I bowed in reply, awkward, fumbling and slow, a thing almost forgotten, mumbling some half-apology. "Sea-kin," he announced, taking my arm by the elbow as if I were a dry flower about to crumble, "I have been sent by the Council to bring you home."

Home is a thousand kilometres away, inaccessible to me. Perhaps he saw this in my eyes because he pressed his hands together again and bowed a little deeper. "I have been sent," he corrected, "to bring you to Yue Taaq."

*

Farii and Yoko rode in the ambulance. Nkagosi and I rode with eight others on the back of a navy truck, heading inland. Low hills of needle-dark winter green stepped in long undulations away from the sea, hard mountains blasted to a soft bulwark by millennia of salty wind. A few cargo bicycles passed us by, heading towards the sea, and one fish truck, coasting down the side of a hill with the casual familiarity of a driver who knows every ridge and switchback and doesn't care if no one else does.

I thought I saw the lights burning in a hilly shrine up an icy path and felt a momentary stab of fear – the soldiers would come, they would shut it down, beat the Medj who guarded this place – and then no. That was in Maze and Lyvodia, where Kun Mi was queen and Georg sat behind his mausoleum desk. Here, the Medj gave thanks to the kakuy of the hill and pine, without consequence.

The truck took us as far as Safaan, a one-track town of red-roofed hearths overhung with heavy cypress trees. Bicycles were lined up outside the communal bathhouse, steam and the scent of thick, foaming white soap spinning from the upper pipes. Across the way, the lights were on in the bakery, flatbreads folding around spinach and nuts for the teenagers in ear-muffling hats and heavy gloves. One station guard huddled inside her office by the railway track, reading something on her inkstone, booted feet up and chin tucked.

"Half an hour," said Nkagosi, as I watched the truck drive away. "You must be hungry."

"Where are they taking Farii?"

"There is a hospital twenty minutes from here. The ambulance will take her there first; then, if she is well enough to move, they will bring her on to Isdanbul. We will go ahead." He waited for me to reply and, when I didn't, bent his head bird-like towards me, as if wondering whether I too hadn't been struck a little too hard by the sea. "Earth-kin?"

Across the way from the station, the wooden gate of a small shrine stood open. A single white lantern hung outside it, swinging erratically in the wind. Nkagosi followed my gaze, let out

333

a little breath, patted me on the shoulder. "I'll get something to eat for the train. You take your time."

The shrine smelt of wet timber. Incense burned in the little ceramic holder. Three rooms clustered tight around a flagstone yard, barely large enough to hold the schoolchildren who came to sing songs and learn the mysteries of the ancient spirits, the great kakuy and the nitrogen cycle. The lights burned in only one window, which I took to be both the office and sleeping quarters of the resident Medj. Another room was raised up a few feet above the earth on wooden legs, open to the elements down one side, woven straw mats on the floor and the trunk of a living silver birch rising up through the middle. Its roots spread out beneath the building itself into the earth below, while its crown reached up through a round hole in the ceiling to plume its branches overhead. Around the hole in the floor through which it descended were offerings. There were a few bags of grain, and a lidded pot containing something that was still warm and smelt of pumpkin, clearly left by someone who knew the Medj's tastes and was willing to occasionally indulge them. There was the shrine's watering can, with a little note on it inviting visitors to water the tree that was at the building's heart, and a scrawled reminder that this month's theme was "renewal" and to please not feed Moonshine the cat. There were a few sticks of incense and bottles of scented oil, an old inkstone, perhaps loaded with suitably contemplative texts – or perhaps not; perhaps it was rich with the kind of scintillating fiction that an honourable Medj might feel a little self-conscious about downloading on their own account but would love to read when the lights were low and no one was looking. There was a woven bracelet of stones and beads, threaded with ancient plastic strings mined from the old landfill sites. A mirror of scrubbed bronze around which were pressed multicoloured shards of more plastic flakes, arranged in a mosaic of ancient and new. A packet of tea. A carved dog, tail wagging and face anthropomorphically split into a friendly grin. A little box of ancient rusted pieces of metal, oiled and scrubbed back into some sort of sacrificial state. Nuts and bolts, an old spoon, a collection of ancient lids in faded green and red. The nib of a pen, and the flaking remains of a circuit board, its use long since lost to time and decay.

A cat meowed, brushing against my legs. I squatted down, held out my hand for him to sniff. "You must be Moonshine." The overweight blue-grey feline contemplated my fingers, found no trace of anything worth licking on them, and, having got my attention, decided that was enough and slunk away. I watched him as he followed an easy familiar path of hop and jump until he was happily on top of the roof of the Medj's small office, curling into a shadow near a hot pipe, a ring of melted snow around it revealing deep red tiles below.

I turned back to the tree, tried to pray, couldn't. I looked for old words, the familiar sounds of the temple, made it a few syllables, stopped. Felt eyes on the back of my neck. Georg would know if I prayed, of course. He'd always know.

I thought of knocking on the office door, asking to see the priest who looked after this shrine. Maybe a cup of tea, a friendly conversation? In Tinics and Bukarest, the Medj had always been horrendous gossips, thrilling in the notion that the drinking of tea and sharing of biscuits could be considered, in its way, a religious duty. "Why I joined Temple!" Lah would say. "Tea, nice music, decent architecture!"

"And the devotion of your life to awe, gratitude, compassion and respect?"

"Yes yes yes – all that stuff too."

I put my hands together and managed the first few words of the prayer for the dead. We had sung it when we'd given Vae's body to the earth and the sky. The tune had been different from the one chanted in Bukarest, which was itself deeper and simpler than the songs sung in Vien, before the temples burned. I tried to hold to Vae's version, to catch at some loose memory of it, but the notes got tangled as I tried to fit word to note, so I stopped, and thought I was going to cry, and couldn't quite believe it. What would Georg say? It would be unacceptable, immediate dismissal. There's no time for such things; utter absurdity. Don't you dare let go!

335

Then Nkagosi was there, a small bag of hot pastries in his hands and a flask of something tucked under one arm, a precarious juggling act waiting to fall. He made a little sound that was the beginning of words, and when I turned he stopped himself and simply smiled. Perhaps the sea had washed something false from my face because he looked and seemed to see someone real. Not Pityr, scrubbing in the kitchens, nor Kadri Tarrad, beaten by Pontus to the chase. He looked at me with kindness, compassion, and for a moment I thought all the things I could not express and did not understand were suddenly present in him, and he had no qualms about naming them, feeling them, even if he didn't know what it was that now burned inside his heart. His empathy was a slap of seawater in my mouth, and I turned away, staring at my feet, rubbed my face to scrunch away salt and fatigue, looked back up and blurted, "Right, yes. The train. Yes."

For a moment, I thought he'd ruin everything and say something thoughtful, or generous, or kind. When was the last time I had heard these sentiments from a stranger's mouth? I would not be able to cope if he did; all my training had been for the opposite – I had no defences against compassion. But he smiled and said: "There's spinach and cheese and nuts and pickles and cardamom tea."

"Thank you."

"Do you need ..."

"No. No – I mean ... no. Thank you. Let's ... let's get this done."

He nodded once more and walked in silence by my side to the train.

Chapter 59

I had never been to Isdanbul.

We arrived at night, by the little four-coach train that wove down along the edge of the water into the city through clinging hill and tight-sliced cutting. The stations we stopped at were quiet: snatches of lone travellers framed in pools of light; a single guard waving us on our way. When the doors opened, I thought I smelt forest through the cold air, heard the steps of the kakuy waiting just outside the light, silver eyes gleaming in darkness, imagined I heard its call in the screeching of the brakes.

Then Isdanbul rose around us, in clinging rows of pinpoint light huddled around the track. Gardens of vegetables and leaf-less winter fruit trees ran away from the line to the hearths and their low yellow lights, growing taller and thicker as we drew into the city. Little wind turbines whooshed busy on top of the highest blocks, and banks of batteries clunked and ticked and whirred in tight coppices of trees between the zig-zagging streets. We rode on bridges cut above the busiest roads of black pressed polypropylene mined from the ancient landfill sites, lined with market stalls and little cafes where the locals drank coffee so thick you could stand a spoon in it, and the cyclists swore and cursed and wove around each other to the jingling of bells and cries of "Move, idiot!" and reproofs of other locals who knew that there was no place for rudeness on their streets and would shout obscenities at you until you understood that fact.

On the edges of the city, I saw regular blocks of buildings

337

laid out in modular stacks, with space between each one like a moat so that when the earthquakes came, the whole thing might shake side to side and not fall, let alone fall on a neighbour. Wide boulevards with trees down the middle; lamps shining above the temple gates and signs at the local stations advertising student shows or concerts at a nearby venue. And yet, here: a knot of soldiers, coming home or returning to the front lines – it was hard to tell – their heads down and eyes up, as if they cannot quite believe that there is peace anywhere they go. Here: guardia on the station steps, watching all who pass by as if they might sniff out subversion like the scent of jasmine on the air. Here: a recruitment sign, defaced, and on one platform a Medj who stands stiff in grey, folded robes and looks lost and utterly alone.

In the centre of the city, the old and new mixed together. Narrow streets ruled by fierce stray cats that curl and rub themselves round the legs of strangers and bite at those who do anything other than try to feed them. The domes of ancient mosques and the tight black stubs of hidden churches where the followers of the old faiths still come to pray, raising up their songs to some creator more benevolent, more caring than the kakuy – or at least, more willing to promise a heaven, as well as a hell.

Some have been converted over the years, turned into community halls or repurposed as museums where you may inspect the ancient texts and artefacts of a long-lost age. Temple built its own premises elsewhere, nestling in between the ancient wooden abodes of centuries-old peoples who clung together through the great burning to build their city again from the fire, as it had been rebuilt so many times before. On the slopes beneath the cracked and teetering tower of Peara, a stepped complex of shrines and halls running up from the sea, where travellers could give thanks to every kakuy of sea and city, of sky and earth you could name. Above the grand bazaar, revellers huddled between the solar tiles, drinking throat-burning alcohol mixed with coffee and breaking bread to the sound of midnight bartering in the maze-tangled streets below. In the quiet streets that staggered and started down to the river, shutters were pulled down against the night and electric trucks groaned as they tried to scale the hills to the first-thing groceries, while cargo bicycles gave up altogether and unloaded in a messy tangle at the wide mouth of the bridge that linked one side of the horn to the other, men and women with sack barrows standing by, arms folded and eyebrows raised at the laziness of their pedalling colleagues.

It was a city that made winter feel like summer, buzzing as the pollen-hunting bees, the sound of war nothing more than an edge to that hum that you thought you caught before some other noise knocked it away.

And then, at the station, was Yue.

She said: All this drama. One day we should just meet for lunch like normal people.

I tried to think of something witty to say, but it had been so long since I opened my mouth to say anything human that nothing came out.

I think she saw that dumbness in me, that mute place where words should have been. Then she held me, in full sight of every-one there, arms wrapped tight; and I held her too, and wondered who this person was who was so unafraid of showing affection, what had happened to Yue Taaq, servant of the Council.

She held on, and I put my arms around her like she was a kitten with a broken bone, terrified of doing the wrong thing. And when it seemed fine, I held a little more tightly and then held her like she was real and this thing between us was true, and never wanted to let go; and there, for a while, we stayed.

When she finally stepped back, she cleared her throat and there was a look in her eye that might have been happiness, or relief, or something else entirely, and I wondered for a moment if she'd finally forgiven me for the day Vae died, or if perhaps she'd forgiven me years ago and I'd just imagined that there had always been this broken thing between us, and never quite forgiven myself.

There was still salt in my hair. She said: Come with me. You're safe now. He can't get you here. Come with me.

*

Yue lived in a hearth a few streets up the hill from the hastily re-occupied Council chambers that pressed to the water's edge. It was a place for civil servants from every department, she explained – quiet, most of the time, especially with the war – too much work for more than the lowest conversations around the table or in the bathhouse as they scrubbed each other's backs and ran soap through their neighbours' hair. Occasionally they partied, incredibly loud and incredibly drunk, and in the mornings after would wake, diagonal across their beds or the beds of their hearth-kin, and pad tip-toe across the hall to their own rooms, and find each other's socks in their washing for weeks to come.

The floors in the downstairs living quarters were pressed crimson earth, still smelling of fresh wax recently laid. The staircase was ancient stone, each step smoothed to a dip in the middle by centuries of footsteps. At the top, it opened to a high skylight, and banks of sage, tarragon, rosemary and mosquito-repellent marigold ran up the wall, padded with green moss. What building the stairs had once served, I couldn't tell, for the corridors that split off from it were panelled wood and bamboo, pressed earth and thin solar glass; the new slid into the frame of the old like the mushroom sprouting from the fallen tree.

Yue led me to a room that seemed to be for a guest: a double futon on the floor, folded; a low portable writing desk beneath a little lamp; a cushion to sit before it and fresh straw mats that still smelt of autumn rain. A sliding door opened to a balcony on which grew crocuses, tulips and mint; another, presumably to a wardrobe, stood closed on the opposite wall. On one shelf, I could see a solar torch, two ceramic soup bowls, two sets of cutlery, two white cups without handles – the fingerprints of the potter visible in the clay – and an unlit yellow beeswax candle. It all reminded me of a moderately priced guestroom in a bicycle-sarai until Yue opened the wardrobe door to reveal clothes that could only be hers. There were only two types: long-sleeved, warm tops and trousers for winter, and short-sleeved tops and light trousers for summer. They had no marks on them or signs of character, and came in sky blue or dark blue. She had two pairs of shoes, apart from the thick winter boots she had left by the door of the hearth, which again conformed to the requirements of either sun or rain and were both dark brown. She had one scarf that shimmered like real silk, grown from the cocoon of the worm itself rather than woven in the bio-labs, dazzling yellow; a gift, perhaps – a token of someone else's idea of her character – whether kept for good manners or fond memories, I couldn't tell. It was a flash of incongruous vibrancy in the austere stiffness of her room.

"I've asked them to give us the bathhouse for twenty minutes," she said, pulling a towel from the top of the wardrobe. "Nkagosi has gone to fetch you clean clothes; he will return soon. I hope that is appropriate? That this ... this is appropriate?"

I mumbled some thanks, suddenly awkward, bumbling, too big for my skin and too small for this place. "I thought I would stay in a temple."

"Of course – of course. I can make that arrangement. Forgive me, I didn't think. All of this is so ... I wasn't ... "

"But I'd rather stay here, if you'd have me."

She nodded once, chewing her bottom lip in a sudden, childish anxiety. Then she straightened up, gestured towards the door. I followed her downstairs, and then down again, to the hollowed-earth cellar where the hearth kept its bath. Damp footprints led away from the cold pool. There was the smell of soap, suds around the greywater drain, hot water ready in the communal tub. Yue dipped her fingers in it as I undressed, testing the temperature, seemed satisfied, rolled up her sleeves and trouser hems and waited for me to climb in. I did so gingerly, not sure whether the touch of water would be a threat, a trauma, a memory of the sea, and instead gasped as the heat broke through every cut and tear, every salt-baked frozen inch of skin and bone, shuddering through me like a train over loose tracks.

"Is it too hot?"

"No. I just need a moment."

She nodded, and as I slowly sank deeper, she scooped up a bar of shampoo and rubbed it into my hair, digging hard

341

with fingertips and occasionally giving an order – rinse – head back – head down – rinse – until every inch of my scalp was pummelled and new.

When she was satisfied, she ordered me out of the tub and splashed warm, clean water over me before murmuring: "Cold tub?" I looked at it with trepidation, warmth still such an alien friend that the idea of losing it seemed suddenly unkind. She smiled, shook her head. "Next time."

She scrubbed me dry with the fat towel from upstairs, then examined my cracked, crimson hands, rubbed something waxy and smelling of spring into them, caressing the thin webbing between each finger and rolling her thumb into the creaking bones of my palms, all in silence, save the tick-tick-ticking of the pipes.

Nkagosi had returned with clean clothes. They were cut in the same severe, brisk style as Yue's own – from the very same market, perhaps – but were warm and smelt of vanilla freshness. I dressed while she cleaned the floor around the tub and pumped water from the greywater tanks into the thin pipes that fed the walls of herbs and moss that ran up the stairs. By the time we emerged, the hearth was sleeping, and even the midnight cats of the city had found some hot pipe to curl up by, a truce declared in their constant bickering as they huddled into the thin heat of each other's bodies. I was exhausted, elated, so tired that it seemed as though I had detached from my own self, become the wind, the breath of the kakuy, floating above human events.

We ate in silence sat opposite each other, cross-legged on floor cushions, leftovers of re-heated beans and grains, thick white yoghurt and hot red spice. I finished first, and when I put my bowl down she took it without a word and refilled it to the top, and I gobbled it up in an instant, and she poured clear water into a cup by my side, and I drank it down, and had never been so thirsty, so hungry, or so full.

When at last I stopped, aching with bloated satisfaction and still feeling a strange hunger – the hunger of not knowing if this feast would ever come again – we sat in the low dark of the kitchen, bowls scraped clean between us.

"Yue . . . " I began, and she shook her head.

"Not now."

"You don't know what I was going to say."

"You were going to say that you have vital intelligence for the Council. You were going to tell me about Farii's defection and the things that needed to be done. You were going to talk about Georg Mestri and the war. Am I wrong?"

"No."

"Not now. Tomorrow. Georg can wait until tomorrow."

I nodded, and thought perhaps Yue was just as tired as me, that she too had left her body behind and was watching this as the kakuy do, apart from it all, just moving air that hummed and shuddered in strange noises.

She twined her fingers in mine as we went back upstairs in the half-dark of the skylight. The hall smelt of moss and linseed oil. The door to the balcony of her room stood a little ajar, letting in a slither of winter air. Her back beneath the blankets was warm; her fingers were cold. I did not think I would sleep, and was dreaming in an instant of the sea, and was strangely unafraid. I do not know if Yue slept, or, if she did, what she dreamed.

Chapter 60

I woke, I thought, from a nightmare, and did not know where I was, or whether I was drowning.

The mind can find reason, calm, a place of safety, but the body still rushes on. In that grey hour before dawn, a thing beats against your skull and says lies, lies, lies. All this reason, all this rationality, this repeated safe thing, these words, lies, lies, lies. Listen to the pounding of your heart; listen to the rushing of your breath and know this civilised safety you have talked yourself into – it lies.

You will never be safe. You will always pretend, when the sun comes up, that it will not set again.

The mattress next to me was cold where Yue should have been. There were birds calling to the morning, and in the distance human voices raised from the high minarets, summoning the faithful of the old religions to prayer. The kakuy are angels, or devils, guardian voi or djinn of fire and sea – all the oldest stories survive because they find their place in the new. There is but one God, sang the chorus to the dawn, and all of us are one. There at least, Temple and the old faiths find a point of agreement, though they will still bicker over the nuance until the tea has gone cold.

The single light by Yue's desk glowed low, but the rising grey through the half-open shutter would soon outshine its dim illumination. A bicycle clattered by in the street below, cargo bouncing on uneven cobbles. A door closed; a shutter slid back. Yue's inkstone was plugged into a hard-wired dataport, the kind

344

we used to queue to use at the Tinics post office when we were children, always discovering as soon as our downloads had finished that someone else had downloaded something better. Someone else would always have something better, when we were young.

I shuffled to my feet, feeling the need to be silent without knowing why. Dressed in the clothes Nkagosi had left me, bare feet on woven straw. Folded back the mattress, laid the pillows on top, heard a temple bell ringing, the voice of a novice calling a prayer for the dawn. In Bukarest, the novices kept such prayers inside the temple courts to rouse only sleeping Medj. In Isdanbul, where the last of the Burning Age minarets still stared proudly down at the sea, the temple felt perhaps a certain need to disturb its neighbours with the best of them, insecurity fluttering in the chilled lungs of the boy in the street.

Yue stood on the little balcony outside, a steaming cup in her hand, the smell of cinnamon and liquorice rising from within. She glanced at me as I emerged, then looked away, as if waiting to see the first lick of sunlight rise above the black-timbered buildings opposite, pushing through the heavy night. I ran my fingers over the wooden rail of the balcony, listened for the ticking of the batteries and the water pipes, heard someone shout at a passing cyclist, another morning of abuse in the ting-a-linging, chain-crunching streets of the city. Said nothing at all.

She did not drink her tea. The temple bells stopped ringing; the faithful scurried to prayer.

All things went in cycles, the inquisition liked to teach. Day and night; summer and winter. Human behaviour too. Lah is an eyeless corpse, swaddled in their infinite robes, laughing like a prophet's bones thrown onto sea-scoured stone. We forget how it felt to suffer, they say. The capacity to forget is how we carry on living. It is our happiness. It is much easier than asking why we had to suffer at all. Round and round and round it goes.

"Farii is awake," Yue said, and any chance we had to continue saying nothing to each other was gone. I watched it vanish with the morning mist, and was grateful she'd spoken before I did, and wished she hadn't said a word.

"Good."

"Weak, but awake. We're going to release her image – an interview, perhaps, the tyranny of Maze, the cruelty of Kun Mi, rebellion, that kind of thing. It will be more effective to do it while she's still in a hospital bed. More valiant, you see."

"Sounds very practical. Cynical, even."

"That," she replied primly, "is war."

Nadira is kicking autumn leaves. She tells her agents that the only thing you can't lie about is how you feel. Lie about anything you need to, do whatever you need to do to get the job done; lie about why you're scared, of course, lie to save your life. But don't pretend you're not afraid.

"It might be worth holding off on Farii's announcement for a few hours."

"Why?"

"There is an order in which things need to happen, I think."

"Do you have a plan?"

"Maybe." Words on the tip of my tongue; they taste like bile and emptiness. "I had a lot of time cleaning dishes to think things through."

"I'm sorry. For that. For what Georg did to you. I tried . . . I had hoped to negotiate . . . but it was just another game he played."

"It's fine. Georg mostly did it to himself. Priests of old would listen to your sins and forgive them. He is in many ways an old-fashioned kind of man. Thank you for trying to get me out."

She watched the light, squinting up into the sky as if trying to spot the sun. I stayed with her a little bit longer, until it hurt to look any more.

Chapter 61

A day of being not human. Or perhaps too human to bear. These things are growing harder to distinguish.

Close my eyes and here it is, here it is . . .

Khasimav, drowning. I did not see him drown and yet I cannot shake it from my mind: the sea, the night, the cold. He is drowning and so am I, reliving, replaying, reliving.

I sit in front of Medj of the inquisition in someone else's clothes and I talk, and they listen. I sit and watch myself speak, and for a little while I am not myself but the wind, drifting in and out of my breath, and the earth, pressed beneath me, and the water in my eyes and the sea in my blood, and it is impossible that I might drown, being made already of the world that will take me into it; it is impossible I should die while crows may feast on me and insects clean translucent wings in the moisture of my lungs. I am a machine for condensing and expiring, a perambulating gas exchange; matter enters my body in one state, leaves it in another. I convert energy to heat, and one day my heat will leave me and other creatures will convert my energy for themselves.

One of the inquisitors asks: "Who do you think Pontus is?"

And in that moment, I am something else instead. A tiny, fleshy thing, a scrambling organism scuttling across the dirt, blind to the forest around, seeing only danger and fearing the things that come in the dark. "I will tell Jia," I reply.

"We are Temple. You are one of us."

We are the same ecosystem. We are the same breath. Sometimes I forget this, and then I remember.

"Yes. And I will only tell Jia."

"May we know why?"

"No. Call it trauma. Call it madness. Call it whatever you want. I will only tell Jia."

"Are you mad, Ven?"

"I think so. I think it's very likely. Don't you?"

The Medj mutter amongst themselves. I had not seemed mad – not until this moment. What smile should I give them? I try to remember how it felt to smile. When was the last time I laughed at anything other than the dark? I think, perhaps, it was with Georg. I think, perhaps, he said something that I found genuinely very funny. Now I'm not so sure. Things that seemed real are only stories, when I try to remember them.

Just in case, the Medj send me to see an emergency counsellor before I am taken to report to the Council. They are a priest called Jaqcs, who adjusts their robes a little tighter against the cold, leans forward over a flask of water to pour me a cup, sits up straight, runs one pink hand over a silver scalp and says at last: "So, tell me why you're here."

"I was a spy, I was betrayed, I escaped, I was captured again, held as a prisoner of war, forced to work for my captors, escaped, nearly drowned, and am now going to destroy it all. The inquisition wants to make sure I'm not insane before I make my report."

Jaqcs clicked their tongue in the roof of their mouth. "Insane is a strong word. Is it theirs or yours?"

"I think I need to commit heresy."

"Why?"

"Might be the only way."

"Well. Always nice to have lots to talk about."

After, inevitably, I am sent to meet the Council.

The building in Isdanbul was not as grand as Budapesht's, a symptom of Council's hurried flight. The street around was cleared of bicycle and pedestrian alike, creating an urban moat of empty space where guardia in heavy hats and gloves like bear paws paced, as much for warmth as duty. The entrance gate was busy with security who didn't have quite enough room to do the tasks they were set to. Bags were searched by two men with elbows tucked in close so they didn't knock against each other; visitors patted down by a woman who'd managed to squeeze a stool, which she rarely got to sit on, into the furthest corner by the door. Nothing electronic came in or out. Even the cables hastily slung down the corridors were guarded by patrols with batons and radios at their belts, as if the technicians who'd installed them weren't quite convinced the whole infrastructure wasn't about to start singing its secrets in operatic binary.

"Do you have a shrine?" I asked Yue.

"What?"

"A shrine. Is there a shrine in this building?"

"Yes."

"May I see it? I would like . . . a moment, before we do this."

Doubt flickered through Yue's eyes, but she nodded and led the way. I felt a little of Kadri Tarrad stir as we prowled through the corridors, counting doors, watching faces, until we reached the small room set aside for prayer and contemplation, sandwiched between a cleaning cupboard and an overflowing office. I stepped inside, removed my shoes and left them on the shelf beneath a line of hooks for coat and bag, bowed to the kakuy stone on its little plinth, took a cushion from its shelf, sat, pressed my hands in prayer, did not pray.

There was room on the straw mats for no more than ten people to sit in contemplation. Only two others sat there now, and the incense stick someone had lit earlier in the day was already burned down in its little ceramic jar. I watched the others shamelessly, their eyes closed, a violation of their privacy in my gaze, an insult they would never know, then rose, bowed again, retrieved my shoes and said to Yue, who waited by the door: "Thank you. I am ready now."

*

They meet me in a room with thick timber walls and a heavy, soundproof door that takes a shoulder's weight to seal properly.

Antoni Witt, who can't quite reconcile his desperate desire for victory with Jia's refusal to start pumping oil from the earth or blast iron from the mountain. No one has seen the kakuy, he whispers, no one has seen them for centuries, we have a war to win – by sky and sea, we have a war to win!

He should have turned traitor, an Anglaes heretic with a one-track mind – but he loves Jia too much.

Krima vaMiyani. No one really knows how much she knows, or precisely what she does with her days. When they told her that her agents had been wiped out in Vien, every Council mole and spy she'd ever snuck into the heart of the Brotherhood, they say one eyebrow twitched, but she still left the office at her usual hour.

Pav Krillovko, chief of staff. He could have been sacked years ago for calling Shahd of the Delta a self-important little bleeder, but for all it was terribly impolitic, there was enough truth in it that Jia kept him on. He is pious in the mornings, outrageous in the afternoon, repentant in the evenings, and what he does at night is his own business, for better or worse.

"I would like Yue to be here," I say.

"She is not cleared for this debriefing."

"I am an inquisitor, not a Council agent. I answer to none of you, yet I am here. And I would like Yue to stay."

Witt looks ready to argue. Pav looks small and tired, skin hanging loose beneath his jaw where he's lost weight. They let Yue stay. She sits cross-legged behind me, a little to the left, where I would sit sometimes when Georg made his pronouncements.

Jia is late. She is often late to things, these days – meetings seem to endlessly overrun. No one can reach consensus.

They have already interviewed Yoko; she swears that Merthe's army is ready to turn, stab Georg in the back. If they strike now, they can have Bukarest before spring, turn the tide. Now is the time, mutters Antoni Witt, for decisive action. If only we'd built our own tanks.

Witt demands: Can we trust Farii? Why has she turned? She seemed loyal enough before.

That was when she thought Jia killed Ull, I reply. That was before she realised who really benefited from the bomb on Kirrk. Her sin has been stupidity and grief, nothing more.

Who is Pontus? Krima doesn't ask the question with much interest. It is a passing thought, barely worth her time. But her eyes are bright moons in a triangle face.

I would like to speak to Jia, I reply.

We are her Council.

Yes. But this is her fight.

Krima huffs in incredulity — her scorn, at least, she is willing to show. Georg sits next to me, right leg folded over left, as he used to before I stuck a knife in him. He's smiling too. I think he is interested to see what I'm going to do next. I close my eyes, try to will him away, but he's still there, in the swimming darkness behind my eyelids. It makes me angry that he got into my skull instead of Nadira or Lah or Yue.

Jia is even smaller than I remember when she arrives. She, who holds the remaining Provinces together by sheer will and clawed fingers, now walks with her neck sticking out in front of her like a pecking bird. Her smile, as she sits at the centre of the table, is like mine — a thing of habit, a half-remembered art folded out of paper. She isn't sure if it's the right smile any more. What will people think of it? Will they see that she is an alien, that she's pretending? Perhaps it would be better not to smile at all, but that doesn't feel right either. I want to talk to her about it, more than anything. Perhaps we can work out something together, some mimicry of humanity that will allow us to pass, accepted and acceptable through the day, without anyone stopping to ask if we feel all right or expressing concern for our sanities.

Someone moves to pour her tea, which she waves away. She leans back far enough to tilt her head up, and her eyes are still alive, glistening, framed in sagging grey folds. "Ven, yes? We met on Kirrk."

"Yes, honoured kin."

351

"They tell me you've been busy."

"Not really."

"No – you have. You have. They tell me you have things you need to say but will only say them when I'm here."

"That's right."

"May I know why?"

"I need to discuss Pontus and heresy."

"And heresy too? How lovely." She speaks like she's discussing a burnt slice of cake. Will someone fetch her a new one? She won't make a fuss if it's impossible, but a war leader in her own capital can dream sometimes. "Well, you have my attention, for the few minutes I can give it. But please be concise. The only reason we're not all hiding in bomb shelters is that winter has slowed even Kun Mi to a halt. But the spring will come and the snow will melt and we will not be able to hold the roads when it does, and time is short."

"Winter is not the only reason the war has slowed – but I will try to be concise. When I was an active agent in Vien, Temple contrived an operation to ascertain the identity of Pontus. Documents were distributed to the prime suspects, ostensibly containing military heresies. They were false. Each file we sent contained a unique error that marked out who had received what – a spelling mistake, for example, nothing that would stand out. It was a fishing exercise. Who would take our bait? It took a while, but eventually the doctored document was given to me in Vien, by Georg Mestri, to verify whether it was genuine. I photographed it, returned it to my handler, Nadira, who concluded that the version I was seeing came from Pav Krillovko. He was Pontus.

"Temple shared this intelligence with Krima, Krima drew up an arrest warrant, but before it could be enacted, it emerged that Pav was not in Budapesht when the document was distributed. He could not have seen it nor have forwarded it to Georg. He could not be Pontus.

"Our failure to determine Pontus' identity at that time was a disappointment, of course. It contributed to my exposure and the

352

death of my handler. It has led to many of your defeats during the war as Pontus continues to transmit vital intelligence to Georg. However that only made the search more urgent.

"Two questions remained: was there any way in which Pav could be Pontus, despite his apparent alibi, and, if not, how could someone else get the document from Pav's system to Georg? Krima vaMiyani was aware of this mystery and pursued it, causing I have no doubt deep discomfort to any and all on Pav's staff who might have had access to his inkstone and the more classified materials within Council premises. But she found nothing."

Krima is stone, her long fingers poised to drum on the table-top, without moving.

"This, of course, put the suspicion on Krima herself. How hard can it be to catch a spy? And if she were Pontus, she would have access to the intelligence that was being fed to Georg, as well as regular access to Pav. There was also her attempt to recruit me in Vien – presumably for Council purposes, but the crudeness of the approach also raised the question of whether this was a counter-intelligence move by Pontus against the inquisition, to sound out whether I was capable of turning traitor. No evidence emerged conclusively either way.

"It is an error for a spy to assume their opposite number is in any way like them. It is a presumption that only clouds investigation. But I had a lot of time in Bukarest to think about how I would go about being Pontus.

"First, consider Council security. Much like Georg, each of you has an inkstone and a fixed terminal secured with biometrics and a passcode. These things are not impossible to break into, of course, but doing so takes time and skill. Nothing electronic is permitted to leave or enter Council buildings unless it has been cleared in advance through a torturous bureaucratic process, which means if you are being hacked, it must happen on site. None of you are able to remove your inkstones, with classified material, from Council premises, and at night they are locked away in a secure charging port. Your networks are isolated from other servers, and your offices regularly inspected. Again, all this

353

would point the finger of blame at Krima, as hers is the department responsible for counter-intelligence and thus the most likely source of any failure in the system; but, then again, insufficiency is not evidence of betrayal. So I ask myself: how would I beat the system?

"The first step is to use analogue technology, rather than attempt a hack. I used it in Vien myself to take photographs of documents using chemically developed microfilm, which I would leave in capsules at dead drops for Nadira to collect. The camera need be no bigger than the end of a spoon, and may be manufactured from mechanical moving parts, rather than electronic ones. I found capsules in Bukarest that resembled the photographic capsules I myself used to conduct my espionage. I also found the microdrone that Pontus uses to send their packages to Georg. They can fly by night and recharge in the morning – a perfectly discreet tool, so long as the weather's not too bad.

"Both these items support the hypothesis that Pontus is using microfilm to smuggle intelligence out from Council buildings – film that would not be detected by your electronic or manual searches – and sending it in drones, rather than transmitted over any network, to Georg.

"We know that Pontus transmits highly classified intelligence, but how did they specifically access intelligence on Pav's inkstone, when he himself was not in the building? Let us eliminate, for now, the notion that Pontus is somehow ... shimmying through the window to access Pav's office and rifle through his private things. And let us eliminate from our list of suspects those staff of Pav's who may have had access to his files while he was on retreat, given that Krima has already investigated them. If Krima herself were Pontus, that same investigation would be a good opportunity to find a scapegoat, so we will cautiously accept its veracity for now. Yet the fact remains that someone must be accessing Pav's inkstone – an item which is either secured and guarded when he leaves or which he carries with him at all times, full of classified material."

"My inkstone never leaves my sight." Pav's voice rises

354

sharply, bristling with something of the old pride. "From the moment I check into the building to the moment I leave, it is attached to me."

I half-nod, raising a hand in placation. "Of course. I have seen your security. Nothing in, nothing out. And you are all experienced – none of you would just . . . leave classified material lying around. Yet there *is* a weakness. Something that makes Pav in particular vulnerable to attack. On Kirrk, I saw you praying to the dawn. Repentance, the gossips say – nothing quite as pious as the man who has repented of past sins. How do you pray?"

"I beg your pardon?" blurts Pav.

"When you pray. How do you pray?"

"That is a very personal question, especially coming from a priest."

"Do you put your hands together, like this?" I raise my hands, palm to palm, touch the fingertips to my lips. "Do you listen to the sky above you, and feel the earth below?" I bow my head in thanks to the breath in my lungs and the ground beneath my feet. "Do you close your eyes?"

I close my eyes, and in my mind Lah whispers: *We give thanks. We give thanks.*

There you are, Lah. There you are.

I open my eyes again, look up to see the whole room staring at me, Pav's eyes so wide they must have ached in his narrow face.

"Council and Temple have always been . . . close. Perhaps too much. In every Assembly and every Council building I have ever been to, there is a room set aside – a shrine – where people go to pray. There's one here, in this building. I imagine, Pav, that when you come to work you pass through security, collect your inkstone, head to your office – but before you reach it you stop. You enter the shrine. You take off your shoes, put your bag down by the wall – not exactly out of reach, but not in your grasp either – kneel before the kakuy stone and close your eyes to pray. I imagine it is a comforting ritual. I imagine you arrive early to ensure you have enough time to catch those few minutes when the shrine is quiet, without singing or the ringing of bells. Just a few people around in the morning, hands clasped, eyes closed, like you. You may only be in there for a few minutes, but it is enough. For those brief moments, your inkstone is not in your hands. It is unwatched."

For a moment, I think Pav is going to splutter, mock, deride the whole idea. His eyes flicker to his colleagues, but Krima is stone, Witt a bastion of folded arm and crossed leg, Jia leaning forward with that same automatic smile locked on her lips, curious and polite. "All right," he exclaims at last. "So for maybe three minutes my inkstone is not in my actual hand. So what? It has never been stolen, and no one can unlock it without my code and fingerprint. Three minutes is not enough to hack a stone. What do you propose?"

"I agree – it would be impossible to hack your inkstone in that time, and you have never noticed its absence. But you do pray in the morning, yes? And in the evening too?"

"A few minutes. A brief ritual. What of it? My inkstone is neither accessed nor stolen."

"The problem with theft is not the stealing of the object – it's that someone almost immediately notices that it's happened. Three minutes of prayer is not long enough to bypass your inkstone's security and photograph classified documents. To do that, Pontus needs several hours at least. My theory is that Pontus steals your inkstone in the evening, as you are on your way out. When you stop to pray, or are in the bathroom or the last meeting of the day – a momentary lapse of attention, a few seconds for Pontus to slip a hand into your bag. That's when they swipe your stone, knowing you aren't going to check it again before securing it away under guard and key."

"How precisely does Pontus do that? I *do* secure my inkstone, every night. Every night it is locked away, and every morning I recover it. You're saying I have been robbed and not noticed?"

"That is precisely what I'm saying. Pontus doesn't just steal – they swap. They replace your inkstone, the real inkstone, with a copy that to all intents and purposes looks the same, which, if you turned it on, would show perhaps an unexpectedly low battery – ah, I see that's happened to you before. You return this inkstone to its dock to charge, and in the morning collect it, and go to pray, and when you are praying, that is when Pontus completes the switch, returning your real inkstone to your bag while you sit in devotion. It is risky, of course. A rare, dangerous risk. Pontus has to stay late, three or four hours to hack the inkstone and leave it downloading its material overnight. They'll have to photograph everything they steal, of course, since they can't smuggle out any digital device containing your archives – that also slows down the process. But for the wealth of material, it's entirely worth the risk. What makes it feasible is your piety. Your piety makes you predictable. It makes you weak. That is how Pontus steals from Pav Krillovko."

Silence in the room. I half-expect a slow hand-clap from Krima, but none comes. In the end, it is Witt who speaks. "If we accept this . . . somewhat fanciful hypothesis . . . explain this: There are no electronics in and out which are not logged. So how has Pontus managed to smuggle in some . . . dummy inkstone, some unauthorised device to swap with Krillovko's own?"

"That's simple," I reply. "Inkstones are modular, made for easy repair. Each component is small enough that you could hide it in a shoe or at the bottom of a purse. Sky and earth, you probably even have a technical department in this building that has boxes of the larger, more difficult parts you might need to assemble a stone. All you need to do is gather each component one at a time, over the course of a few months, maybe a year, and put them together. She builds it."

There is a silence in which even dust in the air dares not ripple.

There is a silence where the forest grows; listen, and you can hear the leaves unfurl.

"The rest is simple," I say, and it is not, and it is the hardest thing in the world. "Temple has every report I ever sent as Kadri Tarrad. These include the times and dates when I was given classified material by Georg – stolen documents sent to him by Pontus. We know the model of drone that is used by Pontus to send Georg information. We know it's likely flight time from Budapesht to

357

Vien. This is enough for you to begin to build a picture of when Pontus stole Pav's inkstone. Prayer is private, but entry and exit times to the building are not. Pontus does not need to have a high security clearance – just high enough that she is regularly seen in the same place as Pav, at the back of meetings or popping into the shrine now and then for a moment of peace. The list of suspects writes itself. On the nights Pontus stole Pav's inkstone, she would have had to stay late to work, those dangerous few hours in which she was hacking his device. Perhaps she couldn't smuggle in the larger components with which to build an inkstone entirely, which means there will be maintenance records of her requesting them – a spare battery, perhaps, or a new screen cover – harmless repairs. Nothing to arouse suspicion, unless you're looking. Line these up and you're done. You have Pontus. It is over. The only question remaining is – what are you going to do with her?"

What does the mountain feel, when the seasons turn? Rain, sun, snow, wind, the slow indentation of the river down its back, the patter-patter-patter of a thousand creatures scuttling across its chest, the moon rises and sets, the shadows turn and turn and turn again, and only the mountain remains.

Do not make me a mountain, I pray. I think I would go mad.

Jia stands, and she is not looking at me. Forgive me stars, forgive me the water that we share, Jia is looking at the woman sat behind me.

She is looking at Yue.

So is Krima, and now Pav too. Only Witt hasn't lifted his gaze from the table, but he'll come round in time. With Jia on her feet, the rest of us rise, Yue last, and for a moment the old woman sways as if this little breath, this room of exhaling people, were a storm too great for her to bear.

Then she says: "Krima. Do you accept what this priest has to say?"

Krima is quiet a long, long time. Then: "Yes."

"Pav?"

"I . . . it merits consideration. It is . . . but it merits . . . it would be worth considering more."

358

Jia's eyes have not left Yue's face. "Is there something you would like to add, Taaq? Is there ... a reason your friend has brought you here, today?"

Yue is silent. I cannot turn to see her face. Even the mountain would break.

"I think," she says at last, "that I would like to negotiate."

Chapter 62

There is a time after.

After everything.

They send me back to Temple.

I think I am escorted, but it is hard to say.

Yue does not look at me as she is led away.

Here, said Jaqcs, here. I find this a lovely spot to sit, beneath the cherry tree.

You can take one of the hot stones we keep by the stove and stick it under your robes, such a lovely sensation, when I was a novice I would put one behind my back and curl over it like a cat, chest to the sky, it was the most wonderful feeling.

Here.

Have some tea.

When the snow falls all around, but you are warm, there is something in the silence, in the way the light is different in winter, it is quite . . .

You probably are insane – your word, not mine – but you've got a few more weeks of good use in you before you crack completely.

Do you want to talk about it?

Maybe later.

Jia has asked that you stay in temple grounds, and I wanted to show you my favourite spot, my favourite . . .

You've really done your best.

I think you need to know that.

Everyone thinks you've done . . . very well.
Really made a difference.
I'll . . .
. . . leave you to it.
. . . we've prepared a room . . .
. . . all spick and span . . .
Well.

        Well.

                I will see you at the ringing of the bell.

When the dinner bell rings I do not hear it, and a novice comes to bring me to the hall. My fingers and toes have gone blue. Jaqcs was right – it is a very nice cherry tree. There are early spring buds, tiny and crimson, on the ends of the matt-grey twigs.

There are prayers, which I mouth.

There are bowls of soup, steamed dumplings, roasted vegetables and thick yoghurt to take away the heat of some of the more liberally deployed smoked spices. Whoever has decided to claim the kitchen as their domain would not have been contested in their mastery. My room is slightly smaller than the attic where I slept on the floor in Bukarest, and clean. The walls are paper bricks lined with bamboo. There is a spider-silk woven tapestry on one side depicting kakuy representing patience, generosity, balance, compassion and so on. It is a bit of a metaphorical stretch, but then, as Lah would say – bums on seats. No point preaching the oneness of the universe, the inter-connectedness of all things and the harmony of being if no one turns up to hear the sermon. Nice bit of singing, biscuits straight from the oven. That joke you know, Ven – the one about the anemone – it's so lame it's almost funny again, yes?

Lah is decaying in a corner, smiling as the maggots wriggle from out their eyes. They'd hoped for crows – lovely creature, a crow, carrion are always so much smarter than your standard herbivore, count to seven, bring its friends, always know which Medj had a soft spot for feeding it leftovers – love a crow. Be eaten by a crow. Couldn't ask for a better end. Not that they have anything against maggots. Whatever gets the job done.

The midnight bell rings, and will not ring again until dawn.

This is an hour to pray.

How hard can it be?

The kakuy don't listen, there is no god who cares – gods are human things – but that's never really been the point.

Pray for yourself.

Pray for something worthwhile.

Pray for good things to happen.

Pray for it to be all right.

Pray for hope.

Pray for forgiveness.

Pray for yourself.

Be someone worth praying for.

Useless bastard, pray.

Empty little eggshell, pray.

Well.

Maybe tomorrow.

Chapter 63

Tomorrow came, and the day after, and the day after that, and on the fourth day they called me back.

Not to Council halls.

To a small house on the edge of the city, pressed behind straw-bale walls, a garden of winter vines, security dressed in civilian clothes and the shutters locked on the low windows. They asked me to wait in the pantry, near the stove, brought me dark brown tea and a honey cake served with a petal on top. Krima came down first, saw my food and drink untouched, didn't bother to sit, barked: "She says she'll talk to you."

I rose without a word, followed Krima up the creaking stairs to a door with a bolt across it, a woman guarding it with a set of keys. Waited for it to be unlocked. Followed Krima inside.

Yue sat on the rolled-up cylinder of her mattress, elbows on knees, head turned towards the thin light that drifted down from the single window. There was a stool opposite her, unoccupied, an empty plate by her side, and a clay cup and beaker of water. She wore clothes of thick winter grey and had no shoes. Her head didn't turn from its contemplation of the light until the door clicked shut, and when she at last looked to see me there was a flicker of surprise.

"Ven. I wasn't sure they'd bring you. I hope it wasn't too far to come."

I folded myself down onto the stool, adjusted it a little so I faced her, pulled my inquisitor robes a bit tighter around my neck for warmth, let my hands hang loose. Krima stood by the door, leant against it with arms folded, a weary bend in the curve of her spine. "Yue," I said. "They are treating you well?"

"Oh yes, fine. It's all pretty procedural."

"Good. I'm glad." And when she said no more: "They said you wanted to talk to me."

"Yes. Of course. You are Kadri Tarrad. I am Pontus. Of course."

These words said out loud were the hard thump of the winter gale that fills your lungs too fast, too deep for breath. I half-closed my eyes, felt the blood in my fingertips. Remembered standing in front of the mirror, learning to meet my own reflection while Vae's hand slipped from mine again, and again, and again. Looked up, and met her gaze.

"What would you like to talk about?"

"I was wondering when you knew."

"Knew?"

"About me. Pontus."

"I see." She waited for me to answer, but I was slow, so slow, trying to fish the words from some distant, crumbling part of myself, memory slipping like dust. Finally: "I suspected you when I was in Vien. Right at the beginning. As a matter of course, you understand. When I first saw you, trailing along behind Jia, I was excited, terrified. Someone I knew – someone who could know me. A single word from you would blow my cover, but at the same time, it was ... I wanted to reach out to you, so of course had to question my own assumptions, practise the paranoia that the inquisition taught. Had to be safe. Then Nadira told me that your clearance wasn't high enough, that the inquisition didn't suspect you, and I was so relieved that I didn't stop to check the obvious assumptions – that my clearance wasn't high enough either, and I was still tearing Georg to pieces.

"I wanted you not to be Pontus. And then when you told me how you knew Georg, it was so damning, such a compromising thing to say that I thought, well, there you go. She can't be Pontus. Pontus would never have said something like that. And besides, if you were stealing intelligence, you would have stolen from Krima, the person nearest you, not Pav. Pav seemed out of your reach – until I saw his devotions on Kirrk. Then everything went wrong, and I didn't have much time to think about these things. I should have been executed in Bukarest. Georg should have executed me. I couldn't understand why he didn't. Vanity, of course. His ... need for power, a playmate, a confessor. All of that, perhaps. But still. He is also a pragmatist, at the end of the day.

"Then I saw you, that night you came to negotiate, and the thought crossed my mind: for Yue. He's keeping me alive for Yue. I am leverage. It seemed inconceivable, but then why had he dragged me to Kirrk? A display of power, of course, game-playing, time-wasting, but what else? Why were you responsible for me on the island? And why had you of all people come to find me in the forest, alone, your military escort still shuffling around in the snow? I thought perhaps you had come for friendship, that you'd seen something in my file, seen my real name – but no. You didn't know it was me until the moment you saw my face. Georg sent you. You had come for Pontus. You were meant to kill me, out of sight, a quiet ending to this little dance. And you didn't."

A little shrug, a little nod. "Georg didn't understand why you were still alive. Why I hadn't put you down. He wanted you on Kirrk to show off – always showing off – but he mainly dragged you there for me. To see how I'd react when he put you in danger. To work out why I hadn't killed the man who had tried so very hard to destroy me. It didn't take much for him to solve it. When he realised that he could use you against me, hold your life over mine, he did. He didn't need to. He already owned my every breath and bone – but he does enjoy power."

"How did Georg recruit you?"

"We met when I was eighteen – I think I said? The same university – he was a little older, on the sprinting team; a brilliant runner. He had interesting friends, with lots of opinions. They talked the usual revolutions. How Temple was bloated, blind and old. How it existed to make sure that nothing changed. No one had seen the kakuy for years. What he said wasn't attractive, but how he said it – that was hypnotic. The first time we made love I couldn't believe someone this remarkable might be interested in me, might take the time to care for me. Nothing he ever does is casual. But when his course ended he went back to Vien, and we drifted apart. We tried to make it work for a few months, but you know how these things are. He encouraged me to go for Council work. He was supportive. Believed in me. I trusted him. I joined security; things fell into place. Georg was working for the Brotherhood, watching me rise – helping me, even. He would feed me titbits from Maze, bits of gossip and things he called "secrets" to make me feel like we were part of some mutual exchange.

"The first time I betrayed Council, I thought I was doing the right thing. Greasing the wheels. Solving a problem. Then I did it again. And again. And one day Georg laughed and said, 'Good thing no one knows about this, otherwise they'd arrest you on the spot,' and it was a joke, a silly little joke; and just like that, I was his. I understood in that moment what I had done, how deep I'd gone. He owned me. He laughed, one arm round my shoulder, chatted about nothing – some sport, perhaps – said, 'Same thing next month?' and it was done. I had become a traitor without even noticing. After a while, he stopped pretending. We stopped having our little dinners. Stopped with the smiles and the solicitations. He would ask me for information and I would do it. Like a dog trained to fetch, I fetched. Fetch, puppy, fetch. Go fetch. He's always seen the animal in people."

"Did you ever believe? In what he said – the kakuy, humanism?"

"Believe? I never really thought about it in those terms. But this I know: one day, the kakuy will wake. They will come from the forest again, some day, and when they do, we have to know how to kill them. It is the only way humanity will ever be safe. Georg was right about that, at least."

She was not looking at me, at anything, not moving, her face a barely living thing, blood turned to crystal ice.

"Why did you sleep with me on Kirrk?" I asked, and at my question Krima stirred, and Yue did not.

"Because I wanted to. Because it was nice. You were available and I knew . . . well, perhaps this is the last time. When Jia is dead and Georg has won, when he no longer has any use for Pontus, he'll put me in some apartment somewhere with guards to watch over me, and sometimes we'll have sex and dinner because he has me. He has my mind and he has my body and that's all there is to it. That is what my future holds. I had spent so long looking for Kadri Tarrad, so long trying to find you, I could feel you, see the shape of you without knowing your face. And when I found you, I already knew you. All such a mess. I was meant to kill you, and even before I knew you were Ven, I didn't think I could. I don't know which you I spared – Kadri or Ven – but I couldn't do it. What mercy would there be for Pontus? What mercy for me? What would Vae say, if she saw what I had become?"

"Who's Vae?" Krima's voice, hard from the door.

I ignored her. "Why did you come to Bukarest?"

"Jia sent me – peace talks. Nothing would ever come of them, of course, but Georg does like to string the old woman along. And he always insists that they send me."

"Why did you really come?"

"To see you, idiot. To make sure Georg had kept his promise. Kept you alive. He asked me, Why does this man matter? Why do you care? I told him we were lovers once; he likes it when it's about sex. He understands that sex – love – these things make people vulnerable. It is much easier for him to comprehend than the truth. I tried to get you out. I did. But he would never let you go." She smiled, held out her hands. I took them. Her fingers were cold, tipped with blue. I squeezed them tight, pressing a little warmth into her. "What a mess!" She nearly laughed, eyes shining, chin twisted high. "What a stinking mess."

"If I asked you, would you help me destroy Georg?" Her eyes lowered back to me, and there was a smile on her lips, tears on her cheeks. "In Maze, the kakuy are waking. The rivers carry plague, swarms of black flies that sit in the corner of the eye and lay their larvae in pink flesh. Fires leap from the furnaces to the schools, the streets, the forests. This war can never end, because the Brotherhood cannot turn back. They have burned everything they have to take what was never theirs."

She looked away and did not answer. I sighed, spoke to the sky, to the earth, to her bare toes pressed to clay. "Temple teaches that the kakuy wake not because they are angry at humanity and the things it has done but because the cycle must not be broken. Anger, shame, guilt – such human things. It is hard to teach that the sky doesn't care. Destroy ourselves, or live in peace – all this will someday end, and the earth will endure, in one form or another, whether humans breathe or not. In Tinics, the forest burned, and then the forest grew, and we were taught to give thanks that we lived in a world where that which is lost can grow again. Give thanks, they said. We are of the forest. We are of the earth and of the sky, boundless and eternal. So give thanks." I pressed my hands around hers, tighter. "Yue – sister of earth and sky; kin of sun and moon. Thank you for saving my life."

Her smile broke into a grin, a laugh that dislodged the tears that ran down her face. "Ven – I've made a total mess of mine."

"On that point in particular, we have something in common. Will you help me?"

Chapter 64

Three days before the end of everything, Jia came to the temple to pray.

They sent me to the main hall a little after breakfast bell, and there she was.

They'd brought out a chair for her to sit in before the altar. The altar carried images of a hundred kakuy, spirits of the cypress tree and the fish creatures that still played in the darkness of the cistern beneath the streets when no humans were there to see them. But the largest image, moulded from ancient sea-smoothed plastic pulled from the deeps, was the kakuy of the water, the place where two seas meet. It had tentacles woven in plastic bags, a crown of metal shards dug from the landfills, eyes of black opal. It was neither beautiful nor ugly, kind nor vengeful. It had clearly been created by someone with a great deal of piety.

The Medj slipped from the hall as I settled down on a wobbly pile of cushions stacked up next to Jia. She prayed a little longer, or pretended to pray – a woman of her profession must be supremely skilled at demonstrating piety while wanting to pee. Finally she said: "I suppose it's sacrilegious to discuss war in a place of contemplation?"

"When I last checked, the falcon didn't care about the scenery if there was something to eat."

A little nod; she found this satisfactory. "Farii is up and about and has done us a lovely little speech about the tyranny of the Brotherhood. We're releasing it this afternoon, and have established contact with Merthe in the north. As soon as the message goes out, she is bringing her divisions over and Kun Mi will have a hostile army in her backside. It has all the hallmarks of a bloodbath. I trust you're satisfied."

"Not really."

She nodded; neither was she. "I had a long chat with my advisers. They are, disappointingly, desperate. We are all desperate. None of us have slept enough. None of us have time to sleep. It makes for terrible judgement." A slight bristling; a tilting of her chin at an unwelcome thought. "How does Mestri do it? You were his assistant for months – does he drink a lot of coffee? Stimulants and hard drugs? How does he run his war?"

"He likes washing in icy water."

"As if I didn't despise him enough."

For a while we sat in silence as the smell of incense drifted on the air with the out-of-tune calling of a novice new to the sacred songs. At length, Jia said: "When this is over, there will be a trial. Quiet, of course – it would be embarrassing to have to admit in public how far Pontus got. But it will be imprisonment, parole at fifteen years if she keeps her nose clean, shows remorse. Five years' probation, never hold any meaningful position ever again and so on. If she co-operates. If your little scheme works."

"I understand."

"She betrayed you. She betrayed your handler. She is directly responsible for the deaths of countless people. She can't argue ignorance. She knew what she did and understood its conse-quences. Would you forgive her?"

"My forgiveness is mine to deal with on my own terms. You cannot mandate it or enforce it with a court order. That's not what justice is for. I'll deal with it when I'm ready, in my own way."

A little sigh, a little shrug. She's heard more laughable things, in her time. "Why did you join the inquisition, Ven of the Temple of the Lake?"

"Why do you ask?"

"You could have worked for Council."

"Council is too political. You come, you go. You have short

370

memories and short-term goals. It's all necessary, of course. Society, culture, all evolve far faster than our genes do. But Temple measures its objectives in the erosion of the valleys and the churning of the glaciers. It is fantastically dull, very hard to emotionally engage in and entirely necessary. I saw the forest burn, when I was young. I would like to see it grow, before I die."

She thought about it, nodded. "Bit self-important, but not completely inane."

"I was taught that when you thought people were talking absolute nonsense, you should always say, 'You are partially right.' It allows everyone to feel that their views are valid and worth consideration, even when they're categorically wrong."

Jia laughed. It was such an unexpected sound that I nearly jumped, held onto my knees and wondered if this was a cackle too far, whether someone so frail should be allowed so much merriment. Found that I was smiling, didn't quite know what to make of the feeling. She patted me on the shoulder, stood up slowly, still beaming, exclaimed: "I like that. I will use that in meetings. So much for the end of the world!" and hobbled away, chuckling as she went.

Chapter 65

All things ended in a place called Martyza Eztok.

It lies at the bottom of a valley of terraced steps, an unnatural hollow in the earth. No river had carved its lines; no great ice age scratched it from the earth. It was as if the talon of some mighty kakuy had descended from the sky to just pick, pick, pick at the land like some yellow spot, ripping out nearly ten kilometres of blackened dust from the flatlands to create an indent through the rock.

The first inquisitors who ventured into it could see chimneys still sticking up from the earth, the buildings beneath them long since collapsed or buried beneath black. Their smooth stacks were shattered, but the rusted remains of some still lay where they'd fallen like clawing fingers. Closer still, and the smell of festering eggs grew, a throat-closing tingle at the back of the mouth, and concrete blocks rose from the shaggy ground, empty windows and cracked walls, pools of brackish water and signs in archaic script. Previous travellers had tied signs of their passage to the fallen lampposts or broken, bleeding pipes that zig-zagged across the ground. Scraps of cloth and woven patches of plastic; bits of ancient fishing line and crumbling wire turning to orange flakes. They were the only living things in this place, catching and snatching at the wind. The walkways of the refineries had tumbled down, nosing into dirt. The great cooling tanks had shattered; the acid in the pipes had eaten everything they'd touched until there was nothing left but hollows and dust.

There was no shrine in this place, no monument to the spirit of rust and the pit. The Medj had argued over whether to build one, to try to re-sanctify the blasted earth, but had eventually agreed that there were some things best left profane. Nothing grew from the yellow muck save brown, scraggy grass that lived only long enough to die. Even the crows kept away.

Nadira had been one of the first inquisitors to risk diving into the abandoned coal mines below, swimming through collapsed tunnel and flooded shaft, unable to see her hand in front of her face as she twisted and wormed her way to the archives the burning ones had hidden within. It had taken the inquisition nearly six years to dig new passages down to the surviving chambers of hidden knowledge, and what a surprise they'd had when the first translations of recovered material started to emerge.

Lignite mining and the great toothed engines that could carve out the belly of the earth.

Essays on storage of radioactive waste; lessons on slag heaps and acid rain.

This is our knowledge, our gift to you, wrote the last of the archivists who had died when the world burned. *Everything we did, everything we made, we made so our children could live better than the ones who went before.*

After fifteen years, the tunnels beneath Martyza Eztok were re-sealed by inquisition order, the recovered material distributed to the anthropological and historical working groups for analysis and classification.

Sometimes, when the wind was right, black clouds of coal dust still spun on the edges of the valley, and the few inquisitors left to guard the mines swore that there were things which groaned beneath the earth that had in their sound something living.

Nine days after Yue was arrested
and Merthe turned her guns against the Brotherhood
I got on the train heading north
towards the mines.

Chapter 66

By the time I reached Martyza, the Council had moved a small army in.

They spread themselves into the villages to the south of the torn-up land, camped in clumps of forest and little knots of wood between the thin, dusty fields that clung to the edge of the hollowed-out, blackened valley. Blood-red bricks and a cracked roof were patched over with sheets of waxed fabric. Portable solar arrays were lined up towards the noonday sun, pickets of mounded earth dug out in the scrappy, broken land beyond. To the north I could see the last standing remains of two ancient cooling towers, their curves tumbled in on themselves like broken smiles. A few signs still lined the muddy borders where fences had once separated the old factory lands from the farms, written in archaic script.

PPE must be

Beware the dog

a better future for

I wasn't sure what "PPE" meant, tried to turn over the ancient dialects to find words that fit, and came up with nothing. Georg would not have been impressed.

An army Medj, head shaven and uniform indistinguishable from anyone else's, met me at the edge of the camp as I pedalled up on my borrowed bicycle. "Inquisitor!" they exclaimed, bowing low. "Welcome to Martyza Eztok."

"Temple-kin," I replied, slipping off my muddy vehicle and returning the bow. "I had no idea there'd be so many soldiers here."

"Brotherhood troops have been seen heading south towards the mines, bypassing Plovdiq altogether. The assumption is they're going for the archives – more heresy, I assume."

"You assume wisely. What is your role?"

"Me?" they answered. "I'm here for sermons and hugs."

In the evening, I shared dinner in a tent with the Medj and a bustle of soldiers, knees stained with dust and coal. They led the prayers. We thank you, earth, for the food we eat. We thank you, night, for the safety you give. We thank you, dawn, for all that will follow.

I wondered where this soldier-priest had been, and what they'd seen in this war, and didn't have the courage to ask.

An hour before sunrise, I woke, freezing cold on the thin mat between my body and the earth, legs stiff inside the barrel of my sleeping bag. I uncurled, wound up the little torch that lay beside my head, fumbled out in the night, trying not to step on too many slumbering bodies, looked to the east and saw a hint of grey that might have been the approaching sun, and tried to remember where the toilet was.

A guard sat hunched like a raven on the broken roof of the little farmhouse, weapon tucked into chest. A low light burned from the makeshift kitchen, where breakfast was already being prepared. I sat on the broken wall on the edge of the compound and looked towards the skeletal valley beyond, wondering what it had been like when the cracked towers and toppled chimneys of this place were living, powerful things. The people of the past had made their own kakuy, spirits of metal and steam, great gods that, for a little while, challenged the thunder itself. They had seeded the clouds and put machines into space. Perhaps Georg was right;

perhaps with steel and oil they could have tamed the earth. Those who survived, at least. Those with the will to survive.

Something moved overhead. I glanced up, tried to pick it out in the darkness, strained my ears for the telltale whine of the rotors, couldn't hear it. The sky was streaked with scudding clouds that opened and closed like tired eyes. Sometimes I saw stars behind them, a promise of infinity – a busy, beaming void. Then it vanished again, and again I looked and thought a tiny point of darkness moved, but when I looked one last time it was gone.

"Brotherhood drone," explained a sergeant in the breakfast queue. "They say the main force will be here by tomorrow."

"Aren't you . . . a little concerned by that?"

He shrugged. "Witt's good at rearguard actions. Didn't think it'd be over some stinking archive, but still . . . " But still, but still. What's a soldier to do, when the inevitable calls?

By daylight, I drift through the camp, half-listening to the soldiers talk. They glance to the north, the flat, broken plain between us and the wide horizon. They do not talk about the approaching Brotherhood forces. One drops his pants to stick his buttocks up at a passing drone, until a colleague hisses that it's one of theirs. They wonder where Merthe is; rumours and gossip from Lyvodia. A few wonder where they will be when the day is done, and are hushed, and go back to talking of little, idle things.

There are muddy crates stamped with the mark of the inquisition being loaded into a truck. They look crudely out of place, each one designed to fit a rack of ancient hard drives or chipsets preserved from static, moisture and time. They should not be slathered in mud or thrown from soldier to soldier like a toy box. There should be Medj here, protecting the history of our ancestors, of the burning ones who died wishing us well.

Old Lah walks beside me and reminisces about the ancient hard drives they've unlocked, piecing together the code of our history. Pornography; bank statements; computer games full of slathering demons and sexy aliens. Family photos. Endless pictures of food on white, round plates with captions full of yellow smiley faces and exclamation marks. Infants beaming up at a camera, at the parent that wielded it. Children running through autumn leaves in red rubber boots, being pushed on swings by cobweb Grandma, come alive again. Lovers, puckered lips, cheek-to-cheek, black background, overlit, over-bright faces and black-rimmed eyes. Friends dancing in the summer streets, drinks in hand; holiday shots across monuments even more ancient than the fires that ended the last great age. Lounging in sunlight on a golden beach. Running, sweaty and out of breath across the victory line. Waving goodbye at an airport, bags packed and guidebook in hand. Thumbs up and big grins. A father who cannot find his child in the ruins of war. A glimpse of someone famous on a bright red carpet, the shot out of focus against the hordes of fans trying to get in close. Wedding photos, confetti, tears; the kind of beauty that can only be born of joy. A woman sleeping in afternoon sun.

It is strange to imagine that the dead were ever young, children covered in cream, teenagers falling in and out of love.

I want to go back to Georg.

I want to sit him down and tell him: You never find what you expect when you dig through the archives. You want nuclear fission and geoengineering. You want oil refineries and investment banking prime-mortgage re-packaged bonds. You want pesticides and herbicides and humanicides and a way to kill the kakuy.

But look, look. Here's what you get.

Three pictures of different kinds of food shared between friends, an out-of-focus shot of two lovers sticking their tongues out at the camera, a screenshot of an ex-boyfriend's stupid text message to share with friends, because you can't *believe* he'd say that shit.

Here's the history of the world for you.

Here's what the burning left behind.

You want gods, and all you get are people.

*

I see Krima vaMiyani.

She nods at me once, from the passenger side of the heavy truck she rides in, then turns away.

In the morning, the truck of crates marked with the badge of the inquisition is gone, and on the other side of the gouged-out valley there are black fumes in the air as an army approaches.

Chapter 67

Once, on the edge of Martyza, there was a church.

It was far older than the coal mines, than the black claw raked through the earth. It did not make itself especially denomin-ational, having at some point in its history been a place of worship for nearly every flavour of monotheism imaginable. Its yellow stones had cracked and fallen away in places, and the roof was long since tumbled down. Moss grew on the piled mounds of fallen masonry, glistening in the morning frost. A hollow stair led to a soggy black below, perhaps a place of corpses and snakes, of ankle-deep fetid water and ancient bones with wet hair on bare skulls, and sometimes children dared each other to go inside, and sometimes they did, and usually they did not, because some darknesses were a little too conclusive.

I cycled there on a borrowed bike as two armies lined up across the scarred field of Martyza. They told me it was far enough away from the main battle lines that I probably wouldn't be mortared to death, that the worst of the crossfire would pass me by. They told me, if it didn't, if the battle raged out of control and soldiers with guns descended upon me, to surrender immediately and grovel for mercy. They seemed fairly sanguine about the whole affair.

"How does a battle begin?" I asked one.

"Oh – they'll probably start shelling us when they've had a bite to eat, and if they don't, we might try shelling them. There's a lot more of them than there are of us, of course, but they've had to travel a long way so they might not be feeling too frisky."

I wondered what "frisky" could possibly mean when two armies faced each other over the black-dust belly of the earth, and decided not to ask.

In the church on the edge of the field, I left my bicycle by the dry mouth of a little bowl where worshippers had once dipped their fingers by the broken door, and sat inside on a stone near a place where once an altar had been, swathed in my priest's robes, and closed my eyes, and waited for the end of all things.

I did not pray, since there are no gods with interests in human things.

But, for a little while, I let my mind be in the cold morning air, and my toes be in the cold morning earth, and my heart beat with the fluttering of the wings of the crow on the wall overhead, and my mind grow slowly, so slowly, with the moss unfolding over fallen stones. And for a little while, that was enough, and I was nothing, and everywhere, and everything, and I was the kakuy.

All around: nothing.

No forest, no hills, no mounds of slagged chemical sewage belched from the belly of a machine. Nowhere to hide, nowhere to run. Just the flatland before the fall into the pits and the dry rasping of brown grass rubbing against the dead stems of its nearest neighbour.

A little snow fell, crystals melting slowly on my sleeve. I watched each one, determined to spot a pair, and soon lost interest. Drew myself a little tighter into my robes, drank tea from a hot flask, felt the knife buried in my boot, listened.

I heard the armies move before I heard him.

They didn't open with shelling, as had been promised. Everyone was in too much of a rush to get the artillery out. I had imagined the belching roar of the Brotherhood's tanks to be an offensive shuddering in the land, a tumour in the ear. But the morning was kind, and the faint snow muffled the rumble of their movement to a distant animal growling as they revved their engines and charged forward. Drones buzzed high overhead, impossible to tell which was on whose side, sweeping back and forth across the field. I wondered where Antoni Witt was now, and what his soldiers thought of the lumbering death shuffling towards them. I waited for the sound of artillery, and the odd big gun fired desultorily into the sky, and no more. The sound of small arms fire when it began was an erratic, far-off thing, odd units skirmishing in strange places, the constant dance of fire-withdraw-fire that was Witt's calling card. I wondered if his troops could outrun a tank. I wondered how much fuel a tank needed to mow down men. I waited, checked my watch, waited.

Put my fingers on the earth and felt the hum of the vehicles moving across it, far away.

Listened for the sound of birds; heard none.

For the crack of animals moving across frost; heard none.

Only the distant thump of unseen shadows, inhuman things, busy about killing.

Understood, for a little while, why Yue wanted to go to prison. Missed for one startling moment my cell in Bukarest. Decided I was, indeed, finally, mad. Drank some more tea.

When he came, he did so on foot, and that surprised me. I heard his stick on stone, striking hard as he approached the church, near enough to cut through the chunking, thumping, rumbling growl of the Brotherhood soldiers pouring across the ruined land to the west. Was Witt even bothering to fight back? Perhaps not. Say what you will of the general, he liked his troops to live.

The man approached at the pace of one out for a hearty constitutional, a pleasant early morning walk. There should have been mist on the ground and bells ringing in the air; he should have nodded politely at people who owed him favours as he passed, a grand fellow about his business.

Instead, he stopped on the edge of the church, listened to a sudden swell of distant gunfire, knocked once with the tip of his cane on the broken porch, stepped across the threshold, a smile on his lips.

"Hello, Georg," I said.

He was surprised enough for the smile to freeze, for the stick to hang in the air for an instant. Then his smile changed; he nodded, beamed, tucked the stick under one arm and straightened a little, as if he could hide his limp from me. "Kadri. Congratulations – I am surprised. Goodness, indeed yes. Well done."

"Tea?" I held out my steaming flask.

"What is it?"

"Jasmine."

"Thank you, no. Are you alone?"

"Regrettably, yes. With so many of your drones flitting about, it didn't seem prudent to bring a whole military convoy with me, however much I would have liked the cover."

"I didn't expect to see a priest so close to the battlefield."

"I don't think anyone expected to see you so close to one either. Not Georg Mestri – not sticking his neck out. But then you expected Yue."

His smile widened, a flicker of something real, something familiar. His eyes roamed round the ruined place, he paced a little forward, a little back, saw no threat as he talked. "Ah. Yes. I did. I do believe this is what it's like to feel . . . flustered. How novel. Are you armed?"

"With more than tea? Are you sure you won't drink?"

A hesitation; a memory in his eye, perhaps, of hours spent in each other's company, playing games, drinking wine, talking of nothing much. He gestured towards a little mound of stone slightly lower and less comfortable than mine, tried to find a comfortable way to perch on it, found it impossible, tried for the sake of the illusion anyway, one leg high, one leg low, smiled again, hands folded, stick tucked into the bend of his hip, watched me, watching him. Finally, he said: "I've never seen you in priest's robes before."

"That would have somewhat blown my cover."

"You look like an ugly duckling, all fluff and a tiny head."

"They're not really cut for style. The sexy Medj with gleaming torso was always something of a myth. How are you doing?"

"Oh, fine, fine – you know. Fine. Busy as ever. You may have spotted the little ruckus happening a few thousand metres from here. Yourself?"

"Could be worse. I mean – significantly better than in recent months. Keeping busy, and so on. I've been reliably informed that I'm going insane. But I'm not of any strategic significance, so it probably doesn't matter."

"Probably not. Where is Yue, out of curiosity?"

"Under close arrest, behind the lines."

"And she's turned, presumably? Her message told me to meet her here, but it showed none of the duress protocols we established."

"She is no longer your agent, as you can see. But then again, all we asked her to do was bring you here – that's hardly so much, given that you brought an army with you."

"What? Oh, yes. Technically I brought the army for Martyza Eztok, for the archives. Yue's message suggested they would be heavily defended. I am beginning to suspect that was also a lie, yes?"

I've left the lid off the flask of tea. It'll be getting cold, ruined soon. Never mind.

In the distance, someone opens up with a high-speed kind of gun, nothing I've ever heard before; they must have dug the designs out of some sealed archive, a hundred bullets a minute, two hundred, pop pop pop, you're dead and you're dead and you're dead, so easy, so much easier if you do it right, just like a game, really, a short story on a winter's morning.

"Witt has brought in a few divisions – enough to make a scene worthy of your attention. It was . . . nice of you to come for Yue personally, when she asked. I wasn't sure you would. Wasn't sure if you cared so much for your assets."

"Yue was more than an asset. She was . . . she is . . . special. She has done more for my cause than you'll ever know. And I'm fond of her. We were friends, when we were young, did you know that? We lived together for a few months, argued about all sorts of things – we had some serious fallings out, in the way you only really can do when you're that naïve and pig-headed. I can still make her favourite dinner. Do you know what her favourite dinner is?"

"What would you offer, in exchange for her?"

"Is that what this is? You've asked me here to negotiate a prisoner exchange? Really? Not a special operations team – not an assassin?"

"You would have spotted an armed bunch of bastards with big guns a kilometre off. And killing you isn't Jia's preferred outcome. But seriously – what would you give for Yue?"

"Oh ... some of the politicals we've got in Bukarest, perhaps? Now that Farii has betrayed us, I imagine she'll be keen to get a few of her last surviving allies out before we shoot the lot of them."

"I didn't know there were any you hadn't shot."

"That's because you're middle management, if that. Secretarial – that's more accurate, isn't it? A competent secretary."

"I imagine you burn through staff at a terrible rate."

He smiled, shifted his position on his uncomfortable seat, found it too much, stood, walked a little back and forth, hiding the limp now, hiding the pain as the weight fell on his injured leg, swinging his stick side to side as if it were just an ornament he carried for fun. I closed my eyes, heard gunfire but nothing human behind it – no screams, no cries on the wind, just the tearing of broken air.

"Do you know this place?" he asked, sweeping his stick towards Martyza. "Do you know what it was?"

"Coal mines. Power stations. A relic of the burning. Nothing grows here, any more."

"Coal mines and power stations," he mused, half-nodding into the grey morning gloom. "The burning lifted people out of poverty in numbers never seen before. It extended the life of man to nearly a hundred years – a century of living. It made it possible to travel the world, to change the face of the planet. It changed what it meant to be human. Our minds expanded as our potential did; we could conceive so big, so far, of so much. Ability was rewarded. We were not afraid of consequences; there was nothing that could hold us back. It breaks my heart to see what we have become. So scared of the kakuy, we barely dare tread on a dandelion for fear it brings down the thundercloud."

"We've understood very different things from the past. All I

384

see are a few people getting rich in paradise, while everyone else chokes and burns. An age of economic tyrants with too much power and not enough care. One man may burn a forest, but he can't make it grow again."

Georg rolled his eyes. "Do the robes make you more pompous, or have you always been like this? There will always be a top and a bottom of society, but at least it will be one of merit. War teaches us that there are generals and there are soldiers, but you too could be rewarded, if you are strong enough."

"To be honest, at this stage all I really want is to go home and have a nervous breakdown. It's not very meritorious, but it'll probably help in the long run."

He scowled, a sudden flare of anger bursting from behind his smile. "Don't you know there's a fucking war on?" he snapped, and I recoiled a little, curling up tighter on my rock, but then the smile was back again in a moment, bright and merry as if we were discussing butterflies or the first buds of spring. "Anyway. All this is academic until Jia's deposed. We'll take Isdanbul then negotiate a settlement with whoever's left standing. Give everyone a chance to calm down a bit, reconsider their positions. In time, the remaining Provinces will see the power of our argument; the strength of it. I do believe in something, you see."

He talked light and easy, but his eyes were to the west, to the rumbling of his army as it growled across Martyza Eztok. Too far now. Too late – all of it, far, far too late.

"All this would be an even more stupid waste of life if you didn't believe." I raised my voice a little, to cut through the barrage of his thoughts. "But I imagine the wrathful kakuy currently poisoning the land in your wake might be a bit distracting – not to mention Farii's rebellion." Not a flicker in his smile, not a flinch, but neither did he reply. "You are worried. About the archives in the coal mines, yes?"

"It's my job to be worried. While it is always ... nice to see you, the thought that Yue lied to me about the level of defence Jia would dedicate to this region is naturally perturbing. It suggests, in the worst case, a trap."

"What do you think is down there?" I asked, following his gaze. "Nuclear? Biowarfare? Cluster munitions? What are you hoping for?"

He shrugged. "I will take what I can get. We can extrapolate a lot from a little. Look at the advances we've made already."

"Perhaps you hope there's a way to kill the kakuy. The great ones, I mean. The ones that come in thunder."

"As I said – I make do with whatever I find."

I sighed, checked my watch, clicked my tongue in the roof of my mouth. Georg stopped pacing, half-turned, looked at me and seemed for a moment to see me, myself. I smiled, put the lid back on the flask of tea, sealed it up tight, creaked side to side, felt the little muscles down my back ache.

"It is a trap, of course," I said, and finally he turned to face me full-on, one eyebrow raised. "Oh, there's an archive down there, full of frightening, terrible things. Even without Yue's invitation, you should have left it alone. You talk about ingenuity, but your mindset is so stuck in the past you can't see the extraordinary advances of the present. You are incapable of appreciating the wonders around you, incapable of ever just being ... all right. Satisfied. Under other circumstances, you could have been an astonishing human being. You could have achieved wonders. But you are not. Instead you are remarkably easy to manipulate."

I checked my watch again, watched the second hand ticking down.

"I wish you'd got here on time," I sighed. "We could have done this differently." He didn't speak, didn't blink. I couldn't remember the last time he'd listened to me so intently. "I am here to commit a terrible heresy. When it is done – if there is anything left – your army will be destroyed and you will lose Bukarest, probably Budapesht too. It's going to be hideous for everyone. But you have a choice. You came here for Yue. That was good of you. That suggests consideration for the life of an agent. I'm here to return the courtesy. Krima vaMiyani would love to talk to you; she is as close to thrilled at the prospect as I think she can physiologically be. Defect now, and you'll have a perfectly comfortable war in a nice hearth somewhere by the sea. Or don't, and watch everything you've built tumble down, and eventually be arrested as a war criminal, perhaps by our side, most likely by your own. Kun Mi strikes me as fond of a scapegoat."

He turned, took a step away, stopped, turned again, rubbed his leg – an unconscious movement, a little leaning – seemed to realise what he was doing, straightened, stiff as a tree. "All right," he murmured. "You've surprised me. Thoroughly and actually surprised me. I'm impressed. You've given me a great deal to think about. Thank you for that."

"I fear that in moments we'll both have a great deal more."

"Even if you did have some sort of trap to spring, I've seen your troops, Jia's little armies. You could bring every soldier she has from every corner of the Provinces here and all you'd do is speed your demise."

"Yes. She knows that. She's old, Georg, but there's a reason she's in charge. Winning was never the plan."

He looked directly at me, his chest square, shoulders back, stick rammed into the dirt between his feet like a flagpole. "Fascinating. I can still see you – some of you – some of Kadri. But only pieces of you; of him, rather. Little parts you used to be Kadri – or perhaps little parts of Kadri that you have used now that you are trying to be Ven. I have always prided myself on being better than people – at knowing them better than they know themselves. You force me to rethink this position. Thank you."

I sighed, stood, stretched, checked my watch one last time. "Too late," I said. "But for what it's worth, you're welcome."

"You know that this can never be a—"

I raised one hand to silence him, and he stiffened, astonished, utterly unprepared for the gesture. "To be clear. There is an archive under Martyza. It was buried in the mines. All the way under the valley, stretching on beneath the earth all around. Tunnels which your army are currently running – in the case of the tanks, driving – directly above."

Here it is.

Here is the moment that Georg's world falls apart.

I thought I would enjoy it.

I thought it would make everything all right. That I would punch the air, laugh, cackle, say something pithy. I thought I would watch him collapse into an old, broken man, and I would feel somehow young again, feel that I had clawed back some piece of myself that had vanished so far into Kadri, into Pityr, into the air and the earth and the forest and into him.

Instead, he took in a single breath, and let it out slow, because even he had to breathe again.

I felt tired.

I wanted to take his hand, tell him it would be okay.

I wanted to apologise – maybe not to him, but to anyone who'd listen.

I opened my mouth to try and find words, and there was nothing.

We stood, frozen in that place, and there would be a part of us always frozen in that place, a shadow of ourselves left behind that we could never find again.

I wanted to say: Georg. Please defect.

Please.

It will just be . . .

. . . it's the sensible . . .

. . . maybe even the right . . .

. . . we can work something out, it'll be . . .

Sorry.

Sorry.

It wasn't ever a game, but in the end that was the story we told to make it . . .

Sorry.

You weren't ever really human in my eyes either. You were always just . . . something else.

Sorry.

Instead, I stared at my boots, and then up at him, and wondered what words he'd find, if it would be kindest to speak, or if he needed a little space. When I was Kadri, I had always known these things, but that was another man, another time.

I thought he'd say the obvious – you wouldn't dare, you never would, the inquisition would never allow it! But Georg was not one for obvious falsehoods. He nodded, tilted his head to one side. Nodded again. Didn't meet my eyes. Then he straightened up and, looking a little past my head, said: "So, are you armed?"

I went for my knife, which is why his stick whipped just above my head as he swung it with both hands, before he turned and, stepping to the side, brought it down across my shoulders. I crumpled beneath it, rolled onto the earth and away from his kick, tangled now in robes – stupid bloody robes for a stupid bloody priest – tried to crawl away from another swipe, couldn't quite make the distance and deflected the weight of his stick across my arm. The pain of it cracked down into my spine, salivated in my mouth, more than just bruising, but the adrenaline kept me moving away as I tried to grab at the weapon, over-swung on its arc, and hold on with one hand while fumbling for my blade with the other. My fingers slipped on the waxed wood, and Georg stepped sideways again, using the weight of his body to pull the cane from my grasp, landed a kick, a little awkward, across my ribs, stumbling back off balance from his own efforts as I rolled away from it, gasping for air. In the moment it took him to steady himself on his feet I scurried onto mine, hands up, and as he swung again I barrelled towards him, fingers aiming for his face, trying to close the distance before the full force of the strike could reach me. The heavy handle of the cane flew past my head, but the tip of it bounced into my skull behind my ear. By then my momentum was too great to slow; I slammed into him, fingers clawing at his face, his eyes, trying to get pur-chase on something soft and squelchy. Georg dropped the stick to flail at my hands, strength against strength, before some more intelligent instinct kicked in and, reaching through my arms, he tried to ram his thumb into the ridged length of my windpipe, pushing me back as I curled away from the choking pain of it.

I let go of his face, dropped myself to his left, went to grab his stick as I rolled away, got one hand round one end, but he had caught the other and for a moment we were tugging on it with all the grace of two muddy, yapping pups fighting over a chewed twig. He pulled a little too hard and I let go, fast, his own strength knocking him onto his backside as the energy between us was released. As he fell, I fumbled for my knife again, felt the warmth of the handle against my calf and looked up to see him swinging for my right eye.

It was somewhere around then that the mines blew.

It wasn't one coherent blast. First one chamber beneath the earth, then another, then another, like a string of beads falling from a necklace and clattering to the floor. The roar – the coherent, concerted roar – was a thing that grew over a few seconds as the separate pops joined together, as the clouds of black coal dust and yellow dust broiled and rolled together and upwards, feeding each other, seemingly propelled by the noise of their own explosion. From the church I could see it rise, and an instant later could see nothing at all as a sideways wall of dust choked in off the flatlands. I squeezed my eyes shut and curled up into a ball, covering my ears, trying to breathe only through my robes, the heat and the scratching, suffocating blackness of it a spider's jaw; nothing but this devouring, this coming apart. The ground bounced and buckled like it was a liquid thing, back on the sea again, drowning again, don't let go, don't let go, I had not realised until this moment that the earth was nothing but broken dirt hemmed in by water and air, we would sink, we would be swallowed whole. I couldn't see Georg, couldn't open my eyes for more than a moment to try and peer through the blackness, had never tasted coal before – is this what coal tastes like? The taste of the past, of a dryness that prickles your tongue, of red tissue burning raw and breath with stones in it. Medj should taste coal, before their ordinations; they should swim through the flooded caves of Martyza and learn the songs of the old gods too, the ones who made people special.

After the first roaring, a falling rain. The earth as it falls sounds like hail on metal. It has notes to it, discordant percussions and strange chords. It bounces on your back, runs fingers through your hair. The dust moves like a living thing as you blink and try to rise, shielding your face from the fog of black and grey, blood thick, greased with yellow, melting the soft whites of your eyes. I coughed and spluttered and choked, staggered a few paces, ears singing; tried to shake the singing out, tilting my head side to side, but the note didn't change. I stumbled to the broken door of the church, half-fell, black lumps of broken world falling all around me, slow, fluttering down like feathers or slamming hard in wet splotches of heavy clay. I coughed, spat the colour of slate from my lungs, staggered a few more paces over the buckled earth, distorted like dunes at the beach, saw only blackness rising from Martyza, heard no guns firing, could not see the hollow, empty place we had ripped through the earth beneath what was left of Georg's army. Could not see the bodies they would find there in the months to come, even their eyes turned black by the dust that caked them when the world had caved in.

I thought I heard something behind me, but it was hard to tell through the ringing of my ears, looked up, up through the dust and the black, to where the cloud of coal blown into the sky was still billowing overhead.

I saw something ripple in it, and it was just the wind.

I saw something spark within it, red like fire, and it was just the light.

Then Georg, face turned to soot, caught my shoulder and tried to hit me, but his weight was off, his ears as bloody as mine, and he missed the punch, and I caught him as he half-fell, sinking with him onto the crackling earth. I grabbed his arm before he could swing again, his stick nowhere in sight, and pointed to the cloud, didn't think I could speak, didn't think he could hear me.

He blinked, not understanding, tracks of thinner grey around the corners of his eyes where moisture was trying to form. He followed my finger, pointing to the heavens, saw the dust, saw the coal.

Saw it catch on fire.

The flame started at its root, where the black cloud still clung to the earth, and spread up like a blooming flower. It leapt through the dust and through the fog, a rippling wall of crimson, spilling in all directions across the battlefield, curling in and rolling out like the all-consuming wave of the tsunami. The earth boiled beneath it, fused to stone; the clouds parted overhead as if frightened by a predatory beast, and still the inferno rushed outwards, tumbled down, tumbled towards us.

And for a moment, in the light that was too bright to look at, the fire igniting in every mote of dancing coal spinning on the air, I saw a creature drenched in blood, and its eyes were the hollow voids of an endless death, and its jaw was a waterfall of dripping oil, set alight. It had no wings, no talons or claws of prey, but it beat vengeance across the sky in crimson and black, dimming the sun as it roared across the field. It consumed the ancient chimneys, boiled the water in the abandoned lake. It melted the tanks of Kun Mi, charred the lungs of Antoni Witt and all who followed him. It ignited the grass in tiny spears of spitting yellow, turned the few standing walls of ancient metal into pools of burnt-silver slag. It roared, and roared again, and its voice was the fire, the storm and the earth. The kakuy of Martyza Eztok was as old as the first iron rod driven into the earth, with a heart of coal and a skin of oil. It knew only how to burn.

I crawled to my feet, called: Georg, Georg!

Georg, come with me!

Stumbled towards the hollow open dark that plunged down to the crypt, broken stairs and broken stones.

Georg!

He didn't move.

Kneeling in the peeling ground, staring up at the firestorm.

And I wondered if he saw it too, the great kakuy of the mines, vengeance set aflame. I wondered if he saw it reach out as if it would set the whole world ablaze, as if it could tear down the stars, boil the moon.

Perhaps not. Perhaps, even then, all he saw was the fire.

I tumbled into the darkness of the crypt, as the world burned.

Chapter 68

After a great fire, rain.

The rain was not the rain of the falling forest. It was the winter rain, sucked in by the air being burned away, a tumult of clouds spinning into the eye of the storm. It was cold, melted ice that sizzled and steamed when it hit the ebony earth. It fell for nearly a day, which is why it finally roused me, the thin stream of slime-ochre water at the bottom of the crypt rising to tickle my nose where I'd fallen. Choking woke me. Then I thought perhaps I slept again, and was awake again, back pressed up against a broken sarcophagus, and wondered if this was me awake at all.

I moved my fingers, and the skin was leather.

I listened to the world, and all I could hear was ringing in my ears.

I looked up, and there was night above me, which seemed a lot like being entombed for ever. But if I was entombed, how was the rain getting in, drizzling sideways into my face? My clothes were sodden, black, singed at the hem.

I unwound myself from some of them, tried to tear off a strip, couldn't get enough grip on the tough, wet fabric, wound myself back up again.

It hurt to breathe.

My tongue tasted of ash.

I sat a while.

Someone would come and rescue me, I decided.

Then I decided that the world was dead.

The sky had caught on fire and the world was going to start again from the ashes. The deep-sea creatures would have their time at last, those that barely needed a sip of oxygen to endure. The cave sprouts of impossible green, the crimson algae that lived beneath frozen lakes – they would come into their own and start gorging on the burnt ashes of this new world, exhaling oxygen as they slithered across the earth. Cockroaches would be fine, they always were, and probably form the basis of new life. I wondered what monuments they would make, and what they would make of the ruins of ours.

I sat a little longer, and no one came.

I started to feel cold.

The sensation was astonishing. I had not imagined I could feel cold ever again.

I coughed, and the pain was like bones puncturing flesh. Our lungs are terribly soft, squishy things.

I tried not coughing, and the cold, which had been my friend, became a dull ache, a restless, heavy thing.

It occurred to me that it wouldn't be so hard to die here.

I didn't have much of an emotional relationship with this outcome, but, resting with it for a little while, I felt a growing conviction that to die in this place would be insufferably dumb. It would have been easier to drown, or freeze in the forest, or get shot in the head, or burn alive. All of these would have been quicker and almost entirely someone else's fault. Still, there were plenty of little insects down here – shiny-carapaced millipedes and green-bellied beetles that got tangled in my hair. They'd probably make something worthwhile from my corpse.

I think I slept a little again, couldn't be sure, woke, angry at myself for sleeping, felt the edge of snoozing, raged and cursed and fought against it, found that I had one hand braced against a broken stair.

Climbed.

It was all right to stop every few metres.

It was all right to lie down and try not to cough, to burn, to vanish into this pain.

Reached the top.

Lay down in the rain.

Listened to the earth, hissing, uncoiling from fire to ice.

Crawled towards the broken door of the tumbled-down church, realised it wasn't a door but just a hollow where walls should have been. Pressed my fingers over stone and found it warm, warmer even than my body, was amazed, and clung a little bit longer, revelling in this strange sensation.

Made it all the way out into the ash beyond. Lay on my back to drink down the grey sludge of feathered soot and water falling from the sky.

Slept again, but felt much better about how far I'd come.

Dawn, the colour of an iceberg.

My bicycle was a melted, shrivelled thing, turned in on itself as if ashamed.

I discovered I was incredibly hungry, and that amazed me. I had no idea that hunger could make itself known over so many other unpleasant sensations.

There was a tickle at the back of my throat, a single delicate hair tickling my epiglottis, but I could neither cough nor swallow it down.

I made it to my feet, walked a few paces, crawled a few, walked a few more. If I could walk more than ten, that made the next ten easier. Then I would stop a while, then walk twenty, twenty-five, then rest again. This was how exercise worked, I seemed to recall. You do a little, then a little bit more. It was hard to find a direction and keep to it. The sun swung, a pendulum, back and forth across the sky. I did not aim for the heart of Martyza, for the place riddled with ancient tunnels. But I supposed it was where I needed to be.

There was no clean cliff where the earth had collapsed. Rather, the land caved in towards the valley in slippery, sodden sheets. Nor was it the black of the fire that had burned away the yellow grass but rather the charcoal, coal-burnt, dust-blazed black of an ancient fuel that had nothing left to give. The rain had liquefied much of the broken soil, creating a sea of dust and mud that stretched to the horizon. Those who had not been crushed when the world gave out beneath them, had suffocated. Those who had not suffocated burned. There were no hands reaching up to the sky; no last pictures of pain. Most had been blasted apart when the sky ignited, and only around the very edges of the broken land were there bodies, black, their moisture boiled away so that, mummified, their limbs had curled in, knees to chest, arms laid across their hearts as if peacefully slumbering as every ligament shrivelled and contracted in the heat. I had expected something more. A scarlet morning over which good people might weep. Carrion, pulling at bare flesh. Survivors howling in their agony. There was none of that. Death was too absolute for human drama.

I walked south, towards where there had once been a camp.

The land beneath me squelched and crackled as the rain fell. Sometimes I slipped, half-tumbling into soft earth up to my knee, my thigh, and crawled out hand-over-hand, and then rested a while, drank down air. My breath was wheezing in my chest. A tank was still burning, near the edge of the field. I stared at it, amazed, wondering how there was still fire left in it. Then I smelt the petrol from its broken engine, and it made a little more sense, and either side of it were the foetal, blackened bodies of its crew, ringing it like flowers round a monument.

I found the first trenches that Jia's soldiers had dug. Some lay empty; in others, bodies were still hunched, wrapped around their guns, suffocated as the oxygen burned away. I kept going. There were no bodies in the forward station, but the ceiling was black, the floor too, all the way across the room – not collapsed, but rather a tongue of scarring as if some timber-licking ghost has wet its lips at the window frames. There was no sign of life. The turbines had melted, the solar panels cracked into a greenish, liquid stain.

I walked on as the sun set, and did not hear them over the ringing of my ears but merely stumbled into their camp because it was on the side of the road, and the road was what I was vaguely following. The tents were untouched by char, sagging under the weight of rain, the waxed fabric bowing and bending in pools that the nurses tried to splatter clear with broomsticks from beneath. For a moment I wasn't sure whose side I was looking at, or what I saw. Stretchers were laid out across the floor, faces without eyes, without skin; the less injured sat in rows, knees hunched up, squinting as if the fire still burned in front of them. No one called for the doctors – there seemed a consensus that this would achieve nothing – and in a buzz of orders and ticking compression batteries alone the camp scuttled on.

I thought of asking someone for help, but there didn't seem much point.

Instead, I found what looked like the end of a line and sat down in the mud.

The woman next to me didn't look up, didn't ask me any questions, didn't blink. She held her knees to her chest, arms wrapped tight, and watched sights only she could see.

There was soup.

I ate too fast, and someone snapped at me to stop.

There was clean water.

I choked as I drank it.

Someone said, "His breathing doesn't sound too great . . ."

Someone told me to lie down on something that bounced.

Someone else shoved something up my nose that tickled. I tried to swat it away, but hands caught mine and tutted and said, "Leave it – leave it!"

I think they gave me something that felt nice, like cherry blossom, but inside.

Sometime later, someone asked: "How are you feeling, earth-kin?"

I tried to speak, couldn't. They gave me water. I tried again. "Terrible."

"I'm going to do some tests, okay? I just need you to . . ."

A little later, someone else leant over, white rags turned black

397

with the soot from my face, my hands, my skin. They'd taken off my robes and manhandled me into some sort of sterile gown that tied at the side. I wasn't sure if I'd participated in the process or not. They said: "What's your name?"

"Ven. My name is Ven."

Chapter 69

There was time in a hospital.

Then there was time in a temple room.

Jaqcs came to me and said: "The fires have burned out now. The rain has stopped. The Brotherhood is in full retreat."

I didn't answer, lay curled on my side, staring at the wall.

A delegation of inquisitors came to me and said: "It was heresy. It was. It was heresy. Blowing the archive at Martyza Eztok . . . we meant it for the best. The longer the war goes on, the more angry the kakuy become. We had to end the war. We have to keep the peace."

Someone turned on the radio, and there was music playing, and it hurt my head.

Someone gave me an inkstone, and the news showed an artist's impression of the great kakuy of the pit, and it looked human, it looked like the kind of creature that cared how humans looked.

I threw the inkstone across the room, and no one asked why.

Then, one unremarkable day, Jaqcs came to me and said, "Merthe has taken Bukarest," and asked me if I wanted to light a lantern at the spring festival, and I smelt the cool damp of unfolding green after rain, and held the thin, painted paper between my hands, and that was when I cried.

So ridiculous, I thought, to cry for the lighting of a lamp. Of all the things to get messed up over, this little, absurd thing, this tiny point of light – it made no sense at all.

They put one hand awkwardly on my shoulder while I wept, and murmured, there there, it's all right, it's all right. You're all right now.

In the evening, we processed down to the water's edge, all the Medj of the city, the temples great and small, and some people came to watch the procession and eat sticky cakes of nuts and honey, and others joined in, dancing and ringing bells, for the spring festival of Isdanbul was meant to be a party, not a serious, chanting affair. There were stalls selling sticks of fruit and piles of hot, steaming bread; competing bands trying to out-blare each other, flags flying from the branches of the newly budding trees. The Medj of the Blue Temple lit their lamp first, from a taper they'd carried down the hill, and that fire was then passed to the next lamp, and the next, and the next, until the flame reached me. I cupped it carefully as the wick caught, then passed it on, until at last the lamps of every priest and novice were lit, and the youngest went into the crowd to pass the fire to the waiting tapers and lamps of the hearth-kin waiting there, and I wasn't sure if I would get through the business in one piece, and Jaqcs stood nearby to say nice things in case I didn't, and they helped me push my lantern out onto the still waters of the strait, to join the others, swimming in light.

In the morning after Bukarest fell, Jia went on the radio and said: This is the beginning of the end. We have suffered, we have endured, but now the tide is turning. The tide always turns.

She sounded tired, but who didn't these days?

Kun Mi's entire second army was gone, along with large parts of the third. The lucky ones would have died too quickly to know how it ended. Council did not report the losses on its side or speak of the tongues of flame that had melted the railway tracks and ripped the nearby villages from the earth.

The kakuy of Martyza had not cared who it killed, the day the sky caught fire.

If, that is, there had been a kakuy at all. All you need to start

400

a fire is fuel, oxygen and a spark. And who was there left alive to report on the details of what they'd seen? Not Georg. Not anyone whose report could really be trusted.

Do you think you saw the kakuy of Martyza? asked Jaqcs as we drank cool water by the temple stream. Do you think you saw the spirit of the flame?

They had found a few ashen bones from Georg's body and the metal head of his stick, wolfen, grinning still, its snarl a little twisted at the edges where it had started to melt, turning from a leer to a sobbing scowl.

Coal dust in the air, I said at last.

Sparks from a gun.

Does it make a difference, when the day is done?

Krima vaMiyani sits, cross-legged, on a cushion by the door of the shrine reading from her inkstone. There is a guard nearby, examining the wall of little prayers inked onto bamboo by the door. I do not know if he is impressed by what he reads. One day, he may be thinking, our civilisation will fall and when people find our prayers they will discover it's all "please let her love me again" or "I lost my favourite necklace" or "just no morning sickness this time round".

I want to take him down, down, to the cold archives beneath the temple, to the tunnels where we keep the past, to show him selfies and pictures of food, jokes and terrible puns in dead, archaic scripts, tell him, look, look – look at people living. Look at how beautiful it is to be alive.

Instead, I follow the jerk of Krima's chin into the shrine, where Yue sits, back to the wall, hands loose by her sides. I ease down next to her, bump my shoulder against hers, mutter, "Hi."

"Hi."

"You heading out?"

"Uh-huh."

"Got everything you need? Toothbrush, spare change of pants?"

"I believe the system provides all that when I get there."

"Take it from someone who was a political prisoner: you'll want your own toothpaste. It makes such a difference."

"I'll be fine."

She has shaved her hair down to a buzz, perhaps unwilling to trust a prison barber. It makes her look younger, a child with tired eyes.

"They let you have an inkstone?"

"They believe that busy, occupied minds are safer than bored, unstimulated ones. So yes, I have an inkstone, and there is a library."

"I'll send you books."

"That's hardly necessary."

"I have eclectic taste."

She smiled, quickly turning her chin away from me to grimace at the painted ceiling of the shrine, where kakuy of sky and star danced in blue above us. "Nothing too philosophical, please. I think I'll get enough of that anyway."

"Trashy romance?"

"If you absolutely must."

"There are some fascinating old-world texts. Girl meets boy, boy is a dickhead, girl falls for boy, girl meets different boy who isn't a dickhead, but in her infatuation can't see the merits of new boy because the first boy is pretty . . . "

"Did you study this? Is this what inquisition training involved?"

"Eclectic tastes," I repeated. "Good for insomnia."

She nodded, unfolded, rose, stretched. I rose too, facing her, a breath apart. She looked past me for a moment, then said: "Don't wait. It's very important to me that you don't wait."

"That's my choice to make, isn't it?"

"You can take good advice."

"I can find no evidence whatsoever to support that hypothesis."

Her eyes flickered to my face as if they would stay there, then danced away again. "According to the priests, everything changes. They say it's the only thing you can rely on."

"Please. I am a professional deliverer of pithy contradictory-yet-demonstrable nuggets of wisdom. And what Temple says is true. The world is vast and everything changes; but that doesn't mean we don't try."

She nodded again, harder, brisk. Smiled at her shoes, smiled at the painted roof of the shrine and finally smiled at me. "Be well, Ven, kin of earth and sky."

"See you around, Yue."

One last nod, an ending of all things. She pressed her hands together, and bowed, and so did I. Then Yue walked away, and in the shrine I prayed for her, and felt that she would probably be okay, and that if she wasn't there were things people could do about it, and that made praying much, much easier.

Later, the forest grew.

About the author

Claire North is a pseudonym for Catherine Webb, a Carnegie Medal-nominated author whose debut novel was written when she was just fourteen years old. She has fast established herself as one of the most powerful and imaginative voices in modern fiction. Her first book published under the Claire North pen name was *The First Fifteen Lives of Harry August*, which became a word-of-mouth bestseller and won the John W. Campbell Memorial Award. Her follow-up, *Touch*, was described by the Independent as "little short of a masterpiece". Her next novel, *The Sudden Appearance of Hope*, won the 2017 World Fantasy Award for Best Novel, and *The End of the Day* was shortlisted for the 2017 *Sunday Times*/PFD Young Writer of the Year Award. Her 2018 novel, 84K, received a special citation at the Philip K. Dick Awards, and her latest novel, *The Pursuit of William Abbey*, has been shortlisted for a Locus award. Claire lives in London.

Find out more about Claire North and other Orbit authors by registering for the free monthly newsletter at orbitbook.net.

Help us make the next generation of readers

We – both author and publisher – hope you enjoyed this book.
We believe that you can become a reader at any time in your life,
but we'd love your help to give the next generation a head start.

Did you know that 9% of children don't have a book of their
own in their home, rising to 12% in disadvantaged families*?
We'd like to try to change that by asking you to consider the role
you could play in helping to build readers of the future.

We'd love you to think of sharing, borrowing, reading, buying or talking
about a book with a child in your life and spreading the love of reading.
We want to make sure the next generation continue to have access
to books, wherever they come from.

And if you would like to consider donating to charities that help
fund literacy projects, find out more at www.literacytrust.org.uk
and www.booktrust.org.uk.

Thank you.

hachette
CHILDREN'S GROUP

little, brown
BOOK GROUP

*As reported by the National Literacy Trust